Squire

– ANTHONY WAYMAN –

To Jaqueline
with love.
Dad.

An environmentally friendly book printed and bound in England by
www.printondemand-worldwide.com

This book is made entirely of chain-of-custody materials

www.fast-print.net/store.php

Squire
Copyright © Anthony Wayman 2011

ISBN 978-178035-033-2

First published 2011 by
FASTPRINT PUBLISHING
Peterborough, England.

Chapter 1

'You are a cheat, sir! You have cards up your sleeve.'

The card room erupted as men leapt to their feet and seized hold of the accused player. He was stripped of his coat and the extra playing cards he carried were laid out on the table for all to see. This was the one unpardonable sin amongst men little troubled by their conscience and it would go hard with the culprit. So hard in fact, that Luke Gregory quietly left the room, not caring to be in any way associated with what might follow for he never gambled at cards and was contemptuous of those who did, though he enjoyed a profitable sideline in trading the promissory notes offered by those in need of ready money.

Although he didn't know it, 1880 was to be a momentous year for him. By any standard, he was a successful man. He was certainly a wealthy one, the head of a group of business enterprises that flourished despite the economic difficulties of the country. He was not, though, a happy man and in moments of personal gloom was becoming increasingly conscious of the fact.

For twenty years, he'd built up the business and achieved the security for which he'd hungered. Now, only the greatest foolishness or misfortune could threaten his position. What then, was lacking? Marriage? He'd thought of it. Was fond enough of the ladies; too fond some might say but, with his single-minded interest in the business and a sailor's reluctance to tie himself to one port, he'd never got around to it.

Did he want to expand his business interests? Not really. There was no sense in growing beyond a point at which he could keep an eye on every aspect and his wharfing, warehousing and trading activities produced a steady, comfortable income that allowed him to be a generous and supportive employer.

Not being of a sociable disposition he had no circle of friends and relied on the newspapers and his partner's daily visits to keep him in touch with the world, and was becoming, he realised, increasingly reclusive, interested only in his wealth. Then suddenly, unable to contain his pent up energies any longer he'd take to the river in a light skiff and row all day, only to curse sore muscles and blistered palms for a week afterwards. Occasionally he might visit a ballet or opera, for he liked music, but he never entertained, lived quietly and plainly and was often thoroughly miserable.

His partner, Sean O'Dowd, known as 'Digger', was a complete contrast in personality and habit and complimented him exactly. Small and brightly dressed, where Luke was tall and formal, he was always out and about and, with a host of friends and acquaintances, was the light-hearted co-ordinator who kept the wheels of the organisation turning smoothly.

On a grey January morning, with little daylight penetrating the gas-lit sitting room at Gresham House, Digger came bounding up the stairs in his usual fashion to find Luke settled in front of the fire still in his carpet slippers, the daily newspapers to hand on the coffee table.

'Morning Guv. You remember that lawyer feller who got five years hard for knocking off 'is client's money? Well, 'e's due out in the morning. Still want ter see 'im, do yer?'

'I most certainly do. I want to pass the complicated stuff to him, if he's up to it. No telling what five years inside can do to an innocent man. You've kept an eye on his family, I take it? Mm. Give him chance to settle in at home then wheel him round and we'll see what's what.'

'Righto, Guv. Charlie'll meet 'im with the cab an' I'll 'ave a natter with 'im before 'and. I'm off up the Dials now. There's a geezer got something for me, I hope. S'orl right,' he added, seeing Luke's look of concern. 'I've got the Murphys with me. I'll be back in one piece,' he grinned as he retreated to the door.

Ten days later, Digger brought Walter Brierly to see Luke. Five years of confinement had left their mark. His clothes hung loosely on him but he had a keen, alert look that Luke found reassuring.

'Welcome aboard, Mr Brierly,' he greeted, rising to shake hands. 'I understand you're prepared to join us in a professional capacity.'

'Mr Gregory, I just do not know how I can thank you for all you have done for my family and myself and I really am most grateful for your offer of employment. As you will know, I am now barred from practice following my conviction.'

'An unfortunate decision,' Luke replied. 'For myself, I'm certain of your innocence. Now let me enlarge upon what Mr O'Dowd has already told you. We operate a variety of enterprises on and around the river but certain activities based here would benefit from the guidance of a lawyer. The one thing I require though is the absolute loyalty of anyone working for us and we'd expect a total commitment from you. How do you feel about that?'

'You have my word upon it. I am so deeply in your debt that I would not dream of offering anything less than my very best endeavours.'

'Good,' Luke said, nodding gravely. 'Your office will be downstairs and I wish you in the first instance to familiarise yourself with our records and accounts and the investments we hold through the Stock and Commodity Exchanges. You have two assistants to fetch and carry for you who'll benefit from your guidance. They're young but willing and intelligent and should one day make first-rate clerks at the very least. Your salary of five hundred a year you may take monthly from the general account, for which you'll have responsibility. Is that satisfactory to you?'

'Indeed it is, Mr Gregory. I am overwhelmed by your generosity, I really am, and I am truly grateful for this opportunity and for your trust.'

'Very well,' Luke said, solemn as ever. 'Mr O'Dowd will find your assistants and show you where things are in the house,' and he again offered his hand, leaving Digger to lead the way back downstairs.

When they were alone, Walter Brierly turned to Digger. 'I really have difficulty coming to terms with this. It all seems too good to be true. I hope I shall live up to expectations.'

'Oh, you'll make out. The guv always picks the winners. I've been with 'im since I was a nipper and 'e's not 'ad me shot yet,' Digger said, with his great grin. 'Just play it dead straight, even if things don't go 'zactly right and you'll find 'im good as gold. Not ter worry if 'e don't smile at yer. 'E never smiles so I does that fer the both of us. Come on and we'll find those lads o' yours', and knocking on the door at the end of the passage leading to the rear of the building he called out, 'Let's be 'avin' yer. Come on Mrs Cherry, chuck 'em out,' and two reasonably tidy youngsters appeared with great pieces of stout hale pudding clutched in their hands as

Mrs Cherry, in her spotless white apron, beamed after them from the doorway.

'Just look at 'em,' Digger said. 'All they ever seems ter do is eat. Now this is Mr Brierly. You're to work with 'im and wot 'e says goes. Got it? The guv'll be asking about yer so watch yer step. They're all yours, then Mr B. Anything you wants ter know, send one of 'em to ask,' and he turned to climb the stairs again.

'All right down there?' Luke asked as Digger flopped down into the vacant armchair by the fire.

'Reckon so. Somethin' on yer mind?'

'I'm visiting the card rooms tonight. Levine's first then on to Ashington's. There's a couple of wild merchants around at the moment and one in particular seems set to win or lose everything, come what may. Name of Barrington and staying at the Alexandra Hotel in Knightsbridge. Got a slight accent I can't place. Offered gold mining shares when he ran out of cash and then won 'em back. Might do it again but I need to know about him beforehand.'

'We've got young Alf at the Alexandra. I'll give 'im a call'.

★ ★ ★

'Come on, Guv, cheer up,' Digger bantered, when he returned. 'It can't be all that bad,' seeing Luke staring morosely out of the window. 'What you needs is a change of air, like we 'ad down Southend that time. That was a bit o' fun that was. Or 'ow about a day at the races? Come on down with Beth an' me next week.'

'Digger, my old friend, I think you may be right. Perhaps I do need a change. Now, what have you got for me?'

'Had a word with young Alf. You know, 'e's the boots there. Had a good butchers round. Said nothing's 'ung up or in the drawers. It's all packed in bags, ready ter leave like, but nothing said to the manager so 'e could be ready to skedaddle.'

'That's worth knowing. Give him my thanks and see him right will you? Off home to the loving wife, are you? Give her my best and I'll see you in the morning.'

Shortly after eight-thirty Luke, resplendent in the evening attire of a gentleman of leisure, strolled into the foyer of Levine's in Marlborough Street. Typical of the smaller and less prestigious gentlemen's clubs it attracted a following of card players who preferred to gamble away from their regular club.

Whist was currently in vogue and several partnerships frequently met to pit their skills against one another. Luke, although a member, wondered constantly how grown men could risk their money, sometimes enormous sums, on the turn of a single card.

He found it fascinating though to watch the faces of the players, the range of emotions reflecting their success or failure. The gleam in the eye of a winner or the angry glare of a loser befuddled with alcohol. Surely, the only time to drink deeply was when relaxing? A bottle of Champagne now, well cooled and shared with a friendly lady was just right but to swill brandy whilst playing cards was sheer folly.

Several quartets had formed up or were moving towards the tables whilst a game of baccarat was already in progress, the players hawkishly concentrating on their cards. The man Barrington was not yet playing but lounged casually against a pillar near the baccarat table. He laughed frequently and loudly and held a half empty glass of spirits in one hand, a cigar in the other. Cautious as ever, Luke had decided to have no dealings with him and settling in an armchair, carefully trimmed and lit a cigar and studied the various factions present.

By midnight, he'd moved on to Ashington's Card Rooms where he was offered property deeds for cash. He spent a little time considering the wisdom of such a trade but decided to take a chance, completed the transaction and went home to bed.

★ ★ ★

'Ah, Mr Brierly. Walter. Just the man. Last night I acquired a property, the deeds to which I have here. I should like you to examine them and tell me what you think. The former owner pledged his estate at the tables and lost.'

Walter Brierly nodded. This was business he understood and he started to sort through the documents as Digger came though the front door.

'We'll invade the kitchen this morning,' Luke greeted him. 'My fire's smoking again. Probably the wind direction.'

'You could try a taller chimney pot, Guv. That'd give a better pull on the flue.'

'I didn't know you were an expert on chimneys.'

'Knows all about 'em now. Remember our kitchen range smoked something rotten? Well, Beth got a builder in who said it were the trees making a down draught and he stuck a few more bricks on top and a bigger pot and that's solved the problem.'

'I'll get George to have it looked at,' and he led the way into the warm, comfortable kitchen with its big central table surrounded by chairs, two of them occupied by Walter's assistants, stuffing themselves with bread and sausage.

'You two eating us out of house and home? Still, you're looking well on it,' Turning to Digger, he said, 'I bought the deeds to a country property last night, at Ashington's, for a couple of grand. A bit of a risk, but they looked interesting. Feller put 'em down to cover five thousand at baccarat to the Honourable Charles Barker. He's never got two ha'pennies to rub together and took my offer like a shot. Let's hope I haven't caught a cold. What a damn, stupid business it is,' he said with feeling. 'The loser went off and topped himself,' and he shook his head at the folly of gamblers in general then abruptly, changed the subject. 'That tea should be in on the tide this morning. Coming down the wharf with me?'

'Why not? Better show me nose on the old patch.'

Finishing their coffee, they joined Walter in his office to see how he was getting on with reading the complicated deeds, written in copper plate script on parchment liberally adorned with red wax seals.

'Everything looks straight forward,' Walter informed them and went on to describe the property as the manor house itself, the demesne, or home farm and a hundred and thirty acres of land. It had been in the same family for nearly two hundred years but three farms and a lot of land had been sold off and there had been a dispute with the church over the matter of tithes.

Much would depend on the condition of the buildings, of course and the quality of the land but the signed and witnessed note of transfer of interest would save difficulty should any other party lay claim to the title. Of interest were the Land Tax Redemption Certificates from eighteen thirty eight, which suggested the owner at the time was wealthy. 'Incidentally,' he concluded. 'The owner also becomes lord of the manor.'

Digger started to laugh. 'Lord Guv, eh? I think it suits.'

'I see. Would you visit and look it over? See what you think its value might be. I've little interest in lordships. Not to my taste at all.'

★ ★ ★

It was to be a busy week for that same evening Luke had word that Benjamin Stanley was using his property as security at the tables in an effort to make good his weekend losses at Acre's card rooms. He already held several of Stanley's notes but if he was putting all his resources at risk then Luke knew to declare his own interest without delay so lost no time in getting to St James with his escort.

For an illegal pastime, the place was well attended even for a weekday evening but the police knew better than to interfere with wealthy and highly placed patrons of a private club. Or, possibly, they were rewarded to 'look the other way' and concentrate on the lower orders playing pitch and toss in the public houses.

Dishevelled and the worse for drink, Stanley was arguing loudly with a group of others in a corner. A large, course-looking, red-faced man held a collection of papers in his hand and was angrily asserting them to be 'worthless and wouldn't cover one half.' Then, catching sight of Luke, he left the group and thrusting the papers under his nose demanded, 'Here, make me an offer on these. Snivelling whore's son, pulling a fast one.'

Stepping back half a pace from the blast of brandy-laden breath that accompanied the demand, Luke took the papers and spread them out on a nearby table. There were two notes, one for a thousand pounds, the other for half that amount and two sets of deeds relating to factory premises at Lambeth and a property at Kingston on Thames.

'There are charges out on both of these', indicating the deeds. 'They're not worth a lot.'

'Don't I bloody well know it, now,' the man stormed. 'Go on; put a price on 'em. I'm not fooling around with bits of damned worthless paper.'

Luke considered and shook his head doubtfully. 'There's nothing to back these notes. There are others I know of for over five thousand. The business is in tatters and that leaves the house, which can't be worth much.'

'For God's sake,' red face expostulated in a hoarse whisper intended for Luke's ear only but audible to much of the room. 'I've got my notes to settle.'

'I'll take a chance on face value,' he said.

'What!' Red face exploded. 'They must be worth more than that'.

Luke shrugged his shoulders. 'I doubt you'll do better on those,' and started to turn away.

'Wait a minute.' Red face was looking desperate. 'Fifteen hundred you say? Make it two thousand, can't you?'

Luke looked even more doubtful. 'That's too much. I'm not interested in a loss.' Then, appearing to relent a little, added, 'Well, a couple of hundred more perhaps, but that's my limit on these.'

'Gold?'

'Banker's drafts. Gold's too heavy to carry.'

'All right. Done.'

A pen was produced, the drafts signed and Luke signalled to his escort. 'Get this fellow out of here in one piece,' and with difficulty the now semiconscious Benjamin Stanley was half carried from the card room. One man, wavering on his feet, tried to stop them, saying he wanted a word with Stanley but Luke gave him a sharp push into a convenient chair, where he remained, blinking owlishly. Hailing a four seater, Luke's escort allowed Stanley to collapse onto the floor between the seats and they set off for the wharf.

'Watch yer feet,' one cautioned. 'Could puke anytime.'

Half an hour later they reached the warehouse with Stanley sleeping soundly but no sooner had they hauled him out than he vomited violently, gagging and choking. He remained on hands and knees swaying and moaning whilst Luke roused the night watch. Bert, with his nightshirt tucked into his trousers and his sparse hair standing on end, appeared in the doorway.

'This is Mr Stanley who has had a skin full. I want you to tuck him away in a quiet corner and let him sober up. His clothes can go in the wash. He'll not need them while he's here and he goes nowhere until I send for him. Oh, and mind he doesn't try to top himself. Tie him up if you have to. Got that?'

'Sure an' I have, Guv. He'll be safe and sound with us. Come on fellers, get 'im inside,' and the heavies helped the groggy man whilst Luke climbed into the cab again with directions for Gresham House.

★ ★ ★

'So what you going ter do with the geezer, Guv?'

'Set him to work for us if he'll co-operate. If he's not interested he can disappear and I'll put a manager in or else sell the lot. Should make a shilling or two either way but I can't say I like the crowd they get at Acres. It's not a place I call at much.'

'Me neither. I've seen a few of them geezers around. Pimps and the like, they are. A few bookies too, but none I'd trust me money with.'

'Fancy wandering round to the factory? See how things are?'

'Yeah, why not? See if I fancies the leather trade fer meself.'

'Smelly business.'

'Well, just so long as it pays, eh?'

Two and a half hours later, Digger flopped into the armchair opposite Luke. 'I needs danger money at this game. Had ter quell a riot at the tannery. That joker 'adn't paid 'is workers on Saturday an' they was all up in arms. Said as they were stayin' put 'til they got their money. A few women there an' they don't arf screech at yer.'

'Mm. Bad was it? So how've you left it?'

'Told 'em the chief 'd been taken ill. Got the foreman to list what was owing. Drew the readies from the bank and paid 'em. Gave an extra day fer 'aving ter wait and 'ad a quiet word with the foreman about keeping things going 'til the chief was back.'

Luke nodded and smiled his appreciation. 'Well done. Well done indeed. That feller's certainly let things go. It beats me how anyone can throw it all away as he has. If he'd known an empty stomach when he was younger he'd see things differently.'

★ ★ ★

'Well, Mr Gregory, it was an interesting visit, I must say.' It was Walter Brierly's turn to occupy the armchair by the fireside as he reported on his visit to Chidlingbrook Manor. A branch line railway service ran from Guildford to the village, which was not large but pleasantly situated in a valley with a small river running through. The Manor, a short distance from the station and clearly very old, was rather uncared for, with rough grazing and woodland round about. A large and hostile woman, who appeared to be the only servant there, had at first refused him entry but a younger woman, who described her position as governess, had spoken with him.

Luke was all attention now. He'd pictured a run down property and was interested in what value Walter might think to place on it, expecting it to be unoccupied, but the presence of a governess, and a young one at that, created a different picture.

'Yes, it was a surprise, I must say. There were two young people present, the son and daughter of the late owner whose wife had died some years earlier. They are twins aged eleven, apparently. Their father, Squire Travers, has been absent from the Manor for some weeks and the household is experiencing straightened circumstances with credit no longer available for even the most basic foodstuffs and the woman in the kitchen was strident in her demands for her wages. In short,' Walter concluded, 'a deplorable situation.'

'Not straight forward then,' Luke commented. 'So presumably no one was aware of the squire's demise?'

'That is correct and I had the unhappy task of relating this and explaining, as best I could, the change of ownership. I am not at all certain that the present position is fully understood.'

'What's the legal position?'

'That is straightforward. You are the owner of the property, including all fixtures, fittings, live and dead stock. Others may or may not dispute ownership of various items but it would be expensive to do so and probably not worth their while.'

'And the occupants?'

'You may require them to vacate immediately.'

'Any mention of who might take responsibility for them?'

'No mention was made and I hesitated to enquire. I did say that I should be reporting to you and that you would make er, appropriate decisions in due course.'

'Mm. Quite so. Mm. It looks as though I'll have to visit rather sooner than is convenient. Tomorrow? Can't leave things as they are. Tomorrow it is. If your helpers can look up the train times they can come for the ride. Er, you said they had no food?'

'I did leave a small amount to help with immediate needs.'

'Ah, yes. Take from the general fund. The problem's mine. Well done and thank you.'

★ ★ ★

They met next morning at Waterloo Station in time for the eight fifteen train to Guildford and Walter was amused at his young assistants, who clearly couldn't wait to get started.

'What class we going Guv?'

'Mr B and I are going first,' Luke replied. 'If you want first class you have to sit still and there's no singing. If you go second, you're still expected to behave. Third? Well, you can't go far wrong in third so what's it to be?'

They conferred briefly. 'Second, Guv,' Tommy said. 'Firds only got wood seats and Sammy's got a sore arse,' and he went off into a fit of giggles and was thumped by his partner.

'Here you are, get singles,' Luke said. 'You never know what might turn up,' and they scampered off to the booking hall to return in triumph clutching the tickets and change.

Taking the two first class tickets, Luke gave them sixpence each to last the day. 'No booze, no baccy,' he warned, 'and we'll see you at Guildford.'

'No, Guv,' and they disappeared in the direction of the chocolate kiosk on the platform whilst Luke and Walter settled themselves into a vacant compartment.

'They're a lively pair,' Walter said. 'I don't wish to pry but as you said, there is much I don't understand and I'm curious about them.'

'No secrets there. They're two of the Doctor's boys. You know the chap I mean? Barnardo. Looks after homeless children over Stepney way. We've met a time or two, and

- 14 -

given him a hand now and then. He found Tom and Sammy were quick to learn and asked us to help fix them up with work, so they moved in. They've been waiting for you to employ them. They know the City side of the river so could be useful as we're mainly based on the South side.'

'Yes, I had heard of Doctor Barnardo. Do you do the same sort of thing?'

'No thank you. I'm no do gooder. He's a regular Bible thumper, always singing hymns and praying from the heart. Got to hand it to him, though. Funny little cove. Irish and full of blarney. A bit like Digger I suppose, very likeable,' and Luke's face relaxed in a rare smile. 'I think he should have gone on the stage. He's one of the most entertaining people I've ever met but he'll never make old bones. He'll burn himself out.'

From Guildford, the single-track branch-line ran up the shallow valley to the village of Chidlingbrook with one other village and a halt beyond, where the line ended at the foot of the chalk hills. Being the largest of the valley villages, Chidlingbrook boasted the principal station with water tower, engine shed and a double siding, where a coal merchant had his yard. A pony and trap was available to carry passengers but being too small for all of them, they decided to walk the half mile or so to the Manor House.

The appearance of more strangers on the platform two days running aroused immediate interest and news of their arrival seemed to precede them but only one man offered them a greeting of 'Good day, genel'men' in passing.

It was indeed a pleasant landscape Luke decided, with the small river running through gently sloping fields and woodland covering the hillside down to the road beyond the last cottage and where the trees receded, a curving driveway led up to a rambling building set back in a shallow bowl in the hillside, with an area of rough grazing in front of it.

'This is it', Walter said and led the way up the tree-lined driveway towards the front of the building, the main entrance made prominent by a pillared stone porch sheltering an iron-studded oak door.

It was an irregular shaped building that had been added to over the years but it gave an impression of age, with the central two-storied part facing out across the valley, presided over by a massive, brickwork chimney. Two wings, added at right angles, extended forward with half-timbered upper stories, partly hung with tiles.

'Been here a while, I should think,' Luke commented, his eye running over the mullioned windows, with their small, diamond shaped panes of glass.

Approaching the door, he pulled the bell handle of dull, unpolished brass and they waited in anticipation. A bell had rung inside; they had heard it clearly but no one was in a hurry to admit them so Luke tugged at the bell handle again and as the sound of the bell inside died away, gave it another pull for good measure.

This time, they heard heavy feet clattering on the stone floor and the door was opened sharply by a heavy-set, course-looking woman of early middle age wearing a long and very dirty apron.

'It's you agin is it? What yer want this time?' she barked aggressively at Walter.

'I, madam, own this property and have come to take possession,' Luke said.

'Oh, you 'ave, 'ave yer. And what about the squire then, and what about my wages, eh? No wages fer weeks past and it's 'igh time somethin' were done about it. I'm not working 'ere on me own for nothing,' but Luke cut her short.

'Step aside, madam, and allow me entry,' and he pushed past the woman, closely followed by Walter and the boys.

- 16 -

'Ere, 'oo do yer think you're shoving? You ain't comin' in ere shovin' folks about,' but Luke ignored her and looked around the hall, a large, oak panelled room with a huge, open fireplace, a broad staircase and various doors leading off.

'Ere, you say you're the owner of this 'ere place, then what about my wages? I'm not going 'till I've bin paid,' and the woman folded her arms across her hefty bosom and glared truculently at Luke.

'And if you were paid you'd leave this house?'

'I will,' the hostile woman replied, emphatically. 'I'm not cookin' and doin' in this place no more. I'm not treated proper, that's what.'

Turning to Walter, Luke said tersely, 'Pay her off.'

'Three weeks you said you were owed, I believe,' Walter said. 'Let's see, now. Three weeks at seven shillings, that will be twenty-one shillings,' and he reached into his pocket for the money.

'I were promised ten shillin. I wouldn't 'ave come up 'ere else.'

Walter looked at Luke, who nodded, and Walter handed over a sovereign and two crowns and made an entry in his note book as the woman flounced away through the rearmost door, slamming it shut behind her.

'Cor, she's a rare beauty, ain't she, Guv,' Tom said. 'Thought she were goin' ter poke yer one, I did.'

Luke nodded. 'Not a pleasant type. Off and have a look round outside and keep an eye cocked in case she walks off with the pots and pans,' and grinning, they scampered off through the front door. Walter, meanwhile, had opened the right hand door leading off the hall and was looking into a pleasant, panelled drawing room, comfortably furnished in a masculine sort of way with deep, leather-covered armchairs and a large desk.

A movement at the turn of the stairs caught Luke's eye and looking up he saw a young woman, hesitating as if trying to decide whether to descend to the hall or not.

'Oh, good morning, madam,' he said, and removed his hat, which had remained firmly in place during his encounter with the woman with the dirty apron.

'Good morning, sir,' she replied, still hesitating.

May I know to whom I have the pleasure of speaking?'

The young woman, apparently reassured, descended the stair. 'I am Miss Hetherington,' she replied, 'the governess. Forgive me, but did I hear you say that you are now the owner of the Manor?'

'Yes, that's correct,' Luke said, guardedly and was glad that Walter had now joined him.

'My name is Gregory. As Mr Brierly has already told you, I purchased this property following the death of the previous owner. I'm sorry you had to learn of this in such a fashion, but when Mr Brierly told me of your situation I thought it best I visit personally.'

'Oh dear,' Miss Hetherington said, dabbing her eyes with a lace-edged handkerchief. 'This has come as a most disagreeable surprise and we are wondering what we are to do.'

'Ah yes. I understand you have two young charges. Perhaps I might meet them?' as he caught sight of them peering down at them, solemn faced and large eyed. Slowly they descended the stairs and Luke introduced himself.

'I'm Peter Travers and this is my sister Lucy', the boy said, giving a stiff little bow and shaking hands formally whilst his sister curtsied and silently offered her hand. 'Is father really dead?' Peter asked.

'I'm afraid so. I think we have much to discuss so do you think we might adjourn to the kitchen, Miss Hetherington and put the kettle on. I'm sure a good, strong cuppa will help.'

'But we never go to the kitchen, Mr Gregory,' came the surprised reply. 'We always take tea upstairs.'

'I rather think those days are over. That was the cook who left us so noisily a short while ago? So, if we want anything we shall have to shift for ourselves. I take it there is no one else in the house?'

'No, there is no one else here and I really do not know if I can be of use in the kitchen, I'm sure.'

'Oh we shall manage', Luke said, trying to be reassuring. 'To me it's the most important room in the house,' and he moved towards the door that led to the rear of the house, Peter and Lucy, watching him curiously, followed.

★ ★ ★

The kitchen was enormous and mediaeval. The only concession to modern needs was a large iron cooking range set into one of the two equally large fireplaces. Walter already had a kettle set on the hottest part of the range top and was energetically stirring up the fire with a long iron poker whilst Miss Hetherington attempted to assemble sufficient cups and spoons clean enough to use.

The whole room looked and smelled, Luke thought, as though it had last been cleaned shortly after it was built. The flag stones of the floor were covered with debris and in places were slippery with ancient grease whilst the huge wooden table that stood in the middle was similarly cluttered and filthy.

'I've seen cleaner stables. It doesn't look as though that woman lifted a finger. How are you coping? That stove looks big enough to power a locomotive.'

'I think we shall raise steam before long,' Walter said, with a smile. 'I should think you could cook for an army on it. Just look at all the different ovens but it needs a spring clean and all these brass fittings should be polished. I'm sure my wife would not be impressed.'

'Well whilst we're waiting for the kettle, perhaps we could go over things again to make sure I have the picture clearly. Could we all find somewhere to sit? Now, Miss Hetherington, you are governess to Peter and Lucy and live in the house?' A nod of assent. 'And you haven't seen the squire, their father, for several weeks?' Another nod and a murmur of agreement.

Looking over at Peter and Lucy, who had settled on stools at the far side of the table, Luke explained that their father owed somebody a great deal of money, not himself, as he'd never met him, and was forced to settle the debt by offering the Manor. That person had then sold the house to him, which is how he came to be there.

'You will have relatives you'll wish to contact and perhaps move to, in due course? Miss Hetherington, are you able to help in this direction at all?'

'Oh, Mr Gregory, I do believe there is an aunt, but she is quite advanced in years. I am uncertain of her whereabouts although I have heard Canterbury mentioned.'

'Do you perhaps then, know the name of the family lawyer?' Walter asked.

'I am afraid not but squire kept all his papers in the desk in his study,' Miss Hetherington said. 'Perhaps there may be something there.'

'Do you mean we have to leave here?'

The question was quietly asked but it hit Luke like a slap on the face. Now here was a problem. This was their home. Did he say 'yes' and be done with it or did he fudge a reply and postpone the unpleasantness? He looked at Peter, who was standing now. 'I had assumed,' he said slowly, thinking hard about what he was saying, 'that you would prefer to live with relatives. Aunts and uncles, cousins, and so on.'

'I don't want to leave here and I don't want to live with Great Aunt Emily.'

Lucy started to sob and Luke looked helplessly at Miss Hetherington who moved over to her side and producing a large, plain handkerchief from some hidden fold or pocket applied it with a practiced hand. The ridiculous thought flashed through Luke's mind that perhaps governesses concealed numerous handkerchiefs and other tools of their trade about their persons ready for instant use. For all he knew, they probably did.

Distant muffled voices and clattering feet announced the return of Tom and Sammy to the entrance hall and Walter went out to call them. They arrived with flushed faces, grinning widely.

'Hey, Guv,' Sammy announced, 'we found an old geezer 'oo flinged rocks at us. Swore somethin' 'orrible 'e did. Said ter get out of 'is yard. Didn't 'it us, though. Reckon 'e's past it.' They thought this event a huge joke.

'The word is flung,' Luke corrected, 'not flinged and come out of that fireplace, you'll get filthy.'

'I'm starving,' Tom said.

'You're always starving. You'll have to wait a while. Have a cup of tea. This is Miss Hetherington and Lucy and this is Peter, who all live here so when you've finished, perhaps Peter could show you around properly without annoying anyone. Walter, I think you and I should take a stroll outside and discuss matters.'

★ ★ ★

It was a pleasant view from the front of the house. Set on a South-facing slope overlooking a shallow valley of fields and trees, only two other dwellings, probably farms, could be seen. The village lay to the right, lower down the valley and the road connecting it to the next one ran a little way below, keeping level with the river some quarter mile distant while on the other side of the meandering stream they could see the raised track of the railway line.

Luke and Walter wandered along the gravelled area in front of the house, their boots crunching on the layer of river pebbles, hidden in places by a growth of weeds.

'Tell me the legal position again' Luke said.

'According to the note of transfer of title,' Walter said, in his lawyer's voice, 'you own the property as outlined in the deeds together with all live and dead stock, trees, shrubs, fixtures and fittings as found. You are responsible for maintaining all rights of way that may exist and are liable for all the usual charges and outgoings that are part of rural holdings, such as taxes that may be levied, poor law contributions and tithes to the church, and so on.'

'And the contents of the house and present occupants?'

'At your discretion entirely,' Walter stated, firmly. 'Fixtures, fittings, live and dead stock means everything that you find here without exception. You are free to demand the property be vacated forthwith and nothing whatsoever removed.'

'Mm. I can hardly turn Miss Hetherington and her charges out with nowhere to go. Do you think it likely there is someone in the family to take responsibility for them?'

'Impossible to say,' Walter said. 'What we need to know is the name of the late squire's lawyer. He's bound to have had one. You could, as you own the contents of the house, legally search for some reference to him, in the desk, perhaps?'

Luke reached his decision. 'They can all stay pending discussion with the family lawyer and we search the desk for his name. They can all be present if they wish. In fact, I shall insist they witness the search.'

'Do we, I wonder, have a key?' Walter asked.

'If we lack a key, we have Master Thomas. That young man has certain talents. No need to force anything.'

'I see,' Walter said. 'At least, I'm beginning to,' smiling and shaking his head.

They turned back to the front door again and met the three boys as they came downstairs from their tour of the house where Miss Hetherington appeared to be keeping an eye on them from the hall.

'Ah, all together, I see,' Luke said. 'Good. Now, it's imperative we consult with your family lawyer,' he said, addressing Peter and Lucy 'and to find his name we shall have to look in your father's desk.'

'You've no right to touch father's things.' Peter was indignant.

'I have every legal right as it happens so you, young man, will do the searching, unless you can remember the lawyer's name. No? Then we must take a look at the desk,' and he led the way into the study and tried each of the desk drawers in turn, but all were firmly locked.

'Miss Hetherington, do you know if we might find a key to fit? No? Peter and Lucy, can you help? No? Tom. What do you suggest?'

Tom looked around the room and settled his attention on the tall, bow-fronted bookcase near the fireplace.' Top of that, Guv,' he indicated. 'I can't reach it.'

Luke walked over to the bookcase and ran his hand along the raised ornamental rim that decorated the front and sides of the top, and produced a small, brass key.

'What did I tell you?' he said to Walter. 'He's a bright lad, is our Tommy,' and Tom grinned proudly and swaggered self-consciously back to stand by Sammy, who nudged him with his elbow.

Walter was impressed. 'But how did you know where to look?' he asked.

Tom shrugged. 'Looked the right place fer this 'ere room,' he said.

'Right, Peter. The responsibility is yours.' Luke said and handed him the key. 'It may take a little while so I'll have a wander around outside. Tom, Sammy, I have a job for you.' Luke looked at his watch. 'Remember we passed an Inn on the way here, near the station? It's twelve fifteen now so take a walk down there and see if you can organise a meal for one o'clock for the seven of us in Mr Brierly's name. Whatever they can offer. Then have a scout round the village but mind you keep out of trouble.'

★ ★ ★

Relieved to be free to look around his latest acquisition, Luke wandered outside. It'd been a prosperous enough place at one time, he thought and it didn't look as though he'd paid over the odds for it. What would it take, he wondered, to patch it up for a profitable sale? A damn good clean for a start and all these weeds cleared away. A lick of whitewash where it was needed perhaps and get all this rough grass trimmed up. Shouldn't cost too much, then he could offer it for sale in the summer.

Perhaps George and his missus might fancy a change of air and move down here to get it organised. He'd sound them out when he got back. 'Now what have we here?' he said, half aloud, and stooped to examine a tiny yellow flower with a green frill of leaves like a collar. Couldn't be a buttercup. Too early, and he struggled to remember the names of plants he'd known as a boy around Dean House. Blessed if he could remember; been too long at sea and in the City but it looked familiar. George would know, but it must be a sheltered spot to flower this early. Peaceful too, with just a few birds around.

Returning inside he found Walter holding a letter bearing the legend 'Paulin, Gage and Pill, High Street, Guildford,' legal people who appeared to have acted for the late squire over some business or other. Good, so that was one problem solved.

'Perhaps you could break your return journey at Guildford and call on them? Might save a little time and the boys've gone to organise lunch at the Inn. I must say, I'm unusually peckish. Must be the country air.'

★ ★ ★

Tom and Sammy awaited them on the bridge over the stream, where they'd passed the time spitting into the water below. 'All set fer one o'clock, Guv,' Luke was cheerfully told.

'Good, but nip over to the station and ask the time of the next train back, will you?'

'Two twenty-three, Guv,' was Tom's immediate reply and he and Sammy fell about, laughing. 'Told yer so,' he chortled.

'I told you, yer mean,' from Sammy, and they leaned against each other and grinned at Luke like a pair of mischievous puppies.

Luke turned to Walter. 'I should've known better than to ask but you see what you'll have to put up with?' and Walter smiled his appreciation of the rapport that existed between the dour Luke and these two bubbling young helpers.

The landlord of the Lamb Inn, a short, rotund man wearing a clean white apron, met them in the doorway to bid them welcome to his house. His look of surprise at seeing Miss Hetherington, Peter, and Lucy did not go unnoticed but he wisely made no comment and ushered them into a side room adjoining the bar, cheerful with a bright fire and a table laid for their meal.

'What can you offer us, landlord?' Walter asked.

'We have rabbit pie and pigeon pie that are fresh cooked and hot, sir and cold beef and cold ham with fresh vegetables and pickles and apple pie and cream, sir.'

'That sounds excellent,' Walter said then, turning to the table at large asked, 'What would we all care to drink?' suddenly realising that he was unprepared for this potentially delicate subject. 'You have mineral waters, have you not?' he asked the landlord.

'Why, certainly sir, and would especially recommend the Zoedone which is becoming very popular.'

'Miss Hetherington, would that be satisfactory?' and receiving a demure acceptance looked to Luke for his order.

'I think ale for this end of the table, if you please,' he said and was quietly amused at the ripple of uncertainty, possibly of disapproval, that showed momentarily on the faces of his adult companions. Dammit, he thought. He wouldn't tiptoe about. A pint or so would be most welcome now and he knew that for Tom and Sammy it had long been a regular part of their diet, being safer than water of unknown origin.

'Which knife, Guv?' Sammy whispered.

'The big one for the meat and the little one for buttering your bread,' Luke said quietly and noticed the superior look on Peter's face at Sammy's admission of ignorance. The whole question of table manners and etiquette was one that Luke was determined to persevere with and he was well pleased with both boy's willingness to learn and with their efforts to eat decently, especially when on show. There was no point, he maintained, in having good employment only to let yourself down by eating with your mouth wide open and spitting fish bones on the floor.

For a small village inn given only short notice, it was a creditable meal and the three guests from the Manor proved to have most healthy appetites. Quite likely they'd been on short rations for some time and had been quietly and genteelly starving, complete with stiff upper lips. The empire could be proud of them, if it cared. Then, sitting back contentedly, he pictured again a small, yellow flower with a frilled collar. Funny that, he mused and chuckled to himself as he caught a glimpse of Sammy grinning over the top of his half pint tankard at Peter sipping his mineral water. The look of envy on Peter's face suggested honours to be even between them.

It was time to be moving or they'd miss the train and catching Walter's eye, Luke began to stir in his chair to give Miss Hetherington time to get the message and rise first. These conventions, Luke thought, and leaving Walter to settle the reckoning, he escorted the party outside.

'May I have a word with you, Miss Hetherington?' and they moved a short distance away, leaving the younger ones standing looking at each other by the doorway.' Am I correct in thinking you have no resources whatever, for food and other necessities, at this time?'

'I am afraid that is the position, Mr Gregory. I was left with no allowance when the squire went away and I have used up the little I had put by and we can obtain no further credit from trades people. They send round from Guildford and deliver the following week and are becoming quite pressing. I really do not know what to do next.'

'Mm. Well, whilst you're looking after the property on my behalf I'll advance you sufficient to cover your needs,' Luke said, gruffly. 'Can you give me an idea of what is owing? There is a shop here, in the village, I take it?'

'There is no shop as such in the village just the post office, which sells very little. Everything is sent in or comes from the farms but they no longer supply us with milk or cheese. There is the baker but again we no longer have credit. You see, I was not responsible for housekeeping arrangements so I have only a general idea of what is outstanding.'

'I see. Well, er, Walter, have you ten pounds to leave with Miss Hetherington who will look after the Manor for the time being. I shall ask Mrs Cherry to come down and tidy the place up. George too, if he feels like a change. They keep house for me in London,' he added by way of explanation to Miss Hetherington, who was looking a little overwhelmed. 'I'll send down a few items first thing in the morning to help tide you over. Now, we must get to the station or we shall miss the train. Mr Brierly will contact you as soon as he's made his enquiries,' and Luke took his leave as briskly as politeness would allow, leaving Miss Hetherington and her two charges staring mutely after them.

★ ★ ★

Chapter 2

Back home at Gresham House, Luke went straight through to the kitchen and lost no time in sounding out George and his wife over a move to the country for a week or so.

'Well,' said Mrs Cherry, who usually did the talking, 'you know you've only to say.'

'No. Only if you'd like to,' and he described the Manor and its need of capable hands to tidy it up. 'The farm belonging to it appears deserted though I'm told there's an old chap doing something or other round the back but I need to know what land belongs to it and what state the buildings are in, that sort of thing. You'd take on whatever help you needed and decide how long to stay. All that I'd leave entirely to you. By the way, I found a small yellow flower there. Funny looking thing with a frill of leaves like a collar. Can't for the life of me put a name to it though I've seen them before, years ago.'

'Probably an aconite,' George said. 'Winter aconites they're usually called, the first flower of the new season. Sometimes they're a month before the snowdrops.'

'Ah, so that's what it could be but we called them something different where I grew up. Probably a local name. Any way, what do you think?'

'It would make nice change,' Mrs Cherry said. 'When would you like us to go?'

'As soon as you can, but I'll need someone to take your place here. All right? Good, then I'm off to get cleaned up. Travelling makes me feel uncomfortable.'

★ ★ ★

The next morning, promptly at nine o'clock, Walter was waiting to report on his enquiries in Guildford. In his slippers still, Luke sat comfortably by the fire, a half-empty coffee cup balanced on his knee and several discarded newspapers within reach. Settling himself down, Walter described his meeting with a Mr Gage, one of the partners who had acted for the late Squire Travers.

'Gage had no idea the squire had died,' Walter said and went on to say that he held a will and was aware there was little wealth in the family as the squire had been selling off land piecemeal, to settle debts he believed arose from unwise speculations and with the continuing fall in land values, had to sell off increasing acreages.

Following his wife's death six years or so ago, the squire had more or less gone to pieces and neglected his estate and family and as for relatives who might take care of the children, and there are, in fact, three of them for there is an older son at school somewhere near Salisbury, he knew only of an elderly aunt of the squire's who lives in constrained circumstances at Canterbury.

His late wife had no relatives so he suggested the family would become the responsibility of the Board of Guardians. He did though, undertake to communicate immediately with the aunt and advise her of the position and will inform me as soon as he receives a reply.'

'Mm. A sorry state of affairs. Let me know as soon as you learn anything, will you. Mr and Mrs Cherry have agreed to go down to Chidlingbrook to get the place straightened out and I should like your two henchmen to show the way and make themselves useful. Mrs Maddocks will move in here meanwhile to burn my toast and keep the fires alight. She's a widow with two small children but I'm assured they're well behaved. Now, I shall ask Digger to introduce you to the wharf this morning as it figures prominently in our activities but he'll shortly be bringing a visitor for a business discussion.'

★ ★ ★

Digger escorted a pale and subdued Benjamin Stanley into the room as Luke tidied away his newspapers.

'Ah, come in Stanley. Take a seat. On Monday you lost your assets at the card table at Acres. I bought those assets in settlement of your debt so I own your factory and your house and you are bankrupt. There are three courses open. The first is to sell everything. The second is to appoint a manager and the third is for you to continue to run the business with the possibility of regaining at least part ownership.'

'You mean get the factory back again?'

'I mean precisely that. You have a thorough knowledge of the leather trade and inherited a thriving business. I'm proposing you resume control of that business and continue to live at your present house but on condition you neither drink nor gamble again. Both brought you low and you must avoid them for the future. You must devote your energies to the business and will be in the tannery office by eight o'clock daily. In short, Mr Stanley, you're going to work as you've never worked before in your life and when you've restored

- 31 -

the fortunes of the business, we'll discuss plans for expansion. Should you fail to honour my conditions I'll appoint a manager and sell your house. Is that clearly understood?'

Stanley nodded and started to offer his thanks but Luke cut him short. 'This is purely a business arrangement. No one outside of this room will know of it. Mr O'Dowd has paid your workforce and your foreman will keep things running whilst you recover from a bout of ill health so it's up to you. I wish you good day,' and Luke stood up abruptly whilst Digger ushered Benjamin Stanley from the house.

'Reckon he'll do it, Guv?' he asked when he returned.

'I hope so. It'd save a deal of bother and could prove profitable. Now, I want to visit the Exchange this morning so would you show Walter round the wharf and fill him in with all the gory details? Warehouses, boatyard, shop? The lot? Young Jimmy with us still?'

'He is that, Guv, now 'e knows 'e's welcome. Follows Bert like a shadow, giving 'im an 'and.'

★ ★ ★

A week later, on the last Tuesday in the month, Walter received a letter from the lawyer in Guildford and having read it, took it upstairs to Luke. Short and to the point but written in an immaculate hand of well practiced symmetry that was itself a work of art, it outlined factually the situation regarding the family of the late Squire Travers of Chidlingbrook in the County of Surrey.

It stated that the only known surviving relative, who resided at Canterbury, was unable to accept or assume any responsibility whatsoever for the family of her late nephew due to advanced age, failing health and scant resource. It further advised that it would be for Luke, as beneficial owner of the property, to decide at what point in time he required said property to be vacated by the family of the late squire.

With Walter gone, Luke stood gazing moodily out of the window at the murky street outside. Every building nearby had at least one coal fire burning against the cold and the smoke from them seemed to be blowing down into the street instead of over the roof tops and away. Then Digger came clattering up the stairs. Where did he get his energy from, Luke wondered?

'Morning, Guv. Tanner fer yer thoughts?' he quipped.

'You can have 'em for less than that,' Luke replied, gloomily. 'I've landed myself a problem with that country place and can't see an easy answer. Here, read this. It's from that lawyer at Guildford.'

Digger read the letter then looked up at Luke, who'd turned back to the window.

'So what's the problem, Guv?'

'Well, it's still occupied,' Luke said, fretfully, 'and to be honest, I was toying with the idea of keeping it as a weekend retreat. You know, somewhere to get away to instead of hanging around here all the time.'

'Now you're talkin', Guv. It's just what yer need, honest,' but, as Luke continued to stare out of the window he went on, 'Look, Guv, me old mate, me an' Beth've been off your 'ands fer ages now, ain't we? You're not going ter get married an' 'ave your own family, or so yer say, so why not take on this one, ready made an' waiting for yer? It'd save you being all lonely on yer tod down there, wouldn't it now? Go, on, 'ave a bit o' fun an' when it gets too much, 'op on a train an' come back up 'ere fer a rest.'

Slowly, Luke turned to face his partner. 'Are you serious? You really mean that?'

'Yes, I do. Take it as it stands. I mean ter say, what's a couple of nippers an' their governess? You can do with all the company yer can get, I reckon, specially now young Roddy's away so much. Go on, give it a go.'

'You know, Digger,' Luke said, with just a hint of a smile, 'I can't think of anyone else who'd come up with a suggestion like that. I wonder if it'd work. They appeared reasonable enough, I suppose. All right, I can but try it. Better have a word with Walter and see what the legal side is,' and when Walter joined them, Luke came straight to the point. 'The proposed solution to my dilemma is to offer to accept responsibility for the occupants of the Manor, as guardian and employer respectively, I suppose. What would this entail, do you think?'

Walter gravely considered the question. 'It is a very generous gesture and comparatively easy to arrange if all parties are agreeable. It would be better for the other side to be legally represented, in the absence of parents, and the formal approval of the aunt should be sought, but I doubt there'll be any problem there. You could then, if you so wished, make a deposition before a judge in chambers but that would not be essential; it would merely formalise the arrangement.'

'He'll keep the lawyers busy, won't 'e,' Digger said, grinning.

'Very well,' Luke said. 'Will you put the proposal forward? Get that Gage fellow to approach the aunt and the two at the Manor and contact the headmaster of the eldest one's school. I shall want everyone's complete acceptance though and I suppose we shall be retaining Gage. I doubt he'll want to work for nothing, but everything must be clear cut and above board.'

Walter left to start work and Digger stood grinning at Luke. 'This'll keep you out o' mischief fer a bit. Fancy a nag or two around the place? I knows of a couple o' likely colts I wouldn't mind bringing on somewhere nice and quiet. Fancies meself as a trainer, I do.'

'Put what you like down there, as long as you arrange your own mucking out but you ought to visit first to see if it'll suit. There's supposed to be a hundred and something acres but what of, I'm not sure.'

'I'll do just that,' Digger said, 'now I knows yer going to keep it. In fact, I'll go tomorrow, if that's all right. Best take Beth along to watch me back, mind. No telling what'll jump out at yer in them there country places. She keeps on askin' about it so it'll give 'er chance fer a nosey round, eh?'

'I haven't looked it all over yet but I think it could be made quite comfortable. By the by, I hear Swayne's giving up his granary and it's for sale or lease. I was wondering if we might have a use for it, as it's on our doorstep. Then again, there's so much American wheat coming up the river now, would it be an idea to set up a flourmill, I wonder? Something like Reeds, but with deep water for direct unloading. There's too much wastage using lighters.'

Digger cocked his head on one side. 'You reckon you ain't got enough ter do, then? Go on Guv, don't go over doin' it. Get this country place sorted out first, then see 'ow yer feel.'

★ ★ ★

The next day, Digger and Beth set out early for Chidlingbrook, leaving their maids to look after their children. Beth was bubbling over with excitement at the prospect, imagining all sorts of fanciful buildings whilst Digger was thinking along racehorse lines and wondering if he'd find anything suitable for his plans.

It was another grey and murky day but dry, so far, and as the train moved steadily South and West, away from the pall of smoke that hung over the built-up areas, the sky began to brighten and by the time they got out at Guildford to change for the local 'bumper', a little pale sunshine was struggling through the cloud, encouraging them to walk the short distance to the Manor. Pausing at the end of the drive, they looked around to admire the sweep of the hills in the distance and the river following the course of the valley below them.

'Cor, it's lovely,' Beth said. 'You reckon this is it?'

'We can always ask,' Digger replied, 'but it looks like the place. You can just make out some buildings from 'ere. Let's go and see.'

Approaching the house just a little diffidently, they were relieved to see George limping his way from the rear yard where the stables lay, and called out and waved.

George, ever ready for Digger's quick humour, waved to them and called out, 'Get off my land. No gypsies or race horse owners allowed.'

'You're looking well,' Digger said. 'The air must be good fer you.'

'That it is and the missus too. Reckon the Guv should've found this place sooner. Come on in. Tradesmen's entrance for us,' and they followed him through the door into the kitchen where Mrs Cherry was up to her elbows in flour, kneading bread on the big, pine table, scrubbed now to a respectable shade of white. There was a chorus of greetings and Beth was organised to put the kettle to boil while the dough was placed by the stove to rise.

'Cor,' Beth said, yet again. 'Ain't it luverly. I likes yer stove. It's a good big 'un and a luverly big kitchen too. Lots of luverly space to work in.' Her animated chatter and obvious interest filled the kitchen and Mrs Cherry was hard put to answer all her questions.

Digger grinned at George. 'Shan't get any peace now,' he said. 'She'll be wanting a kitchen like this one. How's the stables? The guv said he didn't mind a few nags moving in. How're you fixed fer looking after 'em?'

'You know me,' George replied. 'Loves me 'orses .How many you got in mind? There's six good stalls in the yard close by that're cleaning up well. You ready for a look now?' and he got up from the table, all eagerness at the prospect of horses.

'Well, all right,' Digger said. 'Won't be two ticks. Back before the coffee's poured,' and he and George went out and across the yard to the stables, a beautifully constructed range with stone walls and a slated roof covering a hayloft over the paved and cobbled stalls. The task of cleaning and white washing was well under way but, as George explained, there was still much to be done before he'd be satisfied.

Digger was delighted. 'Just the ticket,' he exclaimed and mentioned the two colts he was interested in. 'You'll need a bit of 'elp though, if we fill these up. Best keep yer eye open for a likely lad or two. Come on, coffee time. I can smell it from 'ere.'

'Before we goes in,' George said. 'Do you reckon the guv'd agree to us havin' a pony and trap. One'd come in right handy I reckon.'

'Course he would,' Digger replied. 'You know the guv. If yer needs anything fer the job in 'and, 'e's 'appy for yer ter get it. I'll tell 'im you're looking out for one soonest.'

Back in the kitchen, Beth and Mrs Cherry were discussing the workings of the stove, coffee cups in their hands. 'Help yourselves,' Mrs Cherry directed as Digger and George seated themselves. 'There's biscuits in the tin.'

'This is a bit of all right,' Digger said to George. 'How much grazing is there?'

'About forty acres, I'd say. Some is plough that's rough seeded itself and needs working on but a goodly bit is old ley that should come up sweet in the spring. There's some below the orchard next to the Home Farm, as they calls it, the ground that runs down to the river in front and the rest at the end of the wood beyond the house. There's more stables and barns just below the yard belonging to the farm but the house is empty and a bit shabby but the buildings aren't that bad. Old Joe keeps chickens down there. He's worked here since he was a boy, so he says. Must be eighty if he's a day.'

'Well, we moving in? Digger asked Beth, mischievously. 'Lovely stables. Just what I need.'

'You and your horses,' Beth replied. 'Wouldn't mind it 'ere, though. Can we have a look around inside?' she asked Mrs Cherry.

'Of course you can. We'll go together directly. Ah, here's Miss Hetherington and her charges. Smelled the coffee. Let me introduce you,' and Digger and Beth received their formal bows and curtseys from Peter and his sister.

'I was wondering,' Miss Hetherington said, addressing Digger, 'if you are able to tell us what the position is regarding Peter, Lucy and myself.'

'Go on, Diggs,' Beth said. 'Tell 'em what the Guv has in mind,' and, nothing loathe, Digger explained the idea they'd decided upon.

'You mean we can stay here?' Peter asked. 'All of us?'

'Just so long as you accept the guv as your guardian. He's decided he likes the idea of visiting weekends instead of staying in the City all the time and 'e's happy fer you all to stay if you want as long as you remember 'e's the chief. Some lawyer from Guildford'll be asking you about it before long but this gives you time to think about it.'

'I think it's a lovely idea,' Beth said, 'but you have to decide for yourselves.'

'Yes, it would seem to be a most generous offer,' Miss Hetherington said. 'Have you known Mr Gregory long?'

'Lor, yes,' Beth replied. 'Since we were grubby little tykes down 'ere,' and she gestured to knee height. 'He brought me and Digger up, he did. He's a proper dear so don't be put off if he growls at yer. He's as good as gold underneath, ain't 'e Diggs.'

'Couldn't wish fer better. Mind you, you don't cross 'im. What 'e says, goes. He can be a tough 'un if 'e's pushed and no one shoves the guv around, I can tell yer. Anyway, give it a thought, why don't yer. Now, 'ow about a butchers round. Come on Mrs C., lead the way.'

Beth and Digger stayed until late afternoon, looking at everything the house and surrounds had to offer and it wasn't long before Peter and Lucy relaxed with them, attracted and fascinated by their constant cheerful banter. Lunch in the big kitchen was a lively and enjoyable occasion that lasted nearly two hours with, time after time, everyone helpless with laughter at the endless stream of anecdotes and jokes they related. So animated did things become that Beth, gesticulating with her spoon, accidentally landed a custard laden lump of sponge pudding on her husband's nose.

Miss Hetherington, accustomed to maintaining a dignified and decorous image, as her position required, could not recall ever laughing so much in her life and, for the first time ever, saw Peter laughing too. Mr and Mrs O'Dowd, she thought, were two of the most entertaining people she had ever met.

★ ★ ★

Calling in at Gresham House the next morning, Digger found Luke anxious to hear what he thought of the Manor and was relieved that George approved of the water supply, both from the hand pump in the scullery, which drew from the well, and the spring supplying the yard, which ran from the hill behind the house into a stone trough, before running on again down to the pond near the farm house.

There were many improvements Digger thought Luke would wish to make, like a bathroom with flush lavatory, and described the existing earth closet at the side of the yard, suggesting it would smell worse than Thames mud on a hot day. 'Very traditional, Guv.'

★ ★ ★

In due course, Walter was able to tell Luke that all the loose ends were tied up with regard to his new responsibilities. The elderly aunt had willingly consented to Luke assuming the role of guardian and the headmaster of the school at which the eldest boy was a boarder had written to say that the offer had been 'gratefully accepted' and would he care to visit at his earliest convenience, to meet all concerned, whilst Peter and Lucy, guided by Miss Hetherington, had agreed to accept the new situation.

Conditions at the Manor had so improved for them since Mrs Cherry had taken charge that, in truth, they were far from displeased by the turn of events, despite the sadness that had led to the change.

Satisfied that all was now clear, Luke felt he was free to visit again with a view to planning improvements and he decided to spend most of the following day there discussing with George what needed to be done. He'd then only have to pay a visit to Bramsden College to meet Richard to complete his immediate obligations.

Travelling down alone this time, he began to take more notice of the scenery from the carriage windows and, arrived at Chidlingbrook, of the station itself and the village and its inhabitants for he would, he realised, be making this journey many times in the future and the people who lived there would be his neighbours and a part of his life.

By choice, he entered the house by the back door deciding he'd feel a bit foolish ringing his own front door bell in order to be admitted. George and Mrs Cherry, who were in the kitchen, greeted him warmly and, sitting down at the table and pushing his hat to the back of his head, Luke looked around with approval.

'You've been busy, Mrs C. It's a different place from when I saw it first. Have you got enough help?'

'Oh yes, Guv,' she answered, looking pleased at the compliment. 'Two women come up from the village each day for the general housework and another is responsible for the heavy scrubbing and another one comes in part time for the laundry but if I may say so I think all the bedding needs to be replaced, mattresses and all. We all get bitten in the night you see.'

'Ah, bed bugs. Right, list whatever's needed and we'll have new and you'll get all the bed frames and floorboards scrubbed will you? Vinegar and soda unless you have anything better. And how is George fairing? Got a list of urgent jobs a mile long, I expect.'

'Well not quite that many things are out of place,' George smiled, 'but I reckon we need a builder in to do some tidying up here and there and a carpenter too. There's a few floor boards need fixing.'

'We'll have a walk round in a minute,' Luke said, 'and decide what's what. Are you comfortable enough, living wise?'

'Oh, yes thanks,' George said. 'No problems there apart from the bugs, that is. Reckon we're not begging to rush back to town. Very pleasant spot, this.'

'You mean you'd prefer to stay here permanently?' Luke asked.

'We certainly would,' Mrs Cherry said, firmly. 'If it's possible, that is.'

'Of course it's possible. To tell the truth, it's how I'd prefer it. That's settled, then? You'd like all your things brought down? Good, and you're happy to be steward and take charge of everything, George?'

'Steward? That's a fancy title, Guv. Aye, I can get this place worked up with a bit of help. We've just the one man working outside, apart from old Joe that is and Digger said to look out for a couple of lads for the stable when his 'osses arrive. We've just the one pony at present. I believe 'e told you about it, for the trap, like? Nice little beast 'e is too. Well set up. You want to see 'im?'

'In a bit George, in a bit. You know I'm not very horsey. I'm more interested in getting the house up to date. Let's have a look round and see where we can start. I believe you have a room above the kitchen at this end? You'll need a bathroom and inside facilities. Digger's told me about the black hole outside. We'll take a walk upstairs and work it out.'

On his first visit, Luke hadn't looked upstairs or, indeed, hadn't seen all over the house and he was surprised at the number of rooms, ten in all, on the first floor and four more in the two attics over the end wings, which were set at right angles to the main body of the building.

One room at the back was used as the schoolroom and there they found Miss Hetherington with Peter and Lucy, who stood up when they entered. The atmosphere was a little awkward at first until Luke suggested they each show him their respective rooms with a view to seeing if anything needed doing to them. Structurally, the building appeared sound enough but was in urgent need of redecoration.

Three bathrooms in the modern style were needed, one each in the two end wings for himself at the East end, where he'd have his room, and a similar arrangement for George and his wife in the other wing whilst the third one, for general use, would be in one of the rooms at the back. Water tanks in the roof, a proper cloakroom downstairs, a flushing privy outside and a cesspit well away from the house. He'd have the cobwebs shaken from this old pile!

Returning to the kitchen, they decided the stove might be adapted to supply hot water to two bathrooms and the scullery but there'd have to be a separate boiler house at the East end.

'There's a heck of a lot of work involved in all this, Guv,' George said, looking serious.

'Yes. The place'll be upside down for a bit. Better put the word out and see what it'll all cost. We'll give anyone local a chance, especially with the decorating, but I expect we'll have to go further afield for the plumbing. There's probably someone in Guildford able to cope so you sound out the local folks and see who wants to do what and I'll get something in the newspaper inviting tenders.'

'Righto, Guv, I'll take a ride down to the Lamb and leave word there.'

'Outside, now then,' Luke said. 'Let's see what the score is there. Digger seems to think the land isn't too bad for horses.'

'Well, some of it'll work up in the spring but a lot of the grazing is rough. Horses is choosy animals. They won't just eat any old thing because it looks green. It could do with a flock of sheep over it to chew it all down a bit.'

'And where do we get a flock of sheep?'

'It's coming up to lambing time now,' George said, 'and it's mostly well sheltered ground. If word were put around I dare say there'd be a few takers, specially if you don't ask too high a price.'

'George, I'll leave it in your capable hands. Now, let's have a look at your pony.'

As they approached the stable block and George ushered him into the cosy half light of the stalls, the pony, the sole occupant, looked up from the manger and whickered a greeting.

'Nice little creature,' George said, running his hand over the animal's flank. 'Well mannered and lively.'

'You can give me a run down to the station later on. I shall go back on the seven twenty. Where do you keep the trap?'

'It's down in one of the cart sheds by the farm. There's nowhere up here with a wide enough doorway.'

'Better have a look around the farm, I suppose. In a bit of a state, I understand.'

'It's neglected, that's all. Hasn't been lived in since the land was sold off. The last tenant reckoned he couldn't make a living off what was left, so I'm told.'

Situated about sixty yards or so behind and to the side of the Manor House, the Home Farm stood down hill at a lower level, surrounded by stables, a barn and other outbuildings. It looked forlorn in its unoccupied state, with weeds growing from crevices and everywhere, peeling paint had left exposed wood on window frames and doors but, as with the Manor, the buildings looked sound enough. A lick of paint and someone living there and the place would come alive again.

Looking at the run of the ground, Luke gestured in the direction of the house. 'We'll need a trench dug from up there, straight down through here and out beyond the orchard to take the drainage pipes. I should imagine the cesspit could be dug somewhere down there,' pointing to an area well away from the farm. 'This place can be connected at the same time. No point doing the job twice but we'll have a separate quotation for a bathroom in here as well. Yes. Not a bad place, this. I can see why you're happy to stay. I reckon my weekends'll get longer as time goes on. After we have a few modern facilities, that is,' giving a hint of a smile.

George pulled out his watch. 'I reckoned as much. We'd best get back in or we'll be in bother with the missus. Steak and kidney pud, today, as well. All this 'ere planning and thinking 'as made me hungry,' and they started back for the house where they found everyone already seated at the kitchen table, savouring the appetising smells coming from the stove as Mrs Cherry lifted the muslin-wrapped pudding basins from the steamer.

'Mrs C, you're a cook in a million,' Luke said. 'I defy anyone to produce better fare.'

'Why, thank you, kind sir,' replied Mrs Cherry, smiling and dropping a curtsey.

'No, no, I couldn't,' Luke protested, as jam roly poly appeared. 'I won't be able to move.

Lunch over, Peter and Lucy were allowed to disappear for an hour whilst the adults lingered over coffee and Luke outlined the first stage of the improvements that he and George had discussed.

'So, Mrs C, there'll be wall paper and paint colours to choose. I'm sure you'll be better at it than I'll ever be so you'll just have to tear yourself away from the stove.'

'She'll never do it,' George muttered. 'It'll be pattern book in one 'and and mixing spoon in t'other.'

'Well, George Cherry, as I can't cope with two jobs at once, you'd best get all those dirty dishes out to the scullery so's the girls can make a start on 'em. I've got scones to make while the oven's hot and I'll need this table.'

George shook his head in mock dismay. 'See how badly I'm treated, Guv? No peace for the wicked in this kitchen,' and he dutifully started to clear the table, which gave Miss Hetherington the opening she was waiting for and asked if she might have a word with Luke.

'Of course,' he immediately agreed and they left the kitchen to find somewhere private. 'We'll use the study. We should be undisturbed there. I can guess what you're wishing to discuss. Your position here?'

'Well, yes,' she replied, diffidently. 'I was wondering whether I should seek a new position or not.'

'Would you care to remain in your present post? If so, I'd want to make alterations to the terms of your engagement.'

Miss Hetherington looked embarrassed. 'I find it a difficult subject to discuss,' she faltered, 'but yes, I should very much like to remain here, it's just that, oh, I really do not know how to express myself.'

Luke held up his hand. 'I think I understand. Whatever salary was agreed has not been forthcoming and I believe you were good enough to spend your savings on food and necessities for your charges? Not everyone would've done that so I'd be very glad if you'd continue here and help Mrs Cherry make the house run smoothly.

She's been my housekeeper for some time now and I regard her as a valued friend. Likewise with George who'll take responsibility as steward for the whole property. I doubt Mrs Cherry'll stray far from her kitchen by choice but if you could lend a hand, perhaps by keeping an eye on the cleaning and tidying of the house and keeping the accounts? That sort of thing? How does that sound?'

'I like the idea very much indeed,' Miss Hetherington replied. 'I am sure I can work happily with Mrs Cherry. She really is a lovely person.'

'Good,' Luke said. 'Would forty a year be acceptable? All found, of course, and I wish to reimburse you for your earlier expenditure. Your room in the attic appears to be inconvenient so if you'd care to choose another, please do so and furnish it as you wish.'

Miss Hetherington's eyes had nearly popped out of her head at the offer of the salary for it was far in excess of that normally offered to governesses and was such a huge increase on what she had been earning that she could scarcely believe it.

'I just don't know what to say, Mr Gregory. It really is most generous of you,' she stammered.

'I'm sure you'll earn every penny but I'm relying on your complete loyalty and trust in all matters. There was something else you wished to discuss?'

'Yes,' she answered. 'It's Peter. He used to attend a preparatory school near Woking, as a boarder, but just before we all met you, he was expelled for stealing from another boy's play box and sent home in disgrace. He had only been back here a day when Mr Brierly called and he is afraid that now you are his guardian you will punish him as his father would. He knows there is a letter from his headmaster addressed to Squire Travers on the desk.'

Luke got out of his chair, crossed the room to the desk and picked up a buff coloured envelope bearing a Woking date stamp. He stood for a while in thought, tapping it against his fingers then held it out to Miss Hetherington.

'Give it to him. Tell him to open it, read it and destroy it. As far as I'm concerned, whatever happened took place before I met him so is none of my business. There must be no repetition mind, and he never steals again, at any time, from anyone. Every dog is allowed one bite and this is his. Then, I suppose, I must sort out another school for him.'

'Yes, I will certainly do that,' Miss Hetherington said, rising. 'I think that is a very kind and wise decision.'

'One more thing before you start lessons again. That room upstairs you use as a schoolroom is gloomy and not very warm. Why not work down here? Light a fire and make yourselves comfortable.'

'Oh, that would be lovely. We should all find that much more enjoyable.'

★ ★ ★

Luke spent most of the afternoon walking around the grounds until rain made him seek refuge in the kitchen. The tangled wood particularly interested him for he could see it had once been looked after, the shape of the growth clearly indicating coppicing at some time. There'd be enough timber in that wood to keep a fire burning in the hall for evermore, he thought, without touching the mature trees and thinning out would improve the appearance no end. There was certainly plenty to think about. Different things too, which took him back to his early years at Dean House. What had he most enjoyed doing there? He tried to recall different occasions before the Reverend Banks changed it all.

Yes, rambling alone through the woods. He used to know all sorts of different birds and animals by sight. Flowers and plants, too. What were those funny things that used to stick up inside a kind of mantle? Lords and ladies! That was it, and those earliest yellow flowers that George called aconites, and there they were, a whole carpet of them now, instead of just one.

That's what he remembered, so perhaps he was a countryman at heart after all and needed to leave the city for a while. Leave behind the dirt and noise, the crime and vice, the misery and degradation and the constant battle to gain and then protect that gain from predators. Which, he wondered, was the biggest jungle? The city or the country?

★ ★ ★

Chapter 3

Warmly dressed for the weather, Luke followed the stationmaster's directions for Bramsden College. February, he thought, was just about the least lovely season of the year and this was a typical February, cold and damp with a heavily clouded sky that promised either snow or that peculiarly bitter, icy rain that was so much a part of English winters.

His appointment with the headmaster was for two o'clock and being assured that the college was only fifteen or twenty minutes steady walk, he decided against taking a cab, preferring to get his circulation going after the discomfort of the unheated railway carriage. Even at this hour there were lights in the shop windows, for it promised to be dark early and what few people were about hurried along, clutching shawls and scarves against the penetrating wind.

He was not looking forward to his meeting with Richard Travers but, as his offer of guardianship to the family had been accepted, it was for him to introduce himself though he was aware he was moving, or had indeed moved, into different social strata. He'd always been a working man, accustomed to boys leaving school at twelve or so to earn their keep and though he lived comfortably, was well dressed and had healthy bank accounts he'd never sought to alter his social standing. Many tried but their pretensions always showed.

Being a close observer of people, he accepted the cultural distinctions between the classes and managed not to drop his aitches when speaking but he knew he lacked the confident poise of the well educated and influential. He would, he thought, fit somewhere in the middle tiers of society and here he was, on the way to a college where boys learned how to be gentlemen until they were eighteen and went on, or was it up, to university. So, approaching the imposing front entrance of the main building he was just a little apprehensive, but determined not to let himself down in these strange waters.

He need not have worried for he was politely welcomed by the headmaster in his academic gown and shown courteously to a seat in his study whilst the school and its academic credentials were described. Richard Travers was, though, a problem, as he was so poorly equipped for school life, something Luke saw for himself when they were introduced. He'd seen some sad sights in his time, at a different level, but the miserable looking boy he met looked quite out of place and he suggested they go for a walk to get to know each other.

'Locking up is at six o'clock, Mr Gregory and if you could spare the time to call in at the house before you leave, Richard's housemaster would appreciate a word.'

'Yes, of course,' Luke replied and to Richard, 'Better get your coat. It's a lazy wind outside,' and ushered him through the door.

The headmaster advanced to see him out. 'I hope that you can do something for him, Mr Gregory. That young man is quite a worry.'

'I shall do my best,' Luke replied. 'My immediate impression is that he is exceedingly poorly dressed. Is that a problem?'

'Ah, yes, it is indeed, and is one of the things his housemaster would like to discuss.'

'Well that at least is something easily rectified. Ah, here he is again.'

Of average size for his age the shabby coat into which he had struggled might have fitted him some two years earlier making him indeed, an embarrassing sight in that setting.

'I will be in touch,' Luke said to the head, and shook hands. 'Come along, young man. Let's brave the elements,' and he led the way through the two sets of doors into the gathering gloom of the afternoon. 'We'll head into town. Much too cold to linger outside and I think we should do a little shopping.'

They walked in silence for a while then Luke asked, 'How do you find the school?'

Richard, walking with bent and drooping shoulders, looked up briefly. 'I don't like it, sir. How did my father die?'

'I don't know exactly,' Luke said, half truthfully for this was no time for gory details. 'It will take a little while to discover all the facts but give me a month or so and I'll be able to tell you. All I know is, there was a mishap with a gun.'

'Did he really lose everything? The house and farm?'

'I believe so,' Luke said, trying hard to choose the right words. 'You do realise, don't you, that I had never met your father?'

'Yes, sir.'

'I think we can dispense with the 'sir' bit. I'm known generally, as the 'Governor', a common enough title, but everyone calls me 'Guv' and that includes you, from now on.

The first thing I want to do is get you kitted out properly. I think you've done a fair bit of growing since you first had that coat. We'll look for decent outfitters and see what they can offer but you must guide me as to what is suitable for school wear.'

'Yes, sir, Guv. He looked up quickly in confusion at his mistake and Luke thought he saw the first glimmer of a smile.

'What do you think to this one?' Luke asked, stopping outside a gentleman's outfitters and haberdashery establishment. 'Shall we have a look at their stock?' and not waiting for an answer, he opened the door and advanced to the counter. An elderly man with a tape measure draped around his neck looked up expectantly and Luke asked to see the ready-made selection of youths and gentleman's suits.

'Is the young gentleman attending the college, sir?' he asked, and on being told 'yes', lead the way to the far end of the shop and indicated a very complete range of pinstriped trousers and short, Eton jackets. 'We have everything here that the college prefers, sir,' he said.

'In that case,' Luke said, 'measure him up and we'll discard the present outfit in its entirety.'

'Certainly, sir, very good, sir,' and Luke settled himself on a convenient chair and watched in quiet satisfaction as Richard was transformed from a caricature of a schoolboy to a smart young gentleman scholar.

'Shirts, underwear, collars,' Luke encouraged, and the elderly outfitter bustled fussily about, opening cupboards and drawers and rummaging behind curtains and succeeding in producing everything of a suitable quality and adequate fit.

'Handkerchiefs, ties, night attire, socks, waistcoat,' Luke continued, remorselessly and the pile of clothing on the counter began to assume respectable proportions.

'Clothes maketh man,' he seemed to remember reading somewhere, or something similar, for Richard was beginning to assume a distinctly improved demeanour already. He was standing up straight now and appraising his new image in the full length mirror fixed to the wall. He was an intelligent-looking, pleasant faced boy with the grey-blue eyes and firm, pointed chin shared with his brother and sister. The family features, he thought. Interesting they should all look so alike. Same coloured hair too, but this one looks a lot paler in complexion, at the moment, anyway.

'Oh, most certainly a top coat, and scarf and gloves also, top hat too, yes.' It had taken over an hour, with Richard flitting back and forth to the fitting room to try on different things but the outfitting was nearly complete. Only sports attire now and boots, shoes and slippers, which this shop didn't stock.

The outfitter had started to add up the cost of the numerous items whilst Luke waited patiently, producing his wallet as the pencil reached the bottom of the column of figures and settled on a total.

'That comes to twenty three pounds and eighteen shillings, sir,' the outfitter announced and Luke paid in bank notes and coin on the understanding that the pile of clothing would be parcelled up and delivered immediately to Halliday's House, where Richard boarded at the college.

They were escorted effusively to the door and Luke immediately set a course for the nearest purveyor of boots and shoes to complete the afternoon's work and, that done, announced, 'After all this effort I need a cup of tea so lead me to the nearest bun shop, will you?' and they entered a cosy, bow-fronted tearoom a little further along the road.

'Tea for two,' he ordered, 'muffins, lightly toasted and a selection of cakes, if you please.' Richard, sitting opposite to him, fidgeting with his hands and clearly ill at ease, looked up, caught Luke's eye and gave a quick, shy smile. 'Thank you ever so much for all this,' he said, blushing bright red.

'Only too happy. Look upon it as coming from home, a little delayed. Ah, the tea. Hot and strong, I hope,' and he poured for them both. 'Milk? Help yourself to sugar. I don't care for it myself.'

The cakes arrived next, followed by the muffins. 'Pitch in before they go cold,' Luke urged and helped himself. 'What's the food like at school?' he asked, struggling to make conversation.

'It's not too bad,' Richard replied, hesitantly, 'except on Thursdays when we have milk puddings and I hate them, only we have to eat everything,' and he gave another quick smile. Starting to thaw, Luke decided. Press on.

'You said earlier that you didn't like the school. Would you care to tell me why?'

Richard coloured up again and looked uncomfortable. 'It was my clothes,' he said, very quietly. 'Everyone kept laughing at me.'

'I see. It must have been very difficult for you.'

'And one of the monitors won't leave me alone,' he continued. 'He keeps picking on me and makes me do all sorts of rotten things that no one else has to do. He calls me 'The Pauper', he added and Luke could see that he was seething with anger at the memory of countless humiliations.

'And the name of this monitor?'

'Stanley. He's head of the dormitory and he keeps whacking me for nothing.' The tears started then and Luke was glad they were the only ones in the tea rooms at the time, but he could have wished for more privacy. Richard regained his composure and looked at Luke to assess his reaction, fearful of contempt at his show of weakness, but Luke reached out and patted his hand.

'I understand,' he said. 'Bullies are unpleasant people at any time and Master Stanley sounds a prize specimen. Tell me, do you know where he comes from and what line his people follow?'

'I think they are in leather. He boasts about his father's manufactory and said that he had the strap he whacks me with, specially made.'

'Ah,' Luke said, gravely. 'Benjamin Stanley and Company of Lambeth.'

'Do you know them, sir, I mean Guv?'

'Indeed I do. I most certainly do. You may safely tell Stanley to leave you alone. If he continues to treat you unfairly, you will write to me immediately and I can assure you Master Stanley will suffer an unpleasant surprise. Now,' he went on, his mood suddenly brightening, 'look at those two cakes all on their own. We can't leave them there. You have first choice.'

The walk back up the hill was a more relaxed one, despite the sleety rain that had begun to fall. Reassured and encouraged by his unaccustomed refreshment, his new clothes and the promise of Luke's support, Richard agreed to try his best to settle at the college. His coat pockets bulged with chocolate and toffee, which he planned to share with his friend, another new boy named Robert Weston, whose father was with the army in India, whilst note paper, envelopes and postage stamps were tucked securely into an inside pocket.

Arrived at his house, Richard self-consciously led Luke to the housemaster's study, their appearance together causing a stir of interest amongst the other boys who happened to be around the entrance hall as they entered.

Mr Halliday, the housemaster, a youngish, academic looking man, regarded Luke with some interest and Richard, in his new clothes, with surprise. Luke immediately took the initiative and forestalled comment by bluntly stating that immediate deficiencies had been made good, he was unable to stay long as he had a train to catch and that he wished Richard to come up to London for the weekend after next to attend to certain matters, which he deliberately did not specify. No point, he thought, in beating about the bush with a man so weak and inept as to allow serious bullying in his house.

'Is there any matter that you wish to discuss at this point?'

Mr Halliday opened and closed his mouth, rather like a fish gasping for oxygen, clearly caught off-balance by Luke's assertive manner. Deciding there wasn't, after all, anything he particularly wished to discuss, Luke announced, 'In that case, Richard can show me out. I'm glad to have met you. Good evening,' and he made for the door, followed by a bewildered Richard who was unused to seeing the august person of his housemaster so firmly and cavalierly handled. What was it, Luke wondered, about schoolmasters that caught him on the raw? He'd have to think that one through.

There was quite a throng of curious boys milling about the hallway when they emerged from the study and who, as one, fell silent. Two paces from the door, Luke halted and glared ferociously about him causing most to lower their eyes or look away. A clear lane leading to the front door appearing as if by magic, he resumed his course, accompanied still by Richard, who was acutely conscious of the attention they were receiving and trying to decide whether it was hostile or not. Almost at the last moment, a boy hastened forward and opened the door for them.

'Thank you,' Luke said, and passing through, put on his hat. Richard stood on the step looking up at him, pale and apprehensive. That was it, Luke decided. Schools have a threatening atmosphere that the masters encourage in order to maintain control with minimum effort. That was what he was subconsciously reacting to, the threat, real or implied and that was what Richard had to learn to cope with.

Putting both hands on his shoulders, He said, 'Don't look so worried. You have nothing to be concerned about as long as you follow the school rules. Remember that you are at least as good as anybody else and are probably better than most. I've enjoyed meeting you and will look forward to seeing you the weekend after next. I'll send you a ticket and arrange for someone to meet you at Waterloo then we'll go home together and you can see Peter and Lucy. All right? Here, put this in your pocket,' and he slipped a half sovereign into his hand. 'Remember, if that fellow bullies you, let me know immediately. Understand?'

'Yes, Guv. Thank you ever so much.'

'Off you go inside now, or they'll think you've done a runner. Cheerio, see you soon,' and Luke turned away and started his walk back to the railway station, hoping he'd be in time for his train.

★ ★ ★

On the Thursday morning, there was a letter from Richard, written in a round, clear hand on the notepaper they'd bought earlier that week. It was dignified, short and to the point, describing how his arch persecutor had made great capital of his new clothing, had taken much of his chocolate and given him a dozen with the strap for cheek when he'd protested and to crown it had made derogatory remarks about The Pauper's Governor.

Luke felt his anger rising. Here was some spotty faced bully having a go at him, a bully who lacked the sense to note a change in his victim's circumstances. Had he been one of the crowd in the hallway of Halliday's? This was a personal affront and hearing Walter arrive and enter his office, Luke gave him time to get his coat off then went downstairs, his face bleak, the letter in his hand.

Walter, seeing the storm signals, enquired, 'Is anything wrong?'

'Write a note for me, would you? To Benjamin Stanley Esq. along the lines that his son, as monitor at Bramsden College has systematically beaten and abused my ward, whom he has labelled 'The Pauper', has stolen his property and made offensive and derogatory remarks about myself. This situation to be remedied forthwith. Dress it up as you see fit and have the boys hand it personally to Stanley. Tell them to hang around and watch for reaction. They know where to take it,' and Luke, his expression still angry, stumped back upstairs leaving Walter to pen the note and send it on its way.

An hour and a half later, Tom and Sammy returned from their errand and reported to Walter, who was checking through the stock market prices from the previous day's trading. 'You found the gentleman in question?' he asked.

'Yes, Mr B. No bovver. The gent came steaming out like a scolded cat. He couldn't get a cab so 'e fair ran all the way to the station. Waterloo. Got the nine thirty-five for Salisbury and went second class.'

'Well done. You'd better go upstairs and tell the guv. Go carefully though. He is far from pleased this morning,' and Tom and Sammy, heeding the warning, walked carefully upstairs and knocked respectfully on the sitting room door.

'Come in,' Luke growled. 'What have you got for me?' He was sitting in his armchair, sorting through a pile of papers but paused as Tom and Sammy repeated their story. 'Good,' he said, and gazed absently into space as if picturing the scene then, looking back at the boys standing uncertainly by the door, he suddenly relaxed.

'Come here. Let's have a look at you,' and they advanced obediently towards him. 'Mm, you're looking fairly civilised these days. Are you ready to move in here yet?'

'In 'ere wiv you, Guv?' It was Sammy who spoke, wonder, excitement and pleasure all jostling for a place in his expression at the same time.

'Yes. You can share the back room at the top, but you have to keep it tidy.'

'Cor, fanks, Guv,' Tom said. 'When can we come?'

'Ask Mr B. when he can spare you then get Charlie to bring your things round. That'll be soon enough. I want you to give Mrs Maddocks a hand in the house, like seeing to the fires and other jobs that George used to do. Now, ask Mr B. to join me up here and then bring us coffee, but make sure it's hot. I can't abide coffee that's not really hot.'

'Right, Guv,' and they clattered off downstairs, bursting to share their news with Walter who, shortly afterwards, joined Luke.

'You've certainly pleased those two young men,' he said. 'They're over the moon about moving in here.'

'All part of the civilising process. They've come a long way, no mistake about that but with George away we're short of help here. When they're settled in, I should like them both to have smarter clothes; a suit each, perhaps. What they have now is all right for sculling around in general but there'll be times when a smarter appearance will be appropriate.'

Footsteps on the stair and a knock at the door signalled the arrival of the coffee. 'Can we go up and 'ave a look at the room, Guv?' Tom asked.

'If you go quietly, both ways,' and they tiptoed off with exaggerated, mock care, grinning hugely at Luke and Walter.

'You'll probably be wondering about this morning's drama. It's pure coincidence that Stanley's son attends the same school as Richard but I'm hoping he's gone off to box his offspring's ears, which should solve Richard's problem.

'I see,' Walter said. 'That is interesting and is why I'm glad my own boys were entered as day boys. So often, a school can offer an excellent education but the boarding conditions can leave much to be desired.'

'If I'm not satisfied with present arrangements for Richard, I shan't hesitate to send him elsewhere, which is why I'm looking very carefully at possible schools for Peter. He appears to have certain difficulties and I'm anxious to make the right choice. Funny, all this. A month or so ago I wouldn't have given schools a thought and here I am, holding forth on the subject as if I'd been a family man for years.'

★ ★ ★

Tom was sent to meet Richard at the station on the Friday morning and, feeling proud and important, was waiting for the Salisbury train a good half hour before it was due, which didn't please Charlie, as he waited with his cab.

Assured he would have no difficulty in recognising Richard, he walked impatiently about the concourse but never far from the barrier at the end of platform four, constantly glancing at the slow-moving hands of the station clock.

Two minutes early, the train eased steamily alongside the platform and disgorged its passengers, who streamed through the gate, handing their spent tickets to the uniformed collector as they passed.

'Are you Richard Travers?' Tom asked, already quite certain he'd picked the right person. 'I'm Tom Collins. The guv sent me ter meet yer. I works in 'is office,' and, as instructed, he extended his hand in greeting. Richard, who had expected to be met by an adult, hesitantly shook hands, appraising his cockney companion with interest.

'Have you known the guv for long,' he asked.

'Bout a year or so. Me an' me mate, Sammy, was wiv the Doctor, dahn Stepney way 'till the guv took us on an' now we lives in 'is 'ouse. This 'ere's Charlie 'oo drives us arahnd an' this is Ginger, the best cab 'oss in town. Ain't that right, Charlie?'

Introductions thus made, they rattled off towards the City, with Richard looking curiously about him as they threaded their way through the congested streets, listening the while to Tom's non stop chatter and managing, from time to time, to ask one of the many questions buzzing through his mind.

'What does the guv do?' he asked. 'I mean, what sort of business has he?'

'The guv? Oh, all sorts of fings. E's got ware'ouses by the river, dahn stream from 'ere, below London Bridge, an' barges and lighters an' a shop and 'e fixes fings. Yer know, anyone wiv a problem 'as a word wiv the guv an 'e sorts it out. If yer needs a few 'eavies, frinstance, fer a bodyguard, the guv 'as some real 'ard cases dahn the wharf, an' then 'e 'as interests, like, in the City, 'im an' 'is partner, that is. Shares an' fings, like the railway back there. You met Digger? That's 'is partner. E's a card, 'e is. The guv don't say a lot, 'e jus' growls at yer but Digger, 'e's different. Little bloke 'e is, bout my size an' allus tellin' jokes. Been wiv the guv fer years an' 'oo 'e don't know ain't werf knowin. E tells the guv 'oo's arahnd an' wot's goin' on an' such like. Is missis is all right too. She was wiv the Guv too, when she were a nipper.'

Tom paused for breath and glanced at Richard to see his reaction, and was gratified to note that his recital had suitably impressed his audience and, thus encouraged, added a few further comments.

'Mind you, the guv gets narky if anyone gets nosey. Very private bloke, the guv an' no one pushes 'im arahnd, not if they wants ter stay 'elfy, that is. E's a tough 'un but 'e's fair an' 'e'll do anyone a good turn like, no matter 'oo, but God 'elp anyone wot gets the wrong side of 'im', with which warning note Tom broke off to point out one of the team standing on a street corner who waved to Joe. 'That's Fergus Malone. E works mainly wiv Digger. Keeps an eye on the runners.'

'What are runners?' Richard asked, his curiosity aroused.

'They takes messages an' keeps watch on places an' such like. They could be anyone; nippers, mainly I reckon but I don't know 'em all an' then there's the watchers, 'oo stays in one place. Some of 'em are bootblacks an' there's a coupla flower sellers I knows of,' he ended, a bit uncertainly. 'Well, 'ere we are. This is where the guv 'angs out when 'e's in town. Nice comfy 'ouse. Mrs Maddocks is the 'ousekeeper now Mrs Cherry 'as gorn dahn ter your place.'

Luke was in his sitting room, working methodically through The Times when Richard was ushered in by Tom.' Ere 'e is, Guv, all safe an' sound.'

'Thank you, Tom' and Luke rose from his chair and offered his hand in greeting to Richard, who stood uncertainly by the door. 'Come along in and make yourself comfortable,' he said, indicating the other armchair by the fireside.

'You met Mr Brierly on your way in, I expect. He's our legal adviser and is usually to be found here. You've missed my partner but you'll meet him before long. How is school?'

Richard coloured up and looked down at the floor before replying, hesitantly. 'It's so different, sir, I mean, Guv. It's not like it was before.'

'I take it things have improved?'

'Oh, yes, Guv,' Richard replied, more confidently. 'I don't get bullied any more. All the fellows are ever so much more friendly and even the masters seem to be better. We have a new monitor in our dorm now as Stanley has moved to another house. Guv, what did you do? I mean, he apologised to me for being so beastly. He asked me to forgive him and said if he could do anything for me at any time, I had only to ask him. He was quite different. I know his pater came down to see him,' he tailed off uncertainly, looking confused as he met Luke's eye.

'Perhaps, as the problem is resolved, we should leave it at that? Now, we'll take the three fifteen train this afternoon for Guildford and be at Chidlingbrook by five thirty. In the meantime I wish you to meet everyone here and get to know your way around.

The train journey to Guildford and then on to Chidlingbrook, they passed largely in silence, both being pre-occupied with their separate thoughts as they looked out at the wintry scene. Here and there, patches and streaks of snow clung to the hedgerows where it was sheltered from the feeble rays of the sun that was already setting in a gloomy, overcast sky.

A brisk walk from the station warmed them up and both looked forward to the comfort and welcome of the Manor so, heading straight for the back door, Luke led the way into the kitchen, transformed now under Mrs Cherry's tireless care. As he had anticipated, it was warm and heavy with the smells of fresh baking, a happy enough introduction to the new regime for Richard, who was warmly welcomed by Mrs Cherry and as warmly shaken by the hand by George.

'I should find your brother and sister,' Luke advised. 'I'll stay here and sample home cooking and a nice cup of tea,' and he shrugged off his coat and laid it on the bench seat together with his gloves, scarf and hat. 'I can see you've been busy,' he commented approvingly to George and Mrs Cherry. 'You're well on your way to getting the place ship shape.'

'There's a lot of interest in the village about this place,' George said. 'A feller from the next village has been along to look at the carpentry side of things. He's a wheelwright by trade but his price doesn't look that bad. I've a whole list of jobs and prices for you to look at and the blacksmith in the village reckons as how he can fix up all the hot water. Says as 'e's been studying heating systems, same as they have over in America. Showed me a book and a catalogue of pipes and fittings. Reckons you can heat a whole building from one hot water boiler. Dead keen 'e is to do the job. They all are, come to that. Seems there's not much work about at present. We've had enquiries from lads down here to old men who should have their feet up be the fire this weather. It's worse'n down the docks, I reckon.'

'Mm,' Luke commented, noncommittally. 'We'll go through your list in the morning. It'll be easier than trying to see things in the dark.'

The door from the hall opened and Miss Hetherington entered, followed by Peter, Lucy and Richard and after the usual greetings they all settled round the table and Luke was amused by the way they all attempted to sit on the far side of the table, leaving him the sole occupant of one side.

'Someone'll have to sit near me,' he said, 'otherwise I'll get lonely,' and Mrs Cherry spread everyone around in her best no-nonsense manner, assuring everyone it was quite safe, as the guv wouldn't bite anyone, at least not in her kitchen, which produced some sheepish grins and broke the ice.

★ ★ ★

Luke and George were outside looking up at the chimneystacks when the sound of bleating sheep interrupted their discussion and the first of a flock appeared around the bend of the drive.

'I should've mentioned they was coming,' George said. 'Farmer over the hill liked the idea of lambing here because of the sheltered ground. He's got fifty-eight ewes in lamb and he'll leave a shepherd and his lad to tend 'em. He's paying six pence a head, which is cheap enough, but they'll do the grazing a power of good. He'll have to watch the foxes, though. I've seen two by the trees in broad daylight.'

The sheep quickly spread out on the rough grass in front of the Manor and started grazing enthusiastically whilst the shepherd, a weathered-looking man, approached and, removing his hat, enquired if there was anywhere the sheep had to be kept from. Told that all the grass was for his use he replaced his hat, gazed around, then pointed. 'Look you, bold as brass,' and following his pointing finger Luke saw a fox over by the fence, staring at the sheep. 'Dogs'll see un off,' and placing two fingers in his mouth, he let out a series of short, shrill whistles.

Immediately, both collies tore off in the direction of the fox, which took to its heels, making for cover. More whistles and the collies stopped in their tracks and returned to their stations, watching the spot where the fox had disappeared from view.

'Now they knows, they'll not let un near,' was the confident opinion.

'You have them well trained,' Luke said, impressed.

'Arr. Reet good dogs. Father and son they be, the best pair I ever did 'ave,' and he walked slowly off, clucking and talking to the nearest animals who glanced up at him then went on grazing.

'Never had dealings with sheep,' George said. 'Cattle an' horses aplenty, pigs as well, but never sheep.'

'Well, back to the chimneys,' Luke said and they carried on with their discussion of repair work. By lunchtime they'd completed the task as had Miss Hetherington and her charges, who had spent the morning gathering up the late squire's belongings for necessary disposal.

They were a bit subdued at lunchtime but, afterwards, with money in pockets and purse, all three went off to buy sweets in the village and tobacco for Luke and George. By the time they returned, everything they'd collected during the morning was out of sight.

The weekend passed too quickly for Luke and Richard, who parted company at Guildford on the Monday morning, Luke to take the up train to Waterloo and Richard one in the opposite direction to Salisbury. He was, Luke decided, more relaxed and contented now, with the Easter holiday not so far off and he was satisfied that a pattern of organisation had begun to take shape, with George overseeing everything, Mrs Cherry reigning supreme in her kitchen and Miss Hetherington teaching her pupils and directing the general domestic side of things, with responsibilities, by mutual agreement, overlapping.

★ ★ ★

It had been a busy week and Luke was looking forward to spending the weekend at the Manor so he caught the three fifteen from Waterloo and found the connecting train waiting at the branch platform at Guildford, ready to take passengers up the valley.

The first-class compartments were in the first of the three coaches and Luke was about to enter the compartment of his choice when a voice called to him from the cab of the locomotive. 'That is you, ain't it, Guv?' and a figure in blue overalls and railman's cap stepped down onto the platform.

Luke stared hard at the coal-stained face, then held out his hand. 'Johnny Barron. So you made it. Well done,' and they shook hands, Luke ignoring the grime.

'I'm a driver now,' Johnny said. 'With luck I'll be on the main line before long, on expresses. I've got you to thank fer this, yer know. If I'd stayed on the river I'd be doing time, I reckon.'

'I'm sure you would but it's good to see you. Better get aboard, though. I can see the station master looking at his watch,' and Luke entered his compartment, reflecting once more on how easily the course of a life could be changed.

Alighting at Chidlingbrook twenty minutes later, he saw Johnny leaning from his cab to see at which of the five stations on the branch line he'd get out, and he acknowledged his call of 'Cheerio Guv,' with a wave.

'Evening, Guv. How's the smoke?' George greeted him from his seat in the trap.

'Same as usual, Luke replied. 'The air is sweeter here and no mistake. Everything all right?'

'Just about,' George said. 'Spot o' bother with young Peter though. Playing up a fair bit he is and giving Miss Heatherington a hard time. Seems to 'ave given up washing, too.'

'I'll have a word with him. Can't have that sort of thing.'

As George took the pony and trap down to the cart shed to unharness, Lucy's puppy came wobbling up on its short, fat legs, yapping squeakily and Lucy herself appeared from around the corner in pursuit. Seeing Luke, she waved and called out 'Hello Guv,' and running up, gave him a kiss on the cheek.

'Hello, my dear, and how are you?'

'Very well, thank you, and so is Topsy, but he's chewed your slippers up. You won't be cross, will you?' she asked, looking very serious.

'Well, as long as he doesn't make a habit of it,' Luke said. 'Now, what's for tea? I'm starving.'

'Mrs Cherry's made a great big fruit cake and lots of scones,' Lucy said. 'I helped her to stir things in the bowl because it was very stiff and it made our arms ache so and I've made something very special, all by myself. Would you like to try it?'

'I most certainly would,' Luke said and hand in hand they entered the kitchen, where Mrs Cherry was placing plates and cups around one end of the big table.

Luke had decided early on that he was happy to wander into the kitchen for an informal meal, with the minimum of fuss. After all, it was the hub of the house, spotlessly clean now and a warm and homely place, alive with the gorgeous smells of fresh-baked bread and pies and in the mornings, of bacon, coffee and toast.

'Tea's ready, Guv. Sit yourself down. I'll just get some more butter,' and she bustled over to the cool corner, farthest from the cooking range, where a pile of fresh butter sat on a marble slab under a muslin cover.

Luke helped himself to scones and jam, scones that melted in the mouth and jam that tasted of fruit. This is living, he thought. Different altogether from the town house, though he'd not exactly starved there. Must be the setting and the atmosphere that was so refreshing.

Lucy carried over her special creation that appeared to be a shapeless mound of pastry of a slightly greyish hue from which currants and raisins peeped and with a preserved cherry on the top. Placing it directly in front of him, Lucy looked at it proudly and told him, 'You can eat it all if you like.'

'That is kind of you,' Luke said, 'but surely you're going to have some as well.'

'Oh no, that's all right,' Lucy said. You are quite welcome to have it all.'

'Well, I think it's far too nice for just one person. Why don't we cut it into pieces so that George can have some, too. I happen to know he's very fond of cakes like this,' and Luke thought he saw Mrs Cherry's shoulders jerking. 'Isn't that right, Mrs Cherry?'

There was a slight spluttering, quickly subdued with a handkerchief and Mrs Cherry turned, with perfectly controlled expression and solemnly agreed that George was, indeed, most fond of such delicacies and had been hoping he might be offered some, at which point the unsuspecting George entered by the back door and seated himself at the table.

Lucy slipped onto his lap and the division was carefully made, four ways as it happened, and with the formal declaration that a great culinary success had been achieved, Lucy beamed and promised to make something else, at the earliest opportunity.

'Now,' Luke said, feeling inwardly content once more, 'I shall change into something old and comfortable and have a wander round outside. Where's master Peter got too? I would've thought he'd join us for tea.'

Mrs Cherry and George exchanged glances. 'He's probably in his room,' George said. 'He seems to spend a lot of time there lately.'

'Oh,' Luke said, 'I see,' and left the kitchen to change. He'd have half an hour for a walk round before it became too dark to see and then he'd spend a quiet, relaxing time by the log fire in the hall before retiring early to bed.

Just thinking about it was refreshing. Perhaps he needed the country more than he realised, for the peace and quiet of this house was such a pleasant change from his usual surroundings.

★ ★ ★

Breakfast was served next day in the dining room at eight o'clock, Mrs Cherry carrying in from the kitchen the various dishes that made up this substantial meal. Miss Hetherington and Lucy were already seated when Luke took his place and after their formal but friendly exchange of greetings, they tucked into their ham and eggs with enthusiasm.

'No Peter this morning?' Luke enquired casually, but before anyone had time to reply, Peter slouched into the room and slumped down onto his chair. He was very untidily dressed and appeared unwashed and unkempt. In short, Luke thought, he looked as if he'd been dragged through a hedge backwards. He sat, sprawled on his chair, his chin sunk on his chest, his arms dangling loosely by his side, saying nothing. Luke looked at him quizzically whilst Miss Hetherington and Lucy concentrated hard upon their plates.

'Something amiss?' Luke enquired and Peter pushed back his chair and rushed from the room.

When Lucy had finished eating, Luke asked her to leave the room. 'So what was that all about?' he asked Miss Hetherington.

'Well, Mr Gregory, Peter has always been a difficult boy for at least as long as I have known him. I came here as governess after the squire's wife died six years ago, when Peter was five. He has great difficulty in learning to read and write and his father believed he was being deliberately awkward and used to punish him severely. I'm afraid he's had some terrible whippings but he still cannot read or write properly. He says the words and letters keep jumping about but he's had his eyes tested and no disorder was found so he was sent to a preparatory school but, as you know, was expelled. I believe he is apprehensive of attending the other school at which you have entered him'

'I see. I'd better have a word with him,' and leaving the dining room, went upstairs to Peter's room and tried the door. It was locked. 'Open the door,' he ordered. For a moment, nothing happened, then he heard the sound of the key turning in the lock and, opening the door, went in. Peter was standing just inside the room, cowering slightly, his face pale. Luke studied him for a while. He's scared stiff, he thought.

'So what's the problem? Peter stared at him and said something inaudible. 'Is it about the next school you're about to go to?' Peter nodded but said nothing. 'Because you have trouble reading? Miss Hetherington has told me of the problem.'

Eventually, in little more than a whisper, 'I get beaten if I can't read properly.'

'Hardly the answer if you can't see properly so come Monday we'll ask a doctor friend of mine what he thinks but no matter what, you'll behave like a gentleman and not go upsetting Miss Hetherington or anyone else. Is that clear? Now, tell me, what sort of things are you interested in? What d'you like doing?'

'I like trains,' Peter said, shyly.

'Trains. Railway trains, you mean? I see. What else?'

'I like animals and I've got a garden, too. Joe helps me with it.'

'You must show me later; I'd like to see it, but first off, wash your face and have your breakfast in the kitchen. Can't do anything on an empty stomach then tonight you'll have a good scrub until you're gleaming. If I'm not satisfied, I'll set Big Eva on you. She's a very large lady with a very large scrubbing brush she uses on grubby folks who won't wash. Alright?'

★ ★ ★

Now for a look round and he wandered off outside, interested to see what progress had been made with the cesspit in the field below the farmhouse. Two men and a boy were at work, lining an enormous hole in the ground with a double row of shiny bricks. The line of the pipe-run down the slope from farm and house was marked out, with the turf lifted from a two foot wide strip and laid neatly to one side for later replacement. Giving them 'good day,' Luke asked the purpose of the two separate chambers that were taking shape in the hole.

'Well, sir,' said the older of the two men, 'this 'ere is a septic tank. When one side is filled up it can be left to settle an' go off, like, and the flow sent into the other one. Then, when the first 'un is nice and firm, wi' no smell, it can be dug out and emptied, ready for filling again. Grows lovely taters, does that. Better'n pig or horse any day, ain't that so, Fred?' turning to his companion for confirmation of this most profound truth.

Fred, a man of few words, added his agreement by means of a deep-throated 'Arr', and nodded his head. The boy had the good sense to stay silent.

Thanking them for their explanation, Luke strolled back up the slope to the farm where he saw Peter standing by the end of the implement shed, apparently taking a close interest in the stonework, which he was rubbing with his forefinger though Luke could see he was covertly watching him as he approached. Waiting to be noticed, he guessed.

'Had your breakfast?'

'Yes, Guv,' with half a smile.

'Like to show me your garden?'

This time, a full smile, and he led the way behind the stables and along the path at the rear of the house to a cultivated area showing signs of recent digging. Mostly, though, it was covered with weeds and the remains of last year's planting.

'Joe started to dig this bit,' he said 'but he can't do a lot because he's old, so I'm going to do some.'

'He lives in the village, does he?' Luke asked.

'Yes, but he doesn't come in very early now. He looks after the hens and things.'

'He certainly looks a very old man. Has he thought of retiring?'

'Oh yes, but he said he can't because he hasn't got much money saved,' Peter said, seriously. 'He says it's difficult to walk all the way here, sometimes.'

'Well, when you next see him, ask him if he'd like a pension. It'll be better coming from you. Old people are suspicious of strangers.'

'Yes, Guv,' Peter said, looking very solemn.

'It's a bit early for gardening, I suppose,' Luke said. 'Nip inside and tell Mrs Cherry or someone we're walking down to the village. We'll see if a friend of mine is about.'

Together, they walked the quarter mile into the village, heading for the station, not talking a great deal, with Peter stealing quick glances at Luke.

Chidlingbrook was small enough as stations went but it served the largest village on the line and boasted a ticket and parcels office and a lamp and maintenance store and was staffed by two porters and a station master, the latter newly promoted and proud of his small, but neat and tidy station.

'See what time the next train arrives,' Luke suggested, and Peter went to ask, barely giving the displayed timetable a glance.

'It's the ten forty five up train,' he reported, 'which comes back as the eleven thirty down train for Guildford.'

'Can you not pick it out from the time table?' Luke asked.

Peter looked crestfallen. 'No, Guv,' he said.

'Look at these figures and letters here,' Luke said, indicating the top line. 'Don't worry. Just tell me what you can see. I'm curious, that's all.'

Peter concentrated hard. 'I can see a nought, a six, a three and a nought,' he said. 'Next to it is a nought, an eight, a one and then a five that looks backwards and now the first six has changed into a d.' He looked up at Luke, worried and fearful.

'I see. Don't look so upset. You got the six thirty right first time, which shows you understand figures but the trouble started with the second group, eight fifteen, when figures looked backwards. Is that it?'

Peter nodded, miserably.

'Well, that could easily be your eyes playing tricks, couldn't it. On Monday, we'll get my doctor friend to give his opinion. You'll like him. He's full of fun and what he doesn't know about boys isn't worth knowing. The train's coming from that direction, isn't it? Right. I'll expect you to tell me what kind of locomotive it is. Five minutes to wait, then.'

They first glimpsed the smoke of the approaching engine when it was about a mile away as it rounded a bend and shortly afterwards it eased gently alongside the platform, and the driver stepped down from the cab.

'Ullo, Guv. What brings you 'ere again? Not train spottin', are yer?'

'I was hoping it'd be you, Johnny. This is Peter. He's interested in your trade. Any chance of a ride in the cab?'

'For you, Guv, anyfing,' was the immediate reply and Johnny offered his grimy hand to Peter. 'Any mate of the guv's is a mate o' mine,' he said. 'Hop aboard, young 'un. I'll 'ave a quick word wiv Bob. E's the stationmaster an' it'll stop 'im worryin'. You still a share 'older, Guv? No problem then. Bob'll want ter kiss yer 'and or anywhere else yer fancy when 'e 'ears 'e's got a share 'older on 'is platform.'

Luke watched the train pull out and was conscious of Peter's beaming face as he waved goodbye. 'Throw him out when you've had enough of him,' had been Luke's final injunction and Johnny had waved and grinned before turning his attention to his controls.

The station master was waiting for him by his office door and touched his cap respectfully. 'I understand you are a shareholder in the company, sir,' he said.

'That's right and you're Mr Anstey? It's good of you to be understanding where my boy is concerned. Much appreciated. Of course, I've known Driver Barron for a long time. Very well thought of by Mr Beattie when he was at the depot. I take a close interest in the company and I must say, you keep a smart station. I'll let it be known in the right place. A very good day to you,' and Luke offered his hand, which was shaken by an enormously gratified stationmaster, who flushed with pleasure at Luke's words.

That, Luke thought, is Master Peter taken care of where trains are concerned, provided he doesn't do anything foolish of course and strolled leisurely past the Lamb, hesitated and changed direction. 'Why not?' he asked himself. No harm in a couple before lunch. Nice and relaxing, and he entered the bar, a plain, functional room with whitewashed walls and a couple of high-backed settles by the open fireplace. A mixture of coal and logs, Luke noticed as he approached the bar, behind which a row of casks lay in racks.

His entry caused interest amongst the few assembled there as he ordered a pint of strong ale, served in a pewter tankard. Not a bad brew, this he thought and asked for a cigar to go with it. Not bad either, a mild Havana and he settled comfortably on a stool, leaning back against a pillar supporting both bar and ceiling, slowly exhaling blue smoke.

'A pleasant day for the time of year,' the landlord said, conversationally.

'Indeed it is,' Luke agreed. 'At least you can see the sun when it shines, the air is that clear. I've been breathing smoke and fog all week, so it's a real pleasure to leave it behind.'

Outside, there was a clatter of horse's hooves and loud voices and immediately, the atmosphere changed. All eyes turned towards the door, which crashed open as a large, red-faced man in mud spattered hunting pink and top hat strode in, brandishing a riding crop. He immediately banged this violently on the bar, as if to attract attention, though the landlord was present and attentive enough, but no longer smiling.

'Brandy,' the red faced man ordered, as he and his companion, a tall, haughty young man, similarly attired for the hunt, spread themselves out against the bar. 'Move away,' he snarled in Luke's direction.

'Go to the devil,' Luke replied coolly.

The red faced one turned towards Luke, seeming to swell with rage, his face turning purple with passion, the riding crop coming up ready to strike. Luke continued to loll against the pillar, tankard in hand, cigar in mouth and looked him straight in the eye. The crop stopped in mid air as its owner considered the wisdom of assaulting a stranger.

'And who the devil are you?'

Luke ignored the question and continued to puff at his cigar without removing it from his mouth, ready to hurl the contents of his tankard at the angry face.

'I said who the devil are you?' stamping his foot.

'I heard you,' Luke replied.

'Er, this is the gentleman from the Manor, Sir Brandon,' the landlord intervened in worried tones.

'Ha!' the red-faced man barked. 'The city upstart come to live in the country, heh? Well let me tell you, we don't like your sort round here. Get in my way and you'll regret it,' and he thrust his face forward aggressively. Luke removed the cigar from his mouth and blew a cloud of smoke at him, causing him to step backwards and swear horribly.

'Come along, pater,' the young man drawled, 'no need to soil your hands on such types,' and taking this cue, the red faced baronet stamped towards the door, turning to brandish his riding crop at Luke.

'You mark my words. I'll remember you!' to which Luke replied with a traditional Anglo-Saxon salute, his cigar back in his mouth.

A silence settled over the room following their departure and Luke drained his tankard, his enjoyment gone because of the unpleasant incident.

'Who was that person?' he asked the landlord.

'Sir Brandon Remnold, sir. His estate is across the valley but he bought up the manor land when it was sold off, including most of the village, here. A very difficult man, sir.'

'And the other one?'

'His son, sir. His eldest son, Percival.'

'People to avoid, I think.'

★ ★ ★

Chapter 4

He left then to walk back to the Manor, unsettled by the unpleasantness. In fact, that fellow had fairly spoiled his day and he sat brooding on the wide settle by the hall fire. He'd come down for a quiet, relaxing weekend and found conflict forced upon him. Damn that fat oaf. If he was typical of his neighbours, he'd want nothing to do with them.

His household knew by his mood that something had happened and kept out of his way, not caring to enquire about Peter's whereabouts and wondering if he was the cause but they need not have worried. At half past four, he rushed into the kitchen, face glowing from hard running and excitedly related to an astonished Mrs Cherry his adventures on the footplate of the branch line locomotive.

Miss Hetherington too, on entering the kitchen, was greeted with a description of how he'd been shown all the controls in the cab and how he'd operated them with the driver, who'd known the guv for a long time, and had been shown how to stoke the fire. It wasn't just a case of throwing coal in and shutting the door, he explained. You had to spread the fire evenly and load from the back or a hot spot would develop and turn into holes in the fire bed and then you'd lose steam pressure, and so on.

Never, Miss Hetherington remarked later to Mrs Cherry, had she ever seen Peter so animated and yes, happy, but that was after he'd gone in search of Luke whom he found sitting alone still in the hall, staring at the flames of the fire. Breaking into his black mood with his excited chatter, Peter regaled him with the need to keep the oil cups on the big end bearings of the axles filled with oil up to the correct mark together with other items of a technical nature, and Luke was brooding no more.

'And what kind of locomotive was that?' Luke asked.

Peter drew himself up and struggled to recall accurately this vital information. 'It was an Adams four four nought with outside cylinders. It was three years old and its driving wheels were five feet and seven inches across. I can't remember its boiler pressure but Johnny did tell me. He said I could call him Johnny, if that's all right with you, Guv. He says everyone calls him that and he said he'd do anything for you, Guv. Did you really hide him in a bed when the police were looking for him and they were standing right next to him?'

'That was all a long time ago. The river was a very rough place in those days, much rougher than it is now and it's never peaceful at the best of times. It must be about tea time. I think we should go and hunt up something to eat, don't you? You must be starving by now. You've had nothing since this morning.'

'I had some of Johnny's,' Peter replied, cheerfully. 'We cooked bacon on the back of a shovel in the fire and there's a tap in the cab for boiling water to make tea. It tasted lovely.' A pause. 'Can I tell you something?'

'Go on.'

'At the station, I cleaned some lamps that had red glass in them. When I looked through the glass at the time table, the figures didn't jump, but when I looked without the red glass, they got all mixed up again.'

Luke pondered this a while, weighing it up and testing the logic of it. 'You mean the coloured glass helped you see better?'

'Yes, sort of.'

'That's interesting. I'll give it some thought. Now, let's see what Mrs Cherry has to offer.'

★ ★ ★

Back on his seat by the fire, relaxed now, he carefully filled his pipe, lit it with a wooden spill and settled back comfortably to enjoy a quiet smoke. This seat promised to be his favourite place for the large, open fireplace, with its blazing logs, was somehow coming to represent all he had striven so hard to achieve. Great blustering oafs, like that fellow in the Lamb, were to be found everywhere he reflected and he'd be silly to let him or others of his ilk get under his skin and he turned his attention again to improvements to the house.

Gas lights wouldn't be out of place, he thought, but little chance of being connected out here. That new fangled electric system might have possibilities though. He'd make enquiries, but he was not to be left in peace for Miss Hetherington was anxious to tell him how much happier the children were this evening. She should know, he supposed. She's been around them long enough. 'Must be Mrs Cherry's cooking,' he said. 'Plenty of good food helps.'

'Will you be joining us at church in the morning?' was the next bothersome topic. How was it women found so many things with which to plague a man? Thank goodness he'd never married. He'd have had this sort of thing all the time. No wonder poor old George looked a bit harassed at times. 'As you know, I take the children and they would be delighted if you came too.'

'I'm not much of a church goer, Miss Hetherington. I never seem to know when to stand up and when to sit down and I'm not too keen on clergymen. Still, I could give it a try but if the sermon's boring, don't expect me to make a habit of it. Er, you know I'm taking Peter to see a doctor friend about his eyes. I wondered if you'd care to accompany us? Lucy too, of course.'

'Oh that would be wonderful, Mr Gregory. We should love to come too.'

★ ★ ★

To church next morning, Luke duly went, leaving in good time for matins at eleven o'clock, formally and stiffly dressed for they'd be on show and the newcomer to the Manor would be an object of critical attention.

Luke had hoped they could hide away at the back of the church or at least, lose themselves in the crowd in the middle, but no, for the family pew that belonged to the lord of the manor was of the box type on a raised dais, placed sideways on and directly opposite the pulpit.

Towards this reserved sanctum, Miss Hetherington led the way, looking neither to right nor left and speaking to no one as she passed, followed by Lucy and Peter, then Luke. Strange, he thought. She's not an unfriendly person so how come she has nothing to do with anyone?

This though, was not his favourite pastime, being placed on view and stared at and whispered about. Perhaps he should have brought his pipe and lit up. That'd give 'em something to talk about but, here he was so he gazed around at the congregation seeing how quickly he could make people look away. A silly little game but feeling a bit more cheerful, he winked at Lucy, sitting solemn and lady-like next to Miss Hetherington, which produced a smile and a giggle, quickly suppressed. Then he deliberately held his hymnbook upside down as they stood for the Rector and choir to take their places, the choir on either side of the chancel, next to and opposite their private pew.

It was, as Luke had feared, a tedious, affair. The organ sounded reasonable but the organist played slowly and turned everything into a dirge. The prayers seemed never ending and one, for the well-being of the Prince of Wales, caused him to snort. It was the sermon though, he found particularly irritating, both for its length and its topic, which posed the question, 'Am I my brother's keeper?'

According to the Rector, middle aged, well fed and self righteous, all was well with the world for the church saw to it that everyone reaped as they sowed and enjoyed the bounty of the Lord. Anyone in want had only themselves to blame for their improvidence, and so on. That's right, Luke thought. Keep the rich man in his castle and the poor man at his gate. He would, he decided sooner muck out the stable than listen to such a load of nonsense.

His thoughts wandering, he studied the stained glass windows depicting saints and angels and began to think again of Peter's claim that he could read better through coloured glass. Odd that, for what had colour to do with letters and figures?

Service over, choir and Rector filed out and Luke suddenly realised that he was expected to leave next, the congregation waiting expectantly for him, so he swiftly opened the door at the end of the pew and ushered Miss Hetherington, Lucy and Peter out then followed them down the aisle. The congregation eased itself from the rows of pews, stretched cramped muscles and relaxed from the attitudes of piety and reverence that convention required. Ritual handshakes with the Rector at the door, a baring of teeth in conventional pleasantries and they were free to leave.

Luke felt like flinging his top hat in the air and leading the charge to the Lamb, if it were open, but that would hardly do at all.

'Can we see mother's grave?' Peter asked.

'Of course,' Miss Hetherington said, and Luke followed them to the far end of the churchyard to where a carved stone cross bore the inscription 'In loving memory, Mary Louise Travers, wife of John Travers, Squire. Departed this life, May seventh, eighteen hundred and seventy four. They stood for a little while in silence.

'Where is father buried, Guv?' Peter asked.

'I'm not sure exactly,' Luke replied, 'but I'll get Mr Brierly to enquire.'

'Couldn't he be buried here?'

Luke considered the question. 'I should think that would be possible. When Richard comes home at Easter, you could all go and talk to the Rector and we'll make the arrangements. Now, before we go back, I want to try something. I was looking at the coloured glass in the windows. If I can hold something up close to the glass, you could try reading through different colours to see if it helps. We'll give folks time to go home then give it a try.'

Waiting around for ten minutes or so, they went back into the church and chose a likely window for their experiment, one with a saint in a saffron robe framed in red, blue and green borders. Opening a hymnbook at random, Luke went outside to locate the window whilst Peter stood on the end of a pew and peered through the glass.

It was a basic enough experiment and if another source of coloured glass had been handy, Luke would have used that so he was quite unprepared for the Rector's fury when he returned unexpectedly and demanded how they dared profane his church, and on a Sunday, too.

Hearing the sounds of outrage and seeing Peter suddenly disappear from the window Luke hastened inside to explain and was met by a hostile clergyman who stated that his church was a holy place, a place set apart and his, Luke's conduct, was reprehensible, outrageous and an affront to decency.

'Don't be silly, Rector. Looking through a stained glass window is hardly offensive behaviour and taking a hymnbook outside is scarcely sinful either. Why don't you go home and enjoy your lunch instead of making such a ridiculous fuss. Good day to you. Come along, everyone,' and to the accompaniment of further exclamations of 'monstrous' and 'reprehensible', they made a dignified exit, bemused, puzzled and not a little nettled. Then, as they reached the lych gate and began passing through, they all caught sight of each other's faces and spontaneously burst out laughing.

'The man's a lunatic,' Luke said. 'Don't ask me if I'm coming next week because the answer is 'no'. I'd sooner go for a walk and talk to a goat.'

'I'm afraid he is very uncertain in his manner,' Miss Hetherington said, 'and he sometimes says some very hurtful things.'

'Well of course,' Luke said, maliciously, 'he's a practicing Christian. Give me a friendly Jew any day,' and to Peter, 'How did the words look to you this time?'

'The yellow glass was just ordinary,' he said, 'but the blue was better and I was just going to try the green glass when he came in and shouted at me.'

'So, red and blue could be helpful,' Luke said. 'We can give more time to it tomorrow. At this moment I'm hungry so best foot forward and into lunch.'

★ ★ ★

They travelled by the eight fifteen train to Guildford with only a short wait for the mainline service to Waterloo. Luke was amused by his companion's excitement at this outing, for Miss Hetherington, as well as her charges, found the journey a welcome change from the quiet routine of the Manor. Peter, of course, looked to see if Johnny Barron was driving but he was on the afternoon turn this week, he was told and might even be on a different run.

Charlie, waiting near the cab rank in anticipation of Luke's arrival was surprised to see him accompanied, so Luke went through the introductions, not forgetting Ginger.

'Now you see why you had to bring one of Mrs Cherry's buns,' he said to Lucy. 'He enjoys them as much as you do but hold your hand flat so he doesn't catch your fingers. Best cab horse in London, this one. Isn't that right, Charlie?'

'Sure is Guv. Couldn't wish fer a better one.'

With Miss Hetherington and Luke seated and Lucy and Peter perching on their respective knees, they filled the cab but Ginger didn't seem to mind the extra weight and as there was no hurry he set an easy pace towards London Bridge and into the City. stopping of his own accord at Gresham House. It was Sammy's turn to be door keeper and he had it wide open before they'd all climbed down, standing smiling and waving to them from the top step. Telling Charlie to wait whilst they sorted themselves out, Luke led the way to his sitting room, where a cheerful fire blazed.

'Make yourselves comfortable,' he said. 'I must have a word with Mr Brierly,' and he disappeared back downstairs to arrange for a message to be sent to the Doctor that he'd appreciate a consultation as soon as possible and was about to go upstairs once more when Digger arrived.

'Country air seems ter suit yer, Guv. You're looking brighter.'

'Truth is, I feel brighter,' Luke told him. 'Haven't enjoyed myself so much in years. I've brought the gang back with me so Thomas can take a look at the boy. Seems to have an eye problem I'd like his opinion on.'

'Oh, I'll go up and say how de do,' Digger said, 'but don't suppose yer've heard of 'is bit of bad luck?'

'No, what's happened?'

'His literary agent's done a runner and left 'im without a bean.'

'The silly clown's too trusting for his own good,' Luke growled. 'You've started enquiries, I expect. Let me know if you hear anything.'

'Will do, Guv.'

As Digger passed upstairs, Luke went back into Walter's room. 'Walter, draw a cheque in favour of Thomas J. Barnardo for one hundred pounds, will you? Mark it prominently for 'personal account only,' and while I think about it, open a file on Sir Brandon Remnold of Morden Hall. Unpleasant fellow. Liaise with Digger when you've got as far as you can. Every last detail in case of need and would you also verify the burial site of John Travers? There's a change in the offing.'

'Come on, Guv, your coffee's getting cold,' and in response to the summons, Luke returned upstairs to join in the animated chatter that always accompanied Digger, no matter what company he was in. Luke never ceased to admire his partner for his continual stream of anecdotes and jokes that he could produce, on tap, as it were, and could entertain dock labourers and titled race-going aristocracy with equal facility. He even had, so he claimed, something for the odd bishop but as he didn't know many odd bishops, he was a bit rusty in that department.

As Luke entered his sitting room, he had Miss Hetherington blushing furiously but, like Peter and Lucy, laughing heartily. 'Is he misbehaving again?' Luke asked. 'He's terrible. Lucy, speak to your Uncle Digger,' but as Lucy promptly got her ribs tickled she was incapable of anything but helpless shrieks.

With a level of peace restored, Luke suggested Miss Hetherington might care to take Lucy on a sightseeing trip. They could have the cab all day and Charlie would take them anywhere they wished. Provisionally they'd meet again for dinner at six thirty for he and Peter would await a reply from the Doctor before going out.

This suggestion they greeted enthusiastically and left straight away, Luke, Digger and Peter waving them off as Ginger trotted smartly away, refreshed this time with one of Mrs Maddocks's buns. Digger had decided to make the wharf his next port of call and Luke's plans revolved around Peter at the moment, though he was hoping to visit the Stock Exchange sometime. There was little active trading at the moment and the number of men without work pointed to a period of depression, though the river was as busy as ever and their warehouses bulged with stored goods of every kind.

Oddly, there were many people with money to spare who spent huge sums on gaming, racing and pleasures of all kinds and, oddly again, religion was thriving as never before, but farming wasn't and neither were the unskilled labouring classes. A strange old world, he thought.

'I'll be off then, Guv,' Digger said. 'Guv!' a little louder, and Luke came out of his reverie. 'I'm off.'

'Oh, right. I'm not sure what I'm doing yet. Give me a shout if you find anything interesting.'

'Will do,' Digger replied and, to Peter, 'He gets like this sometimes. Shuts right down while he plans 'is next ten thousand thick 'uns, unless he's just getting old, that is,' as, with his usual cheery, cheeky grin, he moved towards the door.

'Out!' Luke roared. 'Before I set the dogs on you. Getting old, indeed,' then called out, 'Hold on a minute,' and Digger came back into the room, looking expectant. 'I'd like some muscle up here for a bit. Two by day and three at night.'

'I'll get straight on with it,' Digger replied, looking serious for once.

'What's 'muscle', Guv?' Peter asked, looking puzzled.

'Big, strong men, my boy. Bodyguards, if you like. We have a few down at the wharf who keep the pirates off. I feel we should have one or two up here for a while.'

'Pirates, Guv?' Peter asked, his eyes wide.

'Yes, on the river and along the banks. Not so many as there used to be but there're villains aplenty who'd rob and kill for money. Now what can this be, I wonder?' for someone was racing up the stairs and making a good deal of noise about it.

'Come in, Sammy,' in reply to the knock at the door. 'Do you have to gallop around like a berserk elephant?'

'Sorry, Guv. The Doctor's 'ere.'

'Already? Well, show him up, then.'

''E's talkin' to Tom and Mr B., Guv.'

'Well, organise the coffee, then,' and a few moments later, brisk steps on the stairs announced the arrival of their visitor. 'Thomas, I didn't expect you to steam round here this quickly,' Luke said as they shook hands.

'You're one of the very few people for whom I would happily cancel all prior engagements, Guv. Your note said consultation, which doesn't mean casual chatter. And who have we here, then?' he said, looking at Peter over his glasses.

'This is Peter Travers who is my ward. He has a problem with his eyesight on which I'd like your opinion,' and to Peter's surprise and pleasure, the Doctor stepped forward and shook his hand vigorously.

'I'm delighted to meet you, Peter and delighted you're with the Governor. You'll lack for nothing. If I could put all my young folk with him I'd be a happy man. You won't find a finer man to look after you.'

'Stow the blarney and take a seat,' Luke said, with mock severity. 'and let's concentrate on problems for a moment.'

'Yours or mine?' asked the Doctor, with a twinkle in his eye. 'I'll wager I have more than you have.'

'That's one wager I wouldn't dare touch. Ah, here's the coffee. Thank you Sammy. Put it on the table, please,' and Sammy, smiling widely at the Doctor, carefully put the tray down.

'Can I pour, Guv?'

'Go on, then, but only ten spoonfuls of sugar for the Doctor, mind.'

'Indeed no you don't. I no longer take sugar at all,' the Doctor protested.

Coffee poured and handed round, Sammy was urged to depart and close the door, reluctantly returning downstairs.

'The difference in those two is truly remarkable. I think you've done a wonderful job with them and they tell me they live here now.'

'They were ready and it saves travelling back and forth.'

'That's excellent, excellent. Now, what is the problem with Peter?' and Luke gave as full a description as he could, referring to Peter for confirmation and adding the experiment with the coloured glass.

'Until now, he's been labelled stupid and lazy and has suffered greatly as a result but he's neither stupid nor lazy. In fact, he's quite the opposite so, how do we approach the problem?'

'With patience, both of you. I know of several forms of word blindness, which this would seem to be. It is not generally recognised as such and I can well imagine the average pedagogue to be far from understanding. I'm intrigued by the coloured glass and suggest you follow it up in an ordered fashion. My own spectacles are tinted blue, but for a different reason. Now, come over to the window and let me have a look at you. Would you get me a lighted candle?' to Luke, and the Doctor tested the workings of Peter's eyes, getting him to follow his finger, watching the pupils contract against the nearness of the candle flame, asking him to name and identify colours, and so on.

'There seems nothing unusual so far as the eyes are concerned. I suggest you consult a good spectacle maker and follow up the colour idea. You might care to try Dollands, in Bond Street where I get my spectacles. They are very helpful but the important thing, I believe, is not to over concern yourselves about this. It is probably something he will grow out of. Are you at school at present?'

'No,' Luke answered for Peter.' His last school was not a success and I feel it best he has lessons at home 'til he can overcome this problem.'

'Ah, wise words, wise words indeed. Fine. Then I had better be off. There's much to be done,' and springing to his feet, the Doctor picked up his hat, adjusted his spectacles and prepared to leave then, as his own problems resurfaced to occupy his thoughts, he asked, 'I don't suppose you have any employment vacancies at present? There simply aren't enough positions for all those needing them. I'm seriously thinking of seeking work for my young fellows in the colonies.'

'Any particular type of employment?' Luke asked, dubiously.

'Anything and everything,' the Doctor said, ruefully. 'I've got a farmer's boy who wants to go back to the country. I've got carpenters, brush makers, cobblers. I've got girls needing safe positions in service, laundresses, seamstresses and, of course, I have all those who don't have any trade yet.'

'A farmer's boy, you say. Reliable sort is he?'

'Well, yes, I would say so. Pleasant lad. Joseph Ash by name. Came down from Bedfordshire, he says. Why, you haven't got a farm, have you?'

'We have a country place, haven't we, Peter. Not a lot of land at present but Digger has ideas of horses there. George and his wife are looking after it and they certainly need a bit of help around the place. Send the lad round and we'll see how we get on.'

'I knew it. I just knew it,' the Doctor chortled. 'Take your problems to the Guv and he'll come up with something. Now, how about help around the house? Both houses if you like. Very good girls, well trained, anxious to please, just longing for a position.'

'Not my province, Thomas. You know I don't like housework. You could talk to Mrs Maddocks perhaps, and our governess, Miss Hetherington is visiting as well. I could ask her to call round and see you. Now that's all the help I can offer at the moment. Oh, except for this,' and he held out an envelope to the Doctor.

'And what would this be? I'm taking nothing, you know that well.'

'You've been badly let down by someone you trusted. You have family responsibilities and until you take a stipend from your organisation you have your personal commitments to meet.'

'I cannot take it,' then, puzzled. 'How did you learn of that?'

'Thomas John Barnardo, don't ask questions. Just do as you're told for once, you stubborn Irish leprechaun. You're so busy organising other people you neglect yourself. Now come along down and talk to Mrs Maddocks. She has two young children so I'm sure she won't say no to a helping hand in the kitchen. Wait here, Peter. I won't be long.'

And Mrs Maddocks certainly didn't say 'no' to the prospect of a live-in assistant and promised to teach whoever came everything she knew.

'Glad you called?' Luke teased. 'Let's try Mr Brierly. You've made your own introductions, I take it?' he asked, as they entered the office.

'Actually, Tom did,' the Doctor said, 'and made an excellent job of it too.' Tom beamed, for praise from the Doctor was to be valued.

'Tell me, Walter, does Mrs Brierly need a resident maid to help her around the house?'

'I could certainly discuss it with my wife.'

'There you are, Thomas. Now it's up to you. I'll leave you talk together, and many thanks for your help.'

'It is I should be thanking you, Guv. I think I should be calling on you more often.'

'You're always welcome, you know that,' Luke replied, and returned upstairs to find Peter standing by the window of the sitting room, looking far from happy.

'Why so cheerful?' he asked.

'The Doctor said there was nothing unusual with my eyes.'

'That means there's nothing wrong with them. If you were making all this up, the Doctor would have said so. He advised we see a spectacle maker and that is what we shall do and you will play around with coloured glass until you find something that helps. Alright? So off we go.

After a short cab ride, they entered the premises of Dollands, makers of spectacles, telescopes and scientific instruments and Luke stated his approximate requirements to the imposing-looking gentleman who listened so attentively and immediately advised they consult with their Mr Aitchison who was most highly qualified to prescribe for each individual case.

And Mr Aitchison took unlimited pains to be of assistance, spending well over an hour trying a variety of lenses and coloured filters on Peter's eyes. Eventually, he settled on a plain lens for the right and a slightly magnified one for the left but both heavily stained blue. Red was the next most successful colour but blue gave the most settled vision, Peter was certain and his new spectacles would be ready for fitting on Thursday afternoon.

With no cab in sight, Luke decided they'd walk back to the house though the constant jostling of the crowds thronging the streets made progress hard work and they made straight for the kitchen for well earned tea and cakes. Two of Digger's heavies were present, one appraising, with professional eye, the back yard and door fastenings of the rear entrance, the other occupying a chair in the hallway, looking tough, fit and ready for any eventuality of a physical nature.

Leaving Peter exploring a jam-filled creation topped with pink icing, Luke wandered into Walter's room and glanced through the notes of commodity movements during the previous day. Very little movement. Gold was up a whisker and agricultural land prices continued their decline, in line with grain prices generally. Tea and coffee were steady, coal likewise, with shipping prices down a little, reflecting the increasing competition from the Americans.

Nothing much to tempt him he thought though there was no shortage of stock on offer, some at near bargain prices, but there were also many fraudulent companies offering worthless shares. They'd present attractive propositions to the gullible, offer a good dividend, then close the company or reconstruct it under a new name, leaving shareholders with a worthless investment.

Walter and his assistants were out so Luke had the room to himself and, perched on the edge of the desk he idly ran his eye over a list of loans outstanding that Walter had been bringing up to date. These were small sums advanced to various individuals at nominal interest for all manner of purposes from paying off arrears of rent and redeeming tools pledged at pawnbrokers to setting up a market stall and smartening up a run down restaurant.

So little, he thought, yet so important to those concerned and his thoughts wandered back to a cold, miserable November evening when he'd been penniless, hungry and despondent. Pennies to a poor man were worth more than guineas to a rich one, he reflected and to think that titled aristocracy could lose five hundred guineas a night at the gaming tables and not worry, yet five pounds could keep a family for a month and whilst the aristocrat did no work to gain his guineas, a labourer would work fifty or sixty hours a week for less than a pound, in dangerous, dirty conditions and in all weathers.

A strange system governed their lives and it all revolved around money. With enough of it, a man could enjoy every known luxury and pleasure, could purchase influence and power, sample every vice and answer to no man yet, with none, he had less value than a goose or a chicken. He could starve or suffer agonies through illness or accident yet stir no pity from most of the well off, including many of the clergy, who were happy to tell of the good Samaritan on Sunday yet fail to connect their preaching with the poverty and misery around them. Had anyone met a hungry bishop lately? Or one with patched trousers or split boots?

Then the doorbell jangled and the heavy in the hall got to his feet and went to see who was calling and after a brief conversation, knocked on the door to announce that someone wished to see him. The visitors turned out to be one of the Doctor's helpers from his home in Stepney who had escorted a boy and girl to see Luke. The man's not wasting time these days, Luke thought to himself.

A girl of indeterminate age with bright red hair showing from under her bonnet stared fixedly at the floor. The fair complexioned boy of fourteen or so, wearing the home's uniform trousers with the red stripe down the seam, looked at Luke directly but respectfully, cap in hand.

'And who have we here who thinks the floor is more interesting than I am?' The girl continued to stare at the floor, and the helper came to the rescue.

'This is Bridie O'Rourke, sir and she is about thirteen years of age. The Doctor said to be completely honest and to hold nothing back when talking to you. Bridie has a wild temper, you see and will fight with anyone and her language is terrible. She had to leave the Cottage Village because of her behaviour so the Doctor keeps an eye on her himself for she does respect him, if no one else. Bridie is considered too wild and violent for a place in domestic service, although she likes to cook and is very capable when she wants to be. The Doctor has told Bridie that just about her only chance will be to work for you but she is quite convinced that you will not accept her once you have heard what she is like.'

'And she is quite right, unless she has the courage to look me in the eye.'

Immediately, her head came up to reveal a snub nosed, pugnacious face and green eyes staring defiantly at him. Luke paused, weighing her up.

'Can you dance the jig?' he asked, and a flicker of surprise showed in her expression.

'Indeed I can, sor.'

'Give me the steps, then,' and Bridie O'Rourke began to dance, boots clicking on the tiled floor. 'Not bad,' Luke said and joined in. 'Faster, now,' and they began to compete, their feet going faster and faster until Luke called, 'Enough. You have the legs of me there,' and Bridie, flushed and smiling now, looked up at him with interest.

'Well, young lady, you'll do for me. I like your spirit but you'll be working with Mrs Maddocks, my housekeeper and it's her you'll have to please. I like a peaceful house so there'll be no fighting with anyone, you must understand that clearly and the same goes for hard language. And you must be Joseph Ash,' to the boy, who had watched the performance with Bridie with open amusement. 'I understand you want farm work. Is that right?'

'Yes, sir. I don't want to go to no colonies, sir, but I don't like being in the city, sir.'

'I see. Do you know anything of horses?'

'Oh, yes sir. I've bin with 'em as long as I can remember, sir. I can plough a bit, too.'

'The Doctor speaks well of you so if you'd care to join us at our country place you'll be very welcome,' and to Bridie, all for starting work there and then, he insisted she return to Stepney to report to the Doctor and collect her few possessions.

When Miss Hetherington and Lucy returned there was a fresh hubbub as they described their day and made plans for a visit to the Crystal Palace next day, which would allow Luke to have a prowl around the docks and wharves of the river to see how the competition was doing for keeping a close eye on rivals had always been a key to their continuing success.

Always he was careful on such forays, never went alone and took pains to avoid disharmony with those who controlled things on the North bank just as they, for their part, were careful on his patch in the Bermondsey area. Whilst his were honest, straight forward businesses, with no villainy allowed, he had always to be alert to those that might harm the company's interests.

★ ★ ★

'Oh, yes, of course, Miss Hetherington. Of course. Get whatever they need, whenever you see it or why not go off shopping with Beth, or Mrs Metcalfe. They'll know the best places for that sort of thing.' There, caught out again. He hadn't given a thought to the state of their neglected wardrobes, with most items too small or worn out or whatever. He was too busy thinking of warehousing and cargoes for that sort of thing but he had managed to get Ben Driscoll over to speak with Walter about accounts and other matters. Nothing like keeping busy to enjoy a good night's sleep or was there?

He'd placed the hood over the oil lamp on his bedside table as usual, had made himself comfortable and was just drowsing off when he was instantly awake once more, every sense tingling at the unmistakeable click of the door handle turning.

He never locked his door but no one up to any good would think of stealthily entering there, knowing him to be in bed. His hand slid under the pillow and closed over the butt of the little point thirty two calibre revolver he favoured, its hammer resting on an empty chamber. He'd be ready but would pretend to be asleep until he judged it time to act. Then he'd aim low, at the intruder's belly.

The door was opening now, quietly. He couldn't actually see but he could sense movement and knew someone was entering the room. Who the hell was it? Who ever it was, they moved silently and he heard the door quietly click shut again. Dimly, he was aware of someone approaching the bed, could make out their breathing. Short breaths. That meant they were nervous.

Something pale showed and he carefully eased himself half into a sitting position and levelled the revolver whilst groping for the hood over the lamp. The pale object was close now, advancing slowly towards him. Just a pace or so away now, he thought. Any moment and he'd know the answer.

'Guv.' It was whispered. Surely he knew that voice? He whipped the hood off the lamp and there, standing by his bed was Bridie, clad only in a nightdress.

It was hard to say who was most startled. Luke, ready to shoot a possible assailant or Bridie, not anticipating a sudden light. Carefully, Luke lowered the hammer of the pistol then realised that cocking it had moved a round under the hammer and, cursing silently, emptied every chamber onto the bed then carefully reloaded and replaced it beneath his pillow.

'You realise I could have shot you?' he asked roughly. 'Anyway, what is it you want and why have you crept into my room like this?'

Bridie had moved close to the bed now, her head hanging. 'Do you want me, Guv?'

'Want you? What on earth for?' Luke asked, sharply, then realisation dawned upon him. Good God, he thought. The silly little creature was offering to jump into bed with him. He turned up the light and looked hard at Bridie who continued to stand, head down, then saw the first tear fall, silvery in the light, and heard a sob.

Oh hell, he thought. Here was a fine situation. Damn Thomas Barnardo for unloading his problems onto him. Damn himself for being so soft hearted or was it conceit, in allowing it to happen in the first place? What was he to do? Order her out with a flea in her ear? She'd probably be gone in the morning and would probably wake the house anyway and he wanted neither of those courses.

If she made a noise, screamed or carried on he'd have some explaining to do. Everyone would naturally think the worst, even if he was master of his own house. He'd lose a good deal of credibility with everyone. The guv, having it off with his young servant girl. Shame on him. What would Digger and Beth think, or Miss Hetherington? Suddenly it mattered what people thought, mattered a good deal that the Doctor might think he'd betrayed his trust and taken advantage of a child placed in his care. So what to do?

'Sit down. Over here,' and she perched on the edge of the bed, still looking down. 'Look at me,' and slowly she raised her head, looking very doleful. 'Tell me why.' There was no reply. 'Have you done this before?' She shook her head. 'Then why now?'

'The Doctor said I were to do everythin' I could for you.'

'He didn't mean you to go this far, Bridie, but I appreciate the thought,' Luke said, feeling relieved. He'd shock Thomas some day by relating this tale. 'Now listen carefully. I like you a lot but I never go to bed with anyone who works for me, ever, and in any case, you're far to young to be doing this.'

'I am not so,' came the pugnacious reply. 'I knows plenty as does it all the time, younger'n me.'

'Yes, Bridie, I know that,' and he thought of the scrawny girls in their bedraggled finery who loitered around the beer shops hoping to sell themselves for the price of a meal, 'but it's not a good idea. Those girls'll be old women by the time they're thirty, if they live that long. Is that how you wish to be?'

She shook her head. 'I think you'll make someone a fine wife one day, when you're older. You'll meet someone of your own age, you'll marry and likely have lots of beautiful children, but not if you creep into my bedroom late at night. Do you understand me?'

She nodded. 'You goin' to send me away?'

'No, why? Who'd be serving my kippers in the morning if I did that?' A ghost of a smile. 'What I am going to do though, is see you have a good long talk with Digger's wife. She'll explain things much better than I can.'

'She's your daughter, ain't she?' It was more a statement than a question.

'You could say that but now, young lady, I want you to go to bed, your own bed, that is, and let me get some sleep. Off you go now and close the door quietly. I'll see you in the morning.'

★ ★ ★

Chapter 5

Work was progressing well at the Manor and Richard, home from school for the Easter holiday, was intrigued by the improvements taking shape especially the flushing lavatories and bathrooms with hot water on tap and proper iron baths with a white enamel finish. No longer was there a need to splash water around with jug and basin in their bedrooms. This was luxury indeed and the food! He was hard put to accept that this was the same house he'd always known.

He could remember his mother, for he was nearly seven when she died and had become accustomed to a home grown cold as his father pined and lost interest in his estate. Finally, he'd been packed off to a preparatory school, an unhappy experience, and with little to look forward to during his holidays.

Now though, he could scarcely believe the difference. He was unsure of his guardian but he noticed Peter and Lucy were quite relaxed with him and actually sat on his lap. Of course, he was far too grown up for that but still, perhaps he really wasn't as fierce as he looked.

There was though, something that concerned him more. He could accept that his father too, was dead but shouldn't he be buried in the church yard next to mother? He'd just have to speak to the guv he supposed, unless he could get Peter to do the asking, which was how Peter came to raise the subject again that evening as Luke sat by the fire in the hall, casually filling his pipe.

'Guv,' he said slowly, looking very solemn, 'do you think father can be buried near to mother in the churchyard? Only Richard thinks he should be,' he added.

Luke carefully lit his pipe, tamped down the tobacco with his fingertip, relit it and puffed out a cloud of smoke. 'Well, now Richard's home you can all go and talk to the Rector about it and then we can make the arrangements.'

'Doesn't that burn you when you do that?' his curiosity overcoming the more serious subject.

'Not if you do it lightly and take your finger off quickly. Why not go in the morning then we can get an undertaker to do the moving but it's something that shouldn't be delayed.'

Thus encouraged, all three, spruce and tidy, set off to call on the Rector. Luke, standing by his bedroom window looking at the sheep grazing below, watched them go and allowed himself a half smile, wondering yet again what he'd taken on this time.

He wasn't prepared for their return half an hour later though, and one look at their faces showed all was not well and Lucy, bursting into tears confirmed it. Listening intently he felt his anger rise as Richard described how they'd had to remain outside, how unpleasant the Rector had been and how he'd refused their request.

'He said, 'I'll have no suicides in my church yard. Let him stay where he is,' and went inside and slammed the door.'

'He said that to you? I see. Now don't look so glum. That can't be the end of the story by a long chalk. Come and sit down and we'll have a think about it.'

Seated around the kitchen table, Mrs Cherry automatically placed biscuits and milk before them and enquired of Luke 'Tea or coffee?'

'Coffee, I think, no, make it tea.'

With three pairs of eyes on him he felt obliged to offer some sort of reassurance. 'The first course is to enquire if he may legally refuse a burial in the churchyard. If he's within his rights then we'll have to persuade him to change his mind. I'll write to a Bishop I know and seek his advice but I have it in mind to give that high and mighty parson something to think about.'

'What will you do, Guv?' Peter asked, wide eyed.

'I'm thinking hard at the moment. Give me a little time and I'll come up with something. Are you sure you wish your father to be moved? You are, I can see that. Well, one way or another it'll be done so off you go and think no more about it.'

For his part he wandered outside to enjoy the spring sunshine and stood for a while looking across the valley to where the chimneys of Lee Farm showed above a fold in the ground. What was it George had heard? The owner was selling up because he couldn't make ends meet? He'd been the tenant there previously as his father was before him and he'd bought the farm from Squire Travers when it was offered for sale. Borrowed heavily to do so, by all accounts and couldn't meet the interest charges on the loan. So, it had once been part of the Manor estate. Would it be worth getting back again, he wondered? He'd discuss it with George and give it some thought.

Meanwhile, were Squire Traver's clothes still bundled up in the top of the barn? He'd have a look, for a mischievous idea had taken hold in his mind. He'd teach that God botherer to treat his family like dirt.

★ ★ ★

Repairs to the house were now complete and Luke was satisfied that the building was as sound as a building of its age could ever be but there'd been one notable discovery whilst the upstairs floorboards were being renewed. The carpenter working on them approached George in some puzzlement as his measurements hadn't worked out as expected. Together, they realised there was another room upstairs at the rear of the building, completely panelled over. No doorway showed and there was no trace of a window outside.

On his next visit, Luke decided there should be no mysteries and ordered the panelling removed, which revealed a door. When opened they found a room, complete with ancient tester bed, a large wooden stool and an empty wooden chest. The window to the room had been blocked up but for what reason, was unclear.

The room was now cleaned up, the window replaced and the door rehung but the ancient bed frame, stool and chest were left in place. At some time, Luke decided, he'd have the bed restored and use the room for guests.

★ ★ ★

'Mr Gregory, I'm almost lost for words. I just do not know how I may express my gratitude for what you have done for me.' Walter Brierly was clearly agitated and Luke invited him to take the guest armchair in the sitting room.

'Let me guess. Ben's been busy and has given you good news? I thought that might be the case. A very capable young man is Ben. Sometimes I think he can see through walls. So, what's the result of his endeavours?'

'He has produced the evidence that will enable me to restore my good name. He has presented me with the records my ex colleagues kept concealed and has highlighted the false accounting that led to my conviction. I cannot imagine how he achieved this, I really cannot but it means so much to me.'

'Indeed. I can appreciate your feelings. And your late colleagues? What of them?'

'Ben tells me they have fled the country to avoid arrest.'

'Very wise of them, which leaves you free to resume your practice in what are now your chambers.'

'Oh, but I could not. I am in your employ and I could not possibly leave you.'

'I think you might usefully serve both yourself and us, wouldn't you agree?' to Digger as he came into the room wearing his biggest grin.

'What's that then, Guv?'

'As if you don't know. Walter back in his own practice but still advising us.'

'Course. Why not? Keep 'im busy and out o' mischief.'

★ ★ ★

Horace Burlington was a lean, spare man with a worn and defeated look about him as he stood, uncertainly, in the hall of the Manor.

'Good afternoon, Mr Burlington. What may I do for you?'

''Tis about my place, sir. Lee Farm. I'm selling up and I'm bound to offer it to you first. 'Tis copyhold see, as I bought it from Squire Travers.'

'Come into the study. We shan't be disturbed there. May I offer you refreshment? No? I'm not familiar with copyhold. Would you explain it to me please?'

'T'is like this, sir. I bought from the lord o' the manor and I'm bound to offer it back before public sale. I thought Sir Brandon were lord o' the manor now, seeing as he bought land from Squire Travers, but he said not. Got right angry he did. Said as the lordship were with the Manor so I'm offering my place to you in case you're interested. If not, I'll have to place it wi' an agent.'

'Yes, I'm interested. How much land is there?'

'Exactly two hunnerd and twenty-seven acres all told, sir.' Bout half is plough.'

'You have a price in mind?'

'I have, sir, if you'd consider it. I owes nigh on five thousand as it stands,' and as Luke remained silent but looked enquiringly at him, continued, none too confidently, 'I'm asking enough to clear what I owes. To include everything, that is.'

'Would it fetch that at auction?' Luke asked, quietly.

'Horace Burlington shook his head and looked down. 'Likely not,' he said. 'things being what they are and agent's fees and expenses off that again.'

'You know the farm well, of course,' Luke said.

'I were born there. Father moved in when he were a lad. Always said how fine it'd be if we owned the place instead o' tenanting it. We would've made a go of it, I reckon, but for the weather. Three bad harvests in a row set us right back. Even rained at haymaking and spoiled that, never mind the corn. Sprouting in the sheaves it were and not a thing to be done about it. Then the cattle took sick with the pest and the wet weather knocked the sheep up chronic and prices were low even for prime stock.'

'Everything went against you, then. Am I right in thinking the bottom land by the river is good grazing and the slopes don't dry out too quickly in summer?

'That's right, sir. There's a good balance for a mix o' things, if it'd only rain at the right time and the sun'd shine when needed.'

Luke reached for pencil and paper and jotted down a few figures, scratched his head with the pencil and tried again, Horace Burlington watching anxiously as he multiplied and divided. Two hundred and twenty-seven acres of mixed agricultural land, now. Forty pounds an acre bottom price. Mm. Some good land worth more than that. To include the house and barns. Everything. Mm, he pondered and made his decision.

'Would you care to stay on?'

A pause, whilst the question registered. 'You mean at the farm?'

'I'm interested in taking back the Manor lands but I wouldn't want them unoccupied.'

'Stay on at Lee and not have to move out,' the farmer mused quietly, almost to himself then, gathering his wits, 'As tenant, would it be?'

'Er, yes, I suppose that might be the arrangement. My business partner has an interest in horses and will need grass. It'd suit to have the place worked according to need. Grazing, good fences and oats have been mentioned if this is of interest to you.'

'Well yes, sir it is of interest.'

'The deeds, I take it, are with your bank? If my legal representative deals directly with the bank and settles all outstanding charges that would leave you free of any liability whatsoever. He'd then draw up an agreement between us and I suggest that for the first year at least the farm would be rent free with just the tithe payment at some point. That'd give you chance to recover your position, weather permitting, of course.'

'This is very good of you, sir. You're a real gentleman.'

'Hardly that, Mr Burlington. Merely a straight forward man of business, just so long as others play straight with me. Tell me, what staff have you to work the farm?'

'Just my boys, sir. Could never afford to employ help. The girls help the missus, of course, but I don't rely on 'em for field work, though they takes their turn.'

'I see. So you've enough help to keep the place going until my partner tells you what he wants. He would, of course, pay you for whatever you provided for him. That's fine, then. I'm glad to have met you and I've no doubt we shall see more of each other in the future.'

With Horace Burlington gone, a happier man than when he arrived, Luke enjoyed a private chuckle. Digger's face would be a picture when he told him he now had the use of a farm, complete with staff awaiting his orders. For himself, he was well enough pleased with the arrangement knowing full well that negotiations with the bank would result in a healthy discount on the value of the property, if they wished to recover a substantial part of the outstanding loan.

★ ★ ★

'I want you to look outside and tell me if you see anyone you know,' Luke directed Richard and Peter. They were in the sitting room at Gresham House. Breakfast was finished and they were making plans to spend the last day but one of the holiday on the tugs.

Luke, unusually for him, had several times glanced at his watch and checked the time against the clock ticking ponderously on the mantelpiece. Now, at precisely eight forty five, he directed them to the window. There was a joint intake of breath as both boys peered out and again, as one, they turned, with troubled expressions to look at Luke.

'It's father,' Richard said but before he could speak further, Luke cut him short.

'Look again, carefully this time. It's an actor, made up to look like your father. Sorry to give you a shock but I wanted to see your reaction.'

'But he looks just like father,' Peter said, still looking worried.

'Then he's done well and is the man for the part. Nip down and ask him to come up. His name is Morley Richardson. Go on, there's nothing to be frightened of. I'll explain when you come back up.'

Two minutes later, with introductions over, they sat looking curiously at the actor.

'Excellent, Mr Richardson. Excellent indeed,' then, to Richard and Peter, 'You'll remember that unpleasant business at the Rectory and how I said we'd have to give that fellow something to think about? Well, Mr Richardson here is going to have a little fun at the parson's expense. In fact, he's going to haunt him, until either he agrees to your request or leaves the village. He'll keep popping up from time to time and I've no doubt will cause a stir. What do you think?'

Richard, in particular, thought it a 'spiffing wheeze', his face alight at the thought. Peter, though, was not too happy at first but was soon reassured by his brother's enthusiasm.

'The only people to know about this are the four of us and your Uncle Digger. No one else, and I'm relying on you to keep it that way. Lucy knows nothing of it, nor Miss Hetherington, so you Peter, must be very careful not to let the cat out of the bag. Should you happen to see Mr Richardson at any time in the village, you'll not see him, if you get my meaning. If someone says 'Isn't that Squire Travers by the church?' you'll say 'I can't see anyone at all' or 'There's no one there,' that sort of thing. It's all an act to give that parson feller a kick in the britches and I think your father would approve wholeheartedly.'

★ ★ ★

It was cleverly done and Luke was impressed by the actor's resourcefulness. An apparently empty carriage arrived at Chidlingbrook station but as the train drew out, both porter and station master swore they'd seen the late Squire Travers sitting there, 'plain as a pikestaff.'

The Rector's maid, answering the door after dark saw the late squire standing there and promptly had hysterics. Two farm workers about to enter the Lamb Inn fairly fell through the doorway in their haste to report that 'old squire' had just walked past them but his feet had made no sound!

It had meant careful planning, patience and a couple of precipitous flights across the fields to avoid detection but the seed had been sown and the story took firm hold in the village, was repeated, added to and embroidered to the point where people started seeing things that weren't there and only the stout-hearted ventured out after dark.

Then the sexton saw, in broad daylight, the squire standing by his wife's grave in the churchyard, dropped pick and shovel in a panic and fled to tell his tale. The Rector gave a sermon on the subject and spoke strongly against 'the devil's work' but had a fright later that day when he saw Squire Travers standing at the lych gate of the churchyard, pointing at him.

George Cherry was included now in the plot, and was responsible for concealing the actor after his appearances. He casually gave his opinion, one evening in the Lamb, that most likely, 'old squire' was wanting to be buried near his wife, which struck a sympathetic chord amongst those present. No such sympathy was shown by the Rector, who stubbornly discounted his own experiences and the tales of sightings, as ungodly happenings, which called for a redoubling of efforts.

Luke was equally stubborn and quite determined to achieve his purpose. The Rectory became plagued by unexplained nocturnal noises. There were bangs and thumps on doors and walls, the doorbell jangled without warning and something kept tapping on the windows. The maid left in a fright, followed by the cook and the Rector grew uneasy.

Sitting alone in his study one evening, he was disturbed by a sharp rapping on the window and he wrenched the heavy curtains apart to see clearly the ghastly white face of the late squire staring in at him. He was shocked and quickly closed the curtains to lean trembling against his desk, before reaching for the brandy with which to steady his nerves whilst Morley Richardson beat a hasty retreat clutching a length of board under his arm.

A close examination of the garden beneath the window next morning revealed an absence of footprints or marks of any kind, and the Rector began to worry. Then fate took a hand and settled the matter. Hurrying towards the church the Rector slipped on wet leaves and fell flat on his back, almost at Richardson's feet, where he'd been lurking in the shrubbery waiting to show himself. Whether it was the shock of his fall or the late squire standing over him making dramatic gestures of condemnation, this incident was the last straw and the Rector left next morning for a lengthy holiday in the South of France.

Within a week, a curate arrived to minister to the spiritual needs of the parish and just one week later again, that curate received a letter from a Suffragen Bishop advising that, with his approval, he was desirous of conducting the funeral service and interment of an old and close friend who had died away from the village.

And so, the late Squire Travers was laid to rest beside his wife in the churchyard of Chidlingbrook and as a once out of work actor no longer had cause to visit the village, no further sightings of 'old squire' were reported and the events passed into folklore.

For Luke it was a satisfactory ending for he had a deep-seated mistrust of the clergy, the Reverend Banks and his birch having seen to that, and he had a deep dislike of unfairness. The Rector had aroused both sets of feelings and had paid the price.

★ ★ ★

It was a fine and bracing day as Luke set out from the Manor. He took a deep, refreshing breath of the clear autumn air, marvelling at the contrast with the soot-laden variety of the City. Almost like being at sea, he thought to himself.

His Sunday afternoon walks were becoming a pleasurable habit to which he looked forward. He had set himself to explore the locality in every direction, to get the lay of the land, he told himself, but secretly, he enjoyed the exercise and the interesting, ever changing scenery. One of these days he'd head for the distant chalk downs at the head of the valley. Today, though, with plenty of daylight left, he'd explore the valley as far as the next village, or hamlet, of Chiddington.

It would be about three miles or so and he set himself a steady but unhurried pace, wondering what he might find around each bend in the narrow, tree-lined road, the hedges bright with berries and leaves turning colour. He'd gone perhaps a couple of miles when he thought he heard voices ahead, quite a few of them, shouting, and he wondered what might be afoot.

As he rounded another bend he saw, fifty yards ahead, a group of people, men mainly, in two untidy groups and clearly exchanging insults along with a variety of threatening and provocative gestures. So much for a peaceful Sunday afternoon stroll, he thought to himself, wondering if he'd have difficulty in getting past. He was no more than a few yards away when, as if by mutual consent, the two groups closed together and a furious fistfight broke out, the few young women standing by urging individuals on with shrill cries of encouragement.

Luke stood amazed, watching the mill. Almost as good as an Irish row in Dockhead he was thinking when he found himself engulfed by the combatants. His hat went flying and he staggered back as an elbow caught him sharply in the face. He tried to back away but a great lumbering ox of a fellow in brown corduroy trousers swung a hay making punch at him that he only just managed to duck but a blow from the other fist caught him square beneath the right eye.

Luke's temper flared and he hit out with both fists, jolting his assailant to a stop. In a flash he had his jacket off and had slid into that familiar boxing stance. If the bloody man wanted a scrap he could have one, prize ring, Queensberry or public house rules, he didn't care.

'Come on, you ugly bastard,' he snarled and with eyes only for his opponent failed to see that the general melee had subsided and the former combatants had gathered round to watch.

The ox-like man lumbered forward, a trickle of blood coming from his nose, and tried another huge right hand swing. Luke swayed back, felt the rush of the fist past the end of his nose, shuffled to his right and planted a left and a right on the other man's face, and kept moving to his right, making his clumsy opponent keep turning to face him.

He's no foot work, Luke decided, just a big punch. Best to keep him at a distance and sting him, but he quickly began to realise he was neither as young as he used to be nor in the best of condition for this sort of stand up encounter. Better try to end it smartly or I'll be out of puff, he thought and stepped back to take a huge gulp of air. The other man, furious at continually missing with his punches and goaded by the cries of the onlookers, rushed forward, took another left and right to the face but continued on and grabbed Luke in a ferocious headlock, bending him double and squeezing his neck with his full strength.

Blimey, Luke thought. I'm done for now, he'll break my neck. Only one thing for it, public house rules and he struck upwards as hard as his position would allow, catching his opponent in his most vulnerable parts. A grunt, the grip slackened and Luke tore free, gasping for breath, then went at the stricken man with everything he had left, hitting, hitting and hitting again, madly, desperately, regardless of skinned knuckles, determined only to finish the business before he found himself on the receiving end again.

The ox-like man folded up and collapsed in the road and Luke staggered over to the hedge and leaned against a young tree, worn out with the effort. None of the onlookers moved or made a sound. They just stood staring, shocked at the savage beating of the big man who remained crumpled up in the road.

Gradually, Luke's breathing settled down and he eased himself away from the tree, feeling as if he'd been tossed by a bull. The onlookers continued to stare, mute still, as if rooted to the ground. Some of them, Luke thought, looked familiar. Wasn't that young Tompkins who worked in the stable?

'What's this all about?' he demanded, of no one in particular and at the sound of his voice the crowd came alive again and someone bent over the man lying in the road. 'Who's that fellow?' indicating his opponent.

'Jeb Wilson. Works up farmer Harrington's,' a voice said.

'Well, why did he go for me?' Luke asked.

'Dunno, rightly, sir. Reckon 'e thought you wuz a wanting to join in.'

'Well I bloody well wasn't,' Luke snarled, conscious of the pain in his knuckles as he pushed his hands through the sleeves of his jacket. 'Where's my hat? And my stick. Ah, thank you,' and he gently explored the swelling beneath his eye. 'You still haven't told me what this is all about.'

There was a shuffling of feet in embarrassment then a man, a little older than the others said, 'Well, you see, sir, 'tis like this. We be from Chiddington and they be from Chidlingbrook see, and, well we meets just 'ere, on the boundary like, to settle us differences, see?'

'What differences?' Luke demanded.

The spokesman seemed nonplussed and scratched his head, searching for an explanation. 'Dunno, rightly sir, when you comes to think on it. We just does, see? Like we allus 'as.'

'Bloody ridiculous,' Luke snorted. 'Can't you find a better way to spend a Sunday afternoon? And what about him?' nodding towards the man he'd fought and who was now sitting up. 'Not going to be much good for work in the morning, is he?' Luke looked hard at the man. Had he really done that to him? He looked as though he'd been stung by a hive of bees, with both eyes closed, his nose flattened and his mouth, bleeding and swollen, hanging slackly open.

'Best get him home,' and he turned abruptly and started back along the road towards the Manor, suddenly conscious that his torn shirt collar was standing out sideways like a studding sail. He tried to creep quietly in by the front door, intending to settle in the bath for a soak but his luck was out for Lucy came running from round the back, the dog bounding at her heels, trying to catch hold of the stick she was holding.

'Hullo, Guv,' then she stood and stared. 'Your face is all red and you've got a bruise.'

'Not much of one, I'm sure. I'm off to get changed,' and he carried on inside, leaving Lucy staring after him.

Whilst he was able to shrug off his bruised face and half-closed eye, his hands were a different matter. They were stiff and swollen, with the knuckles well skinned and he made no protest when Mrs Cherry insisted on larding and bandaging them, clucking her concern the while. George, though, caught his eye and Luke was forced to grin.

'Do I get to hear what happened, Guv or do I have to go down the Lamb to find out?' he asked.

'You're not going down there on a Sunday night, George Cherry. It isn't proper,' his wife scolded.

'It's up to me, then,' Luke said. 'I got mixed up in an inter-village brawl up the road. Some fellow from Chiddington thought I wanted to join in but I think I'm past it. I ran out of puff in the first round.'

'I've heard about those scuffles.' George said. 'There's reckoned to be bad blood between 'em which was why folks disapproved when we took young Albert on. He's from up the valley.'

'They'd do better to play football instead of thumping each other'

★ ★ ★

Digger of course, fell about laughing when he saw Luke's black eye but sympathised with his swollen hands. 'I don't know what Beth'll say. Probably tell yer ter stay round 'ere where it's safe. At least you won, though. That'll give 'em something ter talk about. So what's life like then, apart from when you're scrappin' that is?'

'Oh, pleasant enough. Back and forth by train can be tedious. Still, nothing's perfect and I've a fair bit to learn yet. Some farmer called round and gave George seven pounds. Said it was a tithe payment as all such came to the lord of the manor. Thought they went to the church myself but I'll not be complaining.'

'The corn price is down again,' Digger said. 'We've just had a shipment in from Canada and good stuff it is too.'

'It's causing problems round about, no doubt of that. Wet weather, poor harvests and so on. Still, not my problem. All quiet down the wharf?'

'Reckon so. We're busy enough. Steady flow o' readies just like you said. I still don't know how you did it, when I think back.'

'We had a bit of luck but there's plenty hard work gone into it as well you know. Anyway, must keep busy. No slacking off yet. What do you think to chartering our own shiploads instead of waiting for others to come upstream looking for a berth? There'd be a better return on bulk stuff like wheat.'

Digger grinned. 'Guv, you just never stop do yer. I reckon the time could be right fer that, an all but I'll leave you set it up. Just give me yer orders and I'll see it done.'

★ ★ ★

So the year for Luke had been a busy one and he'd found himself engaging in totally new activities such as attending the speech day and prize-giving at Bramsden College. He hadn't enjoyed the occasion, had felt out of place and uncomfortable, making small talk with masters and his relationship with Richard was still rather stiff and formal.

'Definitely a duty visit,' he told Digger. 'Glad to get away.'

Now, though, it was Christmas and a lively household it was proving to be for Peter and Lucy were active and lively youngsters in their own right and so full of energy he was hard put to keep up with them. Richard, home for the 'hols', as he termed them, and at that in between stage of trying to be a mature young gentleman, whilst more than half of him insisted on running riot with his younger brother and sister, was accompanied by his friend, Robert Weston.

A month or so earlier, Luke had received his letter asking if he might invite Robert to stay as his father was still in India. His earlier holidays, spent with an unbending and disapproving maiden aunt, had not been happy occasions, so here he was, a pleasant, friendly boy, immediately at home in the relaxed atmosphere, adding his contribution to the excitement of decorating the hall with ivy and berried holly and streamers of brightly coloured paper.

Logs of ash and apple wood were stacked by the fireplace and in the kitchen, Mrs Cherry and her helpers were busy preparing what seemed to Luke, enough food to feed the village twice over.

Gradually, as the needs of the small estate were identified, help had been taken on from the village. Maids to work in the kitchen and house, a laundress, a gardener and his assistant to provide vegetables and to keep the surrounds of the house tidy and a stableman as well as Joseph to tend the horses for, apart from the pony there was now a cart horse and two spindly-legged young fillies that Digger was sure had racing potential.

Also, and this was to be Luke's surprise, four sturdy cobs were due on Boxing Day morning, his presents to his three wards and to Robert, as he felt he should be treated as family, which would keep the staff busy enough, though he intended that each should tend their own animal, from mucking out to cleaning tack.

They had a tack boy, employed for that purpose in young Albert, who'd turned up one day, soaked through from walking the length of the valley in the pouring rain, looking for work and George had lacked the heart to turn him away, though just what work he could be given he wasn't sure.

'Reckons 'e's thirteen years old but 'e's little bigger than an eight year old, and a skinny one at that. There 'e stood,' George had related, 'with his hat in his hands looking for all the world like a half drownded rat, so the missus dried 'im off and fed 'im up and he helps round the stable, cleaning tack and the like and running messages for the missus.'

But Digger had been delighted. 'Just the sort of feller I'm looking for,' he'd greeted him. 'Built like a jockey.'

'A bad lot, that family,' someone warned. 'They lives up beyond Melbury in a hovel decent folks wouldn't put pigs in. The old man, 'e were a terrible drunkard no farmer'd take on. Took 'imself off a year or so back and left 'is missus to it, wi' four young 'uns to bring up. She makes baskets and the like out o' rushes and withies. You want to watch 'un or 'e'll pinch the nails out o' the 'oss's 'ooves, so 'e will.'

Albert though, made no move to steal anything but made himself useful by helping generally, occupying a cubby hole in the hay loft during the week and visiting home on Sundays, carrying a well-filled basket, courtesy of Mrs Cherry.

The now renovated Home Farmhouse remained unoccupied and, apart from the horses and poultry, they kept no stock, with hay and oats bought in as needed. The orchard was replanted, except for a couple of huge cider apple trees and, in George's opinion, the grazing had improved no end following the regular visits of the sheep flock. Reasonable progress for the first season, Luke reckoned.

★ ★ ★

Peter, returning from visiting Old Joe at his cottage, reported carol singers assembling by the Lamb Inn. It was likely they'd call at the Manor but in the meantime, there was much toing and froing between the different rooms as everyone busied themselves with mysterious packets and parcels that eventually were laid beneath the tree, standing opposite the front door by the stair, where the ceiling was highest.

'Is it true, Guv, that the date of Christmas was changed?' Richard asked.

'Yes. The sixth of January was Old Christmas Day,' Luke replied as he steadied a bowl of punch on a small table. 'Shift your rudder, dog or you'll have this lot over.'

'Why did they change it?'

'Something to do with the number of days in the year. I know Christmas used to be called Yuletide and that big log that's about to go on the fire is the Yule log. If you'll give me a hand with it? There, and before it's all burned we have to save a piece to go on the fire next Christmas eve.'

'Why do we do that, Guv?' It was Lucy's turn with the 'whys?'

'Oh, just a custom, I suppose. Carrying something over from the old year to the new. I remember we did it when I was a boy, years ago.'

'Where was that, Guv?' Peter asked and, as Luke settled down on his favourite seat and reached for his pipe, he found himself telling of his early days at Dean House and remembered with affection the Reverend and Mrs Appleton. The dog saved him from having to tell how that chapter of his life had ended when the Appletons retired as he gave early warning of approaching footsteps.

The scrape of feet and clearing of throats outside the door announced the arrival of the carol singers and Lucy asked, 'Can we light the candles now, Guv?' and the long tapers placed ready by the fire were eagerly seized to start the lighting of the sixty candles on the tree, to the accompaniment of robust singing from outside.

By the time the first carol ended the tree was a blaze of light, the big oak door was opened, and the carollers invited in. Twenty or so men and boys, led by Jackson the blacksmith, some bearing candle lanterns, came trooping self consciously in, doffing hats and nodding greetings and formed themselves up in an untidy group. A fiddle sounded a note, a couple of flutes took up the tune and everyone joined in 'God rest ye merry gentlemen.'

The 'Seyn Day' carol followed and as the last note faded, the door from the kitchen opened as if on cue and Mrs Cherry appeared, bearing a tray piled high with small meat pies, followed by her two helpers carrying more. Jugs of ale and cider circulated, were emptied and refilled as hot mince pies were passed around and a merry party of carollers took their leave of the Manor and sang their way back to the village, well fortified against a long tour of every farm in the parish that would keep them out well past midnight, and the household tidied up and made preparations for an early night.

Wandering into the kitchen, Luke found the indomitable Mrs Cherry busy with more preparations for the morrow, determined it seemed to leave nothing to chance, as if that was at all likely. George, returning from lighting young Albert to his bed, nodded in conspiratorial fashion to Luke.

'All's set for Boxing Day, Guv. They'll be brought up before first light and put inside, all labelled so's they'll know whose is whose.'

'Well done. We shouldn't see 'em for much of the day then. Let's hope they'll be able to sit comfortably for dinner,' and they chuckled at the time-worn joke.

Breakfast on Christmas day seemed to start at around seven o'clock and just go on, an informal kitchen meal and Luke, for his part took ham, toast and coffee to his usual place by the hall fireside. Presents from under the tree, apart from those tantalising stockings explored early in bedrooms, would be distributed after church, attendance obligatory for all.

Cards passed round at the breakfast table next morning announced 'I've been waiting in the stable for ages,' and as one, four young people dashed for the door, leaving Luke to chuckle and pour more coffee, wondering once more at this change in his lifestyle.

A visit to the warehouse for the New Year shindig completed the festivities, with snow beginning to fall as they left for their return to Chidlingbrook and by the time they arrived at the Manor it was a white and silent world and Luke was glad to warm himself by the log fire.

First class, he thought. Everything kept just so in their absence with a blazing fire, boilers stoked up, stables and ponies cared for. Shows what a contented staff can do he mused, which was as well for heavy snowfalls followed, with enormous drifts, one of which completely blocked the railway line for several days while lesser ones required much shovelling to allow easy passage round about.

★ ★ ★

Luke was looking out of his sitting room window towards the end of the month, enjoying the view and the relaxing scene as the sheep below munched steadily at the grass, showing green once more as the snow had melted, the shepherd and his lad with their dogs moving easily around them.

Suddenly, a large fox appeared and ran directly through the flock, causing consternation amongst the ewes, who gathered together in worried groups. The dogs had started in pursuit but were instantly called back and urgently set to round up the flock but before they could manage this, the leaders of a pack of hounds appeared directly below, chasing after the fox.

The bulk of the pack appeared, some following the scent, others running flat out, with tongues lolling, belling as they ran. The sheep panicked and scattered in all directions and the huntsmen and followers, riding directly after the pack, with no regard for the flock, transformed the once tranquil scene into one of chaos. Luke was aghast. To him it was as if the fleet had sailed into London Pool and fired broadsides into the peacefully assembled shipping.

By the time he got outside, the hunt had passed on, save for a lone hound who lolloped after his comrades holding a back paw clear of the ground. Sheep were standing around by the fences and at the edge of the wood and the shepherd, hatless, was examining one of his dogs, which had been savaged. His lad, who'd been knocked down and ridden over, got painfully to his feet, looking dazed and shaken. Of the other dog, there was no sign.

'This is a right how do you do,' Luke said to George as everyone from the house and yard came out to look and help. 'Mrs Cherry, see to that lad, will you? Get him inside. Give him a hand, someone. Now, shepherd, what's to be done?'

The shepherd got to his feet, with bloodstained hands, an angry flush on his face. 'Look at me dog, sir. E's torn to ribbons,' and taking off his coat he carefully wrapped it round the injured animal.

'I'll take 'im,' George said. 'He's breathing. We'll have him mended in no time. You'd best round up your animals. Come on, lads, give a hand. Go round the fences and move 'em into the middle, all together.'

It had been quite a stir and it took the rest of the day to account for all the sheep. One was dead from trying to force its way through a gap in a fence and one had a broken back leg and was carried to a loose box, where it was splinted up and bedded down in straw. The missing dog, the younger of the two, reappeared by nightfall, looking nervous, and the shepherd's lad was tucked up in bed with cracked ribs and concussion.

'That there fox knew what he were about,' was George's opinion. 'He knew if he ran through the sheep his scent would likely be lost, never mind them running helter skelter all ways. Tis the hunt's business to go round stock and that lot didn't give a tinker's cuss by the looks of it.'

'Who pays for the damage?' Luke asked the shepherd.

'Don't rightly know,' that gentleman replied. 'Sheep belongs to my gaffer an' 'e's a tenant of Sir Brandon's so 'e daresn't say ought. The dog's me own, tool of the trade, like, an' 'e'll not be fit for work for weeks. Don't reckon as any will want to know about that.'

'And your lad? He'll be laid up a while.'

The shepherd shrugged. 'There's them as'll say 'e should 'ave got outa the way quicker.'

'That's not good enough. It happened on my land and it shouldn't have happened at all,' so Luke instructed Walter to correspond with the master of the hunt regarding compensation for the injured parties. Had he proposed a walking tour of the moon, this request could not have met with more ridicule and mirth amongst the local gentry who supported the hunt and a highly facetious and insulting reply was eventually received.

'The customs of the rural areas are decided by the landowners,' Walter advised Luke, and basically, what they say goes and few can afford to argue.'

'Well I can so I'll be one of the few. Sue them in court. Start things moving for I'm damned if I'll be dictated to by a load of hoity toity layabouts who've never done a day's work in their lives.'

'The sheep were not your property so you have suffered no personal loss. Neither was the shepherd, nor his assistant, in your employ.'

'Mm,' as Luke considered the legal niceties. 'Then how do I stop that whole business happening again?'

'An injunction restraining the hunt from trespass upon your land might be sought,' Walter suggested. 'It will cause a few raised eyebrows I dare say. Fox hunting is widespread and approved of by royalty and the upper classes.'

'Damn royalty and damn the upper classes. I have a right to live in peace where I choose, when I choose and how I choose. Get one of those injunction things and the sooner the better.'

Luke had worked himself up into a most unusual lather and Walter hastened to acknowledge the instruction as Luke departed through the doorway, only to reappear. 'Who's around this morning? Sammy? Tom? Send one of them down to the Manor. Send them both, if you like. They're to tell George to go and see Farmer Tate and to buy his sheep and take on the shepherd and his lad at whatever wages they were getting. Just let that fat barrel of lard scatter my sheep!' and Luke stomped off upstairs, calling for coffee as he went.

'Cor,' Digger said, as he entered the hallway. 'Did I hear the quarter deck voice? Who's going ter walk the plank?'

'The guv is irritated by a letter that arrived this morning,' Walter replied, handing the offending missive to Digger. 'I fear we shall have to tread carefully this morning.'

He need not have worried. As quickly as Luke's anger had risen, so it subsided and by the time both Digger and the coffee had reached the sitting room, the letter was out of mind and it was news of the wharf that occupied his thoughts.

★ ★ ★

A court injunction restraining the hunt from entering or trespassing upon Manor lands became effective and Luke's name was reviled in the locality. This worried him not at all, but immediately, all his employees who lived in the village, left him. They told George they would no longer work for an outsider who interfered with country customs and, in any case, Luke wasn't gentry so they'd have nothing more to do with him for what proper gentleman would raise his hat to a village woman?

Whether this had anything to do with Sir Brandon threatening eviction, should anyone continue to work at the Manor, Luke didn't know, nor did he particularly care but the taunt of him not being gentry caught him on the raw. After all, what had a load of village labourers got to be stuck up about but George was refused service at the Lamb Inn, to his enormous disgust and the coalman refused to make further deliveries. Even the village postmaster tried to refuse service but, as a public servant, had to reconsider when threatened with legal action.

Luke quickly set about replacing essential staff and as Sir Brandon's influence didn't extend beyond the boundaries of Chidlingbrook, the wages offered attracted an eager response. Two secure wagons, one loaded with coal, the other with coke lay in a siding at the station and with their own tipping cart they had an independent supply and with all other necessities sent in from Guildford and two of the Doctor's girls to live in, the Manor hardly noticed any inconvenience.

Interestingly though, Jackson the blacksmith called after dark for a quiet word with George. He was, he said, totally opposed to this action against the Manor but was in a difficult position as he was farrier to all the farmers and the hunt and rented his forge from Sir Brandon. He would be willing though, to see to any horse taken out of the village when he did his weekly rounds to outlying farms.

Then young Albert, or Ticker, as he was generally known, asked if his mother could have employment and George decided he'd better discuss it first with Luke.

'I've not heard a good word about the family,' George reminded him. 'Young Ticker's all right, mind. Never puts a foot wrong but there's three more of 'em and they're pretty wild be all accounts.'

'If mother's working, who keeps an eye on 'em? I see your point but it's only folks round here give 'em a bad name, isn't it? And they've walked out and left us. Be mud in their eye if we gave her work. We'll take a chance. Spell it out straight and offer a week's trial and we'll make our own judgement.'

So Mrs Donkin came to work at the Manor. She was a tiny woman with blackened teeth who was seldom without a sacking apron and another sack over her shoulders. She was appointed to take over the tidying of the outside areas, the yard, the poultry and the beehives in the first instance and as far as work was concerned, she was a marvel.

'I reckon she can shift more work than a man and in half the time,' George reported. 'Talk about gets on with it. You know, she can pluck a chicken in about three minutes flat, clean as a whistle and have it ready for the oven in another five, trussed neat as a butcher'd do it.'

'Worth keeping on, then?'

'Reckon so. I was wondering if we couldn't find her somewhere to live and save her having to walk in every day. That end cart shed is better than she has at present, be all accounts. Reckon we could let her use that?'

'George, I'll leave it to you. Fix her up with whatever she needs in there. It'll be little enough, I'm sure.'

★ ★ ★

The formal invitation to attend the annual speech day and prize giving at Bramsden College lay upon the breakfast table and Luke, having read it once, kept glancing at it as he finished his kippers and toast, wondering if he really had to attend for he'd found it a tedious business last year.

There'd be windy speeches by the pompous and the prizes would be handed out by some retired general or other. The one last year had believed that school days were the best days of one's life, which showed him to be a fool at the very least. There'd be a mediocre luncheon and a cricket match in the afternoon.

Tedious stuff indeed though the cricket might be mildly entertaining and Richard would be pleased he was there but he knew no one and had no wish to stay longer than good manners required. Oh well, he supposed he'd have to make the effort but he'd take some protection with him this time, all the way and not just as far as the station, for there was no telling who else might have the occasion in their diary and it was easy to become careless.

Three weeks later, accompanied by two of Digger's men, and with the July sun shining brightly, he set off for Salisbury, resolved to fulfil his guardianship duties with a good grace. Probably because he feared the worst and had no high expectations of the day, he was pleasantly surprised by his reception, with Richard waiting to greet him along with scores of other boys whose people were expected. Apparently, parents were never referred to as such but were entitled the mater and pater respectively or perhaps as one's governor, which, Luke supposed, simplified matters for Richard in his academic world apart.

The day was planned differently this year with tolerable coffee served in the hall whilst visitors and masters circulated informally, chatting and discussing the scholastic performance of the pupils who hovered deferentially nearby. There was still to be a prize giving though and speeches to listen to with polite resignation but luncheon for the visitors would be served in a marquee by the cricket field and, according to Richard, promised to be an improvement on previous occasions. Clearly, there'd been a fresh approach to the staging of this annual event and Luke began to feel happier at attending.

Under Richard's guidance he made the rounds of the gowned and mortar boarded masters who taught him in lower school, and was not displeased with what he heard. The headmaster, busy spreading himself equally between all the visitors, more numerous this year than last, Luke noted, made a point of speaking to him early on, commenting favourably upon Richard's progress.

'He has now, of course, a new housemaster as you are probably aware. You must be sure to meet him; he is unfortunately delayed but will be here directly,' and having delivered himself of this advice, bustled off to spread himself further.

'Bit busier than last time, I think. More like a fashion parade in here. Can we move outside? Ah, Stanley, good day to you,' he greeted Benjamin Stanley. 'Warm work in here. I'm escaping outside,' he added, as they shook hands. 'Was that his son?' Luke asked, when they were well clear of the crowded hall.

'Yes, Guv. Did you see how red he went when he saw you?'

'Can't say that I did,' Luke replied. 'You may as well meet Jed and Charlie and Luke led the way to where his two companions were trying to make themselves inconspicuous in an angle of the wall, no easy feat for both were big men.

'I should just wander around as if you belong here,' Luke advised them. 'Say you're with me should anyone ask and join us for lunch in that marquee. At one o'clock, did you say?' turning to Richard.

'That's right, Guv. I really think we should return inside soon though, if we are to get decent seats.'

'If that means a quiet corner at the back, I don't mind.'

'I think all the big fellows will sit there, Guv, if they don't have guests. I think we shall have to sit nearer the front. Oh, I wish we had a swimming pool. It would be lovely to jump in and cool off.'

'I know what you mean and I think I'd join you,' Luke replied. Is there nowhere nearby you can swim, then?'

'You have to go miles and then there's not much water. I think the head is going to make an appeal for funds so we can have a proper pool of our own,' and that was indeed the case. During the next hour and a half's proceedings when, on behalf of the governors, the headmaster delivered his report on the school in general, described achievements and outlined plans for the future, he made his bid for donations towards the cost of a swimming pool before inviting visitors and their sons to adjourn to the marquee for refreshments, the rest of the college lunching in the refectory. A smart word that, for a dining hall. He'd have to try it over the servery at the wharf and raise the tone a little.

A reasonable spread and an improvement on last year but he was glad to escape again from the crowded, stuffy marquee and stroll with Richard towards the pavilion and cricket pitch where the stumps were set ready for the game between the first eleven and the masters.

'Guv, are your men armed? I mean, do Jed and Charlie carry guns?'

'Yes,' Luke replied, 'and they're both excellent shots.'

'Have you got a gun, Guv?'

'Yes, but I'm not such a good shot.'

A silence, then, 'Could I see your gun, Guv?'

'I suppose so, if no one's looking. You keep it to yourself, mind.'

'Yes, Guv, of course,' and his eyes widened as Luke carefully slipped a small calibre revolver from the inside pocket of his coat.

Keep your finger off the trigger and don't wave it around. The hammer's resting on an empty chamber, which leaves five shots. It's only a point thirty two calibre but it's light enough to tuck away and useful close to.'

Richard handled the small black weapon with awed care. 'Have you shot anyone with it, Guv?'

'No, and I hope not to,' at least not with this one, he thought to himself. 'It's merely a precaution, that's all. Just in case of need, nothing more than that,' and he put it back in his pocket.

Later, as the wickets fell, Luke scribbled a note that he asked Richard to hand to the headmaster. That gentleman, engaged in speaking with each of the guests as they left, held the note in his hand as Luke and his escort approached.

'Mr Gregory, this is really more than I could ever have hoped for. It really is most generous of you.'

'I'll send down a surveyor to discuss the project. Would tomorrow or the next day suit?'

'Indeed, Mr Gregory that would be marvellous. This really is the most wonderful news.'

'I'd wish for things to be quietly handled, mind. No call for publicity, that sort of thing. Don't care to have my name bandied about.'

'Oh, well, yes, I quite understand. Indeed yes,' and with handshakes they parted, Luke to share a compartment back to London with his large and silent escort and the headmaster to continue his round of effusive farewells to departing visitors.

★ ★ ★

Then news came that Old Joe had been turned out of his cottage. He and his few possessions were dumped in the road by Sir Brandon's bailiff and the old man was found sitting there in a state of shock. George took the pony and trap down and with Peter, brought him up to the Home Farm House.

When Luke heard of this piece of unpleasantness, his expression hardened. 'That's a low trick. Just because he's on pension from here. Well, he'll not score. We'll build him a cottage on our land. Find a level site somewhere and whilst you're at it, mark out another for Mrs Donkin. I'm not keen on her living in a cart shed.'

'Right Guv,' George said, with a chuckle. 'I'll find someone in the next village to make a start. We'll show the blighter.'

★ ★ ★

Chapter 6

Luke didn't often visit the refreshment rooms of railway stations. They were, in his opinion, places to avoid. The coffee was always atrocious, even in the first class rooms where one paid more for the dubious stuff, and the tea was nearly as bad. As for ever eating anything in one, he'd rather not. On this occasion though, accompanied by two of Digger's heavyweights, he had nearly an hour to wait for a delayed train that would bring Ben and Dessy back from a mission to Birmingham.

He had no need to meet the train personally but on the spur of the moment had decided to do so. He was interested in the news they'd have for him and as the station was Euston, which was just about the grandest of all those in London, he decided to risk the worst their coffee pot might offer.

Seated with his companions at a corner table in the second class refreshment room he casually glanced at the other patrons fortifying themselves against the rigours of journeys to come. No one he knew of course, just the usual anonymous faces to be seen anywhere, though a man with a suntanned face seemed to look hard at him before returning his attention to his plate.

'Telegram for Mr Gregory,' a uniformed Post Office messenger boy called, looking around expectantly and Luke raised his hand to attract his attention. 'Mr Gregory, sir? Of Gresham 'ouse?'

'That's right.'

'Would you sign 'ere, please Guv?'

Luke signed the receipt book and handed over a shilling tip. 'Ta, Guv,' the messenger said and bustled away.

'Mm. From Walter. Ben's taking a later train. Gentlemen, we needn't linger here,' and he rose to his feet and started for the door. As he drew level, the man with the suntanned face rose to his feet and spoke.

'Excuse me, sir. I could not help but hear your name called out. Are you, by any chance, Mr Luke Gregory?' The voice was almost anxious, the expression hopeful.

'I am. Do I know you, sir?' The heavies moved in close.

'You do not recognise me? I am Algernon Parrish. We once sailed back from India in the same ship. I thought you looked a little familiar when you first came in but could not be sure.' He tailed off, in face of Luke's unblinking expression.

'Algy Parrish? Well I'm blessed,' as he dug back into his memory. 'Of course I remember you,' and he extended his hand, and the heavies relaxed. 'This is a surprise. It must be what, thirty years or more? And you were able to recognise me? Remarkable, and what brings you to this country? I can see you have an Indian tan.'

They had to move aside then to allow people to walk by. 'Be better if we sat down again, I think. Room at your table? Make yourselves comfortable again,' he said to his companions, who returned to the corner table. 'And who have we here?' as he lowered himself onto the seat to find himself next to a dark complexioned boy of some twelve years or so who was politely rising to his feet.

'This is my son, Frederick,' Algy Parrish said. 'We are here to look for a school and have only just arrived. Our boat, sorry, ship, got into Liverpool last night and we travelled straight down.'

'Where do you plan to stay? Have you anywhere in mind?'

'Well, no. We were about to start looking around.'

'Then you must stay with me,' and he turned to signal the heavies. 'Bear a hand with the luggage, would you?' and with cabin trunk and several bags safely stowed they set off for Gresham House.

'This really is most kind of you and what amazing good fortune to meet someone I know. This is the first time I've been back since I went out again after school and it's Fred's first visit. He is not looking forward to going to school, but there really is no choice in the matter if he is to receive a decent education.'

'Oh, I thought the Indian service had excellent schools now.'

'They have, but not, unfortunately, for Eurasian boys. Fred's mother, you see, was an Indian lady. Yes, I committed the unpardonable social sin of marrying outside of the club. I have no regrets personally but it has led to difficulties for Fred.'

'I see. You'll find this a cold old place after so long away. Will you return to India?'

'I have little choice, I fear. I have but a minor administrative post and it is my sole means. I am determined, though, to find the best school possible for Fred before I leave as he will have to spend his holidays there. I don't suppose you know of any that we might consider?'

'Indeed I do but we can talk about it after you've settled in, for here we are.'

★ ★ ★

Seated comfortably before the sitting room fire after an excellent dinner, with Frederick in bed, Luke felt ready to talk. True to his nature, his thoughts had been racing ever since Algy Parrish had accosted him in the refreshment room. How could he use this situation to advantage? He'd no contacts in India and India was a wealthy country, or at least, there was wealth to be had there through trade.

Here was a man who knew the country but was unsuccessful in life, who'd ruined his chances of promotion by marrying locally and had saved every penny of his salary to pay for an English education for his son. With his wife dead of malaria, Fred was all he had.

'How is your command of the language?' Luke asked.

'Pretty fair, really. I'm just about fluent in Hindi, Gujarati and Marathi and can get by with Urdu and Sindi. You know, I just cannot get over your kindness. It must have been providence come to my aid, meeting you again like this. I hope you won't mind my saying how I admire the way you have got on, when I think back to peeling potatoes with you on deck all those years ago. Fred asked me how I knew you and I told him exactly how it came about and how you punched me on the nose after I hit you. I must have been a thoroughly unpleasant person.'

'I'm sure there was no need to rake that up.'

'But then you were so kind to me afterwards. That was something I have never forgotten.'

'Mm.' Luke was beginning to feel uncomfortable. The man was pathetically grateful and self-effacing to the point of embarrassment, so he made a fresh effort to change the subject. 'Have you done any trading out there?'

'Well, not what you would term trading. Bartering, yes, all the time. Not everyone uses money.'

Luke took the plunge. 'Would you care to represent our interests in India, as agent? Secure commodities, see cargoes onto ships, that sort of thing?'

'You mean work for you?' There was excitement, wonder, disbelief, in the question.

'Yes. Of course, you'd need to think about it but in the morning you can take a look around the warehouses and see something of what we're about.'

'I should really be most interested to visit them but I must start looking for a school for Fred. I have my passage booked from Liverpool in two week's time. You see, I cannot afford to remain here for long.'

'Ah yes, the school. I think we can soon fix that up and there's no need to go all the way to Liverpool. You can leave from the river here.'

'But my ticket is already paid.'

'No problem. Walter will arrange matters. Just let him have the details,' and he went on to describe Bramsden College and how Richard found it not too bad a place and suggested he arrange a visit for Friday when he could spend the weekend at the Manor on the way back. 'I go down there every weekend unless there's something pressing here.'

'This is just too marvellous for words. What can I say but thank you?'

★ ★ ★

In truth, Luke enjoyed showing his visitors around the wharf and its associated enterprises and basked in the open admiration Algy Parrish showed. To have risen from galley boy on a sailing ship to running this bustling enterprise, was to him, miraculous. Even his partner paid the closest

- 139 -

attention to him and addressed him as 'Guv', just like everyone else, but they were clearly very close friends. No persuasion was needed for Fred to go off with the tugs and, well muffled up, he spent a fascinated day up and down the river.

'You are sure he'll be all right?' his anxious father asked.

'Perfectly,' Luke replied. 'You've no need to worry and he'll be escorted back home when work finishes.' Which assurance was fulfilled when he reappeared at seven o'clock that evening to describe a thoroughly enjoyable day to his father and 'no thank you,' he was not hungry as he had eaten at the warehouse with the others and could he please go again?'

★ ★ ★

On the Friday, father and son visited Bramsden College and arranged for Fred to start there after his father had sailed. He'd be in the same house and dormitory as Richard, would spend his holidays at the Manor and, as Luke put it, 'He's joining as one of the crew so he's my responsibility now,' and Algy Parrish sailed for Bombay from the Pool in greater comfort than he'd arrived. A tidy arrangement Luke decided and looked forward to profitable trading with India, now the company had its own agent there.

★ ★ ★

Miss Hetherington returned early from church in a distressed state. It being Sunday morning Luke had preferred to potter around the grounds whilst she had attended as usual, accompanied by Peter and Lucy. With the service about to start, Sir Brandon Remnold and his eldest son had marched up the aisle and ordered Miss Hetherington to vacate the private pew, loudly proclaiming it to be for the use of the most prominent family in the parish, not for some outsider who'd moved into the Manor with his mistress.

It was Mrs Cherry, full of outrage, who tracked Luke down in the vegetable garden to tell him of this latest turn. 'He certainly throws a low punch,' Luke said, 'and who's the mistress I've moved in with? He's not suggesting I'm involved with Miss Hetherington, is he?' as the realisation dawned on him.

'This is not the first time it's been said, Guv,' Mrs Cherry went on, fairly quivering with indignation. 'That old Rector started it, accusing Miss Hetherington of being old squire's mistress, which is why she keeps herself to herself. It's not good enough, Guv, him saying such things about the poor girl and 'er a clergyman's daughter too.'

'I absolutely agree,' Luke said, firmly, to both demonstrate his support and calm Mrs Cherry down, 'and something will have to be done about it.'

Satisfied, Mrs Cherry marched back to her kitchen to pass on reassurances and sympathy to Miss Hetherington. Whether or not that lady had enjoyed a liaison with the widowed Squire Travers, Luke cared not one jot. That was none of his business but he was annoyed that Sir Brandon was getting at him through others who couldn't defend themselves. The mark of a true bully, he thought, as he turned his attention once more to the vegetable garden.

Until he walked out, they'd had a full time gardener to provide vegetables, with the area of level ground between the rear of the house and the foot of the wooded hillside laid out in neat rows of many varieties but he'd have to take on someone else soon if it was to stay productive.

The previous gardener had suggested a wall around the garden to keep the warmth in to give earlier crops and to keep rabbits out and that idea had caught Luke's imagination, progressing to heated glasshouses in which to grow all manner of interesting things. He really wouldn't mind, he thought, having grapes and peaches and even oranges growing here so yes, he'd get George to set someone on with building that wall as a first step.

'Ah, Mrs Donkin. Everything all right? Don't expect you to work on Sunday as well, you know.'

'A few odd jobs'll not 'urt, sir. It's 'bout this 'ere bit sir, I was 'oping fer a word. Now you've no gardener I was wonderin' if you'd give me a try at it, sir.'

'You mean take on the vegetable garden?'

'That's right, sir. I've 'ad years o' practice at it. 'Ad to, see. 'Ad to grow all me own stuff if I wanted things in the pot.'

'I see. Would you manage it yourself or would you need help?'

'I've got all the 'elp I'd need for this, sir. I've three young 'uns as'll turn to and 'elp, never mind Albert. I know folks give us a bad name but be better if they give us a chance instead, like you've done, sir.'

'Very well,' Luke said. 'I'll talk to Mr Cherry and if he's happy you can take it on.' With Mrs Donkin gone, Luke found his thoughts returning to Sir Brandon and his continuing unpleasantness. He didn't usually attend church services so this morning's episode had to be a deliberate provocation but how best to handle it, he wondered, then began to chuckle. Yes. If the fat blighter wanted his pew, he could have it, but on his terms, and chuckling to himself still, he wandered into the kitchen for a drink.

'Oh, Miss Hetherington. I'm so sorry to hear of that fellow's insulting behaviour. I shall accompany you to church next Sunday and he can address his remarks to me. Can't be pushed around by that type, can we?'

★ ★ ★

There were three visitors at the Manor the following weekend, two of Digger's experts and Liam Donavon, who worked in the boatyard. They spent much of Saturday night away from the Manor and slept late next morning, as Luke and his party set out for church.

Arriving in good time, he ushered his group to seats in the congregation, conspicuously leaving the private pew vacant. Again, just as the service was about to start, Sir Brandon, accompanied this time by both his sons, made his noisy entrance and marched straight up the aisle to the manorial pew, a look of triumph on his bloated, red face.

Glaring around at the congregation, he lowered himself ponderously onto the pew, which collapsed in a cloud of dust. The boards of the wooden dais beneath the pew also gave way with the pew sides and door following so all that could be seen of the baronet was a large expanse of trouser seat and a pair of boots waving in the air. Sir Brandon, once he'd been extricated from the wreckage, was beside himself with rage at this humiliation and thundered down the aisle to where Luke was sitting.

'This is your doing, Gregory,' he roared, waving his arms wildly. 'I'll have my day, you mark my words, you damned guttersnipe, you.'

Poker-faced, Luke rose to his feet and bowed formally. 'Your servant, sir,' he said and calmly sat down again.

Sir Brandon spluttered incoherently for a moment, snarled a most ungodly oath and marched from the church, followed by his sons, one of them carrying his father's hat, out of shape now, having suffered in the fall.

Peter, sitting next to Luke, was having difficulty containing his laughter, as were others in the congregation, judging by the suppressed choking noises from all around. With a big effort, Luke managed to keep a straight face, though he was sorely tempted to laugh out loud. Not until they were half way home did their pent up mirth burst out and in the middle of the deserted road they leaned against each other, helpless with laughter, the tears streaming down their faces, their ribs aching.

'How did you do it, Guv?' Peter asked, as they gradually recovered their composure.

'Who said I had anything to do with it?' Luke asked, in mock surprise. 'I think it was death watch beetle or ship's worm responsible,' which set them all off again.

★ ★ ★

It was Friday evening and Luke was walking towards the Manor from the station. His week had been tedious and he was looking forward to changing into comfortable clothes and relaxing, hopeful that nothing else of an unpleasant nature had occurred in his absence.

The first handful of mud caught him squarely in the back of the neck. It was a cracking good shot but he wasn't prepared to applaud the thrower's aim, as he realised what had happened. Stopping to look around, he was pelted with more mud, cow dung and several stones, by a group on the other side of the hedge.

Should he run for it? Most undignified. He'd go straight at them, but the ambush had been well prepared and he had a bank to climb first. More muck hit him as he started forward and all he saw was the back view of several youths as they ran off, jeering as they went.

He stood for a while not sure what he should do. He had little chance of catching up with them and would probably make a fool of himself if he tried. Scraping off the worst of the muck, he carried on towards the Manor, growing more and more angry as he went. He could guess who was behind the attack; there'd be no prizes for that but to be pelted with muck by village louts, well that was close to the end. Seething with rage, he walked into the kitchen and Mrs Cherry's jaw dropped when she saw the state of him.

'I walked right into it,' Luke said. 'They were waiting for me and I'm not best pleased.'

'I should think you're not, indeed,' Mrs Cherry said. 'It's disgraceful and on top of what they've done to poor Joseph. George is with him now. Several of them set on him for no reason.'

'Where are they? Through there?' indicating the back room next to the scullery they used for anything and everything and on entering saw that Joseph had been well and truly rolled in the muck with George helping him clean up.

'Did you get a good look at them?' Luke asked. 'I'd like a quiet word at a convenient time.'

'I knows two of 'em,' Joseph replied.

'In that case there'll be a reckoning,' Luke said. 'I'm no more prepared to be pushed around and set on here than I am in the City,' and he walked off to get himself cleaned up.

The rest of the weekend passed without incident but as Luke set out for the station on Monday morning he was again caught by mud-throwers, this time from a different ambush and was compelled to return to the Manor to change. His mood was far from friendly as he caught the later train for Guildford. Personal assault was something that had to be answered and if the idea was to drive him from the village, someone was wasting their time.

The answer Luke came up with was a well practiced one. If someone started on you, first make sure who they were. Warn them firmly and give them chance to back off. If they didn't, well, on their heads be it so, on the next Friday evening, when he got off the train at Chidlingbrook, he was discretely followed.

His assailants had run off towards the village so, if they tried the same caper again they'd run straight into the arms

- 145 -

of a group of fleet footed and able supporters to whom Luke's instructions were precise. He wanted no one hurt but he wished to know exactly who his persecutors were.

Close to the scene of the first ambush, he was once again pelted with mud and missiles. Half expecting the attack he ran straight at the hedge behind which the mud-throwers had hidden themselves. With jeers and taunts they ran off towards the village, and capture.

There were five of them, all village lads of sixteen or so and they were no match for Digger's trained men, who cut their belts and braces and bundled them roughly along the road to where Luke awaited them. Busy holding up their trousers, they offered no resistance and made no attempt at escape.

Wordlessly, Luke walked along the line of discomfited youths, looking intently at each face so as to be sure of recognising them again. That done, he nodded to his men who marched their captives off towards the village whilst he continued on to the Manor.

At the Lamb Inn, the luckless group was bundled through the door into the bar, the acknowledged social centre of the village and though it was too early for many to be gathered there, the message given was plain and would be relayed to everyone by closing time.

'These've made trouble for the Manor. It'd best stop and you'd best leave our guv'ner alone.' Simple words but spoken by Jess Harper, a large, battered exponent of the prize ring, there was no mistaking the warning. Then the group withdrew and left on the next train. Luke had made his point and no more mud was thrown in his direction.

★ ★ ★

A letter from Richard lay amongst the morning's post on the breakfast table. Not a common event but he usually managed two a month, which wasn't bad for any youngster at school, and Luke smiled to himself as he recognised the neat writing on the envelope.

A pleasant lad. He was growing quite fond of him, he realised. There were the usual preliminaries telling that he was well and managing to keep out of 'Old Soggy's' bad books. That would be the Latin master, if he remembered correctly. The main item though, was serious, for his friend Robert was leaving the school very shortly. His father, retired now from the army in India had, in Richard's vernacular, 'gone smash', having made an unfortunate investment on the stock market, which had left him ruined and unable to keep his son at school any longer.

He poured his coffee, pondering, and hardly noticed Bridie as she placed his kippers before him but gathered his wits in time to thank her as she left the room for it wouldn't do to upset the fiery little thing this early in the day. There'd be broken crockery in the kitchen for certain if she felt slighted.

Now what company had failed recently, of any importance? None he had an interest in or Walter would have told him. There were always the fraudulent ones, of course, those specialising in duping the unsuspecting. Gold mines in the arctic and such like.

So Richard was to lose his closest friend. That wouldn't be good for the boy. In fact, it could be disastrous for him. They were very close and disasters should not be allowed to happen if they could be avoided. Breakfast over and slippers replaced by boots, he went downstairs to Walter's room and posed his question.

'Who's failed on the exchange lately?'

Walter pursed his lips. Putting on his legal face, Digger called it. 'The only one in the last month was Dongara Goldfields, registered in Perth, Australia,' he replied. 'They were newly quoted and had some connection with Consort Minerals.'

'What do we know of them?'

Walter reached for the index to his files, found the reference and thumbed through a large book. 'Consort Minerals, ah.' He looked at Luke. 'One of the directors is Charles Lansdown'

Luke considered. So, if Charlie Lansdown was involved it meant almost beyond doubt that the company was fraudulent. 'I'd like to know the details,' he said, 'and would you send a telegram to Richard at school, please. "Advise R's father contact Mr B immediately with share certs. Imperative no delay. All not lost. Guv." Get Sammy to send it straight away, would you?' and without explanation, returned upstairs, leaving Walter wondering what it was all about.

He was growing used to Luke's ways but often wished that fuller explanations were forthcoming, though he usually managed to piece together most events when they were over.

'Morning Walter,' Digger sang out as he passed the door and made for the stairs. 'The Guv in?' and without waiting for a reply ran on up and joined Luke who was, as usual, when thinking, standing by the window, apparently looking out but in reality, seeing nothing.

'There's a letter from Richard on the table,' Luke said as he returned Digger's greeting and moved over to his favourite chair. 'I shall try to help so have invited Robert's father to call on Walter. If it turns out he was caught by friend Lansdown or one of his associates, then a little leaning will be required to obtain a refund. Should you happen to see that slippery gentleman you might care to make him uneasy, in a general sort of way?'

'Most happy to do so,' Digger grinned. 'He squirms something lovely if 'e thinks 'e's in it,' and that was how it was left, until Tom brought the information that Luke required concerning the failure of the Dongara Goldfield Company. After paying out one reasonable dividend that had attracted many more investors, the shares of this newly floated company doubled in value. The bulk of them, mainly owned by the parent company, were then sold off to eager buyers, after which, the mine announced that the reef, if there had ever been one in the first place, had run out, and the Dongara Goldfields Company was restructured and given the new title of Dongara Mineral Company. This effectively left investors with worthless shares in a defunct company.

'A clear case of fraud, I believe,' Luke told Walter. 'If a Major Weston calls to see you and has those shares, take them at their highest former price. Draw from the general fund and credit his bank account. You might also offer your services as investment advisor. The man appears to be out of his depth in that field.'

'May I ask what you will do with the shares? They will be quite worthless.' Walter was looking concerned and not a little puzzled.

'I shall obtain a refund from those who issued the certificates,' Luke replied, 'plus expenses incurred and I shall not be available should the major call.'

Major Weston did call, a tall, stiff, straight-backed man, grey haired and still showing the deep tan of his many years abroad. He had received a telegram from his son urging that he contact him at school when he'd been persuaded to swallow his indignation at his private affairs being made known to strangers, and to call upon Walter at Gresham House.

He arrived grim faced and on his dignity, struggling to maintain his pride in the belief that it was all he had left after a moderately successful lifetime of service. Walter was at his most charming and worked hard to ease the tense atmosphere but he quickly saw the wisdom of coming straight to the point, after the initial pleasantries.

'I understand, Major Weston, that you hold share certificates of a failed company. Do you have them with you?'

Without a word, the major produced an envelope from an inside pocket and handed it to Walter who took out the fussily printed documents and examined them. 'Ah, yes,' he said. 'Dongara Goldfields. Certificates of five hundred shares. Let me see, seven in all, dated January of this year. You would have paid three thousand, one hundred pounds at that time, received an interim dividend of four per cent in April when their quoted value rose to twenty five shillings per share.'

Major Weston sat stiff and motionless in his chair opposite Walter's desk, a beaten look on his face as he listened. 'I am authorised to offer you the full price for your shares at their peak value,' Walter said. 'That will be four thousand three hundred and seventy five pounds.'

Major Weston stared. 'I beg your pardon,' he said, in disbelief.

'I can offer you the maximum quoted price for these share certificates,' Walter said. 'They reached their highest value on the thirtieth of May, at exactly twenty five shillings per share.'

'But these shares are worthless,' the major said. 'The company is bankrupt, utterly finished.'

'Quite so,' Walter replied, evenly. 'Nevertheless, my instructions are to offer you the full price for them, should you wish to sell them. Payment to be in gold or by credit to your bank, as you may decide.'

Major Weston, sitting up even straighter now, was having difficulty believing his ears. 'You mean you are serious? That you actually wish to purchase these shares?' Then, collecting his wits, 'Of course I would wish to sell them but surely, no one in his right mind would buy them? They are utterly worthless.'

'I can assure you, sir, that my principal is of completely sound mind and knows precisely what he is about,' Walter replied, a little stiffly.

'I am sorry. I meant no offence whatever, but this is the last thing I expected to hear. May I enquire who your principal is? May I not meet him? But why should anyone wish to do this?' Major Weston, from the depths of dignified despair was struggling with his emotions.

'My principal is not available at present and I have no knowledge as to the reason that he wishes to make this transaction. I am merely his legal adviser and conduct business on his behalf. If you would be good enough to sign this certificate of transfer and advise me of your bankers we may complete this matter.'

In a daze, Major Weston signed the transfer document and named Martin's Bank in Lombard Street as holder of his account. No longer so stiff, his hand appeared to tremble and he rose to his feet, looking down at the desk as Walter made out the credit note to be taken to the bank.

'Should you desire advice on investments for the future, I would be happy to be of assistance,' Walter said, looking up with a smile. 'There are many areas of reasonably certain stock exchange activity with which we are conversant, should you, in due course wish to consider them,' and reaching for the bell pull behind his chair, gave it a tug, which brought Tom into the room, smartly turned out in a sober, well cut suit and gleaming white collar.

'Tom, would you accompany Major Weston to the Central Bank and present this note to Mr Swinburne. Ask him to kindly arrange things immediately with Martin's.'

Still not fully in command of himself and scarcely daring to believe the sudden transformation of his affairs, the major was ushered out, leaving Walter sitting at his desk, strangely satisfied and wondering, for perhaps the hundredth time at his employment by this most unusual organisation.

★ ★ ★

Digger, in the course of his peregrinations about the City came upon Charles Lansdown sitting with a group of his cronies in a bar frequented by the 'fast' set and, being Digger, broke in upon their conversation without difficulty.

'Well, well, well. Charlie Lansdown. I'm surprised you're still in town.'

'Why? What do you mean?' retorted that individual, a pale, flabby man wearing expensive clothes and several jewelled rings on his fingers.

'Been doing a little restructuring, I hear.' Then, very softly, 'You caught the governor fer a packet.'

Charles Lansdown went even paler. 'You're not serious. I didn't know that, honest.'

'Honest, Charlie? You don't know the meaning of the word. What I do know is, the guv made enquiries about Dongara and he had a very nasty look on his face. I'm surprised you haven't heard from him.'

'God!' exclaimed Lansdown. 'What am I going to do?'

'Best to see 'im before 'e sees you. Four thousand shares I think 'e said. Trading at twenty five shillings each at one time. Course, a little sweetener might 'elp but that's up to you. Best o' luck,' and Digger wandered off to chat to a man even smaller than himself, with the bowed legs of a jockey.

Walter's first visitor next day was an agitated, pale-faced man carrying a heavy bag, flanked by two large companions for protection, and the general fund was duly replenished, standing at rather more than previously.

Two days later, Luke received another letter from Richard, bubbling over with joie de vive this time for his friend Robert was no longer leaving the school. I don't know how you did it, Guv, it said, but thanks, awfully. Robert wanted to write to you but I said you would prefer him not to. I hope that was right. 'That was indeed, quite right,' Luke said out loud, although he was alone.

★ ★ ★

It was towards the end of the Christmas holiday that a white-faced Robert came running back to the Manor late that afternoon to meet George, as he crossed the yard from the stable.

'Something awful's happened,' he gasped out.

'Something worse'll 'appen if you go waving that gun around like that. Is it loaded? Let me see. Oh, that's all right. Now, what's the problem?'

'It's Richard. The keepers from the Hall have got him. They said he was poaching but he wasn't at all.'

'You mean they've got hold of him? Taken him up the Hall?' George was aghast. 'The guv won't like that. We'd best go and tell 'im.'

Luke was sitting comfortably before the fire in the hall, teacup in hand, his stockinged feet thrust out towards the flames from the burning logs. He'd spent the afternoon pottering around the wood and up the hill, enjoying the peace and quiet and noting the different birds and small animals that lived around there. A pleasant place, he was thinking, when George entered from the kitchen, followed apprehensively by Robert.

'Er, sorry to disturb you Guv but we have a spot o' bother.'

Luke lowered his cup and looked keenly at them both. 'Richard?' he asked, noting his absence.

'Yes, Guv. The keepers from the Hall have taken 'im. They said he was poaching but Robert here says different.'

Luke looked at Robert. 'Tell me what happened.'

'We were up by the trees near the boundary,' he began, swallowing nervously, 'and Richard shot a rabbit. It fell over and then got up again and ran across into the field on the other side. We were sure that it was hit and wounded so he went after it, to put it down properly, but as soon as he got on the other side, the keepers came running up and got hold of him and they picked the rabbit up and said he'd shot it on Sir Brandon's land.'

'The rabbit was dead, then? Mm. Was he carrying his gun when he crossed the boundary?'

'Yes, sir.'

'Harness up, George. We'll have to visit the Hall. I'll go and change and join you in the yard.'

'Shall I come too, sir?' Robert asked, anxiously.

'Yes, you'd better. You can say exactly what took place.'

It was impossible to tell what Luke's feelings were during the drive across the darkening valley to the Hall and whether he was angry or concerned did not show as the trap drew up to the front door of the mansion and he walked calmly up the steps and pulled the bell handle.

There was no immediate response so, after a reasonable delay he tugged at it again. This time, heavy footsteps were heard inside and the door was opened by the estate bailiff, who looked Luke up and down insolently.

'Trades people round the back,' he said, offensively.

Ignoring the insult Luke said quietly, 'I wish to see Sir Brandon.'

'Like I said, tradesmen round the back. Maybe he'll see you there, maybe not,' and he closed the door again and noisily shot home the bolts. For a moment, Luke stood still, looking at but not seeing the closed door in front of him, controlling his anger. Then, abruptly he turned and walked briskly along the front of the building and round the side, through the stable yard to a rear door he guessed might lead to the kitchens, and rapped hard on the knocker.

Almost immediately, the door was opened by a maid holding a lantern and he was ushered into a large room with a long, deal table, which he guessed to be the servant's hall, and there he was asked to wait. Five minutes later footsteps on the stone floor approached, a door was flung open and Sir Brandon entered, followed by his bailiff.

'Well, and what do you want?' he demanded.

'I understand you hold my boy,' Luke replied, calmly.

'I have a poacher in custody. Yours, is he? Well, well, well. How very interesting. Now we'll see you hop, Mr High and Mighty Gregory.'

'He wasn't poaching,' Luke answered, ignoring the taunt. He merely went to retrieve a wounded animal, that's all. I'd be obliged if you'd hand him over to me.'

'Would you, now,' Sir Brandon sneered. 'Would you, now. Well, not so fast. First, we'll see what the constable has to say and then we shall have to arrange a court hearing. Three months in the House of Correction might well fit the bill.'

'That would not be an appropriate course to take,' Luke replied, struggling hard to keep his temper. 'As I have already told you, Richard was not poaching.'

'I'm magistrate here and I decide the facts.'

So that was to be it. This unpleasant and overbearing creature intended taking full advantage of the incident in order to hit at him.

'You're barred from hearing the case because of your personal interest in it. That's the law and it's my duty as guardian to seek the release of a minor on a surety. I therefore ask you to name that surety and release the boy to my custody.'

Conflicting emotions showed in the course features as the man weighed his advantage against his position as magistrate and his desire to score against Luke and finally, with a cunning look about his eyes, he agreed, set the surety at ten pounds and sneered, 'We'll look forward to the hearing in court.'

'It would be preferable not to pursue this course at all,' Luke said, not so much in the hope of a prosecution being dropped as to encourage it. He'd made a decision and was already planning his course of action.

The journey back to the Manor in the well-filled trap was a silent one. Richard, without his treasured gun was slumped abjectly against the side, Luke was preoccupied with his thoughts and George and Robert decided silence to be the wisest course.

Changing once more into older, more comfortable clothes, Luke resumed his seat by the fire in the hall and stared at the ever-changing pattern of flames, his mind working around this new and unasked for situation. The sound of a scuffed footstep made him look up. Richard was standing nearby, the light from the fire showing a look of misery on his face.

'Guv,' he began. 'I'm ever so sorry. I honestly didn't think it would lead to trouble like this.'

'Mm?' Luke said, switching his thoughts from plans and strategies to what Richard was saying. 'Oh, yes. Come and sit,' and when Richard had joined him on the settle, went on, 'Don't worry about it. It's just one of those unforeseen occurrences. Not your fault.'

'You mean you're not angry with me? Richard's voice showed surprise. 'But what if I go to prison for poaching?'

'You won't go to prison,' Luke assured him. 'That fellow was trying to frighten you. You'll have to appear in court mind, but you'll be well represented. Anyway, why should I be angry with you? As I understand it, you very properly went to finish off a wounded animal, to prevent it suffering. You had no idea those keepers were waiting nearby for just such an opportunity. I'll write to Sir Brandon in the morning and ask him not to prosecute. He'll refuse, but he'll have had the opportunity to be reasonable.'

They sat then, in silence for a while then Richard said, very quietly, 'He had Dixie shot.'

Luke stiffened. 'Tell me more.'

'Dixie followed me when the keepers took me up to the Hall. I heard one of them say he was hanging around the yard and Sir Brandon shouted 'well shoot the blasted thing' and a bit later I heard a shot.'

'He'll pay dearly for that. Very dearly indeed.'

'What will you do, Guv?'

'You'll see. Every man has his Achilles heel.'

But Dixie hadn't been shot and was whining at the door later that evening, muddy and wet but unhurt, with a piece of cord attached to his collar, long enough to have been a leash.

★ ★ ★

'I'm assuming the charge of poaching will be pressed.' Luke told Walter, 'so I want Richard properly represented. A Q.C. if necessary, but someone who'll tear their evidence apart. I believe that's our best defence as he was on someone else's land with a newly shot rabbit and a gun. Then, I want to study the file you have on that fellow at the Hall.'

A great deal of painstaking research had gone into the compilation of that file and just how the information had been gained, Luke hadn't asked, but Ben and Dessy had spent some time in Guildford and they were expert at ferreting out useful facts. It was useful facts he now required and the most useful one of all revealed that Sir Brandon Remnold's finances were in a most parlous state. In fact, he was head over heels in debt and the deeds to the Hall and the estate were held by the Land and County Bank in Guildford's Market Street.

Despite falling revenues from his estate, due both to the farming recession and a lack of investment, he lived extravagantly, hunted, drank and gambled and visited London frequently where he stayed at his club in St James.

Ah, now this could be what he wanted, if it was accurate. A note in the file referred to a clerk named Smithers who, for a consideration, had revealed that, with falling land values, the likely market price of the entire estate of Hall, four farms and nearly seven hundred acres of land and most of the village of Chidlingbrook would be insufficient to cover the loans outstanding from the bank and the directors were seriously concerned.

That note was dated six months previously so what was the position now? Unlikely to be improved, Luke thought, pondered the possibilities a while and made his decision. There was little hope of Sir Brandon changing his mind as he'd been hostile from the start. Now, he'd declared war on him, which left no choice but to fight back. Very well, off with the gloves.

'Walter, I want you to negotiate as soon as possible with the Land and County Bank at Guildford for the transfer of Sir Brandon's loans and mortgages to ourselves. I believe the directors might be pleased to relieve themselves of those particular liabilities.'

'I shall leave straight away,' Walter said, knowing that Luke's 'as soon as possible' meant just that. Once he'd decided on a course he expected immediate action and the bank, which was not a large one, was most happy to recover much of its capital from a City company called Gresham Estates and wrote to Sir Brandon informing him of the transfer of interest.

★ ★ ★

A keen, sharp young barrister, a junior in the chambers of Munro Maitland Q.C., was briefed to represent Richard in court two weeks later. Luke was prepared, as a matter of principle, to do everything possible to defend his own and if a barrister appearing before magistrates at the Petty Sessions, to speak in a case of alleged rabbit poaching might be seen as over doing things, he was unworried, for he knew the matter went deeper.

Richard and Robert, by then back at school, journeyed down to Chidlingbrook the evening before, ready to appear next morning as defendant and witness. Both were very much on edge when George met them at the station in the trap.

'Now don't you worry, either of you,' he reassured them. 'The Guv knows what he's about, I can tell 'ee that. He knows fine well it's him Sir Brandon is out to injure and he'll have something up his sleeve, never fear. A pound to a penny there'll be a surprise or two tomorrow so you just follow instructions and watch the fun.'

'But he's asked Sir Brandon not to prosecute me,' Richard persisted.

'Ah, that's his way, you see. If anyone makes trouble for him he gives 'em chance to back off or put things right. Then, if they carries on he hits 'em, very hard, and they're out for the count.'

★ ★ ★

The first person Luke and his party saw outside the Guildhall next morning was Sir Brandon Remnold, who glared maliciously at Luke.

'I would appreciate a private word with you, Sir Brandon,' Luke said.

'I'm sure you would, Gregory. Anything you've got to say can be said here and now, in front of my lawyer and my friends, but much good it'll do you.'

'I would merely ask you to withdraw your charge of poaching against my ward and spare him the ordeal of appearing and the possibility of his good name being tarnished. This business is of no benefit to you whatever.'

'Ha!' Sir Brandon's exclamation was at once contemptuous and triumphant. 'So, Mister High and Mighty Gregory. Singing a different tune these days are we?' he sneered. 'Don't want good names tarnished, hey? The whelp of a suicide and a City guttersnipe aping the gentry? Good names my arse!'

'Steady on, old man,' one of his companions cautioned. 'You're going a bit strong.'

'Huh! I'll see him crawl back whence he came with his tail between his legs. That's all the fellow has there.'

A few smirks and sniggers greeted this course and juvenile insult but Luke merely raised his hat politely and walked steadily on inside, taking a seat towards the rear but, catching sight of Richard's troubled face said, 'Ignore the comments of a blackguard and remember, he who laughs last, laughs the longer,' and Walter nodded his agreement as reassurance.

They were joined then by James Caville, their barrister, gowned and bewigged as befitted his status, who advised that Luke and Robert should wait outside the courtroom until called to give their evidence and the magistrates entering then, they all stood up and Richard took his place to make his plea of 'not guilty.'

The two game keepers were called to tell how they had seized the accused on private land in possession of both a rabbit and a gun and accompanied by a dog and had taken the accused to their employer, Sir Brandon. James Caville asked only perfunctory questions of the first keeper, establishing that the rabbit had been dead when seized and the name of the field in which it had died. The second keeper though, faced a different tack when he was cross-examined.

'You were waiting, as I understand, for the accused to cross what you are pleased to term the boundary between the Manor lands and those of the Hall?'

'Yes, sir'

'Why?'

'To catch un trespassing after game, sir. That being my orders, sir.'

'Did you see the accused shoot the rabbit?'

'Well, not zactly, sir. Trees were in the way.'

'I see. Would you please tell the court, then, why you seized the accused?'

'Well, sir, Jack says, that's my mate, sir, there 'e goes, the bugger, an' 'e runs out after un an' I runs out too an' I sees young Master Travers wi 'is dog and gun and a dead coney.'

'Ah yes. The gun is here. Yes, exhibit 'A'. Good. What of the dog? The one that you claim was present.'

'Well, sir, Master ordered un shot, sir.'

'Shot? Oh, I see. And did you shoot it?'

'Well, no, sir. I were inside wi' young Master Travers, a guardin 'im, see, 'till the constable were fetched.'

'Ah well, the rabbit then, the er, coney, as you call it. Should not that be here?'

'Well, sir,' the under keeper replied, unhappily, scratching his head. 'E were 'et.'

'You mean you ate the evidence?' and there was a roar of laughter from the public benches at the rear and one of the magistrates was seen to stifle a smile.

'In that case, you may stand down.'

It was now the turn of the defence and Richard was skilfully taken through his evidence. He stood up well to cross examination by the clerk of the court, as did Robert when called upon to corroborate Richard's explanation.

'Finally, and to convince your worships beyond all possible doubt that no offence of poaching took place, I call Luke Gregory to the stand.'

Luke entered the courtroom erect, unsmiling and confident, took the oath and identified himself, giving the Manor as his address, then turned to face the barrister, ready to answer his questions.

'I understand, Mr Gregory that you are lord of the manor of Chidlingbrook?'

'That is correct.'

'Did the accused have your full permission to pursue game upon land to which you hold title?'

'He did.'

'The land upon which the accused was seized, wrongfully, I believe, is known as Black Acre. Who owns that land?'

'I do,' and Luke produced from his inside pocket a sheaf of documents, liberally covered with wax seals and red and blue ribbons, which he handed to the barrister.

'I hold here, your worships, the deeds of title to land lying in the parish of Chidlingbrook, amongst which is included the aforementioned Black Acre, and I offer them for your worship's perusal. I would submit that, no matter on which side of the boundary the rabbit was shot, the defendant was on land to which his guardian holds title and rentals owing to that title are sufficiently in arrear as to nullify the tenant's exclusive right to game, in accordance with the Game Act of 1880. The accusation of trespass in pursuit of game would therefore appear to be made in error by a malicious and misguided neighbour who would clearly do well to consider the gravity of his position.'

James Caville was enjoying himself, an influential fish in a small pool.' There is now a matter of wrongful arrest to be considered, or more properly, the abduction of a minor and his subsequent imprisonment by the complainant, a most serious offence in law and one that your worships may feel warrants a hearing in a court of assize.'

The magistrates looked concerned, conferred together, then with the clerk of the court and with no more than a cursory glance at the title deeds, dismissed the charge of poaching against Richard who, bemused but thankful that his ordeal was over, smilingly joined Luke, Walter and Robert at the back of the room.

'Right Walter, let him have it,' and Walter made his way over to where Sir Brandon, looking baffled and blustering noisily about 'some damned lawyer's trick,' stood with his cronies, and handed him a sealed envelope.

Tearing it open he read it through then read it again and stood as if transfixed, staring at Luke who, not deigning to look his way, moved towards the door and the chill air outside.

'There's a table booked at the Clarence for lunch,' he said and set a brisk pace along the High Street. 'Er, Champagne, I think,' Luke said to the attentive waiter who was taking their order, which pleasant, if over-rated wine matched perfectly their lightened mood after the tension of the court.

'George said you'd spring a surprise Guv.' Richard's eyes were sparkling with relief and Champagne. 'Old Bully Britches looked as if he'd been struck by lightning when we left and he wasn't half rude to you before we went in. I bet you've given him something to think about.'

'You might say that,' Luke replied, straight faced. 'Tell them, Walter. They may as well know.'

'Sir Brandon has been served notice of foreclosure,' Walter said. 'He has been given seven days in which to repay all his mortgages and debts, failing which, he must vacate the estate in favour of the Governor.'

'You mean that you'll own Morden Hall and all that land? Golly. No wonder he looked sick. Will you go and live there?'

'No thanks. Far too big for my tastes. Now go easy on that stuff. Remember you're due back at school this afternoon. You have to return as sober, well behaved young gentlemen,' and they both pulled a face in response.

★ ★ ★

Chapter 7

Luke returned to London, arranging for Walter to handle matters arising. There was a tentative approach by an intermediary seeking to reschedule the debt repayments but the ultimatum remained. Sir Brandon either cleared all outstanding loans and interest or vacated the estate and there being no further contact, an agent was appointed to make a full inventory, it being Luke's intention to offer it for sale.

As usual, when he found himself taking strong action in defence of his interests, he felt no sense of satisfaction. He had no personal use for Morden Hall. He just wanted a peaceful neighbour who'd leave him alone, so he didn't visit his latest acquisition and remained aloof from events.

Relaxing before the log fire in the hall just over a week later he was disturbed by footsteps in the porch and a moment later, the jangle of the doorbell. Being closest, he got to his feet and opened the door to find a young man standing there whom he thought he recognised.

'Come in,' Luke invited, standing back to allow the visitor to enter. 'It's Mr Remnold, isn't it? Francis Remnold?'

'Yes, sir, that's right. I, I'm sorry to disturb you, sir, but I wondered if I could talk to you, about the Hall, I mean.' Flustered, Luke decided. Agitated. 'It's about my mother. I know we have to leave, sir, but I don't know what to do. You see, mother is bed-ridden and I wondered if you would allow us a little longer to, to make arrangements.' He tailed off lamely, having delivered his request in a rush of words.

Luke considered a moment. 'You'd better come and sit down,' he said. 'In here, I think,' and he led the way into the study. So this was the younger son. Not a bit like his older brother. At least he could give him a hearing and he ushered him to an arm chair. There, he perched nervously on the edge of the seat, fiddling with the brim of his hat and looking around as Luke turned up the oil lamps on the mantelpiece.' So you wish to remain longer at the Hall,' Luke said, as a way of reopening the conversation.

'If that would be at all possible, sir.' At least, this man, whom his father had so decried, had not thrown him out and appeared remarkably civil.

'Had you any length of time in mind?'

'Well, n,no sir,' Francis stammered, 'only I haven't been able to arrange anything for mother yet. Father and Percival, that's my brother, sir, have already left.'

'Leaving you to solve the problem alone. I see. Your mother is bedridden, you say. May I enquire why this is?'

'It was because of a riding accident, sir. She fell and injured her back and has been unable to walk for years.'

'Ah.' Luke was looking keenly at Francis Remnold, trying to weigh him up. Slim, dark haired, average height, rather tense but honest eyes and he was respectful without being obsequious. 'May I enquire your age, Mr Remnold?'

'I am eighteen, sir,' came the surprised reply.

'You will understand that I sought no quarrel with your family?'

'Yes, sir. Mother and I both know that.'

'How well do you know the estate? House, land, farms, that sort of thing?'

'Oh, very well indeed, sir, although I have never been involved in running any part of it. I was never thought capable of that sort of thing,' he added, rather wistfully but with a clear tinge of bitterness showing. These were strange questions and he had yet to receive an answer to his original request.

'I had in mind to sell, of course, but would you care to manage the estate?'

The realisation of what was being offered only gradually dawned on Francis Remnold and he stared at Luke, mouth open in astonishment.

'You mean me, but I hadn't, I mean,' he stammered in confusion.

'Such a role would solve your problem, would it not? You'd continue to live at the Hall and you'd take responsibility for the administration. What d'you say?'

'I can only say thank you very much, Mr Gregory. This is really unbelievable. I never thought anything like this could happen.'

'Life has its surprises. There'd be certain requirements, naturally. Firstly, I don't wish either your father or your brother to set foot again on any part of the estate. Secondly, you'd give your fullest attention to the estate and I'd expect you to seek advice and to discuss your plans with me. The responsibility would be yours, you realise. There's a problem?' for a change of expression showed in the young man's face.

'It's just that Norris would prove difficult. He's the bailiff, sir. He has already told me, ordered me, actually, to find the money for the men's wages but I have none. None at all.'

'Is that fellow still around? Then dismiss him first thing in the morning and give him no more than a week to clear off. I owe him no favours whatever but you'll need to keep a close eye on him whilst he's around. His sort is capable of all manner of mischief.'

Francis gulped. Dismiss Norris, his father's closest supporter and ally, a man who never concealed his contempt for him?

'You're not happy about that, I can see. Do it this way. Send for him. Make him come to you then tell him his services are no longer required. No arguments and no explanations. Tell him you want him out within the week and his salary may reflect the shortness of notice given. I'll send you sufficient funds for wages but you'll do the paying out. Now, when you've looked through the agent's inventory come over and discuss things with me. What about your own expenses? I quite understand,' as Francis immediately looked extremely uncomfortable and taking twenty sovereigns from the desk drawer he handed them to that overwhelmed young man, ushered him to the door and with a handshake, wished him 'good night.'

Returning to his seat before the hall fire and refilling his pipe, he allowed himself a smile and a chuckle. Installing the despised younger son as master of the estate should set tongues wagging and provide salt for the father's wounded pride and of course, he would be pleased to do exactly as Luke desired.

With the agent paid off, the world knew that matters were settled but when word got around that Norris had been given notice by young master Francis, who had paid out the wages that week, speculation knew no bounds.

Norris, though, was not prepared to take his dismissal from 'that young whelp' and he offensively informed Francis Remnold that 'here he was and here he stayed and if he knew what was good for him he'd make no move to cross him.' Which response was duly relayed to Luke, who raised his eyebrows.

'I see. Very well. Tell him he'll be evicted if he fails to leave by Friday. Now, what are your thoughts on the agent's notes?'

'Well, sir, according to the agent, everything is in better state than it really is' and went on to tell how run-down the estate was with nothing spent on maintenance or repairs for years and with the land overstocked and overworked to produce as much income as possible. The tenants at Higher Farm and Downs Farm had difficulty meeting their rentals, which were the highest in the area and whilst Norris saw to the Home Farm, that was in a poor state as well. Church Farm, in the village, was run-down with very little land in good heart and the mill was empty and almost derelict.

'Mill? I didn't know there was a mill.'

'Yes, sir. An old water mill about half a mile downstream. It hasn't been used since the gearing broke and father said it wasn't worth repairing. Everyone round about says it's haunted.'

'I see. So what about the farm implements?'

'There are three carts and two drays at the Home Farm but not enough sound wheels for them all to be used at the same time. The harness and working tack needs replacing and the horses are too old for heavy work, except for the hunters, that is.'

'Mm. Do you hunt, Mr Remnold?'

'No, sir. I prefer not to.'

'You have a horse that you ride?'

'No, sir.'

'You'll need one. If the hunters are not to your taste, sell them and find something for yourself. The tenants of the farms you mentioned will be responsible for their own tools and implements I should imagine so offer to review their rental conditional upon agreeing to co-operate with improvements. If loans are required or expenditure by the landlord is appropriate, draw up their requirements and I'll see what may be done. Now what about the Home Farm? Will you run it after Norris has gone?'

'I, I really don't know, sir. I should like to try but I have no experience.'

'Well, give it some thought. It'd be a good idea to tidy up the equipment in any case. Wheels and carts, that sort of thing.'

'Yes, sir. I'll see to that straight away. Oh, I have a letter for you, from mother. She wonders whether you could possibly call to see her. She would call upon you were she able but she very much wishes to meet you, sir,' and Francis handed over a small, plain envelope.

★ ★ ★

Visiting bedridden ladies was not to Luke's taste and it showed in his expression as George drove him to the Hall in the trap and that was something he must learn to do for himself.

He was greeted at the front door by Francis and was led up the staircase, at least twice as wide as the one at the Manor, to a first floor room. There he was introduced to Lady Remnold, who sat, propped up by pillows, in a four-poster bed.

'It is most kind of you to call, Mr Gregory,' she said. 'Won't you sit down?' and Luke lowered himself onto the high backed chair placed near the bed and awaited events. What, he wondered, could this pale, worn-looking woman want with him?'

'I should first like to thank you for not only allowing my son and myself to remain here but also for acting as you have.' Luke listened warily, wondering just how to take that last statement. 'My husband is a brute, Mr Gregory and I never thought it possible to be free of him. I was born here, you know. This has always been my home and the gravest error I ever made was in agreeing to marry Brandon Remnold. My maiden name was Morden, Mr Gregory. Is it, perhaps, one that you recognise?'

Luke thought for a moment. 'Yes, I've heard it,' he replied, cautiously.

'Josiah Morden, barrister at law and magistrate? Adviser to goodness knows how many government departments during his lifetime? Yes, Mr Gregory. He was my great uncle and only occasionally visited here. He could not abide my husband but I remember him speaking of you. He told of a most remarkable young man who one day appeared in his court, a young man engaged in commerce by the river?'

Luke stirred in his chair. What was this woman getting at? She couldn't be that much older than himself. A bit unhinged, perhaps? 'I understood that gentleman to be without relatives,' he replied.

'Were you, Mr Gregory, a beneficiary under his will?'

So that was it. What a very small world it was. Who would have predicted this turn of events? 'Not personally,' Luke replied, stiffly and very much on his guard, which was true enough, though he had control of it.

'Please do not look so concerned, Mr Gregory and pray forgive my inquisitive nature but one in my position is poorly placed to satisfy her curiosity. I was well aware that nothing would come to me on my great uncle's death. My husband would have had it all, to the very last penny, as he squandered everything else that I valued. My inheritance, my home and my health. Yes, he was the cause of my present state. He forced me to ride a horse that he knew I could not manage and when the inevitable happened, he laughed, Mr Gregory, laughed at me lying in the mud with a broken back and continued to mock me and deride me ever afterwards.'

Luke shifted again in his chair. Listening to a bitter woman give vent to her feelings was not his idea of a pleasant afternoon. 'I understand,' he said. 'That was indeed, unfortunate.'

'At least you have the good taste not to say how sorry you are for why on earth should you be?' Bitter indeed, Luke decided. He would make his escape as quickly as possible.

'I was intrigued, you know, to learn of your arrival at the Manor. I knew the Travers only slightly, you will understand. You will, of course be related to the family but from what part are your people, Mr Gregory? I cannot place the name locally.'

'People, Lady Remnold?' Luke was weary of this conversation. 'To what people do you refer?'

'Your family, Mr Gregory. Your family connections.'

'I boast no family connections,' Luke stated flatly. 'As you are no doubt aware, I am not considered a gentleman. Certainly not by the village population. I am a common fellow engaged in commerce and have no social standing whatever. Now, was there some particular matter you wished to discuss with me?' he asked, abruptly.

Lady Remnold looked sharply at him, surprised by his tone. 'Forgive me,' she said. 'Yes. It is about my son, Francis. I had no idea that he intended calling upon you and, to be perfectly honest I was greatly surprised that you not only received him but entrusted him with the management of the estate. You realise that he is quite inexperienced in such matters and is not yet of age?'

'Yes.'

'Why have you done this, Mr Gregory?'

'Either I disposed of the estate or appointed a steward. It suited Francis to accept that position.'

'And if he should fail in this task?'

'He won't fail.'

'He has not succeeded in dislodging Norris.'

'He will. By midnight on Friday Norris will be gone.'

'You sound very confident, Mr Gregory.'

'I am. My own knowledge of estate management is minimal so I ask advice from those who know of such matters. Francis will do the same. I assure you, he will not be unsupported. If you are so concerned at his inexperience may I suggest that you take some part in affairs? I'm sure you could manage to travel in a carriage. There are new carts to be ordered and horses to be traded so perhaps you might help there. I must leave now for I also have much to do. Good afternoon,' and getting quickly to his feet, Luke left the room, made his way out of the building and bade George make all plain sail, his irritation clear to see.

★ ★ ★

On the Friday, by ones and twos, a dozen large and capable looking men assembled at the Manor. Only two had gone there directly from the station, the others taking more circuitous routes to lessen the attention that strangers in the area would attract.

They were, to a man, of a watchful, silent disposition and might easily have been mistaken for police officers in plain clothes, had it not been for their air of relaxed competence. These were some of Digger's handpicked and highly trained team of bodyguards, recruited especially for this profession. Gone were the days when men from the river undertook such duties along with their normal work and each man could box and wrestle and prided himself on his physical fitness.

Digger would supervise the evening's proceedings but the first move would be made by Francis Remnold whom Luke instructed to wait until after dark then call upon Norris and demand to know why he hadn't vacated his house as required. Depending entirely upon his reaction would be the response from Digger's team waiting nearby.

Luke had not intended involving at all but, either from a perverse desire to enjoy the last laugh or just to watch the fun, decided to go along and allowed Peter to accompany him and George in the trap.

All day, in between lessons, that young man had taken a keen interest in the assembling heavies, some of whom he knew from his visits to the wharf. Long before Luke's return from the City in his usual train, accompanied by Digger, he'd mastered several wrestling falls and arm-locks and levers from the amused experts present.

Seated on a dray the party left the Manor and made their way across the valley, following the rutted track that served the Home Farm and the rear of the Hall. Francis Remnold met them by the stables and greeted Luke nervously.

'Do you wish me to call upon Norris now?'

'First allow Mr O'Dowd to position his men. No dogs near are there?'

'Only his setters but they are round the back.'

'Very well, then. If he's violent, resist as much as you wish and help will quickly be with you. If he shuts the door in your face, knock again until it is opened then walk away and leave matters to the others. All set, Digger? Right, away we go,' and Luke settled himself against a wall opposite, from where he had a clear view of the door.

'What will they do, Guv?' Peter whispered.

'Just wait and watch,' Luke replied, quietly. 'They all know their business.'

The front door of the Home Farm opened abruptly in answer to Francis's heavy knock, to reveal Norris, in his shirtsleeves, holding a shotgun.

'And what do you want?' he demanded, aggressively.

'I wish to know why you have not vacated this property as instructed.' Francis's voice was firm and sounded confident but he was forced to step backwards as Norris moved forward, brandishing his gun.

'Because I don't choose to, that's why and as for taking instructions from the family runt, I'll not stand for it,' and he hawked and spat, offensively. 'Just get yourself back to your mother, you milksop you, and remember this. I was appointed bailiff by the master and it's for him to say whether I stay or whether I go.'

'But I am master now,' Francis replied, a little less confidently, but Norris deigned not to reply and turning his back on him went inside and shut the door. With a quick glance in Luke's direction, as if for reassurance, Francis again banged on the door with the heavy iron knocker as the first of Digger's men moved towards the doorway, pressing themselves closely against the wall.

A pause then the door was flung violently open and Norris, the shotgun in one hand, strode furiously out onto the porch and seized Francis by the throat with the other. Next moment, his legs were jerked briskly from under him and he found himself flat on his face with his arms twisted painfully behind his back.

Ten men surged quickly inside and with the minimum of fuss began carrying furniture outside. There was a scream and raised voices as Norris's family were disturbed by Digger's men. Norris, recovering his breath after his sudden fall, demanded to know what was happening. Digger strolled casually up to the prostrate man. 'You were required to vacate by this Friday. We are the removal men come to assist you.'

There was a gasp, followed by a flood of unflattering expletives.

'There's a dung heap nearby,' Digger directed the heavies who held Norris's arms. 'Throw him on it and keep him there 'til we've finished. Such language, indeed!'

'Carts, Guv?' one of Digger's men asked.

'Oh, yes. Francis? A couple of carts if you please. They should suffice with our dray, I think.'

In a remarkably short time the house was cleared of every article and stick of furniture the Norris family owned and, together with the protesting and frightened members, was loaded onto the wagons.

'Fetch him up,' Digger ordered and Norris, subdued now and liberally daubed with dung and wet straw, was led up to the lantern-lit wagons.

'You were offensive to Mr Remnold just now,' Digger reminded him. 'I think you owe him an apology, do you not?'

'Be damned if I do,' Norris snarled.

'Oh dear. Cesspit lads. We'll wait for you. We've plenty of time.'

'No, not that. All right,' Norris capitulated. Dung heaps were bad enough but to be dunked in a cesspit would be the end and when he had humbly begged Francis Remnold's pardon for his insults, Luke strolled forward into the circle of light.

'Evening, Norris,' he greeted. 'What a foolish man you are. I trust you'll be wiser for the future and never show your face round here again. If you do you'll be most uncomfortably handled. A covered wagon awaits you and your goods in the railway siding and the ten o'clock train will take you as far as Guildford. From there you'll make your own arrangements. The furniture removers here will assist you and escort you. Good night,' and Luke stepped back into the shadows, almost falling over Peter, who'd craned forward to see all that was going on.

And so, true to Luke's prediction, Norris the bailiff moved out that same Friday and Digger and his removal men returned by the late train to London.

★ ★ ★

Once again the annual speech day had arrived and Luke, familiar now with the ritual of the occasion was more confident and assured since becoming a school governor. Possibly his generosity had something to do with it but it flattered his vanity to be treated respectfully by staff and scholars alike and it certainly hadn't hurt Richard's position at any point. A rising star now, he would be a monitor next term and might even be in line for the House captaincy when it fell vacant whilst Fred, settling down surprisingly quickly in this new environment, was beginning to make his mark as a cricketer.

'Oh Guv, Robert's pater is coming,' Richard told him, then, catching Luke's glance, grinned and blushed. 'His father, I mean,' he corrected himself. 'He very much wishes to meet you.'

'Well, doubtless we'll bump into each other during the day,' and excusing himself from the crowded marquee where coffee was being served he wandered in search of more peaceful surroundings in the coolness of the main school buildings. Why was it necessary he wondered, for the umpteenth time, to be so overdressed in such warm weather and he ran his finger round the inside of his collar to ease his discomfort.

At least, it was cooler inside and he wouldn't mind a quick dip in the swimming pool, but that would have to wait. So, what was it they were wanting to do in here, he mused as he entered the main hall. Build a gallery at the back for additional seating so that the stage could remain permanently erected at the other end? Yes, it could work, he supposed. Look a bit like a non-conformist chapel if they weren't careful, but it would make more space, which was the whole idea.

'Hello. Who are you?' he asked as he caught sight of a figure sitting alone in the corner. The boy stood up. Skinny little nipper. Must be first year. 'Not joining in the fun outside?'

The boy looked up for the first time. 'No, sir,' and as quickly, looked down again.

Red face, eyes swollen with much weeping by the looks of it, Luke noticed. 'Mm. You don't look too happy, young man. Something wrong? Care to tell me about it?' The boy looked up again and his shoulders shook with a huge, silent sob.' Come on. Sit yourself down and let's have it,' Luke encouraged, lowering himself onto the fixed, pew-like seat against the wall. 'Tell me your name for a start and how old you are.'

'Paul Eugene, sir, and I'm thirteen, sir,' followed by the huge, silent sob.

'Have you been here long? I mean, are you missing home? Oh, my name is Gregory, by the way.'

A quick, sideways glance. 'Two terms, sir.'

'Oh, as long as that. Can't be home sickness then, surely. You must have made a few friends by now. So what brings you to sit here alone instead of joining in outside?'

'I, I can't sir. I have to stay here, sir. I'm to be expelled, sir.'

'Expelled? Good gracious me. What have you managed to do in two terms to earn that distinction.'

'I cheated, sir,' and again that huge convulsive sob.

'Cheated, eh? What, at cards? Surely not. Tell me more,' and, bit by bit, Luke extracted the sorry tale of his widowed mother who, left with few resources, was sacrificing everything to give her son a good education. Desperately anxious to do well and please her he'd cheated in the end of term exams by writing notes on his shirt cuff and hiding a crib list up his sleeve, but had been caught by a vigilant master. He was now to be made an example of for the benefit of the whole school and was to be 'dealt with' later, the speech day delaying execution of sentence.

'At least, your motive was a worthy one,' Luke commented. 'Wrong tactics clearly, judging by the fuss. Your father was French, you say. Mm. Your mother know about it yet?'

'I don't think so, sir,'

'Well, expulsion seems a trifle harsh. Obviously not used to cheating or you'd be better practiced and wouldn't have been caught. Take my tip and give it up. The only successful cheats are those who make a study of it and are unworried at the possible consequences. So what's to be done, I wonder. Whose house are you in?'

'Nelson's, sir.'

Nelson's, eh? Well that's a step in the right direction. You remain here, as instructed, and I'll send someone to talk to you. See if we can't change things a bit and getting to his feet Luke strode from the hall, replacing his top hat as he left the building.

'Ah, Richard, a moment if you please.'

'Guv?' replied that young man, quickly detecting that something was up.

'That boy in the hall, Eugene, I believe. What do you know of him?'

'Oh, the Frog. Not much, Guv. Why?' Richard sounded disinterested.

'In your house, I understand and up to his neck in trouble.'

'Well yes, Guv. He was caught cheating. Deserves everything he's going to get.'

'And what is that?'

'A public thrashing after prayers and thrown out in the morning. The head is making an example of him. People like that lower the tone of the school.'

'I see. And is that just?'

'Just, Guv? I don't understand.'

'It seems very harsh treatment to me,' Luke persisted. 'Have you thought about it or are you blindly accepting of it? You'll be a monitor soon, won't you? Should you not be taking an interest in such matters?'

Richard's tendency to blush had largely disappeared but now, suddenly and unexpectedly under pressure from Luke, his colour rose. 'I hadn't considered it, Guv,' he said. 'I, well, he's only a first year and, well, I don't see much of them,' he tried, lamely.

'What is the purpose of attending a school such as this? Ever considered it? Why, when many boys of your age have been earning their living for years, are you here? What is the idea behind it all? Answer that and you'll see what I'm getting at.'

Richard stood, perplexed. He knew well enough Luke's philosophy of life, understood his basic beliefs and had done his best to accept and support them all, often in the face of difficulty in this environment, isolated from the working world. Ever honest and straight forward though, he was prepared to admit he didn't know, rather than fudge a reply.

'Guv, I just haven't given it much thought.'

Luke, seeing his obvious discomfort, relaxed. 'I don't suppose I would have in your place. Let me put it this way. I've heard the object of schools like this is to produce leaders of men at all levels of administration and commerce. Army and navy officers and the like, government officers in the colonies and so on. No matter where you end up, you're likely to have men subordinate to you and for whom you're responsible. Without those men you couldn't do your work and you certainly couldn't run a colony on your own. You depend on them more than they depend on you. Even the smallest and least significant of your followers has his part to play, maybe not this year but the next or the one after that. Think back to when you and I first met and look at your position now. See what I mean?'

Richard saw, and this time he flushed bright red.

'You know what you have to do?' Luke continued quickly, to spare him embarrassment. 'Leadership is not just condemning faults in others it's understanding them. Ask about the reason, look for the extenuating circumstances and put in a word for the little shrimp. I'll look out for you later,' and with a smile of encouragement he started to turn away.

'Oh, Guv, before I go, could I introduce you to Robert's father? He's just over there, look.'

'Of course,' and Luke allowed Richard to lead him over to where Robert and his father awaited them.

The boys watched with interest as their respective 'governors' doffed hats, shook hands and exchanged conventional pleasantries. 'Might I impose upon a few moments of your time, Mr Gregory?' Major Weston asked.

'By all means, sir. You have something you wish to do?' Luke suggested to Richard, who looked at Robert.

'Yes, Guv. Would you give me a hand, Rob?'

Luke and Major Weston strolled off together, both conscious of the formality and reserve between them and each attempting to weigh up the other.' I have much to thank you for, sir,' the major began. 'My boy has enjoyed your generous hospitality over the holidays and of course, there was that other business. I am most deeply grateful for your rescuing me from a most serious predicament. I simply cannot understand how you were able to influence matters on my behalf or even why you should take such trouble.'

'You were the victim of a well planned fraud by a group of known blackguards who make their living by such means. I desired that matters be corrected and they were pleased to oblige. As to why? Your son Robert is my boy's closest friend, and for him to lose such a valuable friendship would have been unthinkable. He made a difficult start here and Robert was the only one to stand by him. Such loyalty is to be admired.'

'You are generous in your comments, sir, and I shall be for ever in your debt. Should there ever be occasion when I might return, in some measure, your services to me I beg that you will allow me the opportunity of so doing.'

'I shall not hesitate and I thank you.'

Both men stopped their leisurely pacing then, as by mutual consent, and faced each other, struck, perhaps, by the stiffness of their conversation and Luke allowed himself one of his rare smiles.

'We must sound like a pair of solemn old Presbyterian ministers,' he said. 'It was my pleasure to be of service. Are you now permanently in this country?'

'Yes. I felt I had soldiered long enough and could look for no further advancement and with Robert at school here and fast growing up I have decided to look around for somewhere to settle. Not sure what I shall do with myself, of course. Have to get used to having time on my hands and all that.'

'Mm. Your boy happy at this school?'

'Appears to be. No complaints to speak of. Just the usual schoolboy moans and groans. Milk puddings and Latin. That sort of thing.'

'Much the same with Richard. He's hoping Robert can spend some time with him this holiday. Is that agreeable to you?'

'That is most kind of you. To tell the truth I have little to offer at present until I'm properly settled. Are you sure it will not inconvenience you?'

'Not at all. We have room and to spare. Would you not care to join us? You'd be most welcome.'

'That is indeed kind. I should enjoy that greatly,' so a friendship was made, for each had taken to the other and they spent most of the afternoon in conversation together, taking occasional interest in the cricket and continuing their wide-ranging exchange of views until, with both sides out, the cricketers left the field and the visitors began taking their leave and drifting away. Richard and Robert had joined them in the marquee for tea, both intrigued to see them still together.

'I've spoken to my Housemaster about that business, Guv. I asked him if it might be reconsidered and he's promised to speak to the Head. I told him you were concerned about it.'

'You did? Well, it's true enough. You'll let me know the outcome? Well done.'

★ ★ ★

Francis Remnold was waiting for Luke to finish his breakfast, later than usual that Saturday morning for he was sleeping longer and more deeply on his weekend visits and saw no reason to leave his bed before he felt ready. Very relaxing, this place, he decided and good for the soul.

'Ah, Francis. Sorry to keep you waiting. How are things?'

'I think I'm managing, thank you, Mr Gregory,' he said, a little uncertainly.

'Have you spoken with the tenants, yet?'

'Well, yes, I went to see them and offered to review their rentals, as you suggested. They were very suspicious and Meredith asked if my father knew I'd called,' he said, colouring up.

'Treated you as if you were five years old, hey? Understandable but it won't do. Anyway, you made the offer so say no more about it and wait for them to broach the subject but take full rental next quarter day. You'll see a change by and by, mark my words. Now, Home Farm. Any thoughts on that?'

'Well, to be honest, sir, I don't think I have enough experience to run it properly. You see, sir, I've never really done anything on the estate. I only left school a few months ago and as I'm unable to go up to university I hadn't really any plans,' he tailed off, uncertainly.

'I understand. Not to worry. I'm probably expecting too much of you too soon. Wouldn't know where to start myself, at that. Barely know a pig's trotter from a horseshoe so you must give yourself time but many routines will be followed as they always have. Last year's corn stubble will be ploughed, will it not? A different crop will follow? Give thought to it all. Talk to George and you'll make out. You've eleven men and three boys, have you not? Wages ten shillings a week and four for the boys? That's less than usual, I believe. What staff have you at the Hall?'

'Well sir, there's mother's maid, who's been with her since she was a girl. I don't think she has been paid a wage for years but she won't leave. There's old Pru in the kitchen and a girl to help her and two maids who clean and do the laundry I think and a boy who does the boots and sweeps up.'

'There were two keepers a short while back. Anyone else you know of?'

'Well, no sir, I don't and I'm not really sure what the men do on the Home Farm. I was always told to keep away, you see, sir.'

'You'll have to ask 'em. Make a note of what they say they do and let 'em know there'll be changes in the offing. Organise the Hall as you see fit. You're master there now and you'll take no nonsense from anyone but the less the world knows the better. Let folks think what they will and guess the rest, eh? One more thing. I'm trustee of your great great uncle's estate with absolute discretion so propose making you a beneficiary of it. It'll give you a personal income of two hundred a year separate from anything the estate might produce.'

'Mr Gregory, I, I don't know what to say. This is just too incredible for words. You must be the most honest person alive, to offer this and after all the unpleasantness, too.'

'Nonsense. It's merely natural justice. I seek to deal fairly with everyone and hope they'll return the compliment.'

'But shouldn't mother have the money? I mean, I only met Great Uncle Josiah twice, when I was quite small.'

'You are the man of the house so yours is the responsibility. Let me have a note of your banker and your preference as to a monthly or quarterly arrangement. Incidentally, with regard to Lady Remnold, I know of a particular surgeon who would willingly visit for a consultation. If you'll mention it and let me know? Now, let me show you the improvements we've made here. You may wish to think about something similar at the Hall. I can't speak highly enough of our water closets. I shudder to think how we managed before.'

★ ★ ★

To employ a woman on 'man's work' in the garden was flying in the face of convention. To pay her the same rate as a man would earn for that same work was a heresy unheard of and Luke's already tarnished name picked up a few more blemishes but he could afford to do as he wished, how he wished and ignore his critics. He had nothing but praise for Mrs Donkin and her unceasing efforts and had no regrets whatever at taking her on. Her family, despite all predictions, caused no problems, were well behaved, polite and helpful though he was not to know they'd been threatened within an inch of their lives if they so much as put a foot out of place.

All he needed to know was that vegetables were being grown for the kitchen to a high standard and that all was peaceful and with the kitchen garden wall nearly completed the higher temperature created by its shelter was immediately noticeable. Some of the stone for the wall was quarried from the nearby hill by the masons, mainly as decoration, Luke thought as it was fairly soft limestone but it blended well with the red brickwork.

It was when the brambles and saplings were cleared away from the quarry site that they found the cave. At least, it looked like a cave but it had the remains of a heavy door at the entrance, one that had once fitted tightly. Intrigued, Luke had it tidied up to allow entry and, with lamps, he and the boys went in for a look around. It was man made, judging by the tool marks on the sides, was high enough to stand upright and went straight into the hillside for about twenty feet before widening out into a circular room twelve feet across. A narrow channel, little more than a groove, was cut into the floor, sloping gently to the outside.

'I wonder what the purpose of this place was?' Luke asked of no one in particular. 'Ah. I have it. It's an ice house. In winter you pack it solid with ice and it melts so slowly there's still some left in summer for when you need it to cool your drinks or whatever. You know that hollow up on the hill that fills up in wet weather? I wouldn't be surprised if that wasn't dug to collect ice from. Much easier to slide it down hill than carry it up from the river. Interesting. I think we'll try it out this next winter. We'll need a new door, though. Volunteers to sweep the place out?'

'Ugh, look, Guv. There's bats all over the ceiling. Can we get rid of them?'

'They're harmless. Leave 'em alone.'

'They gets in yer 'air, Guv,' Ticker said.

'Nonsense. That's an old wife's tale.'

★ ★ ★

Francis Remnold held out the letter to Luke. 'I opened it as you instructed but I think it is really for you, sir,' he said. It was addressed to Sir Brandon and bore a Guildford postmark and an embossed crest. 'The Bishop's Palace, eh? Signed by the Chaplain to his Grace. Ah, so the Rector is taking another living and the Bishop wishes to commend a successor. Can't say I shall miss that fellow. What has this to do with us, then?'

'I believe the Rectory stands on Manorial land, sir, and some of the glebe is jointly held with the lord of the manor so the Bishop needs your approval before appointing anyone to the living. It is all very complicated but mother understands it better than I.'

'So we have some say in the matter. If we don't like the look of the Reverend Doctor Greenway we can say no thank you? We'll be stuck with him for a good many years so we need someone who'll fit in. Be a better if they sent us a doctor of medicine instead of one of divinity. Tell you what, write to the Bishop on my behalf and delay the appointment. I'll enquire about him from someone I know and talking of doctors, Doctor Lambourne is visiting next weekend and will call on Lady Remnold on Saturday afternoon, if that's convenient. He's an eminent man and may prove helpful.'

★ ★ ★

Miss Hetherington was waiting in ambush for Luke, wishing to discuss matters of importance. 'Oh, er yes, of course. In the study?'

'There are two things really, Mr Gregory. I feel that I have taught Peter as much as I am able. He has made a lot of progress now that he can read without difficulty and I am wondering what more I can do.'

'Ready for school, is he? How does he feel about that?'

'He is not at all keen, Mr Gregory. I think he has too many unhappy memories of his last school.'

'Would a tutor be the answer, do you think?'

'Well, this brings me to the second problem. Neither Peter nor Lucy meet other children at all. Their father would never allow them to associate with the village children and Peter was away at school for much of the time and there is no one of Lucy's age near enough to visit. Now, of course, Peter is home all the time and has the same problem.'

'I think Peter should try another school. He'll miss out if he doesn't. He could travel daily to Guildford. Doesn't have to board, if that's the problem. Suggest it to him and see what he thinks.'

'What a good idea. Yes, I certainly will.'

'Which leaves Miss Lucy and her social life, eh? There surely must be families round about. Use the pony and trap and go search 'em out. I reckon you could do with getting out and meeting a few new faces yourself, couldn't you?'

'I had wondered about that possibility, Mr Gregory but unfortunately I do not drive.'

'Ticker can drive you. Give him something to do.'

'Very well. I will make enquiries and see if we may find someone suitable to visit.'

★ ★ ★

'Ah, Stephen. Good to see you again and you, Mrs Lambourne. Come along in. How's hospital life? Keeping you busy, are they?'

'Oh, we are much better organised these days. Surgeons are no longer overworked if they specialise,' Stephen replied. 'I only attend during the day time, unless there is something really urgent, so I manage to enjoy a home life,' and he gave his wife a hug.

'Good, good. Let me show you to your room. We shall just have time for a walk round before lunch, if you'd care to see what we have then I shall ask your assistance.'

Though he was always pleased to see Stephen Lambourne, whom he'd known since he was a medical student at Guy's Hospital, Luke had his purpose in issuing the invitation to visit the Manor.

'Lady Remnold has been bedridden since a riding mishap years ago and I believe an up to date opinion would be helpful,' he told Stephen. 'Ticker will drive you over to the Hall. I don't care to visit socially so I'll stay here and entertain your charming wife.'

Some time later Stephen returned and straight away approached Luke. 'It's not ethical to discuss a patient Guv, but I believe you knew what I'd find.'

'That the lady can walk? That she's not bedridden?'

'How did you know?'

'Tell you the history of her accident, did she? I can vouch for her husband being an unpleasant character. It was because of him I once called at the Hall after dark. I saw the silhouette of a woman at an upstairs window wearing an angular bed cap and the maids wear round, close-fitting ones. I later visited Lady Remnold and noticed that she wore an angular bed cap. I also noticed movement beneath the bed covers so guessed she used her fall as a means of avoiding her husband. He's left but she's in a corner and needs an eminent surgeon to help her walk again.'

'Guv, you put your finger right on it, every time. She realised you saw through her, you know. She's both grateful to you and in awe of you.'

'In awe?' Luke was startled at the suggestion. 'Hardly. I have no people, don't you know. No social connections of which to boast. Not in her class.'

'Well, she thinks you are some kind of magician who transforms hopeless situations by the wave of a magic wand.'

'Ridiculous, but how have you left things?'

'I have recommended a course of treatment and exercise that should enable first tentative steps to be taken within a day or so,' Stephen said, looking up at the ceiling. 'Her maid was the only person in the know. Very loyal to her mistress and won't breathe a word. Funny old world, is it not?'

★ ★ ★

It was a warm October Saturday afternoon with the leaves turning colour and everywhere bright berries in the hedgerows as Luke settled under a large beech tree at the edge of the vale and admired the view. He'd begun walking the land that went with the Hall and was surprised how extensive it was, with many acres of mature woodland.

He'd been sitting for about ten minutes, enjoying the peaceful surroundings, when a squirrel scampered by, stopped to look at him, groomed its face with its front paws then began scrabbling around in the leaves and twigs close to his foot.

Fascinated, Luke kept perfectly still until the squirrel suddenly sat bolt upright, twitched its tail and rushed up a tree. What disturbed him, Luke wondered, then heard a voice. Who, now, was coming to disturb his peace? It was a young voice, singing? No. Shouting? Not really but talking out loud. Odd, he thought and settled back against the trunk of the tree.

The voice came closer. It sounded like rhymes, he thought. Poetry? Could be but who on earth would be walking around here reciting poetry? He hadn't long to wait for into view came a boy, dressed in the usual farm worker's corduroys who'd been walking along the ridge overlooking the vale and, not noticing Luke, stopped almost in front of him. He was, Luke decided, making up poetry, trying his lines aloud to see how they sounded and gesticulating with his hands in accompaniment.

'The leaves so full and green and pure,

Will one day die and disappear,

Like all things that we see around us, no, er,

Though sun may pale and sink in winter,

The brightest stars will shine and, and,'

'Scinter,' Luke offered, from where he sat listening.

The boy leapt as if stung and whirled around, his eyes wide and mouth open, a look of horror on his face. He stared at Luke and gulped.

'I seem to have startled you,'

The boy gulped again and continued to stare in horror at Luke, whether from shock or embarrassment at being surprised declaiming his poetry, Luke didn't know.

'So you have a taste for poetry,' Luke said. 'Did you learn much at school?' Still no response, beyond the horrified stare. 'You don't need to be so concerned,' Luke tried again. 'Do you walk this way often? It's my first visit to this part of the wood. Must say, it's a lovely view.'

'I, I'm sorry, sir. I didn't know you was 'ere. I'm not poaching, sir, honest. I, I won't come again, sir, I'm sorry.'

'Nothing to be sorry about,' Luke said. 'You're doing no harm and this is a beautiful wood. Come and sit here. Tell me about your poetry.'

Slowly, hesitantly, as if approaching a monster that might at any moment devour him, the boy moved closer and sat under the tree.

'I've seen you before somewhere, haven't I? Church choir, would it be?'

'Yes, sir.'

'Thought so. What's your name?'

'John Hurle, sir.'

'Well, John Hurle, I'm glad there's someone intelligent in the village. Luke Gregory', and Luke held out his hand. 'I'm pleased to meet you. Most folks seem to spend their time killing things or throwing mud at people.'

Nervously, John shook hands with Luke. He was still recovering from his surprise and sat wondering what awaited him.

'How old are you?'

'Twelve, sir.'

'So you've left school. Where do you work?'

'At the Hall, sir. On the Home Farm, sir.'

'Ah. Tell me about your poetry. It sounded good. Do you write it down?'

'Oh no, sir.' John was immediately agitated. 'Father'd skin me. You'll not tell 'im will you, sir,' he pleaded.

'No, of course I won't. I have no dealings with the village. So why doesn't your father let you write poetry?'

'He says it's a waste of time, sir. He says it'll give me ideas above me station, sir. He said it's for girls and old women, sir.' John answered, looking down.

'I see,' Luke said and thought back to another occasion, years before, where a boy on a barge wanted to draw and paint but was beaten if he did so. 'What's your mother think about it?'

'She'd let me, sir, but she daresn't go against father, sir. He'd hit 'er too.' There was a trace of anger in his voice then, and he looked down again.

'You're not the first to be in this position. I've met it before and you're not the first poet to work on the land. Did you know that?'

'No, sir.' He was immediately interested.

'His name was John, as well. John Clare. Died about twenty years ago. I've a book of his poems, all about the seasons, and the countryside he saw about him as he followed the plough. The one I like best is called Autumn. Goes like this,

'I love the fitful gust that shakes

The casement all the day

And from the mossy elm tree takes

The faded leaves away.'

Very much like the poem you were working on just now. How did it go?

The leaves, so full and green and pure

Will one day die and disappear.

That, young man, is good stuff. Father should be proud of you. You have talent and talent should be encouraged. I'll lend you that book. You'll enjoy it.'

John's face was a picture of conflicting emotions. Here was praise and recognition, encouragement too, and temptation. Dare he read a book of poems at home? Would father rage if he knew who'd lent it to him? He would and he'd get a leathering and no supper. He'd best not.'

'I daresn't, sir. Father wouldn't let me.'

'Mm,' then, 'Mm,' again, as Luke pondered the problem. 'There was another country poet, named Burns. Scotsman. Heard of him, have you? Quite famous and he started work on his father's farm when he was nine.'

He liked this boy and sympathised with him. He also had mischief in mind. 'Do you have an older brother? Big lad, mark on the side of his face?'

'Yes, sir. That's Ronald, sir,' then, after a pause, 'He threw things at you, sir, but only because he were told to, sir.'

'I thought I saw the likeness and I never forget a face. He'd best not cross me again. He won't get off lightly if there's a next time.'

'He won't do it again, sir, honest. He's scared of what might 'appen to 'im.'

'Very wise. Tell me, what work do you do at the farm?'

'Sometimes I lead the horses, sir but mostly I keeps the yard tidy, sir, and clean the boots. Mr Norris called me the mucker out, sir.'

'Do you enjoy it? I mean, would you choose to do something else if it were possible?' The mischief was beginning to take shape now.

'I don't know, sir,' John answered, cautiously. 'I've never thought, sir. There's only the farm, sir, and father said to work there, sir, the same as he does, sir.'

'I see. Well, I think I've sat here long enough. I'm ready for my tea. I've enjoyed talking with you and you keep on with your poems, understand? Good day to you,' and Luke started back, his thoughts centred on creating a stir, all in a good cause, of course.

★ ★ ★

Chapter 8

'Ah, Francis. Good day to you,' It was Saturday morning and Francis Remnold was making his weekly visit to report to Luke on all matters relating to the Hall, the estate and the village, for which he now had responsibility. He was completely under Luke's spell and was ready to do exactly as instructed, not so much because he had no choice but because he was awed by him.

Luke knew this and congratulated himself on appointing a willing vassal to serve his interests. Others had forced him to take on more than he'd intended so, true to form, he'd seek to call the tune whenever it suited him.

'Everything in order? Good. Now, what do those two game keepers do these days?'

'They tell me they are keeping the vermin down, sir, and watching out for poachers.'

'I've no interest in raising birds for the pleasure of shooting them so I suggest they become woodsmen if they wish to remain in our employ. There's a lot of fine timber in the wood and I think it would show a return for organised management. Some of the bigger trees are crowded and could be felled and young trees planted in their place. What do you think?'

'Yes, sir. I think it would be a good idea. Father didn't cut any trees down because he wanted shelter for the pheasants.'

'I thought that might be it so organise your men to map every fully grown tree and name its type and mark all the empty spaces round about where new trees may be planted. It's a long term harvest but a harvest just the same. You attend the corn exchanges on market days, do you not? No? You should. Talk to dealers and farmers and note everything that affects prices. Now, you'd probably find an assistant useful. Someone to jot down figures and take notes and messages, that sort of thing. A likely lad is the one who sweeps up in the yard. Young Hurle. What do you think?'

'Well, yes sir, if you say so. He's a bit dreamy and is always being shouted at.'

'I'm not surprised. He's a budding poet. Met him in the wood last week. Needs a chance to better himself. Someone to take him under their wing and encourage him. Think you could do that? There'll be a fuss but you can handle that. Just tell his father straight that you want him to perform other duties and take no nonsense about it. There's a book of poems here he'd like to read. Not allowed such things at home but you could find him a quiet corner where he can read in peace.'

'Well, of course, sir.' Francis was smiling widely, now. 'It sounds a bit like my father not allowing me to read books he thought unmanly. Perhaps I may have a look too.'

★ ★ ★

Luke now turned his thoughts to the proposed appointment of the new Rector.

Francis Remnold had been along to meet the man and was far from sure that Luke would be happy with him so

Luke had written to Suffragen Bishop Quinney who, as ever, was happy to oblige him.

Luke wanted someone who'd be an asset to the place. Someone who'd take as much notice of ordinary people as of the local gentry. He wasn't keen on the clergy as a breed and the thought of some useless incumbent riding to hounds three days a week and lecturing his congregation on Sundays as to how they should keep their place, nauseated him. This was a plum living with a stipend of four hundred pounds a year plus certain grazing rights so the Bishop would want to favour some pet of his and once installed they'd have to put up with him.

Turning all this over in his mind, he wandered outside and looked out over the valley. It really was a treat to have such an open view after the closely packed buildings of London. He particularly liked it when the moon was full and lit the landscape with such a different light. Funny, that. He hardly ever saw the moon in London.

Now who would this be coming up the drive in a trap? Surely it wouldn't be Francis calling again. Good Lord! Her Ladyship.

'Good afternoon, Lady Remnold. This is a surprise. I'm delighted to see you recovered.'

'Thank you Mr Gregory. It is kind of you to say so but not such a surprise, perhaps. I really am grateful to you for making this possible. I cannot express the enjoyment of being out and about once more.'

'Can I help you down? You will take tea?'

'Why thank you. I shall enjoy that.'

Showing Lady Remnold into the study, Luke caught sight of Lucy on the stair having a peep to see who the visitor might be. 'Oh, Lucy, would you ask Emma to bring tea to the study, please and you might care to join us if you're not busy,' knowing that she wasn't, but was just curious. Delighted to be included, Lucy made her best curtsey to Lady Remnold then sat demurely on a hard chair, with feet together and hands in lap, as convention required.

She had never met Lady Remnold and was intrigued to be in her company but Luke, ill at ease with her was glad to have Lucy present as a foil. If there was to be verbal jousting, as he feared there might be, Lucy's presence would ensure that it remained amicable. She would also serve the tea and pass the scones and cakes around, which'd be a relief to Luke.

'I may speak freely, Mr Gregory?'

'Of course, Lady Remnold. I would not wish it otherwise.'

'Francis has told me of your concerns over the new Rector and I felt that I should offer my view. If the Bishop's choice is opposed it could lead to a great deal of ill feeling, you know. The reasons for objecting would be closely examined and might easily lead to a civil action for defamation, were they not based upon hard and proven facts.'

'Ah. A good point. I hadn't thought of that.'

'I do believe careful consideration is given before such appointments are made and I hear there is consternation at the palace over your reluctance to accept the Bishop's nomination.'

'Ruffled ecclesiastical feathers, have I? No harm in that if it keeps them on their toes. So, we're expected to meekly accept whoever is thrust upon us, are we? Can't say I like that overmuch.'

'It is the custom, I suppose.'

'Yes, well, thank you for that. I'll bear it in mind. Do have another scone.'

'There is another matter that I feel I should mention. Francis is of course deeply involved in following your instructions and is coping far better than I ever expected. I do wonder though, at the wisdom of appointing a village boy as his assistant. I'm afraid it doesn't do to raise the ploughboy above his station.'

'Oh? Why not?'

Lady Remnold looked surprised that Luke should question such an obvious truth. 'It causes discontent, Mr Gregory. Village life is finely balanced, you know and as long as everyone respects their position they remain content.'

'Content' with mundane work, low wages and lack of fulfilment? That is the condition idle landowners depend upon, is it not? Those who do no work but rely upon the labours of others? I have no respect for such, Lady Remnold. I don't recall who it was asked, 'When Adam delved and Eve span, who was then the gentleman?' but I've never heard a convincing answer.'

'You misunderstand me, Mr Gregory. I know how country people think and they resent those who move away from the customary patterns of life.'

'As they resent an outsider, especially if he's not gentry, eh? Oh I know how they think, if you can call it thinking. More like stumbling from one prejudice to another. That boy has intelligence and ability and it would be an injustice not to help him realise his potential. I call that social responsibility and if it causes a stir in the village, I'm glad of it.'

'But what will you achieve by it, Mr Gregory? What good will it do the boy in the long run?'

'Only time will tell, Lady Remnold. Who knows what he may one day achieve? Who knows what any one of us may achieve and that goes for Francis. He too has intelligence and ability. Would you deny him the chance to develop his talents to the full?'

'You are persuasive, Mr Gregory but I have the gravest doubts over the wisdom of what you are doing.'

'We will agree to differ then, Lady Remnold. More tea?'

★ ★ ★

The letter from Bishop Quinney arrived at Gresham House and Luke opened it with interest. His concern over the appointment of the clergyman at Chidlingbrook centred around his wish to be left in peace at the Manor. Rectors could be influential people and having removed one nuisance, he was keen to avoid another one moving in.

The Bishop assured Luke that he'd made the most careful and diligent enquiries concerning the Reverend Doctor Greenway. All reports pointed to him being of a thoughtful and caring nature. He was of the evangelical school, was unmarried and did not ride to hounds. His previous ministries had been exacting ones in non-genteel parishes of Portsmouth and Birmingham, in consequence of which, his health had suffered. He had no private income but was a fine organist and an authority on church music.

Mm, Luke thought. Perhaps not so bad after all and no grounds on which to base an objection. Oh well. Let them get on with it. There were more interesting things to consider, like the design of the heated glasshouses he planned for the Manor. Iron frames seemed a good idea. Much stronger than wood in the long run and more ornamental. More expensive too, and he pursed his lips whilst considering the cost differences.

Now, if the boiler house that provided hot water and heating at his end was enlarged, would one big boiler take care of the lot or would it be better to have two smaller ones?

He'd need someone reliable to tend them and George had enough to occupy him. He'd have to think all this through.

★ ★ ★

'Guv, there's a boy at the door asking for you.'

'I'll come through. Thanks, Peter,' Who would this be, Luke wondered. 'Ah, John,' and Luke gave a rare smile of greeting. So here was the cause of Lady Remnold's concern, much more smartly dressed now for his new role.

'Mr Remnold said to bring you this note, sir, and I've brought your book back sir, and thank you very much for lending it to me, sir.'

'Find it interesting, did you? Good,' and Luke scanned the note from Francis, who was unwell and asking would Luke mind if he did not call today? There were no problems at present and he would report fully as soon as he felt better. 'Can you ride a horse?' he asked John.

'No sir. Not properly, sir.'

'Care to learn?'

'Oh, yes please, sir.'

'Right. Now, first of all you need to know who everyone is. This is Mr Cherry who is in charge here when I'm not around. This is Mrs Cherry, the best cook in the country and this is Peter Travers. Don't suppose you know each other do you? No, I thought not. And this,' to everyone in the kitchen, is John Hurle, Mr Remnold's right hand man at the Hall. I expect we'll see him around from time to time so feed him up Mrs C.'

'I'll make a start now, Guv. Tea or coffee, dear?' and Mrs Cherry placed biscuits and cake on the table as Luke and Peter sat down for an early snack.

John, completely overwhelmed, was persuaded to sit down too and help himself, which he nervously did and

Luke enjoyed a silent chuckle at what he was doing. Let it be known in the village. He'd show those clodhoppers a thing or two and he reached out for pen and paper to scribble a quick note in reply to Francis Remnold.

'Now then, John. Take this up to Mr Remnold and if he has nothing for you to do, get changed into something old and come back here and we'll get you in the saddle.'

When John had left, his pockets filled with biscuits, George caught Luke's eye and they both laughed. He knew exactly what Luke was up to and would go all the way with him, willingly.

'Peter, would you do the honours when he comes back? You know all the basics, just like George showed you. Unless you'd prefer Ticker to?'

'No, Guv, I'll do it.'

'Good, but teach him carefully. I want him to be able to ride safely.'

★ ★ ★

That might have been the final straw for those who felt John Hurle to be getting above his station for that next week he was set upon and rolled in the mud. He returned home thoroughly upset, plastered from head to foot and his new clothes spoiled.

Francis reported this to Luke on the Saturday and Luke frowned. What a silly business it was. If he'd brought in an outsider to assist at the Hall, there'd have been no particular problem. Because it was someone from the village, resentment, as Lady Remnold had predicted, was aroused.

'They like playing with mud round here, don't they. Interesting but this is the opening you've been waiting for.'

'I'm afraid I don't understand, sir.' Francis looked puzzled.

'How do people see you? What do they say about you, behind your back? What was it that farmer said to you when you offered to discuss his rental? You've always been the also ran, have you not? Looked down upon? Thought to be of no account? Those lads were really rolling you in the mud and want to see what you'll do about it.'

'I, I hadn't thought of it in that way.'

'So now's your chance to make them all sit up and take notice. You need to indulge in a little play-acting. Go raging up to the ones responsible; they work on the Home Farm, don't they? Take the carriage whip with you, wave it about and look really angry. Let them know they've offended you. Demand an explanation. Threaten to take the cost of the boy's clothes out of their wages. After all, you paid for them. Say that because of what they did, he was unable to take an important message for you and so you lost money. That sort of thing. Lay it on good and thick then go round the corner and have a good laugh.'

'I, I'll try but I really am not much good at that sort of thing.'

'Which is why it'll be play-acting but they'll not know that. You have to be seen to assert yourself, Francis. Carry this off and you'll have few problems for the future. Let it go and they'll find ways of putting on you, without a doubt.'

★ ★ ★

Luke, out for his Sunday afternoon walk, paused at a field gate to look at the cattle grazing nearby. They were young bullocks, he decided, of a heavy beef breed. Looked healthy enough. Prime stock, he thought. He'd ask George about them when he got back.

'It is you. I knew it was you, you damned scoundrel. I've been looking for you and now I've found you.' Luke turned at this sudden interruption and saw a dishevelled-looking man pointing a double barrelled gun at him. What now, he wondered and tried to appear unconcerned. 'You're going to pay for what you did to us. You've ruined the family. You've taken everything we had but you're not going to live to enjoy it. You're going to wish you'd never left the city.'

Did he know this fellow? Luke looked hard at him. 'Percival Remnold, I believe?' and not waiting for a reply continued, 'Waving a gun around is in no one's interest. I suggest you put it down.'

'Not until I've settled with you, Squire Gregory.'

'Oh? What's to settle?' Best to stay calm and keep him talking. He might get a chance to grab that gun. But was it loaded? It looked ancient and one hammer was missing.

'You tricked father out of the estate. It was all right until you came to the village, trying to play the country squire. You're no gentleman and never will be.' His voice was rising as he spoke and in his agitation he came closer.

'I tricked no one. Your father forced trouble on me and well you know it,' and Luke looked away then suddenly turned and knocked the gun aside with his stick. Surprising how fast you can move when you have to he thought and seizing Percy Remnold by the coat lapels, he slammed him hard against the gatepost. Slowly, he sagged and collapsed on the ground. Good grief, Luke thought. He's light as a feather. He picked up the gun, an old percussion muzzle loader. Hadn't been fired in years. Would probably burst if anyone tried it and he threw it behind the hedge.

Percy Remnold sat with his back to the gatepost, his hands over his face, sobbing. So what now, Luke wondered, relieved that the worst was over. It wasn't the first time he'd looked down a gun barrel but he couldn't rate it highly as a pastime.

'Get on your feet,' Luke ordered, 'and stop your noise,' and catching hold of his shoulder he hauled him upright. He really was a lightweight, no more than skin and bone. Gone downhill fast but he couldn't leave him wandering around the countryside in this state.

'Listen to me Percy Remnold and listen carefully. You have no just quarrel with me whatever. Your father's finances were in a hopeless state and the bank would have foreclosed if I hadn't. I have in no way ruined your family and any misfortune was brought about by your father and no one else. Your brother and mother are still at the Hall and your brother is working with me to put the estate back on its feet and you're not going to interfere with that. If you're willing to help yourself I'll give you a hand but there must be an end to this sort of nonsense. Is that understood?'

Percy Remnold nodded glumly, completely subdued now.

'Very well. This is what I offer in the first instance. I'll get you something to eat and your train fare but you'll stay out of sight. You'd not want the village to see you like this. You'll get the last train to Guildford from Chiddingfold station and then go on to London. Here's the address of a warehouse at Bermondsey. Ask for Bert O'Riley. Stay at the warehouse until I contact you. You have that clear? Right. Now we'll go to the Manor. You stay in the wood at the back whilst I raid the kitchen, then go over the hill and round the village to Chiddingfold. Don't go anywhere near the Hall. Understand? You can visit later when you're in better shape.'

That got an embarrassment away from the area but Luke was in thoughtful mood that evening for what to do with the fellow? He didn't exactly owe him any favours, but he didn't want him hanging around either. Next thing he'd have Sir Brandon turning up and that he wouldn't welcome.

★ ★ ★

So, Lucy had been visiting and wanted to tell him about it.

'Miss Hetherington arranged it, Guv and we went to tea. Her name is Annabelle and she is just a little younger than me and she lives with her mother in quite a small house miles from anywhere and she is coming to tea next week if that is all right.'

'Of course it's all right. I'm delighted you've found a friend. Does she go to school?'

'No, Guv. She has lessons at home 'cus she's delicate.'

'Mm. You're not delicate are you?'

'No, Guv. Course not, silly.'

'Good. You can bring me a cup of tea, then.'

'Oh Guv, you're always teasing,' and Lucy plonked down on his lap and gave him a hug.

★ ★ ★

A schoolmaster arrived to take over the village school in place of the mistress who'd started when the Board took over the National School eight years earlier. After battling with her reluctant pupils she had now retired and left the village.

A week later the Reverend Greenway moved in at the Rectory. Both arrivals heralded changes in the life of the village but Luke kept well clear. Any formal role that he, as lord of the manor might have, he passed to Francis Remnold, who in turn persuaded Lady Remnold to take a lead.

Mr Aloysius Pike, it was soon learned, was a strict disciplinarian in school and those who'd grown used to the ways of the mistress soon learned to respect the strong arm of the master. He was also an energetic sportsman and organiser of events. When not running about in strange clothing keeping fit, he called meetings in the schoolroom to form cricket teams, football teams, hare and hounds teams and a bicycling club, all in his first month.

In contrast, the Rector turned out to be a quiet, gentle sort of man and something of a free-thinker. He visited every cottage in the village and spoke courteously with those who called themselves chapel, acknowledging their absolute right to worship as they wished, which raised a few eyebrows. Altogether, there was no shortage of topics for discussion at the Lamb.

★ ★ ★

Giving Percy Remnold a week or so to get himself together, Luke sent Charlie to bring him to Gresham House in the cab. Digger had kept him closely informed and it seemed his stay at the warehouse was something of an education to him. Withdrawn at first, he'd gradually socialised with those he found there and had attached himself to John Parsons, closely following his work and talking at length with him. Now Luke had to move him on, permanently.

'Ah, Mr Remnold. Come in. Have a seat. You're looking better, I see. Thank you, Bridie. Put it down here, will you,' as she brought in the coffee. 'Have you had thoughts about the future?' he asked Percy.

'Well, only the vaguest ones really, Mr Gregory but I do wish to thank you for what you have done for me. I had reached the end of my tether and I owe you more than apologies for my misconduct.'

'That's water under the bridge. We have to look forward, not back. I'll speak plainly. You must understand there's no place for you at Chidlingbrook, except as a visitor, so you must decide how you'll make your way in the world. You've had a tolerably good education I should imagine, you're not unintelligent so you might care to consider opportunities in the colonies. Call in at the Colonial Office and see what they can offer. When you've found something that appeals, let me know and we'll discuss how to go about it. You're welcome to stay at the warehouse for as long as you need accommodation. You'll find a few wise heads there. Make use of them.'

'I already have, Mr Gregory and I'm grateful to you for this. I've spoken a lot with Mr Parsons who has told me of possible trading opportunities. I do have one great concern that I need advice upon.'

'What's that?'

'It's father, sir. He is dying and is in the workhouse infirmary at St Pancras. He had a sudden illness and is paralysed down one side. A stroke, I believe it is called. None of his friends would help him. At least, I thought they were his friends. I know how you feel about him but I cannot just go off and leave him. It wouldn't be right.'

'This is family business. Write to your mother and arrange to visit. Find out what her thoughts are. I won't stand in the way of any civilised arrangement. Now, you'll need something for expenses so talk with Mr Brierly downstairs. If I'm not around you can always discuss matters with him or with Mr O'Dowd, of course. Now I must ask you to excuse me,' and Luke stood up to signify the meeting was ended. He brushed aside Percy's thanks and expressions of gratitude and ushered him towards the door.

As far as he was concerned this was a necessary business, something to get out of the way as quickly as possible. At the door, Percy turned and impulsively held out his hand. Luke had not offered this courtesy earlier and was seeking to avoid it altogether but it would have been churlish to refuse, so shook the offered hand and wished him 'Good luck.'

After Percy had left the house, he went down to Walter's room and told him of the suggestions he'd made. 'If you can encourage him to choose some field of employment, preferably abroad, I'd appreciate it and would you get one of the boys to call at the St Pancras Workhouse and enquire about Sir Brandon? Seems he's hit rock bottom and landed in the infirmary there. I'd just like to know the position. Oh, and I'll be going down to the Manor on Thursday, this week.'

★ ★ ★

If Luke had hoped for a quiet weekend he was to be disappointed. No sooner had he walked into the house than he was met by Miss Hetherington, who reported that Peter was in trouble at school and had run off from there but wouldn't say why. Would Luke please talk to him.

'I will when I've had a cup of tea. He's around, I take it?'

'Oh, yes. He's in his room.'

'Tell him to meet me in the study in ten minutes, would you?' and with Miss Hetherington gone to deliver that message, Luke was free to ask George how things were.

'Not so bad, Guv. The ironwork for the hot houses has arrived and work'll start on Monday putting it all together. I reckon we'll have our own Crystal Palace, time it's finished.'

'That's good,' Luke said, looking pleased. 'I'm looking forward to it. Now what about stoking the boilers on a regular basis? I'm wondering too if we'll need someone to look after the plants as well. What d'you think? They'd need to know what they were about and I'm not putting more on Mrs Donkin. She's busy enough.'

'Hot houses is a bit specialised, I reckon. Bit like hot kitchens,' George said, giving his wife a wink. 'Think we'll have to advertise? We'd have to find them somewhere to live, I expect.'

'Problems, problems,' Luke said. 'I think we'll wait until it's up and ready, then see. Now I must go and talk to Peter.'

As he expected, Peter was waiting for him in the study looking as if the weight of the world was on his shoulders. A sensitive fellow, this one, Luke knew. Very easy to squash him down. Very little confidence.

'Now then, young Peter, what have you been up to? Put tin tacks on someone's chair, have you? Come and sit. I'm sure it can't be as bad as you think it is,' and he ushered him over to the chaise lounge and sat with him.

'I got in trouble, Guv.'

'Tell me what happened. Straight, now.'

'I went out after lunch and we're not supposed to and I'll get beaten for it.'

'Who said?'

'One of the boys.'

'I see. Did you know you weren't supposed to go out after lunch?'

'Sort of, Guv. I was dared and then he went and told.'

'Someone set you up, did they? Because you're new, I expect. Happens all the time. Some folks think it's clever. Well, it doesn't sound too bad to me but you shouldn't have run off. That could be serious and you must promise me not to do it again. Understand?'

'Yes, Guv.'

'I'll write a note to your headmaster for you to take tomorrow. I'll explain that you were misled and ask him to be understanding over this. You must apologise for your discourtesy in leaving the school as you did and assure him it won't happen again. You can expect a ticking off and that'll be the end of the matter but you must be careful of whom you take notice and if you accept dares you must take the consequences. That's part of life. Now stop worrying and come and have tea. Come on. Let's see that smile.'

Old Joe was ill, Mrs Donkin reported. She'd called in to see, 'as he 'adn't been outside for a couple o' days and 'e was in bed and looking badly.

'Needs nursing, I reckon,' George told Luke, 'or a doctor. There isn't one in the valley at all. Nearest one's all the way to Guildford, so far as I can make out.'

'Think we should set one up in the village?' Luke asked. 'There's no telling when we'll want one ourselves. He'd need a house though and stabling. I wonder if there's anywhere suitable round about, which was the first topic he took up with Francis Remnold, when he called, drawing on his intimate knowledge of the village.

'The only place bigger than a cottage is the wheelwright's old workshop, next to the post office. It hasn't been used since he left a year or so ago so it's bound to be in a poor state but it used to be held on a tenancy.'

'We can use it then. Have a look round it, will you? See what needs doing to set it up. There'll have to be a consulting room as well as accommodation. I'll advertise for a practitioner and see who's interested. Now, what have you for me this week?'

'Well, sir, there's been some grumbling about wages at the Home Farm. The men have complained they can't live on what they're paid.'

'I'm not surprised. Ten bob a week's a poor wage but it's the going rate. It'd help if they didn't have so many mouths to feed. Ten in a family is nothing I'm told. We'd have to improve production before we could offer an increase.'

Yes, sir. Oh, and my brother has visited, sir. He said he had your approval and he said you've been jolly decent to him. He's gone back to London now to take an examination for the colonial service, in Australia, if he's accepted.'

'Good. Plenty of opportunities there for ambitious men.'

'He also told us about father. Mother doesn't know quite what to do about him. She feels that she cannot just leave him where he is but she doesn't want him at the Hall.'

'And neither do you, I imagine.'

'Well, no sir, I don't,' Francis replied, colouring up.

'I understand. Very well. I'll see that he's moved to somewhere more comfortable. Wouldn't wish one of those places on a dog.'

'You will do that for us?' Francis looked genuinely surprised. 'Mr Gregory, I, I don't know how to thank you enough for everything that you've done for us. Truly I don't.'

'You're giving something in return, are you not? Then say no more about it. Do you like music? Now we have a decent piano someone is coming to play for us next weekend. We thought to invite a few friends for the occasion and if you and Lady Remnold would care to join us you'd be most welcome.'

'Thank you very much, sir. I certainly would and I'm sure mother would too.'

'Good. Lucy is preparing invitation cards so I'll see that you receive one. You've met the Rector I know, so how do you find him?'

'He appears to be a most pleasant gentleman, sir. He called at the Hall last week and spent some time with mother.'

'Mm. And Pike? I understand he's not in the usual mould of village schoolmasters. I've seen him running by in striped flannel. Something of an athlete, I believe.'

'Er, yes, sir, he is,' and Francis started to laugh. 'He is very firm in the schoolroom but out of it, a trifle eccentric.'

'He should provide a measure of entertainment, then.'

'He already has, sir.'

'Oh? Tell me.'

'Well, sir, he was in the Lamb, trying to raise interest in a bicycling group and some of the men led him on. They told him bicycling along roads was no good to them but they might be interested if it was possible to ride across fields, as it would be helpful in their work. Well, Pike offered to demonstrate and they pointed him towards Long Acre, telling him the cows wouldn't mind as they were used to people passing through. They forgot to mention that Arthur was turned out with them.'

'What, the bull?'

'Yes. He's short tempered at the best of times but a bicycle among his ladies really set him off. Apparently, Pike beat him to the river bank by half a horn and was still pedalling when he hit the water, best part of halfway across,' and Francis dissolved into laughter as he once again pictured the scene.

★ ★ ★

That afternoon, Luke was looking over the building of the hothouses. Most of the iron framework was assembled and the glazing had been started. Hot water pipes bolted to the brickwork led to the boiler house, which had been extended and set partly below ground level.

'Something to do with improving the flow of water', George told him. Two boilers now sat side by side there, one for hot water and heating for his end of the house and one for the glass houses whilst outside, a covered coke store was nearing completion. Quite a business-like arrangement Luke decided and wandered back into the partly glazed area, surprised at how much warmer it already was in there, when George joined him.

'Er, Guv. There's something you'd best see,' he said.

'Oh? What's that?'

'I'd sooner you saw for yourself, if you wouldn't mind,' George told him.

'Well, lead on. Let's see this mystery,' and following George to the stable yard, saw Peter walking, or rather, wobbling, towards him, grinning foolishly. 'What have we here, then?' Luke asked and catching hold of Peter, held him at arm's length and quickly realised. 'You're drunk,' he exclaimed. 'What have you been at, young man?'

'He's not the only one, Guv. Come and look round here.'

Leaving Peter sitting against the stable wall, Luke followed George to the cart shed beneath the apple loft and there, in various stages of intoxication were Ticker and his brothers and sister and John Hurle.

'They've been at the mead we had put by in the loft,' George told him. I reckon they've had a drop more than's good for 'em. Powerful stuff that.'

'There'll be some hangovers,' Luke said. 'Their mother know?'

'Joseph's gone down to tell her. She'll go mad at 'em. Reckon they'll not sit down for a day or two.'

'No need for that, I shouldn't think. Peter's the one needs a flea in his ear. Here she comes now. Ah, Mrs Donkin. Looks like they've overdone it a bit.'

'I'll murder 'em,' she said.

'Oh, I wouldn't take it too seriously,' Luke replied. 'There's no great harm done, I shouldn't think, though your youngest looks a bit pale. Tell you what. You take her off and tend to her and we'll bed the rest down here on straw and let 'em sleep it off.'

'Well, if you says so, sir,' Mrs Donkin said, doubtfully. 'They deserves a damn good whipping.'

'Save it for next time,' Luke advised. 'Wouldn't do to make a habit of it. I'll get Peter. He can join 'em here. Joseph, would you keep an eye on 'em for me? They'll probably be sick within the hour, which'll help. Let me know if anyone looks bad. Right, Mrs Donkin. Leave 'em with me. It's not so bad,' he said reassuringly and to George, cup of tea time, I think,' and together they walked up to the kitchen but were barely seated when Miss Hetherington appeared and announced the arrival of a visitor at the front door.

'Who is it?' Luke asked, without enthusiasm. Stray visitors could be a nuisance when you had other things in mind.

'It's Pike, Mr Gregory. The schoolmaster. I feel that he ought really to have called at the rear.'

'Oh, you do? I see. Well, show him into the study, would you, please. I won't keep him waiting long.' With Miss Hetherington gone, Luke exchanged glances with George. 'I don't think the schoolmaster is approved of. I wonder what he's done to blot his copy book.'

Luke soon found out. Pike, he realised, had a fulsome manner and lacked customary tact and deference when meeting strangers for the first time, especially when there was a difference in social status. Village schoolmasters did not enjoy high standing, as their meagre salary reflected and they needed to conduct themselves carefully if they wished for recognition and acceptance.

Pike appeared unaware of this and leapt at Luke with outstretched hand and overwhelming bonhomie. It might have been his study to which he was welcoming a visitor, Luke thought. No wonder the village humorists led him on.

Luke shook hands, and was about to invite his visitor to take a seat when he was pre-empted.

'It's marvellous to meet you at last, Squire Gregory,' he was told. 'Come and sit down and talk to me about the needs of the village.'

Luke felt his hackles rising. Did he show this fellow the door or what? He counted to ten and remained standing.

'I don't care to be addressed as Squire,' he said, coldly.

'Oh, I thought that's how you should be addressed.'

'If a man's a fool you don't have to call him one.'

There was a silence whilst Pike digested this, his expression changing, then he stood up and announced, 'If you consider me a fool, I shall leave.'

'I don't consider you a fool. Sit down and we'll start again,' and Luke lowered himself into a chair. Uncertainly, Pike did likewise.

'You have an off-putting manner Mr Pike. You'll need to amend it if you wish to influence people. From what I hear, you're an effective schoolmaster but out of school, you've laid yourself open to ridicule. That's a pity, because I believe you're well intentioned. You're not a countryman and you've underestimated the intelligence and wit of the villagers. You're an important member of this community. Probably more important than the Rector. You're a sporting man, so when I advise you to play yourself in carefully you'll know what I mean. So far, you've slogged out wildly in all directions in a most unscientific fashion. It's time to settle down and treat both bowlers and fielders with respect. That way, you'll last the innings and gain respect for yourself.'

Aloysius Pike followed Luke's every word closely. Gone was his fulsome, overbearing manner as he recognised the truth of his mistaken approach. He had early realised that his arrival in the village had gone sadly wrong but hadn't understood quite why and so had redoubled his efforts to organise, influence and change the entrenched ways he found but didn't comprehend.

'Do you think I should apologise to everyone for trying to change things?' he asked, almost timidly.

'That's the last thing you should do,' Luke replied, firmly. 'Just go about things gently. Sow a seed here, encourage an idea there. Influence by leading, not pushing. Those interested will join in soon enough. This village is crying out for a football team. It desperately needs a cricket team and umpteen other things. We don't even have a doctor but Mr Remnold is doing something about that. Gain his co-operation and you'll see things happen but don't, for heaven's sake push people about. You'll only put their backs up.'

'Yes, I see. Actually, I came this afternoon to talk to you about a site for a cricket pitch. I was told that you were the person to see about it.'

'Someone misleading you, I think. Talk to Mr Remnold and he'll find you what you want. Get things set up a bit, start small and before you know it, you'll have all the young fellows coming along to show off their skills. Suggest someone propose a captain, then you can pick a team. Get the next village to challenge you or you challenge them and it'll take off.'

'Yes, yes, I see but don't you, Mr Gregory take any part in village affairs? I'm afraid I don't properly understand how everything works round here. I honestly thought that the squire was in charge of everything.'

'In some places that's so. I'm not a squire. The village disowns me so I remain outside local affairs. Mr Remnold at the Hall is the man to discuss things with. Lady Remnold I know, would be delighted to interest herself in your school, were she to be invited. That might be a useful move, don't you think?'

'I see. Yes, indeed. I hadn't thought of that. I didn't think the gentry would be at all interested in such things.'

'Oh, but they are, in a patronising sort of way. The Rector will expect to have a say as well. I think you need to encourage people and let them feel part of things. If you find out what each child's father does and show you recognise the value of their skills, whatever they are, they'll warm to you very quickly. Let them teach you about village life. They'll love it.'

'Mr Gregory, I feel I've learned more in this short time than I have in a year of teaching. I will most certainly follow your advice. I think it is just what I need.'

'Happy to help,' Luke replied, gruffly, getting to his feet. He'd had enough of this visitor and wished him on his way.

★ ★ ★

There was to be little peace for him that weekend, though. He declined to join Miss Hetherington for church, knowing that Lady Remnold liked to share the manorial pew. At least, he used the excuse of making more room for her, should she attend but really, he preferred to wander around the Manor grounds.

He left the vegetable garden and was about to cross the yard when he saw Bridie standing by the gate, clutching a bundle. 'What the blazes?' he said out loud and walked over to her.

'Bridie O'Rourke, what brings you here?'

Bridie looked at the ground and shuffled her feet then glared defiantly at Luke. 'I've left,' she said.

'You mean left my employ?'

Bridie looked down again then up at Luke. 'I don't like it there no more. It's boring and I'm fed up with them little kids. They don't give me no peace.'

'What does Mrs Maddocks think? I take it you've told her?'

'She's always nagging on so I've 'ooked it.'

'I see. You couldn't wait to tell me in the morning, then.' Bridie looked down again but didn't reply. 'Well, come on in and talk to Mrs Cherry but I'm not pleased and you may as well know it.'

Leaving Bridie in Mrs Cherry's charge, Luke walked into the wood behind the Manor and up to the rolling, grass covered hilltop. His mood had changed and he cursed at the cause of it. Why, why, why did these wretched people have to plague him at the wrong time? He'd taken on that handful to help Thomas Barnardo so why couldn't she stay put, at least until the morning. But no, she had to up sticks and bother him here. It really wasn't good enough but what to do about it? He couldn't just send her away. That wouldn't be right but he wasn't having her at the Manor. Things were well settled here apart from which, he'd decide who moved in. Ah, the Hall. They could do with more help in the kitchen. That's it, he decided. She could burn the Remnold's toast and serve their kippers but she'd go there on his terms.

Bridie was still in the kitchen when Luke returned and she looked up at him nervously from where she was mixing something in a bowl. Just like Mrs Cherry to get her to lend a hand. 'Right, young lady, let's sort your future out,' he said. 'I take it you really want to work somewhere else?'

'Yes, Guv. Can I come 'ere?'

'No. I might have considered it if you'd gone about it in the right way but leaving as you did is no recommendation. You'll have to control that temper of yours or you'll find nothing'll go right for you.' Bridie looked down, her lower lip trembling. 'And don't go snivelling into that bowl or you'll spoil whatever it is. If you want a change you can go up to the Hall and show them how to cook properly. It's just across the valley and near enough to borrow Mrs Cherry's recipes but first, though, you'll go back and make your peace with Mrs Maddocks. I won't have you leaving in this fashion. Is that clear?'

'Yes, Guv. I'm sorry, Guv.'

'Very well. You'll take the last train back this afternoon. It leaves at ten minutes past four and I shall expect to see you in the house in the morning.'

★ ★ ★

'There's been a young woman enquiring for you, Guv,' Digger said, after the usual preliminaries. It was a Tuesday morning and Luke had returned to Gresham House after a weekend at the Manor but Digger didn't look quite himself this morning, he thought. A bit edgy. Not his usual self.

'Oh? Who is she?'

'I don't rightly know but she turned up at the ware'ouse late on Friday. Told Bert she wanted to see you most particular. She was that pressing, Bert sent up 'ome for me.'

'What did she want?'

Digger looked uncomfortable. 'I went down straight away and 'ad a word, as Bert 'ad said it was looking urgent.'

'And?' Luke was growing impatient for he was used to Digger speaking freely when they met.

'She said she wanted to speak to you about your son.'

Luke sat up straight. 'She said what? What son? What on earth was she on about? What name did she give?'

'Delia Watkins. She said she knew you at Fairlawn.'

Luke frowned, then glowered. Was he being Shanghaied? He'd always been careful in his off duty visits. He'd relied absolutely on Annie Porter to see there were no mistakes made and in any case, everyone concerned had been well paid for their services. Looked after, was more like it. There should be no comeback at all.

'I've been careful not to sow wild oats,' he said, evenly, looking straight at Digger. 'Oh, come on, now. You know about my leisure moments. There's no need to look so uncomfortable.'

'Well, yes, Guv but I didn't know 'ow yer'd feel about it. You know, others knowing'.

'And who else does know what I've been up to? Come on, let's have it and for heaven's sake sit down. It's not the end of the world. I'm no plaster saint as well you know and you've probably heard worse things.'

Digger looked relieved and sat in the other arm chair by the fireside, then grinned shyly at Luke. 'I thought you'd maybe throw me out,' he said. 'Well, Beth knows; has done all along. Probably Ben and Dessy but I don't think there's anyone else, though there's a few have a guess in and out.'

'This sounds like a try-on to me. I want you to check it out personally. Use anyone you need to but do it quietly and as quickly as you can. If it's just a case of her wanting money I don't mind if you give a bit of help. I'll leave it to you but I don't want shocks like this everyday. What would the Bishop say?'

'As if you cared, Guv.' Digger was grinning now. The worst was over and the guv hadn't exploded but he'd save what else he knew for another time.

★ ★ ★

That came three days later when Digger decided to report again and get it over with.

'It's like this, Guv,' he said. 'It seems like our Delia wasn't careful enough one time and got caught, so she reckons. She's positive it 'appened whilst she was at Fairlawn because she left a few months later, before anything showed. I've checked that with Mrs Porter and it fits. Six years ago, near enough.'

'Go on.'

'Well, she 'ad the baby and her mother looked after it whilst she went back to work. She'd done a turn or two at the Lodge House and knew 'is nibs and his cronies and one of 'em took 'er on full time as his regular. The Hon. Rupert Bridgewood, she said. Well, that was fine while it lasted but then she found she'd got something wrong with 'er and she's not got long ter go. Course, the Hon. Rupert didn't want ter know and dropped 'er p.d.q. so she came looking fer you.'

'Wanting money, I suppose.'

'No, I tried that one. She got right up tight and said 'damn his money.' What she wants, she said, is your name for the boy. Nothing else.'

'But if she's not long to go, who looks after the boy?'

'His father, she reckons. She said she's told the boy who 'is father is and what 'is real name is. Course, 'e doesn't understand it all, 'e's too young for that. Nice little lad though.'

'You mean, you've seen him?'

Digger nodded. 'He's at home, with Beth.'

Luke considered, his feelings in a jumble. Did he really have a son, despite his efforts to avoid family ties? Or was he the victim of someone's scheming?

'What proof is there I'm the father?'

'None, Guv,' Digger replied. 'If you said you didn't want ter know, there's none could make yer.'

'So what do you think? Straight, now.'

'Guv, 'e's the spitting image of yer. Same eyes, same nose, same look about 'im. If I were to lay odds I'd offer a hundred to one on, no messing.'

Luke looked hard at his partner. 'As strong as that?'

'When I took 'im 'ome Beth said straight out she knew who 'e reminded her of and she's dead certain 'e's yours. She said ter say she's delighted and it's the nicest thing she could wish fer you.'

'She said that?'

'Straight up, Guv.'

'It's settled, then. When can I visit?'

'No time like the present. I'll dig Joe out the kitchen.'

Luke sat then, his thoughts and emotions in turmoil. He was excited, proud, shocked even, a strange sensation in the pit of his stomach. A son of his own. He couldn't get over it. Unreal was putting it mildly. How would he explain the sudden arrival of a son? What would people think and say? His mind in a whirl, he walked across the room and stared, unseeing, out of the window, an old habit when he had things on his mind.

★ ★ ★

They travelled in silence to Digger's house at Hampstead and found Beth and a small boy waiting for them in the hall.

'This is William, Guv, Beth said.'

The small boy looked solemnly up at him with big eyes and with trembling lower lip asked, 'Are you my Papa, sir?'

Luke felt himself melt and managed to get out, 'Yes, I'm your Papa,' then picked the little fellow up and hugged him tight. They walked round the garden then, William holding tightly to Luke's hand.

'Mama has gone on a very long journey. It is so long that she won't be coming back. Are you coming back, Papa?'

'Coming back? Oh, I see. I'm not going anywhere, only home for the weekend. Will you come too? We'd have to go on a train to get there but it doesn't take long.'

William looked doubtful. 'I've not been on a train,' he said.

'You'll like the one we'll go on. It's very comfortable and fast,' and then, 'I've got lots of friends for you to meet.'

Back inside, everyone was smiling and looking pleased and Digger slapped him on the back and said, 'Good on yer, Guv,' though quite why, Luke wasn't sure.

'I'll be taking William to the Manor to meet everyone there,' he told them. 'We'll come back on Monday.'

★ ★ ★

The problem of suddenly introducing his five year-old son, 'I'm nearly six,' he told Luke, exercised his mind during the train journey. William sat very close, a little nervous at the strangeness of everything. Only one way to tackle it, Luke decided. Give it 'em straight from the shoulder.

They walked hand in hand from the station to the Manor, Luke pointing out different features of interest along the road. How much registered with William he was unsure for whenever he glanced down at him, William was gazing up at him. Taking a deep breath, Luke opened the back door and entered the kitchen. As he expected, it was warm, bright and full of glorious cooking smells. Mrs Cherry was busy by the stove, George on his stool nearby. Peter was munching a bun to relieve his perpetual hunger pangs and Lucy and her friend Annabelle were icing a cake.

The usual greetings then, 'This is William,' Luke announced and straight away started on the introductions.

'He's been living with his grandmother but I think he's old enough now to join in with us here.'

Mrs Cherry showed great presence of mind whilst everyone else appeared to freeze. Coming straight over to William she shook his offered hand then hugged him tight in greeting. 'It is lovely to see you William. My, you're just like your Papa. How lovely. Now, I'm sure you must be hungry so come and choose one of these cakes.'

'Thank you,' William replied, 'but Papa, should I not shake hands first?' he asked, looking worried.

'Yes, you're quite right. Shake hands with everyone first then choose your cake. Quite right. Good boy,' Luke praised him, quietly proud that William should seek to settle formalities. Lucy and Annabelle were all smiles and happily welcomed William but Peter barely managed to be civil and immediately left the kitchen. Oh ho, Luke thought to himself. Storm clouds gathering there. He'd have to do something about that.

By seven o'clock, William was tucked up and asleep in Luke's bed. He was too unsure of his surroundings to accept any other arrangement. He'd have another bed put in his room for next time until he was ready for his own room.

Peter had disappeared straight after dinner when usually he'd sit with Luke by the fire for a while then tackle his prep for next day at school, but not this evening. Heaving a sigh, Luke knocked on Peter's door and went in and found him sitting on his bed morosely stabbing a pencil into a blanket.

'You have something on your mind,' Luke said. 'Would you care to share it?' Peter grunted but said nothing and continued to stab his blanket. Luke sat down beside him, thinking back to an earlier occasion when his sensitive, mixed up ward had suffered a fit of the blues.

'It's William, isn't it,' Luke stated. 'I saw your face when I introduced him to everyone.'

Peter glanced sideways at Luke then looked away again. 'I didn't know you were married,' he mumbled.

'I'm not married. William's mother died just as your mother died.'

'Is he going to live here?'

'Weekends, when I'm here, yes.'

'He'll get all this, won't he, if he's your son.'

So that's it, Luke thought. He's jealous, envious of William's position.

'Not necessarily. He'd firstly have to want it and secondly, he'd have to earn it just as you'll have to earn anything that's offered when you leave school. If you don't work for something you don't value it. If you want to be a farmer you shall have a farm. Same with Richard and Lucy. As for this house, you can't all have it, can you? Of one thing be certain. No one's going to sit around in idleness enjoying what I've worked for and that includes William. You'll all have a good start but after that it's up to each of you to make his own way. Understood?'

★ ★ ★

'Now then, Richard, why so glum? It's only the start of the holidays,' Luke added, as he helped himself to bacon and eggs from the sideboard.

Richard, nearly seventeen now, was already seated and about to start his breakfast but he clearly was none too happy about something.

'I've done something stupid, Guv,' he said, ever frank, 'and I'm kicking myself for it. I shall look a real fool next term.'

'Oh? Might I ask what calamity awaits you?'

'It's just that, oh why did I have to take notice of him? It's that fellow Chalmers-Reid, in School House, Guv, the one I've mentioned before. Always going on about who his father knows and what circles he moves in; Lord this and Viscount that. He knows I can't stand the sight of him so he's constantly trying to score off me, as well as other fellows. Well, just before we broke up, he was going on about lunching at the Langham Hotel next Thursday with someone or other high up socially and he said to me, 'Don't suppose we shall see you there, Travers. Rather out of reach, what?' Like a fool, instead of ignoring him, I said something about lunching there Thursday and any other day I cared to and a couple of his cronies took me up on it and one or two have even wagered on my being there.' Richard looked down at his plate as he finished, clearly very angry with himself.

'Pass the toast, would you?' Luke asked, then, 'Backed yourself into a corner by the sound of it. So how do you get out of a corner?'

'You duck and weave and side-step, covering up as you go or you go forward fighting and beat your opponent down,' Richard replied, knowing full well it was the prize ring to which Luke referred.

'And which course do you prefer?' Luke asked.

'Well, the second one, Guv but how can I manage that?'

'Lunch at the Langham on Thursday. Face the fellow down.'

'But Guv, the Langham's a top notch establishment. I mean, only important people go there and it's fearfully expensive and you have to reserve a table.'

'Chalmers-Reid is more important than you?' Luke smiled in a challenging sort of way, which added to Richard's discomfiture then, relenting, said, 'Perhaps we could arrange a luncheon party and invite one or two socially acceptable guests to join us and see how we go, eh? Have to keep our end up, don't we?'

'Oh Guv, you are a brick,' Richard said, beaming at him. 'I really am grateful to you but who will you invite? I mean, who would accept?'

'That, I'll leave to your Uncle Digger. I'll scribble a note to him setting out our requirements and let him make the arrangements. I'm sure he'll find a clutch of Lords and Honourables to dazzle your sparring partner. If you take it down to the post office straight away he'll get it in the morning.'

★ ★ ★

The situation appealed to Luke's sense of mischief. For some obtuse reason he positively delighted in harmlessly confounding the pretentious and deflating the pompous, whoever they might be. It was a certainty that Chalmers-Reid hailed from a family of insufferable social climbers and as such, was fair game.

Digger's note arrived on the Tuesday morning and confirmed that a luncheon party was arranged for one o'clock on Thursday at the Langham, with perhaps six or seven guests and had he felt the earthquake, which had shaken parts of London and sent a wave up the river?

Well no, he hadn't noticed anything but he'd seen accounts in the newspapers of damage to buildings in the Colchester area. Miles away from Chidlingbrook and of little interest but Digger, Luke knew, would enter into the spirit of the occasion and work out in detail how best to create the most telling impression for the benefit of the Chalmers-Reid table.

Luke was not, though, prepared for the august gathering who joined Richard and himself on that day. They'd arrived in good time and were shown to their table, the large one on the raised dais at the far side of the dining room and next to, and above that occupied by the Chalmers-Reids and Luke had the satisfaction of seeing the surprise on a certain young man's face as he and Richard took their seats but it was nothing to the expressions displayed when their guests arrived. Led by the head waiter wearing his most impressed demeanour, were Digger and the Prince of Wales, followed by four companions, one of whom Luke recognised as the Earl of Sudville.

'Ah, Gregory, good day to you,' HRH greeted him with outstretched hand. 'Not often I have the pleasure of your company. Glad to see you looking so well.'

'Most kind of you to say so, sir,' Luke replied, shaking hands. 'May I present my ward, Richard Travers?' and Richard, nearly overcome with awe, nervously shook hands.

'Where am I to sit, then? At the end here? Splendid. Room to spread out, eh? Come and sit by me,' he said to Richard who, with legs of jelly, took the coveted seat at the prince's right hand. Clearly, Digger had briefed his guest who, in avuncular mood, set out to meet his obligations wholeheartedly.

★ ★ ★

Chapter 9

The Reverend Edward Greenway called at the Manor on the Saturday afternoon having first enquired of Miss Hetherington whether she thought that might be convenient. He was a shrewd man and was moving cautiously in his new parish but had established that the social structure of the village did not follow the usual pattern and that the lord of the manor did not belong to the traditional squirearchy. He'd also established that the lord of the manor was a man to be reckoned with and that he was believed to control life round about through Francis Remnold.

Luke realised this was a formal courtesy to be observed but one that placed him under no obligation. If he liked the man, all well and good. If he didn't, he'd avoid him for the future. Conventional greetings and formalities over, they settled in comfortable chairs in the study, each trying to decide if what they'd heard fitted what they found. As host, Luke broke the ice by asking how his visitor liked the area. 'You'll find it quite a contrast from city life, as I do myself.'

And so they chatted on, each gently probing, enquiring and building up a picture of the other, seeking points of mutual interest and accord, for an easy relationship would be helpful to both, in the long run.

'I have met your family, of course, at church,' the Rector said. 'Do you not care to attend also?'

'Not greatly. I have reservations over the relevance of religion generally. I don't preach that message, but the whole business is a personal matter in my view.'

'You are tolerant of those who attend chapel?'

'Absolutely. Mr and Mrs Cherry are chapel. Miss Hetherington attends church and I walk around and listen to the birds.'

The Rector smiled. 'I can appreciate your enjoyment of that,' he said. 'I understand you were interested in my appointment when it was first announced.'

'I was. Your predecessor was difficult so I was anxious to avoid a successor in the same mould.'

'And do I meet with your approval, Mr Gregory?' he smilingly asked.

'Time will tell, Mr Greenway. I believe so far, you have done nothing to frighten the horses.' Luke was tired of this verbal exchange. There were more interesting things to do on a Saturday afternoon. If the reverend gentleman wanted to know what made him tick, it would be easier to show him.' Would you care to look around? We're having a hot house built; nearly finished now. I suppose some might call it an orangery when it's planted out. We'll go through the kitchen; might catch the scones fresh from the oven. I love 'em hot.

He was surprised to learn only a short while later, of romance in the air for the Reverend Doctor Greenway had fallen head over heels for Miss Hetherington. That would surely cause a stir in the village but what would Mr Gregory's feelings be? Positively delighted and only too pleased to give the bride away, in absence of any close kin. After all, he'd had some practice at that formality, had he not? Who, though could he find to replace Miss Hetherington? Who would he want to fill her slot in the household? Who would teach Lucy? Mm. Another problem to be solved.

★ ★ ★

The Reverend Greenway called at coffee time. Luke hadn't gone back to the City that morning, finding things to do at home instead. George was a bit off-colour and all was quiet enough at the wharf he thought, so why not?

Sitting together in the hall, the Rector came straight to the point. 'As you know, I move around the village and talk to all and sundry. There is a very strong wish by everyone for a better relationship with you. People think that you will never forgive the difficulties that arose when Sir Brandon was on the scene. It was not altogether their fault that things became unpleasant. When people are threatened with eviction or loss of employment, it can have a very strong impact. Many are really quite afraid of you.'

'They were happy to take his side,' Luke replied. 'All those employed here walked out and let it be known I wasn't gentry so they'd have no dealings with me. Well, I'm still not gentry and don't wish to be and I don't take kindly to being pelted with mud and ordure.'

'I see. No one told me this.'

'They wouldn't. I doubt George will ever get over being refused service in The Lamb. That was a real insult. Cut us dead, they did. Couldn't buy so much as a mint humbug or a jug of milk locally, which is why we have everything sent in from Guildford.

'I see. Things were really unpleasant then.'

'Joseph was well and truly rolled in the muck as well and what had he to do with any ill feeling between Hall and Manor?'

'That sounds most unfair but you do employ a boy named Hurle, from the village, do you not?'

'No. He works for Francis Remnold at the Hall. Oh, all right. So Remnold works for me but they're gentry so the village is happy.'

'Ah. I'm getting the picture,' and the Rector's eyes twinkled. 'I believe most of the men work on the farms round about but if you had work here would you employ anyone from Chidlingbrook?'

'All posts are filled so the question doesn't arise.' Luke was beginning to feel irritated. 'Look, Rector, my obligations locally are met in full, so what are you after?'

'What I would like to see, Mr Gregory, and I beg your forgiveness for my persistence, is a warmer personal relationship between yourself and the village, which might allow you to offer work to those without. You would be surprised how many lack employment.'

'You are indeed persistent,' Luke growled, 'and Remnold engages whatever help is needed.'

'I can see that I try your patience,' the Reverend Greenway said, getting to his feet. 'Perhaps we might talk again, sometime?'

'Perhaps,' Luke replied ungraciously, as he saw the Rector to the door.

The Reverend Greenway walked thoughtfully away, conscious that he'd pushed Luke farther than he'd intended. He'd have to be more careful in future but it certainly was an unusual situation. If Francis Remnold, who lived at the Hall, worked for the squire who was lord of the manor and known to be wealthy, then logically the Hall and estate plus the farms and village belonged to him also.

Only the breakdown in relationships between him and the village marred the scene. He was wealthy and independent so could afford to ignore them. They were still dependent on him but were in an uncomfortable position. That he was a compassionate man was clear. He paid good wages to those he employed and treated the children at the Manor as his own.

That was an interesting story Catherine Hetherington had told him. Not many would have acted as he had but then, he was a free-thinking man and there must be more to this business of young Hurle he was sure. He and the younger boy were friendly so he visited the Manor yet he lived in the village. That might be the chink in the stubborn defence of the status quo. He would have to see.

Luke sat glaring out of the window after he was gone. Why did these holy men have to poke their noses in like this? As a breed they're a pain in the arse, he decided. If it wasn't one thing it was another. Still, he supposed, they'd not much else to occupy their time, though this one might after he'd carried Miss H. off to the Rectory.

★ ★ ★

Luke had hardly settled back in at Gresham house after a weekend at the Manor when the telegram arrived. 'Big problem. Please contact. George.' Now George would never trouble him for anything trivial Luke well knew so this must be serious and, arrived back at the Manor, made straight for the kitchen.

'What's the problem, George?'

'Guv, Francis Remnold has 'anged 'imself. He was found this morning in the stable. Been dead some time be all accounts. Young John brought the news after your train 'ad left.'

Luke sat down at the table, his mind racing. 'Do you know why?'

'Well, Guv, could we step outside, a minute.'

'Never mind all that, George Cherry. I know the ways of the world well enough,' Mrs Cherry put in sharply.

George looked uncomfortable but chose his words carefully.' Seems like on Sunday afternoon, when all was quiet, Master Francis was a seeing to the yard boy in the stable only one o' the men called in for something he'd forgot and caught 'em at it. Found 'em both necked as the day they was born, be all accounts an' doing that what's reckoned unlawful.'

'Good grief,' Luke exclaimed, genuinely surprised.

'Course, it was all over the village in no time and the lad's father went looking for Master Francis who'd hidden away. The constable was called and the fat was in the fire.'

'And we knew nothing of it, of course,' Luke said. 'Just as well. Not a thing I'd want to be mixed up with. How's her ladyship taken it?'

'That I haven't heard,' George replied.

'John around is he? No? Would you go up to the Hall and check things out for me and bring him back here if you see him.'

'Righto, Guv. I'll leave directly.'

'A right how d'you do,' Luke said to Mrs Cherry as she handed him a cup of coffee.

'It's plain disgusting. I really wouldn't have thought it of the young gentleman.'

'No more would I,' Luke said. 'I really am surprised and most disappointed.' He sat then in silence as Mrs Cherry beat eggs and other ingredients in a large bowl with unaccustomed ferocity.

A half hour later, George returned, accompanied by John Hurle, looking pale and upset.

'Sit down,' Luke ordered. 'Something hot and sweet, I think, Mrs Cherry while I talk with George.'

Out in the yard, George took a deep breath. 'No one doing any work up there so I advised 'em to get themselves organised smartly. A couple of 'em wanted to argue the toss, me being there like, giving out orders but their mates soon shut 'em up. I heard one say as 'ow they didn't want trouble with the squire. Doctor's gig was outside. Her Ladyship's taken it real bad. Heart, I was told by her maid. Can't face the disgrace of it. Doctor's with her now. Police 'ave taken the body and a note. Coroner'll have that I reckon. I found young John hanging around the estate office not knowing what to do.'

'And the yard boy?'

'Black and blue. His father walloped him round the village for the shame he'd brought on the family.'

'Not altogether his fault, I wouldn't have thought. Still, not my business. Mm. Can you, for the time being, no. That wouldn't be fair. No. Get Ticker to saddle up and go over to Lee Farm and ask the eldest son, Amos, I think it is, if he'd oblige by coming to see me as soon as convenient. I'll offer him the farm to manage. Think that'll work?'

'Don't see why not, Guv. He must have enough experience under his belt be now. Seems a steady sort of fellow be all accounts. I'll look for Ticker.'

Back in the kitchen, John was looking more relaxed but stood up when Luke entered.

'Sit down, John, sit down. Finish your bun,' and Luke sat down alongside and automatically reached for his coffee cup, empty as it was.

'Another cup, Guv?' and Mrs Cherry as automatically, poured from the pot.

'Mm. A bit of a shock, eh, John? Didn't try anything with you, did he?'

John blushed and looked down. 'Only once, Guv but I said no.'

'I'm glad you did. Well done,' and Mrs Cherry, rigid with indignation, clattered utensils on the stove to register her feelings.

'What, now am I going to do with you, I wonder. You're not going back to sweeping the yard, that's for certain. Have you any ideas?'

'No sir.'

'Mm. What are you, now? Thirteen? Fourteen? How would you like to go back to school, to finish your education? I don't mean the village school. I'm thinking of a bigger one. You've a good brain and a lively mind. You could make something of yourself with the right chance.'

'I'd like to, sir but father'd never let me.'

'Leave father to me. Go and talk to your mother. Tell her I'm offering you a scholarship to Bramsden College. That's the one Richard and Fred go to. If you don't like that idea you could go to the same school as Peter in Guildford. Your choice. Think it over and let me know. All right?'

'Thanks ever so much, sir. I'll go and talk to mother now,' and John scrambled from the table and went out. They could hear his boots as he ran across the yard and down the drive.

'Guv, I think you're a saint,' Mrs Cherry said and dabbed her eyes with her apron.

'No I'm not, Mrs Cherry. Anything but. I was given a chance when I was not much older than him and I was downright grateful. It took me from galley boy to apprentice and set me on the right course. It's only right I should do the same.'

'I still think it's more than anyone else would do and I still think you're a saint.'

'What's this then?' George asked as he came back into the kitchen. 'Been at the onions again?'

'No. It's the Guv. He's sending that boy to school, on a scholarship and I think it's wonderful,' and she broke off with a wail and flung her arms round her surprised husband's neck and wept. Luke quietly got to his feet and disappeared into the hall. Women, he thought. He'd never understand them.

★ ★ ★

Doctor John Fairleigh was still finding his way around the valley. Stephen Lambourne had agreed to find a suitable practitioner for Chidlingbrook and now Doctor John was installed in his house next to the post office and held surgeries twice daily. Not, of course, that anyone had so far attended one. His newness, his youth and his unmarried status served only to arouse suspicion in the narrow minds of the villagers.

It would take time for the ice to break but, given the frequency of accidents round about, it was only a matter of time before he became accepted as a source of help and comfort. Now, he called at the Manor with bad news. He had to tell someone and who better than the squire, he thought.

'Oh, Mr Gregory. I'm sorry to trouble you,' he apologised when he was invited in, 'but I have to report that Lady Remnold has passed away. I wondered if you might know who should properly be told.'

'I'm sorry to hear this. So far as I'm aware her only living relatives are her son, who's in South Africa and her estranged husband, confined to a nursing home. May I enquire the cause?'

'Heart. I believe it must have been weakened by her earlier prolonged confinement to bed. The strain of er, recent events proved too much. Couldn't face the shock and humiliation of it all. Most unfortunate.'

'Indeed yes,' Luke replied, conventionally, though his mind was racing. Suddenly, the Hall was no longer occupied. To what use might it be put, he wondered. 'Er, yes,' as he forced his mind back to the immediate. 'Don't suppose you could let the Rector know? Funeral arrangements. That sort of thing? He'll know who does what. I'll meet expenses, tell him.'

'Yes, yes, I'll certainly call by and tell him,' and Doctor Fairleigh hastened away.

★ ★ ★

'Guv, there's a man at the back door asking for you,' Peter told him. 'I think it's John's father.'

'Right. I'll come through.'

William Hurle was a big man, known to rule his family with a heavy hand. He'd spruced himself up for this visit, even bringing forward his weekly shave.

'Mr Hurle, is it?' Luke asked courteously. 'Won't you step inside?'

'What I've come to say can be said outside,' he said, stiffly.

'As you wish.'

A clearing of his throat then, 'It's about my John. What are you trying to do to un, squire? All this talk o' scholarships an' such. It ain't proper.'

'Oh? Why not.'

'We're country folk. Bin in the village an' round about for years. Our place is on the land as it's alus bin.'

'And if someone isn't suited to the land? Would you force them? I believe everyone should follow the calling that best suits them. If there's no choice there's no more to be said. If there is a choice, the wise man takes the best deal going. Your boy has a good brain. He's quick with figures, he thinks about problems and he deserves the chance to improve himself.'

'That's all well and good for them as 'as plenty.'

'You mean I can afford to speak in this fashion? Well let me tell you Mr William Hurle, I ran barefoot as a boy and was packed off to sea at twelve to get rid of me. Then someone gave me a chance and I took it. Every penny I have has been earned, Mr William Hurle and I've done no one down whilst earning it.'

Luke had found himself speaking with an unexpected intensity, irritated at the suggestion he enjoyed easy wealth and Hurle looked a little taken aback at what he heard. Then, in a softer tone Luke, went on. 'Tell me. Are you content to work for someone else for a low wage or would you choose, if you had the chance, to do something else? Be honest, now. Have you never had a dream of what you'd really like to do?'

'What's the point o' dreamin' if can never come to be?'

'So you have thought about it but you can't see it happening so you push it to the back of your mind. That's fair enough, but tell me, what is your dream?'

William Hurle looked down at the ground and shuffled his boot toe in the dust of the yard. 'To have a place o' me own,' he said, shyly. 'Not a big place, mind. Just a few acres I could call me own,' he ended up, defiantly, looking straight at Luke.

'And what would you do with those acres if you had 'em?'

'Mebbe run a few cows an' pigs an' such an' grow me own feed for 'em.'

'Have you thought of market gardening? Growing fruit and vegetables for the London market? All the good land's being built on now but the need for fresh produce is greater than ever. A box of onions, or carrots or whatever put on the last train out of here would be on sale first thing in the morning. There's an opportunity for the right man there.'

Hurle was looking hard at Luke now, the reason for his visit forgotten for the moment. He'd worked himself up to a pitch, determined to have it out with this fellow at the Manor come what may, even if it cost him his employment and here instead, he was listening to his dream.

'But where would I find the land?'

'What's that field behind your cottage? Three acres or so of grazing isn't it? Goes with the Home Farm here. You could make a start there, if you've a mind to. You're not short of spirit or you wouldn't be here. We'll walk it and look it over.'

Together and in silence, they walked towards the village, Hurle's thoughts in a whirl. Was he really being offered the chance of a lifetime and him expecting to be ordered out of his cottage and dismissed from work? Luke let him lead the way through the cottage gate and along the length of the garden with it's neat rows of vegetables, past the privy at the end and through a gap in the thorn hedge into the field.

'Reasonably sheltered, I'd say,' Luke said. 'Slopes to the South, near enough. Five shillings an acre for two years paid quarterly. After that we'll talk again. You can use the plough and tackle from the Hall to work it. What d'you say?'

William Hurle just stood and stared at Luke, struck dumb, it seemed. 'You mean you'll rent me this ground? I can borrow the plough and horses?'

'That's right. If you want to work your own ground, now's your chance. Keep your place at the farm 'til you're ready to work here full time. Show me you can make a go of it and we'll agree a long lease.'

'You're giving me a chance?'

'Yes. Just as someone once gave me a chance. Just as you're going to give your John a chance. Sounds reasonable, doesn't it?'

'It's reasonable all right. It's more than reasonable. It's bloody marvellous. I don't know 'ow I'm ever going to be able to thank you, sir. Will you come inside and 'ave a cup o' tea? I can't wait to tell me missus.'

After the spaciousness of the Manor, the cottage was tiny, dark and cramped, smelling of washing, cooking and woodsmoke. Mrs Hurle bobbed a curtsey to Luke and bustled with kettle and teapot. Various members of the family moved quietly towards the walls to allow space for their father and Luke to take their places at the table. John, Luke could see was in a corner, trying hard to make himself small, doubtless wondering what Luke's presence heralded.

'You going to tell him?' Luke prompted.

'Come here, boy,' his father commanded and John dutifully stood before him, utterly submissive to whatever was in store. 'You really want to go to school?'

John's face was a picture as he tried to choose the right answer, in case the wrong one should earn him a walloping.

His eyes flicked momentarily to Luke who nodded an encouraging 'yes.'

'Yes please, father, if I may.'

'Very well. You can go but mark my words. You'll do exactly as Mr Gregory says. That understood?'

'Yes, father and thank you. And thank you, sir,' to Luke.

'Good, good,' Luke said, which seemed to fit the bill. How about Friday for a visit there to look around? No, Thursday would be better. My boy's coming down for the weekend. Eight ten train? All spruced up? Good shine on your boots? Good,' and thanking Mrs Hurle for the tea, Luke stood up, narrowly missing the main beam in the ceiling as he did so. Moving towards the door, he noticed Ronald, in his turn making himself small, no easy matter for one of his size. Luke paused. 'Ronald, isn't it?'

'Yes, sir.'

'That business finished? Well, give me your hand on it.'

★ ★ ★

John Hurle was waiting at the gate to join Luke on the Thursday morning. He'd been there since shortly after half past seven, too excited to sit still and terrified of missing Luke. Accompanied by Peter, Luke approached shortly after eight o'clock, well practised in reaching the platform as the train steamed in. Peter, Luke thought, was quieter than usual, wondering probably about John visiting Bramsden College whilst he attended his day school.

Parting at Guildford, Luke and John made for the down line for Salisbury and the South West and, by sheer coincidence found the driver of their locomotive to be Johnny Barron. He stepped down from his cab to greet Luke, his face showing the pride in his achievement at moving to main line locomotives and his pleasure at Luke witnessing his success.

'You've made it, then,' Luke said. 'Congratulations. Well done but this is a monster and no mistake. Rather you than me to drive it.'

'Oh, she runs sweet as a bird, Guv,' Johnny said. 'You get her steam right and she talks to yer.'

'Well, get us to Salisbury on time will you. Two minutes to leaving. We'll go and find our seats,' and to John, 'There's another one took the chance he was offered. Worked his way up from engine cleaner to main line driver. Quite an achievement.'

'Did you help him, sir?'

'I helped point him in the right direction but the success is his alone, by his own efforts.'

★ ★ ★

Arrived at Bramsden College, John first met the headmaster then was taken in tow by Fred, who'd been deputed to show him around until lunch time. In the afternoon he'd join a class to sample the schoolroom.

'Headmaster, you'll recall mentioning a wish for a preparatory department to feed on to the main school?'

'I do indeed, Mr Gregory. Our own satellite prep school would indeed be a real asset.'

'I now have a suitable building vacant. There'd need to be some adaptation, of course but I believe it might serve the purpose admirably.'

'Mr Gregory, I long ago gave up being surprised at your initiatives but this is really exciting. May I enquire the whereabouts of the building?'

'It's the Hall at Chidlingbrook, where I live. Lady Remnold recently passed away and there's no family to make use of it so it's available to our purpose. I'm prepared to set it up if you will undertake to staff it and invite the clientele. Perhaps you'd care to visit and inspect. See what you think.'

'I most certainly would. This is absolutely marvellous. When might it be ready for use?'

'Why not aim for the start of the Autumn term?'

'As quickly as that? This really is marvellous. When may I visit?'

'As soon as you like. Why not return with us today? You would of course, stay at the Manor. You could then take any train back to suit.'

'The grass will never grow beneath your feet, Mr Gregory. That is a most kind suggestion. I will make arrangements immediately.'

The journey back to Chidlingbrook in company with the headmaster was a remarkably light-hearted one. Freed from the constraints of his position, Henry Lampton was something of a raconteur and offered entertaining conversation that included John, whose obvious delight was a pleasure to see.

A quick word with Mrs Hurle, whom Luke introduced to the headmaster and instruction to John to be ready at the same time in the morning and Luke and the head walked on to spend a relaxed evening before the business of the next day.

★ ★ ★

'Guv, do you think I should go to boarding school as well?'

Luke had been expecting this topic to surface, once Peter knew that John might be going to Bramsden College.

'That must be your decision, Peter. If you'd like to go then there's a place for you but you'd have to stick it out the whole time. There'd be no question of second thoughts after a term or two.'

A silence, then, 'What would you do in my place, Guv?'

'I'd ask myself why I even thought of the idea. If it's because John might go I'd ask myself if that's a good reason. I'd then look at how settled I am at my present school and weigh up the daily travelling as opposed to boarding. In other words, I'd decide what best suits me, never mind what others choose. Does that help?'

'A bit, Guv. I just want to do the right thing.'

'Of course you do and you're quite right to talk about it. Could be you're a home bird who doesn't like living away. Everyone's different and if the present arrangement suits you why change it?

A silence whilst Peter considered this, then, 'I think I'd miss everything here too much.'

'I think you would and I'd certainly miss you around the place. Wouldn't be the same at all.'

Peter said nothing but moved up close to Luke for a hug, as he sometimes would if no one else was around. His decision was made.

'There's something I want you to do, though. I want you to show John around your school so he can make his own decision. If I write a letter to your headmaster will you take him with you tomorrow and bring him back again in one piece?'

'John coming to my school?'

'Only to look. Just to see what he thinks of it.'

★ ★ ★

'John's father is asking for you, Guv. He's in the yard.'

'Mr Hurle. Good evening. How's the ploughing going?'

'Very well, I thank you, sir. Tis about that I've called. I've come across a few things you oughter see,' indicating the sack he held in his hand.

'Oh, well bring it in then, and we'll have a look. Come on through,' and he led the way into the back room, Peter hovering to see what it was all about.

Deferentially and uncomfortably, William Hurle followed Luke and, without prompting explained how the plough had snagged on something buried in the ground. He'd urged the horses on and a wooden box had appeared, which split, leaving a trail of objects behind the plough. He'd gathered up everything he could see and had brought them for Luke to inspect.

'Right. Tip 'em out on the table and we'll have a look.'

Spread out was a collection of table ware and utensils, rusty-bladed knives, two-pronged forks, metal plates and goblets, muddy and discoloured.

'This is interesting,' Luke said. 'Peter, take this plate out and scrub it clean for me, would you?' then picking up one of the goblets he rubbed the base firmly with his finger and saw an unmistakeable dull yellow. 'Could be gold,' he said. 'Mr Hurle, you're an honest man. Who knows of this besides us?'

'No one, sir. I've told no one, not even the missus.'

'Good. Tell no one. If word gets out the coroner'll be after it as treasure trove and that'll do none of us any good. Ah, thanks, Peter. Well, just look at that. Pewter with a gold inlaid rim and coat of arms. Very pretty and these knife and fork handles could be silver. I believe this style was in fashion about the time of the civil war. Possible someone buried the family plate to keep it from the other side. I wonder if it was once used in this house? It'd be nice to have it restored to use here. Now, I've trusted friends who'll give a fair valuation and ten percent is usual to the finder. We'll double it and make it twenty. How does that suit?'

William Hurle was completely at a loss. He mumbled, gurgled and finally managed to get out a 'Yes, sir, of course, sir. Hadn't expected that. Don't know what to say, rightly'.

'It'll give you a bit of capital to work with. Peter, whisky and glasses, please. We'll have a drink on this. Oh, and I believe John has decided on school at Guildford and live at home. A wise choice, I think.'

* * *

It was prize giving day once again at Bramsden College. Was it really twelve months since he last attended? It had to be of course but where had the time gone in between? In company with Fred, Luke was strolling around leisurely discussing this and that. Richard was off somewhere helping organise something in his capacity of monitor. Fred, Luke realised had grown considerably since they'd first met and had clearly taken to school life with enthusiasm. His talent as a cricketer had already earned him a regular place in the second team, well before others of his age.

At the fringe of other visitors, strolling with their sons, Luke was suddenly conscious of a slim, dark haired boy raising his cap to him. The lower school were now wearing caps all year round in place of top hats and boaters, which had become the privileged head gear of the upper school. Luke started to automatically raise his hat in polite acknowledgement when his attention was as suddenly caught by the lady with him. Dressed in pink, she made an immediate impression on him in a way he'd never experienced before.

'Oh, er, Paul,' he managed to get out, and offered his hand.

'Sir, may I introduce my mother, sir? Mother, this is Mr Gregory, who is one of the school governors.'

With his hat in one hand, Luke bowed and offered his other, to be politely and gently taken by the lady in pink.

'I'm delighted to meet you, Mrs Eugene. Paul and I, of course, are old friends.'

'And I am delighted to meet you, Mr Gregory. Paul has told me how helpful your ward has been to him since he started here. I really do appreciate this as I have often wondered if it was right for him to attend a boarding school. I so badly want him to have a good education, you see.'

'I think this school offers a very reasonable one,' Luke replied. 'Certainly, I am well satisfied with my boy's progress and Fred here is well settled. Allow me to introduce Frederick Parrish who is also my ward.'

Luke could not take his eyes off this lady and couldn't understand quite why. Of all the women in his life he'd never met anyone who had so fascinated him. She'd be in her early thirties, he thought, was slim, poised and obviously well educated. Refined, yes, with a carefully modulated voice, neither high nor low.

By convention he should now politely disengage himself with some meaningless pleasantry but he didn't want to. He wanted to stay and talk, but what about and how could he with these boys standing there, watching him curiously now. He pulled himself together and let convention rule and as they parted, he felt a most peculiar feeling in the pit of his stomach.

'Are you feeling all right, Guv?' Fred asked, concern in his voice. 'Can I get you a glass of water?'

'Oh, oh, no, thank you. No, I'm fine,' Luke managed to say and put his hat back on. This is ridiculous, he thought to himself, his mind in a whirl and by a great effort of will, he forced himself to recommence his conversation with Fred, something about the relative merits of various cricketing clubs and the vexed question of gentlemen and players that was arousing controversy. Should professionals really be allowed to represent the country or should the amateur gentlemen players retain this honour?

Luke's view, pragmatic as ever held that if winning was all important then the strongest players should form the team, no matter what their background. If winning didn't matter then let the idle rich amuse themselves as they pleased but somehow, the discussion had lost its appeal for both and Fred was glad to suddenly remember something he had to do. Luke was equally glad that he had done so and immediately cast about for a glimpse of the lady in pink.

★ ★ ★

'What's up, Guv? Something bothering you?' Digger asked. It was Monday morning and Luke, back at Gresham House, was standing looking out of the window, his usual spot when preoccupied with a problem.

'D'you reckon I'm too old to get married?'

For a moment, Digger was lost for words, so unexpected was the question. 'You, Guv? Get married?' he said, giving himself time to think. 'Course you ain't. If word gets around you'll 'ave 'arf o' London queuing at the door,' then sensing Luke's mood, he added, 'You're serious, ain't yer. Who's the lucky lady, then? She'll 'ave ter be dead special an' no mistake.'

'I believe she is,' Luke replied, turning away from the window and moving over to his armchair. 'I met her briefly on speech day. Must confess I've never felt anything like it. Might even have made a fool of myself. Mother of one of the pupils. Widow, I know that much, but nothing more.'

'And you'd like to learn a bit more. Want me to open a file on her?'

'Well, I'd hardly put it like that but yes, I'd very much like to know more.'

'Give me what you know and you shall have the answers. Tell Beth, can I?'

'Rather you didn't just yet,' Luke said, almost coyly. 'Rather be sure first. Uncharted waters you know.'

★ ★ ★

October already and Luke sat at the headmaster's desk at the Hall, now a preparatory school, and looked about him, supposing that he'd better have a look at books and records if he was to carry the responsibility until a successor was appointed. Damned inconvenient Horrell having a heart attack like that. Still, these things happened. There was a timid knock at the door.

'Come in,' Luke called and a small boy crept in, a folded piece of paper clutched in his inky hand. 'And what have we here?' Luke asked.

'Please sir, I have to give you this,' he whispered, tremulously.

Luke took the note and read it. 'This boy continues to make no effort in class. He is inattentive, lazy and untidy. His work is a disgrace.' It bore the initials J.B.

'Mr Bradley sent this?'

'Yes, sir,' the boy whispered, cringing.

'So what would Mr Horrell have done if you'd brought the note to him?'

'He'd beat me, sir.'

'Well, I'm not going to beat you, not for untidy work. Tell me, are you unwell? You don't look too good to me. Have you seen matron?'

'She sent me away, sir.'

'Well, we'd better go and find her and give it another try. Ah, Mrs Harvey. This young man doesn't look at all well.'

'Oh, he's always complaining. If it's not one thing it's another and I don't encourage them to waste my time. I'm quite busy enough as it is.'

Luke's surprise must have shown. 'But as matron you're responsible for the well being of the boys, Mrs Harvey. He shouldn't be in class if he's unwell.'

'He'll get over it whatever it is,' Mrs Harvey replied carelessly and held on to a chair back to steady herself.

'Have you been drinking? You have. I can smell it on your breath. What do you think you're about, madam? You're not fit for your position. Pack your bags and leave. Now. You're dismissed. Not a word. Take the next train out,' as Mrs Harvey began to whimper then changed to indignant but slurred protests.

Luke was irritated beyond measure by this state of affairs. Parents were paying for an education for their sons and for their adequate care but there didn't appear to be much of that from what he'd seen. Looking in at the matron's room he saw a young woman in white apron and cap standing near a rack of shelves, holding items of clothing.

'You are whom?' he asked, abruptly, still simmering down.

'Miss Tidy, sir. The assistant matron.'

'Well this boy appears unwell. What do you think?'

'I think he should be in bed, sir. He is often unwell and has no appetite at all.'

'Then please see to it and send down for the doctor. Let me know when he arrives.'

'Yes, sir. I'll need clean bedding and things sir, if you'll excuse me.'

'Of course. Tell me. Could you cope with the matron's duties? Mrs Harvey is leaving, as you probably heard.'

'Oh, yes sir. I know what to do, sir '

'Very well. You are acting matron from now on, on one month's trial.'

★ ★ ★

'So, Doctor. What do you think?'

'I think he is extremely unwell and if we're not careful we'll lose him.'

'Bad as that?'

'Yes. He has a very unsteady heartbeat, swollen glands and a throat infection and I believe he suffers from some kind of blood deficiency. Hard to tell what, exactly.'

'So what do you recommend?'

'Complete bed rest and careful nursing for a start. He needs building up. He's very small and frail for his age. Can't think why on earth he should have been beaten as he has. Enough to kill him.'

'Really? That bad?'

'Yes. That bad. Now I don't know whether you will allow this but I should like him to have at least one glass of red wine every day. Two if he'll take it.'

'If that's what you prescribe that's what the patient shall have. Any particular vintage?'

'No, seriously, sir. I believe it could well be of help.'

'I am being serious. Don't bother with wine much myself. Prefer beer or cider so you must tell me what to get.'

'Oh, sorry. A heavy red would be best. Port even, if you can run to that.'

'No problem. It'll be up within the hour. Now, I should like you to examine every boy in the school. Can you make a start with the younger ones? There are thirty-eight on roll. I just hope nothing else like this shows up. We'll use Matron's room I think. Miss Tidy here is Matron now and she'll call you early in any case of illness in the future.

The examination revealed an excessive use of the cane throughout the school and in each case it was the former headmaster, Bertram Horrell who had wielded it.

'The man must have been a sadist,' Luke commented to the doctor. 'How on earth he came to be appointed I cannot think. We'll have to be more careful next time.'

His first task after lunch then was to write to the head of Bramsden College informing him of the current state of affairs. It was, after all, on his recommendation that Horrell was appointed. Was it because the school had opened too quickly and insufficient care had been taken over staff appointments? There'd been no shortage of applications for placements, which might have encouraged too early a start.

Three o'clock signalled the end of afternoon school and Luke assembled the four assistant masters in a classroom.' Gentlemen I'm extremely unhappy at what I find in the school. I have today seen the evidence of excessive use of the birch and a disregard for the health of the boys. Mrs Harvey has left and Miss Tidy is now acting matron. Mr Jessop, I wish you to assume the role of acting head as far as teaching is concerned whilst I shall take responsibility for administration and all matters of discipline within the school.

There are other areas that displease me and I don't intend that today's disgusting mess shall ever again appear in the dining hall. If I'm wanted, Mr Jessop, send a boy down to the Manor, will you? I shall be in by eight o'clock in the morning, otherwise. Oh, and Eames-Johnson is confined to bed. He is seriously unwell. I think that is all for the moment, thank you,' and Luke left the room to go in search of the yard boy to bring the pony and trap to the front door.

★ ★ ★

All appeared well ordered when Luke stepped inside the Hall next morning. Doubtless everyone was anxious to avoid further upset, though Mr Jessop hastened to meet him.

'The only misbehaviour we have had was from Townley, Mr Gregory. He is a very unruly boy and has been punished for wild behaviour several times. He also bullies smaller boys.'

'Thank you Mr Jessop. I'll speak to him after assembly.' and Luke made his way to the study to make a start on looking through the books and records. A knock at the door. 'Come in,' and a boy crept through the doorway. Don't suppose any of them like coming in here, he, thought.

'Yes? What can I do for you?'

'I've been sent to you, sir.'

'Name?'

'Townley, sir.'

'Ah yes. Mr Jessop describes you as wild, unruly and a bully. What do you say to that?'

'Yes, sir,' looking at the floor.

'Oh. You agree.'

'What's your first name?'

'Adrian, sir,' a note of surprise in his voice.

'And you are how old?'

'Eleven, sir.'

'Eleven, eh? You're a big lad for your age. Now, wild and unruly behaviour doesn't worry me as much as bullying. Bullies are nasty, unpleasant people. They make life miserable for others and they need to be stopped. Bullying is one offence for which I'm prepared to beat you in front of the school. I will not tolerate bullying of any kind. Do you understand?'

'Yes, sir,' a frightened note to his voice.

'I want your solemn promise that you will never again bully smaller, younger or weaker boys. Do I have it?'

'Yes, sir,' anxiously.

'Very well. We'll say no more about it but break your word and you know what's in store. Now, tell me about your wild and unruly behaviour.'

'I don't know what to say, sir.'

'I'm not surprised. It was a difficult question. Where is home? Where do you come from?'

'Godalming, sir.'

'And what is your family interest? What does your father do?'

'I haven't got one, sir.'

'But I've seen somewhere Major and Mrs Townley written down.'

'He's not my real father, sir. That's why he doesn't want me at home.'

'Oh, I see. That's not very pleasant for you. Do you know where your real father is?'

'No, sir,' and he turned his head away as the tears started.

'So you're not wanted at home. I didn't wish to upset you but I need to know why you present problems. There's usually a reason, if we can find it. Tell me. Do you go home for holidays?'

'No, sir. I have to stay here, sir.'

'Why is that, do you think?'

'I'm unclean, sir. I'm a disgrace to the family, sir.'

'Unclean? Can you explain? I don't understand.'

'I'm illegitimate, sir.'

'Well, that's not your fault. You didn't ask to be born and I find that viewpoint ridiculous. No one should have to apologise for that even in this supposedly Christian country. No, it's more important what you achieve in life not where you start from. I've no idea who my family are though I was told someone called Gregory led the mutiny at Spithead. Might have been a relative. There again, maybe not. My partner started at the bottom of the heap and now has the Prince of Wales amongst his friends, we're both comfortably off and happy with life so you must look to your own worth and not be discouraged if someone cries you down.'

Adrian was looking hard at Luke now, puzzled but hopeful, Luke thought.

'So, what can we do to help cheer you up and start enjoying life?'

'I don't know, sir.'

'Well, for a start, there'll be a new headmaster here before long and he'll be very different from the last one because I'm going to appoint him. I'm no schoolmaster. I just happen to own this place. Secondly, if you're here during holiday times, perhaps you might like to stay with me at the Manor. What do you think?'

'Oh, yes please, sir. I'd love to come.'

'Very well but I don't want to hear any more complaints of bad behaviour. Understand?'

'Yes sir. Thank you ever so much, sir.'

'Very well and if I get a good report from Mr Jessop you can visit after church on Sunday. Maybe stay the night and come in on Monday morning. Now off and wash your face and back into class.'

Luke sat for a while then, just pondering, the accounts book open before him, neglected. Were prep schools dumping grounds for unwanted offspring? The workhouse for the lower orders and prep schools for the better off? Possible but this wasn't his trade, though he was looking to profit from it but there'd have to be better safeguards against things going wrong so who'd share the burden? The Rector and Doctor Fairleigh. That was it. Both would be press ganged into becoming governors, but he'd have the place run his way.

★ ★ ★

'So, young man, you're on the mend I see. The doctor recommends a period of convalescence and the best place for that is at the Manor, I think.'

James looked up at him and gave him a shy smile but said nothing. He was a small boy, slim and dark haired with big solemn brown eyes. Give him time and he'll liven up, Luke thought but he really wasn't robust enough for the rough and tumble of prep school life. It would be for the best if he lived at the Manor and went up to school at the Hall by day.

That way he might live long enough to make it to Bramsden. After all, his parents were paying the school and he had a financial interest there. Must look after the stock, be they sheep or scholars. You mercenary hound, Gregory, he thought to himself but, when you came to think of it, what was the difference, really? Schools made a profit from pupils and farmers made one from livestock. Any way, here was Peter in from school, dropping his satchel on the floor and flopping down next to him on the settle.

'Good day at school?'

'Not too bad, Guv. Got loads of prep, though.'

'This is James. William'll be down on Friday so I'm wondering where best to put him.

'He can come in with me, Guv. There's room for another bed if I squeeze up a bit.'

'That's good of you. I want him to stay until he's really well and he could do with a bit of company 'til he's used to us. That suit? And call me Guv when you're here; same as the others. I shall have to write to your parents for their permission, of course and for you to spend holidays here, but do you not wish you'd gone to India with them?'

'The doctor said it wouldn't be safe for me to go because I get ill quickly.'

'In which case we must take extra care of you. Now, do you both think you could go and see how you'll arrange the beds for tonight? I need to talk to George and I'll have a look at your prep when you're ready, Peter. See if we can't make short work of it.'

★ ★ ★

Digger had set his enquiry specialists looking for the lady in pink and now had the answers to most questions. He found Luke attentive and, he thought, strangely vulnerable. 'Well, Guv, the lady is certainly one to respect,' he stated. 'Widow, as yer know. Bin that way nearly three years now. Not well off but maintaining standards and appearances. Lives in a rented house at Portsmouth. Respectable area. Clean and tidy but not much furniture.

Offers dressmaking and piano lessons. One girl of seven and a boy of ten at home. Son at school as you know. No other family to speak of. Late husband's relations don't want ter know, so far as we can tell. There's a brother in Norfolk; clergyman 'e is but not much contact so far as is known.'

'Mm,' Luke said. 'So where do I go from here, I wonder?'

'Why not visit?'.

'Visit? No, no, couldn't do that. Not just turn up on the doorstep. Wouldn't feel right. Mightn't be welcome.'

The Guv, Digger could tell, was quite unusually at sea. Adrift without a rudder, would be his description of someone else's predicament. 'Like me and Beth to call round? Break the ice, sort o' thing? Tell the lady ter watch out fer a strange man with 'orrible intentions?'

'Would you?' Luke was on the edge of his chair. 'You wouldn't mind? You don't think Beth would mind?'

'Come off it, Guv! You know us better than that. As if we'd mind, I arsk you. We'll go first thing in the morning if Beth's got nothing else fixed up.'

So Digger and Beth visited number forty-one Montrose Avenue, a fairly new suburban development of small, semi-detached houses with bay windows and tiny front gardens protected by low walls and iron railings. Giving a gentle rap with the brightly polished brass door knocker, Digger stood back and exchanged glances with Beth. 'Here goes,' he said. 'Get ready ter run if she's got a rolling pin in 'er 'and.'

But Mrs Eugene answered the door without the encumbrance of offensive weaponry and Digger politely raised his bowler hat and introduced himself. 'Mrs Eugene?' he enquired. 'Our name is O'Dowd and we wondered if we might talk with you about someone you met recently. How's that for starters?' he asked Beth, turning to her with his infectious grin.

'It'll do,' Beth replied, laughing. 'Mrs Eugene, you'll find this all a bit odd I don't doubt but you recently impressed a confirmed old bachelor who's too shy to call on you so we've come instead. How's that for a bit more?' Beth asked her husband.

'We're getting there,' Digger replied. 'We don't do this sort of thing every day of the week, so we're having to feel our way and hope you don't set the dogs on us.'

Grace Eugene looked at Beth and Digger in bemused fashion, intrigued, curious and doubtful but reassured by their well dressed appearance.

'Won't you come in?' she invited and ushered them into the front room, one seldom used but maintained as a shrine to respectability. 'May I take your coats?' and conventionally relieved of their outer garments, they all sat down and looked at each other.

'It's like this,' both Digger and Beth said together then burst out laughing. 'Go on, you do the talking, Diggs,' Beth decided and he explained how they came on behalf of Luke Gregory, one of the school governors she had recently met on prize-giving day. Described how he was the guv's business partner and how well they both knew him and how he couldn't bring himself to call on her without her agreement.

'Well, I really don't know what to say,' Mrs Eugene said, showing her gratified confusion. 'I certainly recall meeting Mr Gregory but I had no idea I had created any kind of impression. May I offer you coffee, or tea, if you would prefer?' as much a ploy to gain time to think as displaying hospitality.

Coffee poured and passed round, Beth suggested she tell more about their confirmed bachelor describing how Luke went to sea as a boy and worked his way up and was now wealthy if a bit unconventional. 'He's as tough as old boots but you'll never find a kinder one. Do anything for anyone, won't he Diggs,' she finished up.

'Certainly will. No side to 'im at all. Success never went to 'is 'ead and we've been successful all right. He's got a place in the country and another in the City but 'e's always reckoned he wasn't the marrying kind. He's got a son though and some might not think him respectable because of it, but there we are,' he shrugged.

Mrs Eugene's face showed her continued bemusement and also her interest in what she was hearing. There might well be the possibility of escaping her present difficult circumstances and the thought that someone found her attractive and interesting was profoundly flattering. Nevertheless, she was not prepared to rush blindly into any arrangement, though she had been favourably impressed by Luke at that first meeting.

'Mr Gregory realises that I have a family,' she said.

'Well yes,' Digger said, 'but that doesn't worry 'im. He's got four others, all 'is wards. Treats 'em like his own. Ready made families are no problem and there's plenty of room at the Manor and there's always the stable if things get crowded.'

'Oh, get on Diggs,' Beth put in, 'It's never come to that yet.'

'Yes, I recall meeting two boys at the school who were both his wards. One was an Indian boy, I believe.'

'That's Fred. The guv met 'is father when 'e was at sea. Agent for the company in India 'e is and Fred spends school holidays at the Manor. One of the family now.'

'That sounds wonderful.'

'Ah, the guv's like that. Got one or two others running around there as well, from the prep school in the village. Easy going 'e is unless he's annoyed. Then it pays ter watch yer step.

'So would you allow the guv to call on you, Mrs Eugene?' Beth asked, returning to the reason for their visit.

'I should be most happy for him to do so. Do you know when that might be?'

'When would be convenient?'

'I, I would be happy for Mr Gregory to call at any time, I'm sure.'

'Then what about tomorrow, Wednesday. Same time suit? It would? Right. We'll send 'im down all clean and tidy and on 'is best behaviour.'

★ ★ ★

Chapter 10

Luke had never felt so nervous in his life. He was terrified of making a fool of himself and admitted to not really knowing what to do, probably because he didn't feel in charge and able to arrange things to suit himself. Beth had given him his instructions but he still felt ill at ease, the more so as he rapped with the knocker on the door of number forty-one. His bouquet of flowers felt awkward and he changed them from one hand to the other and prepared to raise his hat as the door opened.

'Good morning, Mrs Eugene. It really is a pleasure to meet you again.'

'And good morning to you, Mr Gregory. It really is most kind of you to call. Won't you come in?'

With those first, awkward formalities over, Luke started to relax, as did Mrs Eugene who had been in a state of excited turmoil ever since Beth and Digger had departed the previous day. That someone like Luke should suddenly appear in her life was such a momentous occurrence that she was hard put to believe it and her other two children, Louise and Julian, were both mystified and curious about their mother's barely suppressed excitement.

'I hope not too grim a picture was painted yesterday,' Luke said. 'I'm well aware that many would not consider me particularly respectable.'

'You need have no fear of that, Mr Gregory. Your envoys are clearly very fond of you and were also very frank with me, which I appreciate.'

'I suppose we are quite close, yes, and I certainly wouldn't wish to mislead you in any way whatever. As Digger probably told you, I divide my time between the City and the Manor, which I consider to be home.'

'Yes, he did explain that. He also told me of your domestic arrangements. I understand you have quite a family already.'

'Oh, well yes. It all sort of evolved. There's Richard, my eldest, whom you met at the school and Fred of course. Peter, who's at school in Guildford as a day scholar, his sister Lucy and her friend Annabelle. Her mother recently passed away so it seemed a natural sort of arrangement. Then of course, there's my son William, who spends the week with Beth and Digger and comes home at weekends. I never married, as you are aware.'

'I do not find that shocking, Mr Gregory. Social convention is so often shallow and yes, hypocritical. I find some of the kindest people are those who do not slavishly pursue conformity. You paint a picture of happy tolerance and kindness of which you are probably unaware.'

'I suppose I seek to sail before the wind whenever possible.

'You have, of course, met Paul at school. May I ask how you found him?'

'A delightfully sincere young man most anxious to please his mother. He recognises the sacrifices you are making to keep him at school and is desperate not to let you down.'

'May I ask how you know this, Mr Gregory?'

'I'm not at liberty to enlarge upon it but you will recall I am a governor.'

'I sense a mystery but I will not pry,' Mrs Eugene said, smiling, and went on to speak of her other children who were at school. Julian was inclined to be difficult, the sort of boy who needed a father whilst Louise was quiet, too quiet sometimes and she found herself over concerned for them at times.

'You're bound to be concerned. Bringing up a family alone is quite a responsibility. I've always enjoyed help with my efforts. Goodness only knows how I would've coped without it. I wonder, would you care to visit me this weekend? See the Manor and have a look around? Bring your children, of course unless you think me presumptuous on so short an acquaintanceship.'

'You are not at all presumptuous, Mr Gregory, just very kind. I should be delighted to visit. The children will be absolutely thrilled, I know. Unfortunately we do not go out very much and never away so this really will be exciting for them. Will you be able to meet them before you leave? I have prepared luncheon for us so there is an excuse to stay.'

So gradually, they broke the ice, sounding each other out, exchanging views and opinions, sometimes formal and stilted, sometimes in more relaxed fashion. So long did they linger over lunch that they were still seated at the table when Julian and Louise returned from school and both stood staring at Luke in surprise until their mother made the introductions and told them of the coming weekend visit. They were polite and cautious with Julian never taking his eyes off Luke and resisting all attempts at conversation. Louise was more forthcoming and shyly asked, 'Are we going to stay all night?'

'Yes. That's the general idea. You won't mind that, will you?' and she shook her head. 'I usually travel down with William by the four ten from Waterloo. We change at Guildford and arrive at Chidlingbrook by half past five. How would it be if we met at Waterloo and travelled down together? I'll arrange tickets, of course.'

'That sounds absolutely splendid,' Mrs Eugene said. 'We shall really look forward to our visit,' with which Luke took his leave and set out on his return journey to the City, strangely satisfied and not a little excited. He liked what he'd found and was fairly certain his interest was favourably returned.

★ ★ ★

William, now a confident eight year old, came rushing up the stairs on the Friday afternoon to be picked up, whirled around and plonked down on Luke's lap. This had become something of a ritual and he animatedly told of everything he'd done that week. Then Luke had to tell what he'd been up to even though they often met up during the week. It was a happy arrangement that worked well, with weekends spent at the Manor, often with Rory and Lizzie joining them.

'We have visitors this weekend,' Luke told him and William's face fell. He was slow to accept change and disliked interruptions to his routine. 'I'm sure you'll like them,' Luke reassured him and described Mrs Eugene and family. 'We'll meet them at Waterloo and you shall show them our train and which will be our seats. They don't go on trains very often so you'll have to help them,' which responsibility appeared to please William.

Charlie took them then to the station in good time to catch the four-ten train to Guildford and Luke soon spotted Mrs Eugene on the concourse. All were dressed in their best clothes and Luke hoped that Julian and Louise had with them older clothes that would allow them to enjoy the freedom of the grounds without too much restraint.

Introductions made and William, well versed now in such formalities shook hands all round and said how pleased he was to meet them and hoped they would enjoy their visit. 'Our train is at platform three,' he confidently explained. 'Papa has reserved a compartment. Would you like me to show you?' and he importantly led the way, Luke and Mrs Eugene exchanging smiles while Louise looked pleased and Julian glowered.

At Chidlingbrook, they walked from the station in company with Peter, who usually took the same train, and Luke deliberately entered by the back door, determined to avoid any pretentious show. Everything appeared as he expected with Mrs Cherry by her cooking range, the table covered with her cakes and puddings and Lucy, Annabelle and James happily making teatime inroads.

Introductions made and bags dumped in the hall, Luke settled his visitors round the table, explaining that this was snack time and dinner would be at seven o'clock. A tour of the house next with everyone joining in, visitors shown to their rooms and Luke settled himself by the fire in the hall with William on one side and James on the other. Julian though, maintained a truculent stance throughout his stay though Peter tried hard to encourage a more cheerful involvement but without success, much to Mrs Eugene's embarrassment.

'I really am so sorry, Mr Gregory. I just cannot understand him at all.'

'Not to worry. Who knows what goes through a boy's mind. Just give him time and he'll come round,' at least he hoped so as he walked slowly back to the Manor after seeing his visitors off at the station on the Sunday afternoon.

He'd enjoyed the weekend. He did indeed like Grace Eugene and found her very pleasant company. He liked her daughter Louise and of course, he knew Paul but what of Julian? Would he want that young man as a responsibility? He'd done his utmost, it seemed, to ruin his family's visit and had certainly upset his mother by his behaviour. What, he wondered, lay behind it? Thomas. That's it. He'd offer an explanation. Yes, he'd have a word with Tom Barnardo.

There was no need however, for an explanation arrived in a letter of apology from Mrs Eugene who again expressed her regret at her son's disappointing conduct. Once home, she had sought an explanation and he had erupted hysterically.

'You're going to get married, I know you are and I don't like him. He's not my father and he'll beat me,' and he'd rushed from the room.

So, that was it. Looked like he'd have to sort something out if he wanted a peaceful courtship and that, Luke realised was what he did want. Yes, he'd like to marry Grace. Of that he was certain, provided she'd have him, set in his ways as he undoubtedly was. He'd have to do a bit of adapting. Wouldn't be able to make all his own decisions, not without discussion first. He didn't think William would mind, secure as they were in their relationship and Peter and Lucy would scarce be affected. Annabelle not at all, unless to her benefit.

Accommodation though. He'd have to give thought to that for he'd like to keep his end of the house as it was and ideally, offer the other end to his wife to be for her own private rooms. The answer? Offer George and Mrs Cherry a cottage on a site of their choosing. Quieter, more privacy, their own place. What could be better?

Now, would a weekend house party be an idea? Digger, Beth and Roddy to play the piano. Who else now? Grace and family of course. He'd set Digger on Julian. If he couldn't manage a change of heart there really would be a problem. It'd be a full house but with the Home Farm set up for guests they'd have room enough.

Never having been one to entertain or fuss over visitors Luke was now organising an 'occasion', much to his household's bemusement. That great banqueting table out in the backroom would go back in the hall. Dark oak, solid as a three deck ship of the line and at least a couple of hundred years old with its great bulbous carved legs. Impressive without a doubt and there'd be seating for all with room to spare and that Mrs Dawson proved helpful in the kitchen, if he remembered rightly. Been in service at some time so she might like to lend a hand. Mrs Cherry would say and Beth was sure to pitch in and set the girls to help. What else did he need to think of? He really did want things to go well. That was it. He wanted to impress, to put on a show, and why not?

★ ★ ★

And a lively weekend it turned out to be. Like a shindig down the warehouse, Digger thought. A bit more respectable perhaps, with not much sitting around but that was how Luke liked it. Primed before hand, Digger set about Julian but with little success. The glowering expression remained as before and he confided his puzzlement. 'Something wrong there, Guv. Got a spiteful side I don't much care for.'

'I just cannot understand the way he is behaving,' his mother said.

'I'd hoped Digger would manage a change of heart. He's certainly tried hard. Ah well, we'll see. Worn out, Beth?'

'Not quite, Guv. I'm good for a couple o' rounds yet. There's more fun to be had in this house than anywhere else I know,' she said. 'Our place is quiet as a church compared.'

'You'd best take Adrian back with you then. He'd break your peace and quiet.'

'He knows how to enjoy himself and no mistake. I think I'll leave him with you. He'd miss you. Thinks you're the best thing since steam engines were invented.'

'I'm just astonished at everything I see and hear,' Grace put in. 'There is such a wonderful atmosphere.'

'You approve then?' Luke asked 'Wouldn't get you down after a while?'

'I certainly do approve and no it wouldn't get me down, at all,' she trailed off, suddenly conscious of what Luke might be asking.

'Will you marry me then?'

Grace clutched involuntarily at her throat at the suddenness of the proposal then gathered her wits. 'I most certainly will. You wonderful, wonderful man.'

'Well done, Guv,' Beth said and gave him a kiss and Grace another. 'Just what I've been waiting to hear for years. I'll get Digger to announce it.'

Arm in arm, Luke and Grace were immediately the centre of noisy interest with cheers and congratulations all round, with the exception of Julian.

Digger, seeing him standing apart and looking glum, went over to him. 'It's the best thing could happen,' he assured him. 'My word on it. Come on over. He won't bite yer,' and he led the reluctant Julian over to where his mother and Luke stood smiling together. 'Ere, Guv. Someone wants ter shake yer 'and,' relapsing into his riverside speech. 'Come on,' to Julian. 'E's pleased as Punch to 'ave yer in 'is family, ain't yer, Guv?'

'I most certainly am,' Luke said and held out his hand. Reluctantly, Julian shook hands but his expression of disapproval was plain for all to see.

★ ★ ★

They would have to tell Paul, of course and Richard and Fred but would it be better to write or to visit? They decided to visit and travelled down together, Grace conscious of the handsome diamond ring on her finger, meeting first with the headmaster, who offered his congratulations and good wishes.

For Luke, it was not a daunting task and he light heartedly told Richard and Fred that he was to marry and while Fred was smilingly accepting, Richard looked thoughtful.

'Does that make Eugene a sort of relative?' he wondered.

'No, not a relative,' Luke told him, 'just a fellow resident at the Manor. It'll take some getting used to, but it needn't affect you in the slightest and you'll decide for yourselves what sort of relationship you have with Mrs Gregory.'

'But you'll be his stepfather, won't you, Guv?'

'Yes, so he'll be more likely to get a clip round the ear than either of you,' which made them smile.

For Grace Eugene it was a more delicate task, or so she felt and approached the subject diffidently. 'Paul, I wonder what you would think were I to marry again,' which came as such a surprise he was unable to answer straight away as he tried to weigh up the implications.

'I, I, well, mama, of course, if it is what you wish you must do so but it is so unexpected. I hadn't really thought about it, that you might remarry, I mean.'

'Of course you hadn't dear. It is all quite sudden but you will remember introducing me to one of the school governors on speech day?'

'You mean, not Travers' governor? Oh, mama, that is wonderful, truly wonderful. You really mean it? You are going to marry him?'

'You wouldn't mind, dear?'

'Mind? Of course I wouldn't mind. I owe him so much. I wouldn't be here now if it wasn't for him.'

Mrs Eugene looked at her son in astonishment. 'Paul, I am so pleased that you approve but I really do not understand. Is there something I should know?'

'Yes, mama, there is. I was told I should forget all about it and start afresh,' and he related his earlier unhappy predicament

'Oh, Paul. That is the most wonderful story I have ever heard. I think we both have so much to be thankful for.'

There were happy handshakes all round then as they looked at each other and wondered what changes might follow. They would, of course, all meet up that next weekend at the Manor for a first full family get together, another house party, in effect and Luke felt himself looking forward to it with pleasurable anticipation.

★ ★ ★

The weekend started well enough when William, Rory and Lizzie burst whooping and chattering into the kitchen, followed by Digger and Beth.

'Look, Papa. I made this for you,' William announced. 'You can write all your important things in it,' and he proudly produced a scribbling pad sewn together with string, the cover decorated with a circus clown hand coloured with crayon.

'You made this all by yourself? For me? Well that is clever of you and most kind,' and he gave his little boy another hug. 'Grace'll be down on the next train and the boys too I expect. Bit of a house full but we'll manage.'

'Well, if anyone can cope, Guv it's you,' Digger said.

'It's Mrs Cherry has the coping to do. I still don't know how she manages, do you George?'

'Oh, it's having a steady 'usband behind her, that's the secret,' George said.

'Is it indeed, George Cherry. I'll have you know it's because I'm well organised and don't allow idle layabouts to hinder me. Come along. I need this table clearing. I can't get on if I've no room.'

'We'll leave you to it, George,' Digger said, grinning widely.

William, still wanting Luke's attention, held his hand as they moved from the kitchen to the hall, where Luke settled in his usual spot, William on his lap.

'That blonde lad's not short of energy the way he's racing around. Is he ever still?' Digger asked as he joined Luke by the fire.

'He is in the kitchen. One healthy appetite I'm told. Mrs Cherry believes he has hollow legs.'

'There's no one better to fill 'em. Fancy a problem?'

'Go on.'

'His nibs needs to leave town fer a bit. Wants to leave, actually. He's under a bit of pressure one way and another and he's not feeling too well. Any chance of a quiet week here?'

'He's welcome if he takes us as he finds us. I'm not laying on anything special for him, entertainment wise. Author of his own problems, that one. When does he want to come?'

'Soon as you say, Guv. He'll make it worth your while.'

'If he comes, it's as my guest and he takes whatever I throw at him. Anyway, I owe him for that business with Richard.'

'Good on yer, Guv. Early next week? Give yer chance to clear the house a bit.'

'Not coming with a gang, is he?'

'Alone,' Digger replied. 'Just a valet. Seems he wants a break from his hangers on. Can't say I blame 'im, either. Some of 'em are pretty rum types despite their titles. I'll come down with him with a couple of the lads to keep the curious away. I've a decoy the spitting image so the news hounds'll be in one direction chasing a coat of arms whilst we take a four seater in the other.'

'Sounds good. Wearing what he stands up in, is he?'

'A couple of trunks'll come down beforehand.'

'All worked out, eh?'

'As ever, Guv,' Digger grinned.

'Shall have to move myself out, I suppose. Give him my end.'

'Hadn't thought of that Guv, sorry.'

'No problem. I can sling a hammock anywhere and get a night's sleep.'

★ ★ ★

'If you want Mrs Dawson full time, Mrs Cherry that's fine by me,' Luke told his ever bustling cook cum housekeeper. On the go from six o'clock that morning, she had been organising a continuous breakfast, starting with Richard, Fred, Paul and Peter, who were following the hunt that morning.

Everyone, Luke decided, would, follow their own inclinations and do as they pleased until dinner time, planned for seven o'clock that evening. For himself, he had Grace to spend time with and together they strolled about arm in arm, talking and planning, deciding how the house would be run once George and Mrs Cherry had moved into their cottage at the end of the orchard and finally deciding that their wedding would be a quiet affair in the anonymity of St James' Church at Rotherhythe, with only immediate family and friends present.

Returning to the house for tea and scones by the fire, Luke was feeling pleasantly relaxed and happy with life, unaware of tensions building elsewhere. All had appeared peaceful as he and Grace had strolled around. Small boys were jumping into piles of hay and straw or running around the river bank throwing stones into the water and the girls had gone looking for wood mushrooms and flowers to pick.

Then William, with tear-streaked face was seeking Luke's attention.

'Julian pushed me over and I've hurt my hand,' he complained.

'Getting a bit rough out there are we?' Luke suggested unconcernedly as he examined a grazed and grubby hand. 'I think a good wash and a bandage is called for,' he decided but William seemed unimpressed.

'He said things to me and Adrian said he shouldn't.'

'Oh and what did he say?'

'He said I'm a bastard and he called me Bill the bastard and bastard Bill and he wouldn't stop so Adrian hit him and then he said I'll get you and Adrian ran off back to school 'cus he said you'd be cross with him and I don't like Julian.'

Luke and Grace sat silent and shocked at this recital then Luke covered his eyes with his hand and muttered 'Oh God!' but it was Grace who reacted positively.

'Oh William I am so sorry you have hurt your hand. We'll go and clean it up and put something on it,' and leading William away left Luke to make his own decision.

'Trust something to come along and spoil things,' he muttered to himself, rose to his feet and made for the back door to see how things were, puzzled at how someone of that age could say such things.

The boys were back from riding and were off-saddling and rubbing the ponies down in the yard, with Joseph keeping a discrete but critical eye on things. James was standing alone by the stable door looking pale and anxious. Of Julian there was no sign.

'Have a good day?' he asked the horsemen'

'Fine, thanks Guv. Only saw one fox and I think he got away,' Richard replied.

'I think Paul wants a cushion next time,' Peter joked

'I'm not used to riding,' that young man confessed ruefully, 'but it was good fun.'

'Alright Jimmy?' to James who nodded and gave an uncertain smile.

'Is William better?' he asked nervously, coming closer.

'Oh, he'll live,' Luke replied, wondering what was coming next.

'He was ever so horrid to William and he hadn't done anything at all. He's not a nice boy and I don't like him.'

'Who's that then? Julian?'

'Yes, sir. He pushed him over and said nasty things to him and he wouldn't stop until Adrian made him.'

'That's right, Guv, if I may say something,' Joseph put in. 'Horrible he were. 'Ad to stop 'im chucking stones at the chickens and 'e kicked the dog as well. Really got it on 'im 'e 'ad.'

'I see. Where is he now?'

'Ran off round the back when 'e got thumped. Served 'im right too, if you don't mind me saying so. Deserved it proper 'e did.'

'I see. Well I'd better find him and hear what he's got to say for himself.'

The young man in question was standing in the corner of the cart shed when Luke appeared and to his experienced eye a good, solid punch had been landed with blood still oozing from Julian's nose.

'You need cold water on that. It'll stop the bleeding. Come on up to the stable.'

'I'll get even for this. I'm going to tell my mother,' with heavy emphasis on the 'mother.' I hate this place and I hate everyone in it.'

'Well thank you for that but if you're half a man you'll get yourself cleaned up first, then we shall all be interested in your side of the story. Always two sides to everything so come on up to the stable and clean up.'

Julian though had no intention of tidying himself up and went in immediate search of his mother to complain of being brutally assaulted by that oaf from the school who has no business being here in this house and so on.

Grace though, with set and determined face took her erring son by the scruff of his neck and marched him into the cloakroom where, by the howls of protest he was subjected to mopping up operations of a not too sensitive nature. Been there before, Luke thought as he and William watched Julian being bundled upstairs with his braces dangling and minus his blood-stained shirt and jacket. Father and son looked at each other and grinned.

'I just don't know how to apologise enough,' Grace said when she returned downstairs alone. 'I have never been so ashamed in my life. I never thought it possible that any child of mine could behave in such a reprehensible manner. What you must think of my family I cannot imagine. Poor William to have such things said to him and in his own home too. I feel utterly humiliated and the only thing I can do is to leave on the next train.'

'Oh, no need for that, my dear. We're big enough to rise above such things are we not Billy Boy?' giving William a squeeze.

'But I cannot possibly stay with Julian in his present mood. He will not be satisfied until he has ruined the whole stay for everyone.'

'Then he mustn't be allowed to ruin things. How would it be if he spent the evening at the prep school, up at the Hall. He'd be quite safe there amongst the other boys and would be supervised by the teaching staff. If he slept there he could join you at the station in time for your train tomorrow. Who knows, he might even enjoy himself.'

'Well, I don't know. Do you think he could? It certainly would be a solution and it would be a shame for Louise to leave early. She is so enjoying herself.'

'Then consider it settled. As soon as Richard and Paul have tidied up they can escort me to the Hall. William, would you ask Joseph to harness up the trap, please?'

'You crafty old so and so,' Digger said, chuckling. 'We heard about that unpleasant little feller. Rory said they all kept out of his way because he was spoiling their games. Something wrong with 'im and no mistake.'

'Can't say I'm looking forward to having him on board full time but if it gets too bad I can always swap him for one of Thomas's lads. Couldn't have the little ray of sunshine spoiling the evening as well. Never met anyone like it before. Causing his mother no end of upset as well. It's never normal.'

'Well, with him out of the way we should have a decent evening of it and if ever I saw spaniel eyes fixed on you it's that fair 'aired one.'

'Had to put things right, you know. Thanked him for standing up for William like that. Got the makings of a good lad that one. Now who's this? Ah, Mr Pike.'

★ ★ ★

HRH arrived on the Tuesday a little before midday, accompanied by a valet, Digger and two of his men. He looked grey and tired and a lot older than his forty or so years. Luke met him outside the front door and formally bid him welcome.

'I'm most grateful to you Gregory. I feel the need for a little peace and quiet. Been overdoing things lately I think.'

'We can certainly offer you peace and quiet, sir,' Luke replied. 'Come along in. Your room is ready. Er, all folks know is that a Mr Wales is visiting. Something in the City. Quite influential so the Guv is putting himself out a little. Just a little, mind.'

Digger laughed and HRH joined in.

'Capital, capital,' he said. 'I feel brighter all ready. Oh, and I must thank you for er, seeing to that wretched man Brown. No more than he deserved and flying a pair of his tartan drawers from the castle flagpole was masterly. Caused no end of uproar mind, but no one knew anything at all. I understand the merest mention of washing on the line is sufficient to send him into paroxysms of rage. Splendid. Absolutely splendid.'

Coffee by the log fire, introductions to members of the household, luncheon, a nap on his bed and HRH was looking for distraction.

'May I suggest a walk?' Luke offered.' It'll give you an appetite. We can see Digger on his way and maybe have a look at his future Derby winners. They're over at Lee Farm, just across the valley there.'

That agreed, they set out on an amble along the road into the village and to the station then on to Lee Farm. Horses were not Luke's strong point but HRH knew promising thoroughbreds when he saw them and expressed both interest and surprise at Digger's animals.

'So this is where he hides them away. Wise man and fortunate too, enjoying such privacy. Everything I have and everything I do is on public view. I must confess I find it extremely tiresome at times.'

'I can well believe that,' Luke said. 'I wouldn't enjoy such publicity at all. It's the quiet life for me every time.'

Surprisingly, the week passed quickly and uneventfully and by the Friday, HRH pronounced himself greatly refreshed and ready to face the trials and tribulations of his usual existence. Bored stiff, most likely, Luke thought, relieved at the prospect of having his own room back again. Still, it'd been an interesting experience and he'd seen a different side of the future king.

★ ★ ★

A week or so later and Digger, as usual, galloped up the stairs to join Luke for their usual morning coffee and chat but found him staring morosely out of the window.

'Now then, Guv. What's up? Fine bright day an' all that.'

'Read that,' Luke replied, indicating an opened letter on the nearby table.

'Blimey, Guv. That's a bit of a shaker, 'en it?'

'Unexpected, certainly and no explanation. Sent the ring back as well, which makes it final, I should imagine.'

'You reckon it could be that little 'orror of 'ers?'

Possible but we could've worked around him. A nice strict boarding school would have answered, I'm sure.'

'Well all I can say, Guv, me old mate is I'm really sorry. I really am. Beth won't believe it I know.'

'I shall write of course and seek an explanation. Try to set things up again.'

'You want me to go and visit? You've only to say.'

'Well thanks but I'll write first and see what response I get.'

Luke's letter though, was returned marked 'Gone away, no forwarding address', which left him more bemused than ever, but he agreed that Digger should undertake a few covert enquiries, purely to confirm that Grace had in fact, moved house. Before long he had his answer. The house was empty, rent paid up to date and no forwarding address left.

'I wonder if the boy is still at school?'

'You want me to check?'

'No, I think not. I'll hear from Richard some time I expect. I've had my answer. No point in flogging a dead horse.'

'You going ter be alright, Guv?'

'I'm not going to take to the bottle or jump over a cliff, if that's what you mean. No, I'll get over it. A bit humiliating I suppose. One minute telling the world I'm getting married and the next that it's all off. I daresay I shall always be puzzled by it but in the meantime there's work to be done. Shall probably go up to the Lodge for the evening and enjoy a bit of reliable company.'

'That's the stuff, Guv. I'd join yer if I weren't married and respectable.'

★ ★ ★

It had not been a good harvest as Luke was well aware. Rain had delayed both cutting and leading, there had been insufficient labour on hand for those brief periods when harvesting had been possible and several fields had spoiled, with seed sprouting in the sheaves. As luck would have it two really sunny days that would have made all the difference had been Sundays but working on Sundays was strictly taboo.

That made no sense to Luke for, as he often remarked, ships didn't stop sailing on Sundays, servants still waited on their masters and policemen patrolled their beats. Hospitals didn't shut down on the Sabbath so why should corn not be harvested when livelihoods depended on it? The problem was, this rule had been made in a hot dry country but was being applied in one with very damp and uncertain weather. At times religion just made no sense. No sense at all.

He was not surprised then when Farmer Meredith from Higher Farm called to announce that he planned to leave the farm at Michaelmas. Poor harvests, low prices for produce and workers looking for higher wages had finally proved too much. He was not as young as he was, had no son to take over from him so it was best to call it a day.

Here was a problem, Luke realised for farming was in the doldrums generally. Few could risk the cost of setting up with the present dismal prospects. Rent, taxes, tithes, wages and interest on loans and mortgages would have to be found. Seed, horses, tools, implements and stock would be needed before any return was possible and that before so much as a loaf was put on the table.

A gloomy prospect indeed as an unworked farm would quickly run down. But then, problems were there to be overcome and most problems could be turned to advantage so, how could he profit from this situation? An idea had been at the back of his mind for a while now and this might be the time to try it. The way these farms were run was, in his view, old fashioned and inefficient and he wasn't even a farmer. They were mixed, in the hope of giving an income all year, if only a small one and they were inflexible, with the same old crops being tried each season and the same livestock as their grandfathers had reared.

There was a mix of land that might be suitable for some uses but not for others. Parts were chalky others had clay. Some parts were well watered and others dried out in summer. Now, if the various farms worked their respective acreage to best advantage and all the farm workers formed a flexible pool of labour, in one farming company, the whole might become profitable. He'd see what George thought.

George, though, had his doubts. 'They won't like it, Guv. They don't mix, you know, farm with farm. The same men've worked at the same farms for years. Be all accounts they used to go along to the hiring fair every year or so and get taken on by the same farmer to do the same work for the same pay or less.'

'And if a farm stands empty they live on fresh air? I'm told there's no work round about because farmers can't afford the wages, unless they pay a pittance to casuals at harvest time. It's a bit like the docks. Everything stuck in a rut.'

'Well that's true enough, I suppose. Wouldn't hurt to get 'em all a bit organised.'

'I've been reading about the new machinery they use in America. Some of it here might speed things up and if we did things on a bigger scale it could work out. I was really surprised to hear some were still threshing corn with flails and sowing the stuff by hand the same as it always used to be done. Talk about traditional. No wonder they can't make a living. Anyway, I'll give it a bit more thought.'

'I reckon they've followed the old planting law too long,' George chuckled. 'You know, Four seeds to a hole. One for the rook, One for the crow, One to rot and One to grow.'

★ ★ ★

Sitting comfortably on the settle by the fire in the hall, Luke was idly watching the ever-changing pattern of the flames and the way they lit up the surrounding stonework of the fireplace. Funny thing, he thought as his eye was attracted to certain stones at the back, close to the right hand corner. Might almost be steps. Eighteen inches apart maybe and offset as they ascended. Mm, he mused. Slightly different colour as well. Odd. Very odd. And the thickness of the wall between the fireplace and the staircase. Massive, as was the whole structure. Perhaps he'd get someone to look it over. Someone who knew about old buildings. What were they called? Architects? Archaeologists? Something like that. Walter would know.

Then Peter came in from school looking unwell and Mrs Cherry suggested he should be in bed. 'Best see what the Guv thinks,' she said to George who accompanied Peter into the hall

'You do indeed look rough,' Luke agreed. 'Best get yourself in bed and I'll send down for the doctor.'

'Almost certainly diphtheria,' was Doctor Fairleigh's opinion. 'There's no telling how it will develop at his age. He's a strong boy but it's a nasty complaint and can all too often prove fatal. There's none in the village so he's probably picked it up at school. Is anyone else here feeling unwell?'

'Not so far. Infectious, isn't it?'

'Very. I should isolate him if you can. Nothing to be done but keep him warm, give him plenty to drink and keep your fingers crossed. I'll contact Dr Lambourne and see if any new treatment is to be recommended. I know there is research in hand, especially in Germany, but I've not heard of any result yet.'

Next day, James was unwell and showing all the symptoms with a headache, high temperature and sore throat and Luke sent a telegram to Beth asking her to keep William away from the Manor until all danger had passed. Enquiry showed that eight boys from Peter's school were also affected and Guildford prepared for an epidemic.

★ ★ ★

Peter was ill for about a week then began to recover. James, though, was more badly affected and began to sink. He had great difficulty breathing and could not swallow. His temperature remained high and a membrane began forming in his throat, a sure sign of a terminal infection.

Luke was worried and upset. He was fond of this little fellow and was really saddened by his plight. Dr Fairleigh could offer no real help beyond recommending careful nursing. The illness would have to run its course, which in James's case, with his weak constitution, meant certain death.

Luke though, was a stubborn man and refused to give up hope. After all, he and Beth had pulled Digger through a bad dose of cholera so why could he not do something for James? He moved him into his room so he'd be close during the night and assembled a collection of spirits; rum, whisky, vodka and gin. Strong spirits would dissolve many things. Sore throats could be eased so why should it not clear

James's throat of that clinging membrane and stifling mucous? If only he could clear some of that rubbish away, but how? He was too weak now to cough it away and could scarcely breathe and had little time left.

What he needed, Luke decided was a tube. Something hollow. Where would he find one? Ah, yes, an elder tree with its pithy old stems and he went off in search of one. Not bad, he thought, as he whittled away with a knife, drawing the soft pith out to leave a hollow tube eight or nine inches long.

Now, a saucer from the kitchen, a couple of small cups and a bucket. Mrs Cherry was tempted to ask what he was up to but noting the expression on his face decided not to. A swig of rum for himself and he placed the tube in James's mouth and against a mass of mucous and sucked hard. Nothing for a moment then a load of rubbish came away and he gagged as it came into his mouth. Ugh! He spat into the bucket and reached for his rum, rinsed his mouth and spat. Shuddering, he tried again and three times successfully cleared solid mucous from James's throat.

Now to get some rum down him, or would vodka be better? It was eighty per cent proof. Strong stuff. He'd give it a try. With a spoon, he carefully fed it into James's unresisting mouth. He gasped and tried to struggle, went red in the face then sank back onto the pillow, but his rasping breathing sounded easier. Just a little, at any rate, Luke thought.

He'd try a drop of rum next. This time, James coughed and brought up both rum and rubbish. It seemed to be working, Luke thought and felt encouraged. Now, hot, sweet tea. Get something warm inside him, and he hastened down to the kitchen.

Dr Fairleigh called in to see how the patient was and found Luke plying his tube.

'Good God, man, you're drawing it out?' He was stunned. 'That's highly infectious, you know. There's no telling what it'll do to you.'

Luke rinsed and spat then took a swig of rum. He was feeling light-headed from his ministrations. 'Ah well. He's breathing more easily. We'll both be tight as drums by nightfall but at least we'll go out merry.'

'I rather think you will. Let me see his throat. Well I'm blessed. I see an improvement undoubtedly. Mm. Pulse is still rapid. Well, sir. What can I say but keep up the good work?'

For three days and nights Luke kept at it. He put hot poultices on James's neck, poured warm liquids into him and removed the rubbish that kept appearing in his throat. On the morning of the fourth day, after dozing in a chair, he noticed James looking at him and he saw a ghost of a smile. It was Digger all over again. James would pull through.

He was dreadfully weak and had to be hand fed for best part of a week but each day saw an improvement. Peter, still away from school and recovering well was allowed to visit and helped Luke with his nursing chores. Good lad, Peter. A kind and gentle side to him, Luke thought. Odd, though that John Hurle had escaped infection whilst Peter hadn't.

Dr Fairleigh was impressed. I don't know how you managed it, Mr Gregory, indeed I don't but you deserve a medal. Will you let him up now?'

'Why not? What do you say, young James? Down to the kitchen and see what Mrs Cherry can offer.'

★ ★ ★

Arthur the bull was, by any standards, a magnificent animal. Massive, light brown in colour, beautifully proportioned and possessing a most imposing set of horns, he was the only bull in the village and belonged to Farmer Pearson at Church Farm.

Only one man ever handled him, Harold Wiggins, the head cowman and he, it was said, sometimes had difficulty with him for Arthur could be a savage. There was no other bull within hearing distance simply because he refused to tolerate any rival. One unfortunate from over the hill, scenting cows ready for service, broke out of his paddock and visited Ten Acre early one morning. As he struggled to break through the hedge to challenge Arthur's supremacy, Arthur charged him flat out and killed him stone dead, breaking his back and goring him 'till he ceased to move. Arthur was treated with a great deal of respect.

When James had recovered from his illness he was encouraged to walk around the village in the mornings to help build up his strength. Fortified by pockets full of Mrs Cherry's biscuits and buns he would set out to wander the locality and it was then that he discovered Arthur.

Every so often Hal Wiggins would hitch Arthur's nose ring to a control pole and take him for a walk as he'd become bored and irritable when not turned out and it was on one of these occasions that James met cowman and bull.

'Hello, sir,' James greeted, politely. 'Is that a bull?'

'It is indeed lad and a dangerous one so don't come too close.'

'I think he's beautiful. Can I stroke him?'

'I don't advise that, lad. There's no telling how 'e'll take it. Very uncertain temper 'e has, see?'

'May I walk with you, sir?'

'Well, if you like, yes, but stay by my side. You from the Manor, are you?'

'Yes, sir. I'm James. Would you like a biscuit? I've got lots with me.'

So this was the little chap who nearly died and would have be all accounts if squire hadn't worked miracles. 'Well, ta,' he said, accepting the offered refreshment.

'Would your bull like one, do you think?'

'I can try him. His name's Arthur, by the way. Pass one over. 'E'll either say yes or no.'

The vote was a definite 'yes' and Arthur was looking for another one.

'He liked that, didn't he. Can I give him one?' James was animated.

'Well, go on then, but be careful. Too good for a bull mind. Who makes 'em? They're delicious. Wouldn't get anything like 'em even at Christmas.'

'Mrs Cherry makes them. She's the best cook in England, the guv says.'

'Reckon 'e could be right at that. Now how many's that 'e's 'ad? You'll 'ave none for yourself.'

'I don't mind. I'm not hungry.'

The walk over, James accompanied Arthur and his handler back to Church Farm and watched Arthur into his pen, a secure, half-covered brick and stone enclosure.

'May I please visit Arthur again?' James asked.

'Well, I should think t'would be all right as long as the gaffer don't mind, but you must never go in the pen with 'im. No bull can be trusted, y'know.'

★ ★ ★

A couple of weeks later Farmer Pearson, leaning heavily on a stick, presented himself at the back door of the Manor asking to speak to Luke.

'Er, sorry to disturb you like, sir, but has your lad said anything? The little one, James, because I've never seen the likes of today's doings.'

'No. He hasn't said anything particular. What took place?'

'Well, sir, 'tis like this. Arthur, my bull was due to be turned out today, into Ten Acre, his usual patch. His handler is my 'ead cowman, Wiggins. He had 'im hitched to 'is pole as usual and they'd started off for Ten Acre when all of a sudden Arthur turns on Wiggins, gores 'im through the leg and tosses 'im into the hedge bottom. A couple o' women saw it 'appen and they started screaming blue murder as Arthur was still going after Wiggins, trying to gore 'im.

The hedge there is on a bit of a bank and though Arthur were on 'is knees trying to reach 'im he could only manage to rake him up and down with the tips of his horns. There were no men about so I went out to catch 'old of 'is pole and pull 'im off but 'e'd got it between 'is feet and when I caught hold o' the end he gave me such a kick as I thought e'd broke me leg. So there we 'ad it. The bull in a frenzy, Wiggins's missis shrieking 'er 'ead off awanting someone to pull 'im off, me flat on me back in the road holding me leg, and a crowd o' women all adding their noise but not doing a lot.

Then up walks your lad, goes straight up to Arthur and takes hold of 'is ear, 'is ear, mark you, next to those great horns an' 'e says, 'Come along, Arthur. Please don't be cross.' There was dead silence then, all round. Bull stops 'is roaring and backs off from Wiggins until the end of the pole caught on the road. Your lad unhitches the pole so it's not dragging on his nose ring and says, 'Poor Arthur. Are you upset, then. And your poor nose is bleeding.'

He takes out 'is 'andkerchief and starts dabbing at Arthur's nose and then, believe it or not, that great lump o' beef sat down on his haunches like some damn great dog whilst your lad mopped his nose and said soft things to 'im. I tell you, I've never seen anything like it in me life nor 'ave I ever heard of anything like it. Then, your lad says to me 'Where should Arthur be Mr Pearson?' and I tells 'im Ten Acre.'

'I will take him there for you. Come along Arthur. Up, there's a good fellow,' and Arthur gets to his feet and follows your lad up to Ten Acre and through the gate to his cows. It were nothing short o' miraculous, I'll tell you that for nothing. Course, we could get Wiggins out o' the hedge bottom then and get the doctor to patch 'im up. Quite a mess all told but it could 'ave bin worse, much worse. It's the talk o' the village. Quite a hero your lad is and you say 'e's made no mention?'

'This is the first I've heard of it,' Luke replied.

'Well, I was wondering if I mightn't shake him be the hand and give 'im a little something.'

'By all means. Come along in. He was reading in the hall just now.'

James was, in fact still reading in the hall and politely rose to his feet as Luke and Farmer Pearson approached.

'I hear you've been playing the hero today, young man. Getting a bull off someone and putting him in his field,' Luke said. 'Mr Pearson here is extremely grateful to you and wishes to thank you,' which Pearson, in an evidently rehearsed and wordy speech proceeded to do and passed over to James a wash-leather bag containing five sovereigns.

'That is very kind of you, sir,' James said but I do not wish for a reward. Arthur is my friend and would not hurt me.'

'Well I'm blessed,' Farmer Pearson got out. 'That's what I call modesty. No, no, lad. I want you to keep it. 'T'is little enough for what you did, no matter how you managed it. There could 'ave bin a lot o' people 'urt 'ad you not come along. No, you keep it,' which insistence, from a farmer noted for his care with his money, showed the depth of his feelings.

When Luke had seen Farmer Pearson out to his trap he went back to the hall and sat next to James. 'You really are full of surprises, young James. You make me proud to know you.'

James said nothing but gave one of his shy, enigmatic little smiles.

Chapter 11

Luke stood at the front of the Manor looking out over the valley and turned at the sound of a horse approaching on the driveway. It was a large, black animal, a hunter, he believed it would be called but if it was an imposing animal, the rider was even more so.

Riding side-saddle, it was obviously a lady but one dressed somewhat as a man, in a tailored black habit, cravat and shiny black silk top hat. Heavy featured with a red, bucolic complexion, holding a large crop in a leather-gloved hand, this was clearly a forceful personality, he concluded. Neither was he disappointed.

'Morning to you,' the rider boomed. 'I'm looking for Squire Gregory.'

'My name is Gregory,' Luke replied.

'Cecelia Burberry-Harcourt,' the rider announced. 'Mind if I hop down?'

'Not at all,' Luke agreed, wondering what this visit heralded. The name was vaguely familiar. He remembered hearing that a Lady Cecelia somebody or other had returned from India and taken up residence at the family seat following the death of her brother. Harcourt Hall, was it? Something like that.

'Glad to meet you,' Lady Cecelia boomed at him again, this time at close quarters, offering to shake hands in distinctly masculine fashion. No dainty finger tips here. My word no. A firm grip, alright. Bet she could crack walnuts in that hand, Luke thought. She was a very large lady, broad of shoulder and hip, impressive bosom and the start of a double chin. She'd just about be a match for Big Eva at the warehouse.

'I'm pleased to meet you also,' Luke replied. 'It is Lady Cecelia, is it not?'

'Right first time. Heard a lot about you. Thought I'd call in; introduce meself. Been away years, you know. Grew up round here. A few changes. Have to get used to it again.'

'Er, yes. Won't you come in? May I offer you refreshment?'

'Good of you, good of you. Horse alright here, is he?'

'He'd probably be happier in the stable. Ah, there's Joseph. I expect he heard you arrive,' and he signalled to him to approach.

'Would you look after Lady Cecelia's horse, please, Joseph.'

'Yes, Guv. Anything special for him, ma'am?' he asked.

'Water and hay. No oats. He's full enough of himself as it is and slacken his girth. Be wary, mind. He bites.'

'Yes, ma'am,' and he led the animal away as Luke escorted his visitor into the house and invited her to take a seat in the study.

'What may I offer you? I have an excellent single malt.'

'Spoken like a soldier. Man after me own heart. Was afraid you'd offer me a thimble of coffee and an arrowroot biscuit, ha ha.'

'I shall certainly offer you coffee, if I can find someone to bring it,' he said, handed his visitor her glass, then went to the door to see who was about. 'Ah, James. Just the man. Would you bring coffee for two, please and see what else Mrs Cherry can offer.'

Lady Cecilia was looking around appraisingly. 'Gad, but you've a comfortable place here. Like it. Never been in before. Didn't see much of the Travers, you know. Understand he died. Heard you kept his family on. In trade, aren't you?'

Her staccato comments and bluntness might have been off putting, offensive even but Lady Cecilia was so obviously of an amiable disposition that Luke was not at all affronted.

'Yes. I work for my living. Always have done.'

'Nothing wrong with that. A few round here need to get off their backsides. Too many airs and graces for my liking. Understand your gels ride astride. Heard you damned for that. Not the thing, you know. Not lady like. Can't think why the devil I don't try it meself. Damn. I will. Get meself a pair of britches and give 'em more to gossip about.'

'I'm no horseman myself but my steward is an old cavalry man and he believes it's safer to ride astride. He's certain we'd never have beaten the French or the Russians if our cavalry had ridden side saddle.'

Lady Cecilia let out a whoop of laughter. 'Damn right he is. A wonder some of the old women who led 'em didn't order it, ha ha.'

The coffee arrived then, James carefully carrying the tray, walking slowly so as not to spill anything. 'Thank you James. Can you put it down here, please. Well done. You've got a steady hand. Lady Cecilia, may I present James Eames-Johnson? James, this is Lady Cecelia Burberry-Harcourt.'

'How do you do, ma'am?' and James politely offered his hand.

Lady Cecilia rose from her seat and shook his hand vigorously. 'Pleased to meet you, young fellah. Ride to hounds, do you?'

'No, ma'am. I'm only just learning to ride. I would need a great deal more practice before joining the hunt.'

'Well, you're honest about it. No flummoxing. No pretence. Like that. Like that,' and Lady Cecilia resumed her seat and picked up her glass again as James, with a smile, left the room.

'Yours is he? Heard you'd got a few around the place. Don't know anything about boys. Girls neither, come to that. Odd thing. Should've bin the feller. My brother should've bin the gel. Read poetry, that sort of thing. Never got married. No one to leave the place to. Only me. Doubt I'll get married. Frighten all the fellers off!' this last with, Luke thought, a tinge of sadness. Certainly, the lady appeared to be one of nature's mistakes and he could well visualise her laying about her lustily with a sabre in a cavalry charge, had things been different.

'Come to the point. I ride, you know, to hounds. Hunt's not allowed across your land. Dispute with the master, years ago, what? Change your mind, would you? Courtesy assured, you know. Sheep wouldn't be scattered again. Promise that. Blackguard, that feller. Not missed at all, what?'

'Yes, he was difficult. Forced my hand and caused all sorts of unpleasantness. If the hunt is considerate I'd have no objection whatever. Have a drop more. It is rather good, isn't it and you must try these scones whilst they're still warm.'

'Good for you. Much appreciated. Like your style, like your style. No side. Down to earth. Good to know you.'

★ ★ ★

'There's a young man waiting to see you, Guv,' Mrs Cherry announced as Luke and William arrived in the kitchen that Friday afternoon.

'Anyone we know?'

'No. We've not seen him before.'

'Looking for work, is he?' Luke asked, shrugging out of his coat.

'I wouldn't think so, Guv, not the way he's dressed,' George put in. 'Top hat and all. Had a dog with him, though. It's all right, dog's in the stable. Joseph is looking after it,' as Luke raised an eyebrow at the thought of visiting dogs invading the house.

'He called earlier, this morning,' Mrs Cherry added, 'but when we told him you weren't expected until this afternoon he said he'd call back. Wouldn't stay, would he, George? We invited him to stop but he insisted on going. Very polite, mind. Can't think where he'd spend the day round here, dressed like that, I'm sure.'

'I'd better go and meet this interesting visitor,' Luke decided. 'I'll be back for a cuppa. In the study, is he?'

As soon as Luke opened the study door, his visitor leapt to his feet and stood looking directly at Luke, a mixture of anxiety, nervousness and defiance showing on his face.

'Good afternoon. I'm Luke Gregory.'

'Good afternoon, sir. My name is Nicholas Hurlingham. I apologise for calling like this but I was hoping that you might be able to advise me. My Aunt Cecilia said I should come and see you. She said you are the one person whom she knows who would know what to do.'

'Aunt Cecilia? That is Lady Cecilia?'

'Yes, sir. She isn't really my aunt. I believe she is some sort of second cousin but I've always called her aunt since I was small.'

'I see. So what can I do to be of help? No, first things first. I understand you called earlier in the day. When did you last eat?'

'This morning, sir,' he replied, looking sheepish.

'I thought I recognised signs of starvation. Tell me, are you still at school?'

'Yes sir. Eton College. I was supposed to return there today but decided that I must try and solve my problem first.'

'I see. Well, problems should never be faced on an empty stomach. They always appear worse that way. Come along and sample the delights of the kitchen. We don't stand on ceremony here so leave your things in the cloakroom and come and join the gang for tea.'

The kitchen was, as usual at that time of day and at the end of the week, filled with ravenous youngsters in from school or wherever, all tucking in to Mrs Cherry's cooking. Luke made the introductions, starting with William, who was nearest, Lucy, Annabelle, Peter, James, and Adrian.

'And here, we have the most important people in the house, Mr and Mrs Cherry who look after us and keep us organised and without whom this house would be a dreary place.'

'Oh, Guv. Get on with you,' Mrs Cherry scolded, but looked pleased, nevertheless.

Fortified by fruit cake and scones, Luke decided that his visitor was ready to divulge whatever problem troubled him.

If Lady Cecilia had commended the visit he'd make the time and effort to help, if at all possible.

Seated once more in the study, Nicholas explained that his father had died a week or so ago and he had come down for his funeral and his father's brother, his Uncle Godfrey, his aunt Agatha and cousin Hubert, had also arrived and stayed at Hurlingham Court, where he lived with his father when he was not at school. His Uncle Godfrey had told him that as there was no will he is now his guardian and would live there and run the estate.

'I see. That is not an arrangement with which you are happy?'

'No sir, I am not. I hate Uncle Godfrey and Aunt Agatha and as for Cousin Hubert, swaggering around sneering at me as a mere schoolboy and poking around in all father's things, I could kill him.'

'You are certain there is no will?'

'I am told one could not be found but I am prevented from making enquiries because I am under age.'

'Have you no other relative to whom you might turn? You haven't mentioned your mother. Has she, perhaps, predeceased your father?'

'Yes sir. Mother died when I was very small and I am unaware of any other relative, apart from Aunt Cecilia.'

'So how old are you, Nicholas?'

'Fifteen, sir.'

'Six years to your majority. On the face of it, your uncle's move is the logical one. Is there some reason, apart from your dislike of him, why his presence is unacceptable to you?'

'Yes sir. He is a scoundrel,' and he went on to relate how his father never had anything to do with him as he was a ne'er do well who had squandered his own inheritance, had enormous debts through gambling and had already started to sell off his father's things and his mother's jewellery and that Hubert was even wearing his father's watch.

'I think it is so unfair and wrong and there is nothing I can do about it.'

'A classic case of the wicked uncle, it seems,' Luke said. 'You're right when you say there's nothing you can do about it. No, no, bear up. Hear me out. I know you're upset but give me a moment. Because of your age there's nothing that you, personally can do but I believe the law can offer assistance. As I understand it, you as the only son, inherit the estate when you become of age. In the meantime I believe you can be made a ward of court to protect your interests so we must seek legal advice about it. Hopefully, your father's estate would then be administered by trustees and Uncle Godfrey would be prevented from selling so much as a blade of grass without the court's permission. Does that sound a little more hopeful, do you think?'

'Yes, sir but how am I to ask for legal advice? I'm supposed to be back at school and Uncle Godfrey won't help me, I know.'

'I'm sure he won't but Aunt Cecilia and I will. Tomorrow we'll meet with Lady Cecilia and clarify her relationship to you then, on Monday you can come and talk with my legal advisor and we'll take it from there. There's nothing to be done before Monday so, if you prefer not to return home you're welcome to stay here for the weekend. Am I right in thinking you have a dog with you?'

'Yes sir. She's called Daisy and I've had her since I was ten but Uncle Godfrey said I have to get rid of her. Do you really think they can be made to leave? I mean, go and never come back?'

'I think there's a fair chance if a strong enough case can be made to the court but that's what we have to talk to a legal eagle about. Mm. Daisy, you say. I like that. A lovely name for a dog. Did you choose it?'

'Yes, sir,' Nicholas said, shyly.

'Well, I'm sure that between us Daisy won't have to be got rid of. What a dreadful thing for him to say. He sounds a proper cad.'

'Aunt Cecilia called him a bounder. She said he always had been and always would be.'

'I've not the slightest doubt Aunt Cecilia is correct in her opinion,' Luke said, smiling.' but would it be an idea to send a telegram to your school telling them you're delayed? Save them contacting Uncle Godfrey, and keep him in the dark?'

'Yes sir and thank you ever so much. I really am grateful.'

★ ★ ★

'Some sort of cousin. Twice removed, I think. Make sense, does it?' Lady Cecilia was frowning, doing her best to work through the complexities of family relationships. 'Father's sister married Benedict who had two sons and a daughter, that's your father, your Uncle Godfrey and Aunt Patricia,' to Nicholas. 'That makes 'em my cousins, doesn't it? Didn't see much of 'em, mind. Help, does it?'

'It certainly does,' Luke decided. 'You're either a second cousin or a great aunt or something like that. It's enough to go on so we'll go up to town and see what we can do.'

'Knew you were the man for the job,' Lady Cecilia stated emphatically. 'Down to earth. Practical man. Everything at your finger tips. Come with you, shall I? Like to see that feller sent about his business. Scoundrel. Don't care for the type.'

'We'll be leaving on the eight-ten train. Can you make it?'

'No trouble. Leave me horse with you, can I?'

'Of course. Joseph'll see to him.'

★ ★ ★

'Would it be possible,' Luke asked Walter, having outlined the problem, 'to have Nicholas made a ward of court to protect his interests?'

'Oh, most certainly, especially in the absence of a will. We should have to apply to a judge in chambers in the first instance, for an interim order pending a full court hearing should the case be contested and I would recommend we approach Mr Justice Pevensey at Lincoln's Inn. He is a judge in the Chancery Division. Now are you certain there is no will?'

'I really don't know, sir,' Nicholas replied. 'Father didn't mention one and it's, well not something one asks about.'

'Of course not but do you happen to know if he had a legal advisor, at all?'

'I'm afraid I have no idea, sir.'

'I see. Very well. I'll write straight away to arrange an appointment. It might take a day or two but we'll see.'

Taking his cue, Luke ushered the visitors up to his sitting room for coffee to allow Walter to write the note and have Charlie deliver it as quickly as possible.

'Do you really think something can be arranged quickly?' Nicholas asked, clearly extremely worried at the prospect of Uncle Godfrey's depredations at Hurlingham Court.

'Well, we're moving as quickly as possible but the law is a slow and tedious business. You'll have to be patient but there's more we can do in the meantime. As soon as my partner arrives we'll get him to organise a bit of research on Uncle Godfrey and see if we can't find someone who acted for your father. If Uncle Godfrey has guilty secrets, we shall soon know of 'em so not to worry. We're pretty well organised.'

'Damn right you are,' Lady Cecelia exclaimed. 'Wouldn't know where to start meself. Lawyer of your own, too. Knew you were the right feller.'

★ ★ ★

Mr Justice Pevensey was a thin, spare, severe-looking individual with a high forehead and receding hair. He regarded his visitors intently over thick-lensed spectacles as they seated themselves opposite his enormous leather-topped desk. Walter though, remained standing and respectfully named everyone before outlining the reason for their visit.

'No will, you say?'

'None has yet been found, Your Honour.'

His Honour considered. 'It would be helpful to establish your late father's wishes as to his estate,' he said to Nicholas. 'There is always the possibility that his brother, your uncle, was named as a beneficiary or as a trustee or executor but also we need to establish by what right he is disposing of assets. You say that your father's bailiff has been given notice?'

'Yes sir.'

'And he is a trustworthy man?'

'Oh yes, sir. He has looked after the estate for many years and father relied upon him absolutely.'

A pause. 'I shall make an interim order freezing your late father's estate pending a full hearing in, shall we say, three weeks time. You are now, from this moment, subject to the protection of the court pending the outcome of that hearing. At what school do you attend?'

'Eton College, sir.'

'Eton, eh? Harrow, myself. You will remain at Eton College until called to attend at court. Your family bailiff will be invited to resume his duties and your uncle and his family will leave the estate immediately and account for all and every item removed or disposed of. His claim to any part of your late father's estate will be established at the hearing. If a will can be found, that will be helpful. How does that suit you?'

'Oh thank you sir. Thank you very much. This is more that I could have wished for.' Nicholas was overjoyed, his relief and pleasure clearly showing as he turned to each in turn to express his thanks for their help and support and Mr Justice Pevensey's severe expression relaxed in a smile.

'It would be helpful and indeed would expedite matters were the Court Sergeant to be shown to Hurlingham Court. He will need to hand the order personally to Uncle Godfrey and ensure his departure and the reinstatement of the bailiff.'

'Happy to oblige,' Lady Cecelia boomed. 'Love to see the look on his face. Man's a cad sir. Bounder. Deserves horsewhipping.'

'Quite so, quite so,' His Honour observed and rang the desk bell to call his clerk to show the party out and prepare the necessary order.

★ ★ ★

'Any luck with your enquiries?' Luke asked Digger as the latter settled himself comfortably in the armchair by the fireside. 'I can see you've got something to tell me,' for Digger was wearing his biggest possible grin.

'You'll just love this, Guv. You'll love it. Our Godfrey has managed to dodge the law more than once by the skin of 'is teeth. He sells dodgy insurance policies to gullible old ladies, 'as been mixed up in racecourse frauds, has at least two aliases, several thousands in gambling debts and by rights should be doing time. Slippery fraudster is a generous description of 'im.'

'Any proof that'll stand up in court?'

'Buckets of it. Walter'll 'ave a field day but if 'e twigs we're on to 'im 'e'll do a runner. Still, 'e'd be very foolish to show up in court.'

'Well done. Any sign of a will yet?'

'Not yet but we're working on it.'

★ ★ ★

Lady Cecelia had thoroughly enjoyed herself when she conducted the Court Sergeant to Hurlingham Hall. The presentation of the writ to Uncle Godfrey requiring him to vacate forthwith and take nothing with him led to some huffing and puffing but, with no option, he and his family had departed. She had relieved Hugo of the pocket watch, she gleefully told Luke and had demanded Godfrey list all items so far disposed of, for the benefit of the Sergeant who magisterially noted everything in detail. The bailiff had been reinstated, with instructions to secure the estate and allow no trespassers whatsoever, pending the formal court hearing.

'A damn good day's work,' was how Lady Cecelia summed up proceedings, 'and all thanks to you, Squire Gregory. Wouldn't have known where to start, meself but you had it all at your fingertips. That boy owes you a great deal, a great deal. So do I. Can't abide a blackguard like that fellah.'

One week later, Digger greeted Luke, grinning like a Cheshire cat. 'We've got it, Guv. Found the legal man who acted for Nicholas's father and he holds a valid will. He said there was a copy and that should have been available at the outset. Anyway I've arranged for 'im to attend the hearing with the will and between you and me, everything is left to Nicholas with no mention whatever of Uncle Godfrey. What d'yer make of that, then?'

★ ★ ★

There being no notice by Godfrey Hurlingham of any claim against the estate of his late brother, the party once more assembled in the chambers of His Honour, Judge Pevensey. The will was presented and attested by the solicitor who had acted for Nicholas's father and Nicholas was formally declared a Ward of the High Court until he attained his majority at age twenty-one.

That formality concluded His Honour required to be informed of proposals for administration of affairs on a day-to-day basis and looked to Lady Cecelia as a relative for an answer. Walter had done his work well and had discussed this issue with everyone so Her Ladyship was ready and boomed, 'Propose Squire Gregory to act on behalf of the court in all respects. Very experienced. Can vouch for him personally. Knows what he's about.'

'I see. Is this a proposal acceptable to all parties and is it subject to review? What other testimony is offered? I need to be sure, you see that the interests of the ward are fully protected.'

'I, I am very happy about this, sir, I mean Your Honour,' Nicholas said, hesitantly.

'Mr Gregory was a confidant of the late Magistrate Morden for whom he undertook assignments of a confidential nature,' Walter, in his turn offered.

His Honour sat up straight and looked directly at Luke. 'Morden? Josiah Morden? Are you then the Gregory from the riverside? Tar and feathers?' and the austere judge let out a cackle of laughter. 'Had the club in stitches over that escapade. Say no more, say no more. Had a very high regard for you. Very high indeed. You're in safe hands, young man, safe hands indeed,' and His Honour dabbed at his eyes with a silk handkerchief, so Luke once more found himself with a new responsibility.

'Find somewhere for lunch, shall we?' Luke suggested, relieved to be away from the legal atmosphere of 'Chambers'.

'Fancy lamb chops, meself,' Lady Cecelia boomed in her tally ho voice, 'and I'm standing treat and no arguments. Come along Cousin Nicholas. Celebration time,' and she clapped that young man heartily on the back, causing him to stagger. Luke and Walter exchanged amused glances and dutifully followed behind but then, Luke posed a question.

'Advise me Walter. Should anything happen to Nicholas, who would be next of kin? Would Uncle Godfrey have a stronger claim than Lady Cecelia? You see what I'm getting at? I've an awful suspicious mind.'

Walter stopped walking and stared at Luke. 'Good Lord. You don't think? I mean. Good Lord. That had never occurred to me. Of course, as a minor he cannot make a will so yes, Uncle Godfrey could well have a very strong claim indeed.'

'Give it some thought, would you? Perhaps go back to His Honour for guidance or whatever. It might be a good idea were you to accompany him back to college and have a word with someone. They'll need to know the outcome of this morning's work but I'll set the lads on Godfrey's trail. We need to keep an eye on him, I think.'

★ ★ ★

Dr J. Bentinck-Searle, DD, MA, the card read. Historical and Archaeological Research. Ah, Luke realised. This would be the museum fellow Digger was on about. Doctor of Divinity as well. Mm. We'll have to see then.

'Right, show him up Tom and bring us coffee, would you?'

Doctor Bentinck-Searle was a small, wiry man with a ragged moustache and untidy hair, a domed forehead and thick-lensed spectacles perched on the end of his nose but no clergyman's dog collar. Free Church? Possibly and yes, Luke decided as he greeted his visitor, he could well fit in with a museum. One could almost smell the dust of antiquity on his clothes but, however that might be, his conversation was interesting from the start as he described his consultancy work.

'So you'd be happy to look round the old building in which I live. It puzzles me and I'd be interested to learn more of it.' Already Luke had decided to accommodate this learned gentleman in the guest room, the one that had been sealed up behind the panelling. No one liked sleeping there for some reason. Guests always mentioned how cold it was even with the heating on and Mrs Donkin had several times told George she thought someone was watching her from the window as she worked in the kitchen garden below.

'Could be one of the girls dusting round,' George had thought but he'd told Luke nevertheless. 'Best to keep 'im in the picture,' he informed his wife.

Now, Luke had got round to organising someone to poke about the place and give an insight as to age and who might have lived there before the Travers. It was probably all in the deeds but he had little interest in wading through a box of old papers. He'd probably not make head or tail of it anyway.

So, Doctor Bentinck-Searle was starting his researches by walking around outside the building, looking at the brickwork and pacing out measurements and generally getting the lie of the land. Inside, Luke indicated the fireplace and what he thought to be a pattern in the stonework, above the cast iron fireback.

'This is a most interesting building,' the Doctor exclaimed. 'There is so much to see and explore. Could you tell me how to get to the cellar?'

'Cellar? I didn't know we had one. No one's ever mentioned one.'

'Oh, there is assuredly a cellar beneath. Properly called an under croft you know. No building of this antiquity would have been without one. Hear this?' and he tapped with his heel on the flagstone floor. Hollow. And here, it's solid,' and he again tapped with his boot heel on the floor. This, of course, is the original part but what purpose it served I'm unsure. The two wings were added at a later date, probably in the sixteenth century. Those old fireplaces in the kitchen tell the tale without a doubt. This one is a hundred or more years earlier.

'As old as that? It's certainly big enough to climb up. A cellar, now. I've really no idea where the entrance might be.'

★ ★ ★

Doctor Bentinck-Searle was a thoughtful man when he joined everyone for breakfast next morning. 'That room in which I slept, or rather tried to. What do you know of it?'

'It was sealed up. Window blocked. Door covered with panelling. It came to light when we had the upstairs floorboards replaced. You didn't sleep well, then?'

'I had a disturbed night. There most definitely a presence in that room, Mr Gregory. I wonder if anyone has commented upon it previously?' he asked, head on one side, his fork poised in mid air.

'Yes, Doctor. No one enjoys sleeping there though the bed is reported to be comfortable enough.'

'Yes, a fine piece of furniture. Of the same period as this table and both in excellent condition. That tends to confirm my belief that the first floor and wings were added shortly after the Reformation, in the mid to late fifteen hundreds or thereabouts. But that room. Sealed up, you say. Interesting. Interesting. I shall return to London this morning and conduct a little archival research.'

'You don't care to stay longer?'

'Oh, I shall return, never fear. Your property has caught my interest. Indeed this whole setting has. There is history here for the finding without a doubt.'

'Does that mean that room is haunted, sir?' Peter asked.

'Quite possibly. Nothing to worry about though. Echoes of the past, that's all. Bell book and candle will settle the matter and help some poor soul find peace.'

The girls looked apprehensive but Peter was intrigued. 'What does that mean, sir?'

'Oh, just that possibly someone died in that room and for some reason didn't pass on as they should. A Christian service is generally all that is required to help matters. You must remember this is a very old house and many, many people will have been born here and died in their beds as well. All part of life you know.'

'Mother died here I know,' Peter said. 'She has a grave in the churchyard next to father.'

'Ah, sad, yes but that is life and we know that is not the end of matters. There is assuredly another life after this one of that I am quite satisfied but come, this is not a cheerful subject with which to start the day. We have a cellar entrance to find and I would welcome the opportunity to clamber up into the roof space to examine the structure. There may well be a date carved into a roof timber somewhere. Fascinating subject this, you know, history.'

'There we are then,' Luke put in, glad that the conversation had taken a more positive turn. 'Peter to find the cellar and the girls to look for a date under the roof.'

'Oh, we're not going up there,' they both exclaimed. 'It'll be all cobwebs and spiders and things. Ugh. Peter can go up there instead.'

★ ★ ★

The next Wednesday, with Luke following his customary routine of reading the newspapers in the comfort of Gresham House, Doctor Bentinck-Searle reappeared.

'Ah, Mr Gregory,' he greeted Luke. 'I have been researching at Chancery Lane among other places and have much of interest to relate.'

'Well, please take a seat, Doctor. I'm at your service.'

'Firstly, the original building was an ecclesiastical one until it was sold off in fifteen thirty-seven. That was when all monastic foundations worth less than two hundred pounds were closed down. You have perhaps noticed that it is on a similar alignment to the church? No? And that hollow in the field down near the river? A pound to a penny that was once a fish pond to supply the clerics with fish on Fridays. Anyway, the extensions would have been added after that date by the new owner, a wool merchant from Guildford, one Hezekiah Tate as far as I can gather.

You see, after the Norman invasion in ten sixty-six all Saxon held land was forfeit to the invaders and much of what is now Surrey was handed to Bishop Odo of Bayeux, who was the new Archbishop of Canterbury. Oh, in the first place the Manor of Chedbruch, I think it was, but the writing is indistinct, was held by one Weolfric, a king's thegn. Doomsday book describes the Manor House as being near to the church with quite a substantial landholding, something like eleven hides of arable plus woodland and common grazing but what I really wished to tell you was that the present Manor House was probably built as a chantry or possibly a friary or nunnery with the income from the land going to Odo and his churchmen.'

Here, the doctor sat back and beamed at Luke who was struggling to take in all this information.

'I see, I think,' Luke offered. 'So the Manor goes back a long way but I thought you said it was near the church. We must be nearly a half mile from there.'

'That's just it. Your present house is not the original Manor House. That, I believe is what you now call Church Farm and I am most desirous of visiting there to examine its structure'

'Pearson's the farmer there. He'd have no objection but I'll speak with him before hand naturally. When had you in mind?'

`Well, I had hoped it would be possible today. There is so much to see and one find is leading to another. Most interesting and indeed, exciting. Have you, by the way, found entry to the under croft?'

'Well, Doctor I certainly welcome your enthusiasm and interest. I'll pen a note to Pearson asking that he offer every assistance and er, no we haven't found a door leading below but there is a hollow-sounding wall beneath the main staircase. It would require a builder to break through I believe but perhaps you'd give an opinion before we go that far.'

Certainly, certainly. We must be sure of what we are about before we knock holes in things. Oh, and there is one more thing if I may make mention,' he added, cautiously. 'I wondered if I might present my account, to meet expenses, you will appreciate.'

'Of course. Mr Brierly downstairs will accommodate you in that respect and please do not hesitate to take an advance if that would be convenient. You will be staying with us this evening? Would you prefer a different room?'

'Most kind of you and no, the same room will be more than satisfactory now that I know what to expect.'

★ ★ ★

Not knowing what to expect or what new discoveries awaited him when he arrived back at the Manor, Luke was not best pleased to learn that Peter had again walked off from school.

'So what's the reason this time?' he asked, his irritation plain to see.

'I hate it,' Peter replied, defiantly.

'Tell me why.'

'It's all that Latin and stuff and I'm sick and tired of John.'

'What has he to do with it?'

'I'm just tired of him.'

'So you've fallen out and legged it again. You disappoint me. I thought you to be settled now. Seems I was wrong. You'll get Latin at any school you attend and it's not so bad once you put your mind to it so I'm not accepting that. You've had a fall out with John. So what's that about?'

Peter looked down and shuffled his feet. 'He keeps following me about.'

'Of course he does. He thinks you're a wonderful fellow. If it wasn't for you he'd not be going to school the same as you. Look at the difference between you. You live in a Manor House and will one day pass as a gentleman. He lives in a farm servant's cottage and was all set for work on the land. He wants to better himself and that's downright difficult. There's so much to learn like speaking properly, using a knife and fork properly and so on and he's relying on you to show him, just as you showed him how to sit a horse. So you get in a huff with Latin and take it out on him. Is that it?'

Peter kept his gaze firmly on the floor. The guv was annoyed with him and he had the grace to realise it was his own fault.

'Monday you go back to school and accept whatever penalty is imposed and you will not just walk away from difficulties. If you've been unfair to John it's for you to put things right, understand? You're in a privileged position so the responsibility is yours. Think it over and if you were in the wrong don't be afraid to apologise. There's nothing unmanly in that. Quite the opposite, in fact,' and Luke abruptly left the study and went upstairs to change.

He was quietly pleased later that evening to see Peter and John sitting together doing their 'prep' for Monday morning so clearly, Peter had put things right. Nevertheless, this situation must be resolved and Luke had made his decision. Peter was growing up fast and would benefit, at least socially, from joining Richard at school as a boarder. It would be no bad thing for him to leave John to make his own way at his own pace as a day scholar. They could remain on friendly terms, but social standing was important after all and he thought back to Lady Remnold's disapproval of the ploughboy rising above his station in life.

No, Peter must have the same advantages as Richard whilst John was being given his chance but dammit, now the girls wanted to go to school. Well then, why not, he asked himself as he sat in his usual place gazing at the smouldering logs on the hearth. He'd get Miss Hetherington. No, there he went again; Mrs Greenway to advise. There was bound to be a suitable academy for young ladies somewhere around.

★ ★ ★

'Ah, Mr Gregory. There you are. This is amazing you know. Truly amazing. So much history all in one spot.' It was the enthusiastic, irrepressible historian seeking his attention now. 'Do you know, you have a perfect example of an early mediaeval tithe barn at Church Farm? The lower courses of stonework could even be Saxon with Norman building above. It's all very run down of course but the evidence is there, all clearly to be seen even down to post holes cut in the chalk, for Saxon timber work, you know.'

He stood back, face aglow with excitement awaiting Luke's approval or comment or at least his interest, all of which he was happy to give. This man's enthusiasm was infectious and in truth, he was more than a little interested in what was being discovered.

'Doctor come and sit down and have you eaten lately? Dinner is an hour away yet.'

'Oh, no time for that. Far too many things to look at and think about. Do you know, I believe the roof timbers to be chestnut and look in fair condition and the roof is of rag stone which must have been carried from some distance for there's none like it around here. A few holes needing repair of course but the farmer keeps his hay and straw there and it appears to be dry enough.'

'Helpful was he?'

'Oh yes, once he had your note. He didn't know much about the history of the farm though he was born there and took over from his father. He did say nothing had been altered for as far back as he knew. Grumbled a bit about the whole place needing money spent on it but I should imagine that's not unusual.'

'Passing on a message, I think. Yes, the whole estate needs a tidy up, one way and another. He's mainly a dairy farmer. Cows, bullocks and a few pigs and sheep. See his bull, did you? Quite an animal that.'

'Oh yes. His pen is mostly stone built. Only a hundred or so years old if that.' and Luke smiled to himself as he realised this historian viewed the world purely in terms of construction and antiquity with the occupants of but negligible interest.' I was not invited to view the farm house but it is clearly of early construction. Would that be a possibility do you think?'

'All things are possible but we must respect the man's privacy and of course Mrs Pearson would have to be consulted. Leave it to me and I'll see what can be arranged.'

'Oh, yes, yes, of course. Privacy. Mustn't intrude. Of course not. Bad form. Definitely bad form but about the under croft here. I have a theory that the entrance would have been on the other side of this wall, possibly opposite the front entrance here which would be under the present staircase, would it not? The ground plans of similar buildings suggest that as a possibility.'

'That'd be in what we call the back room, which was built on at a later date you thought?'

'Oh yes without a doubt. At the same period when the whole building was extended.'

'Then that's where we shall explore tomorrow. I'd sooner have the mess out there than in here. Now, would you care for a drop of this before we dine? It's a very fine malt. Smooth and mellow.'

★ ★ ★

'Good Lord, Peter. What have you been doing?' for that young man had appeared looking dishevelled and dirty with black cobwebs sticking to his shirt.

'Been up in the roof, Guv. Right up to the ridge, above the top rooms. I couldn't find a date anywhere but I did find some of the carpenter's marks that Doctor Searle said to look for.'

'Very good. You'd better go and tell him. He's in the back room searching for a blocked up doorway to the cellar or whatever.'

Peter was back almost immediately. 'He's found it Guv. He splashed water over the plaster and the outline of a doorway showed up.'

'Wonders will never cease. I'd never have thought of that. Let's have a look.'

The table and benches in the back room had been moved out of the way to allow access to the inner wall and there, clearly showing, was the outline of a rounded top doorway about four feet or so from the floor. Both George and Joseph were with Dr Bentinck-Searle, who was industriously scraping damp plaster away from the underlying stonework.

'So you were right,' Luke commented. 'We're just about opposite the front door here.'

'Yes, yes. You will realise that this was once an outside wall and the floor here has been raised but even so, the doorway would not have been much taller. People were quite short when this was built.'

'So now to open it up. What tools have we got George? We'll have a go ourselves. No need to call a builder I shouldn't think.'

'Hammers, chisels, crow bars and shovels all in a barrow outside, Guv.'

'Then what are we waiting for? Bring 'em in Joe. Right, Doctor, tell us where to start.'

'First, clear the plaster from here then ease out the small stone you'll find under the top of the arch. That will be the finishing stone, the last one used when the doorway was blocked up. After that, work from the top down,' and Doctor Bentinck-Searle stepped back to watch the work of opening up the ancient doorway.

'We shall need lights,' he suddenly said, which sent Peter and James scurrying off to find candles and lamps.

'Will there be ghosts there, Papa?' William asked quietly, catching hold of Luke's hand.

'Shouldn't think so, not with Doctor Searle here. He knows all about such things,' which reassured William sufficiently for him to pick up a candle ready for lighting.

'Be a good idea to move the stone and plaster out of the way, don't you think? Keep the floor clear as we go?' which prompted a flurry of tidying up from the bystanders.

There was a fair sized hole now and George stepped forward with his lamp and shone it through. 'Steps leading down,' he announced, 'but looks empty so far as I can tell.'

More hammering and chiselling and within the hour the doorway was cleared and all the debris removed. 'Dusty old job,' Luke commented. 'Doctor, the privilege is yours. You have first look before we all come rushing down.'

Quite what they had expected find, Luke wasn't sure. What they did find was a completely empty room cut into the solid chalk with just the one entrance and no windows. At one end was a protruding squared-off lump of rock and running the length of the far side a flat shelf of stone roughly a couple of feet from the floor.

'Just as I thought. This was a chapel.' Doctor Bentinck-Searle was fairly dancing with excitement and satisfaction. 'Altar there at the East end and seats for the aged and infirm members of the order. Closed off as a Catholic relic by the new Protestant proprietor and then forgotten about. Seen it before. And what have we here? A drainage channel crossing the floor. I will hazard a guess that this is an overflow from your well to prevent flooding during very wet seasons. But just look at the vaulting of the ceiling! Remarkable. Portland stone without a doubt and early Norman. So, there we have it. Eight hundred years old if it's a day.

★ ★ ★

'Ah, Digger. Come and listen to this. I have it all worked out now.' Luke was in one of his get up and go moods, when everything had to be done immediately if not sooner, once he'd settled on his course of action.'

'I'm all ears Guv,' his partner replied as he took his accustomed seat in the sitting room at Gresham House.

'I'm going to run the estate as a farming company. One large business instead of several struggling farms. I want to put each and every acre of land to whatever use best suits. Cows and milk at Church Farm with a new dairy. Horses at Lee Farm, fruit and vegetables at the Hall Farm, and arable at Higher Farm. What do you think? Oh, and pigs in the woods and sheep wherever.'

'I think you're going ter turn the place upside down,' Digger grinned. 'You reckon folks'll go along with it? Set in their ways they are, according to George.'

'If the pay is right they'll change their ways.'

'I reckon they will at that. You've proved it often enough. Interesting though and don't tell me. They'll all turn to and work where they're told. Right?'

'Right. Flexible work force. Whatever needs doing wherever, they all pitch in. Results and profits are what I'm after. They moan about the weather being against them. I want to beat the weather.'

'That'll be a tall order, Guv.'

'Mechanisation. That's the answer. A steam traction engine, seed drills, threshing machine, reaping machines.

Instead of taking a week to cut a field of hay with scythes, it can be done in a day. Less time for the weather to hold things up. Seed drills can sow evenly in half the time and I reckon if we thresh the corn as it's cut, with the machinery in the field, it won't be ruined by rain when it's waiting to be carted to the stack yard. And there's different seed varieties to try and different crops. You know, they save seed back from one harvest to sow for the next? There's been no change for years. Probably hundreds. New blood and new strains could work wonders.'

'Sounds ambitious, Guv. I can see you've bin reading it up but it's going ter set yer back a bit, ain't it?'

'I can always tap you for a loan. No, it'll work out a bit at a time. It won't happen over night. I'll start with friend Pearson and get him organised with a proper dairy. Clean and hygienic. No more piles of muck to plough through and if he doesn't like it well, we'll see.'

'It'll keep you out o' mischief. Beth said you'd find something ter keep you busy. Reckoned no disappointment'd keep you down. Not heard any more, I suppose?'

'Only that the lad left the school shortly after. Address in Norfolk somewhere or other.'

'You want me to make enquiries?'

'I've thought about it but it was all pretty final. I do wonder, mind. Still can't work it out but that's life I suppose. Now, can I take Lee Farm off your hands? You'd still keep your nags there of course but that land could be working harder I'm thinking.'

'It's all yours, Guv but our Horace won't like it. He's about retired now or thinks he is.'

'We'll come to an arrangement I'm sure.'

★ ★ ★

'Rector. Good morning. Come in. Take a seat.' It was Saturday morning and Luke had enjoyed a good night's sleep and a substantial breakfast following an uneventful week in the City. Life was interesting here at the Manor with so many things to occupy his mind and the Rector was proving to be the sort of cleric with whom he could rub along.

Settling onto the offered chair but declining the offer of coffee the Rector was quick to note Luke's relaxed mood and inwardly heaved a sigh of relief for he might, if the conversation went well, touch upon irksome matters.

'You have something on your mind,' Luke prompted.

'Yes. There are one or two things I would like to mention if it is convenient.'

'Fire away,' Luke invited.

'Firstly, an unimportant matter really. It concerns the Glebe land held jointly between incumbent and lord of the manor. It's an unusual arrangement apparently but Doctor Bentinck-Searle tells me it is to do with the Manor's ecclesiastical past when both offices were held in common, connected, I suppose with the Rectorial tithes going to the lord of the manor.

'Ah. So you've met our historian.'

'I have indeed and a very interesting person he is. Quite eminent in his field, you know. An authority on church architecture among other things.'

'He's certainly thrown light on this place and village history generally. He's along the river this morning ferreting around the mill. Apparently, that's as ancient as this place. Told you about the tithe barn at Church Farm, has he? Over the moon about it. Described it as an absolute gem. To me it's just an old ruin but anyway, the glebe.'

'Oh yes. The Return of Owners of Land states it to be about twelve acres or so of grazing that somehow remained partly with the church itself and I wondered how the arrangement worked and whether a better use might not be found for it.'

'Pearson grazes it at present but I've no idea what rental he pays. I suppose it's shared between us. Leave it with me and I'll ask George to enquire. Actually, I'm planning one or two changes to improve the estate and the Glebe might well be included.'

'Well thank you for that, which leads me on to a possibly associated matter. You may know perhaps that Brownlow, who kept Hill Farm, passed away last week?'

'I didn't, no.'

'The funeral was on Monday and his widow is desirous of moving to live with her daughter so wishes to sell up. It would seem that the farm is part of your estate but because of ill health and other difficulties, no rent has been paid for some little while. Mrs Brownlow fears that you might now demand all back rent and tithes be paid before she is free to vacate and you might even take her to law to recover outstanding amounts.'

'Hill Farm? Right on top of the ridge towards the downs isn't it?'

'Yes. About midway between here and Chiddington.'

'I'd heard of it, of course. Didn't know Remnold had it. I'll get George to visit and discuss matters but I'll not be harrying anyone over the place. I'll buy her stock if it helps.'

'That will be an enormous relief to Mrs Brownlow. You know, I had anticipated all manner of difficulties in broaching the subject but well, you have made my task so uncomplicated.'

'Like to keep things simple if I can,' and Luke moved restlessly on his chair as he wondered how Hill Farm would fit in with his plans.

The Rector noticed the change and hastened to mention one more matter before Luke tired of this meeting, well aware that he had saved the worst 'til last. 'I have one real problem that concerns me deeply and I'm not sure that I should be sharing it with you.'

Luke said nothing but looked enquiringly at his visitor.

'You will recall the tragic end of young Mr Remnold I know. The young person who was involved with him has never been allowed to, shall we say, live the episode down. He has suffered continual derision and persecution and has reached the point where he finds life just not worth living. In short, he tried to end his life last night but was discovered in time and the doctor managed to resuscitate him. His only hope is to make a fresh start away from this village.'

'And you want me to arrange the fresh start.' It was a bald statement, Luke inwardly cursing that once more he was expected to pick up broken pieces and do something with them. Was he being put on? Probably. Was it his place to provide a solution? Possibly. He had the resources. Did no one else? Probably not. The Rector saw the inner debate and prepared for a rejection. After all it was none of this man's business what the villagers got up to.

'Where is he now?'

'At the Rectory.'

'Put him on a train and someone will meet him at Waterloo. No questions will be asked and he'll be safe enough if he follows instructions. I'll send a telegram so you'll have to let me know the time of the train. Problem solved.'

'Mr Gregory, I feel my thanks to be utterly inadequate but you have them anyway.'

'Well perhaps you might do something for me by return. Shortly I shall be looking for someone to learn about steam traction engines. If you come across anyone interested in such things perhaps you could let me know?'

'I shall announce it from the pulpit in the morning.'

'My thanks for that. Anything more? There is, I can see. Come on. Out with it.'

'Well, two things, actually. The previous occupant of the Hall was a shooting man and kept the woodland for that purpose; cover for pheasants and partridges and so on. Well, he stopped the village bodger from making use of the timber, which put him out of work. He's an old man now but one of his sons is interested in the trade and knowing you don't keep birds to shoot, wondered if it might be possible to start up again.'

'And he couldn't ask me himself? Couldn't face that devil of a squire who'd likely put the dogs on him? And what, may I ask is a bodger?'

'I had to enquire that myself. They're wood turners, making legs for chairs and tables, for the furniture trade, but this one also had a side-line in charcoal burning.'

'Well he'll just have to come and tell me what he has in mind and he doesn't have to dress up in his Sunday suit to do so.'

'I think it is seen as showing respect and the young man in question was involved in throwing mud at the squire so he is a little diffident about calling at the Manor.'

'Harrumph', Luke grunted. 'If he was one of that little lot he probably helped roll Joseph in the muck. He'll get nothing from me 'till I know he's made his peace with him. And the other thing?'

'The church has a peel of seven bells but they cannot be rung as they are unsafe and need rehanging.'

'And I should see to it? Is that what you're telling me? Fabric of the church, I suppose. Well, best get it done but I think I shall be unavailable when you call in future!'

★ ★ ★

Chapter 12

Now to look round the hothouse and the grounds generally. One way and another his plans were taking shape without too much bother. Good planning was it? More like having the funds to pay for it all. Perhaps that was why neighbouring landowners were hostile. It was surprising what filtered back down the grapevine but, so what? Let 'em say what they liked. If they got off their rear ends and did a day's work they might have fewer money problems. His musing was interrupted by the sound of horse's hooves on the driveway and he wandered round to the front to see who might be visiting.

'Ah, Lady Cecelia. Not chasing foxes today?' he asked facetiously knowing it would be taken in good part.

'Wrong season. Month or two yet.'

'Well come on in and have a seat. Drop of the usual?' as Joseph took charge of her horse.

'Need it. Need it. Come to talk. Things to discuss. Know you're the right man.'

What now, Luke wondered for Lady Cecelia was looking serious and possibly not her usual self.

'Come to the point. Short of money. Have to sell up. Not as much in the bank as I thought. Brother spent it on books and what bit o' land goes with the house doesn't bring in much. Death duties too. Have to face it.'

Luke was by now accustomed to Lady Cecelia's abrupt manner of speech, with no words spared for flowery small talk. Straight to the point and no nonsense was her style.' I see,' he said, mind racing. Was she after a loan or was she offering her place for sale? 'Have you taken advice? I mean, are things as dire as you fear? Is there no way you may economise? Trim your sails, so to speak.'

'Been all through that. Legal man holds a mortgage. Didn't know about it when I took the place over. When brother died, you know.'

'Oh. I see. I do see. That does make things a bit awkward. What staff have you?'

'Housekeeper and a man outside. Looks to the horse, you know. Girl comes in to help clean. Grazing's let. Bout seventy acres. All that's left. Rest sold off.'

'So you have wages, upkeep and day to day living expenses. Have you listed all your outgoings? Often, when you tally everything it's not as bad as it seems at first.'

'Done that. Here. Know I can trust you,' and Lady Cecelia delved into a pocket and produced a neatly written list of her expenses together with her assets as she saw them.

'Good God!' Luke exclaimed. 'They're charging you seven percent interest on your mortgage? That's robbery. Two or possibly three percent would be more like it. That needs sorting out for a start. Don't suppose your legal man advised anything helpful? No. Thought not. Leeches, most of 'em.'

'All beyond me. Never had to deal with money. Father paid the bills so long as I kept out of sight. Embarrassment to the family, you know. Couldn't marry me off. Wrong shape. Not made for corsets. Packed me off to India. Plenty of lonely hearts there. None lonely enough though. No dowry to go with the title.'

Here was the perennial problem of what to do with the surplus daughters of impoverished gentry. Denied a proper education. Bound by social convention. Unable to train for a career or even take meaningful work, they were entirely dependent on their family. Take away the family and the unfortunate woman was in real difficulty. Luke had heard it all before and Lady Cecelia was just one of many. Nevertheless he liked this blunt old girl and would help if he possibly could but with his own plans to fulfil he wasn't in a position to be generous.

'What would be your first choice? I mean, if you could wave a magic wand, what would you wish for?'

'Stay as I am. Live out me days without fuss. Keep me horse as long as I can ride the damn thing. Don't ask much. Not as badly off as many. Know that. Never starved. Always had clothes. Should've been a fellah. Know that too.'

'Firstly, I suggest you renegotiate the mortgage and reduce the interest charge. Secondly, your land could possibly produce more income and thirdly you may well find items to sell off? If your brother spent money on books it's possible they could be resold?'

'You've set me thinking. Knew you were the man to talk to. Never say die, eh?' A pause, then, 'Er, bit out of me depth, though. Where do I start?'

'Lady Cecelia, I'm most happy to offer my services. Have another glass. I'll get someone to sort out the mortgage Monday morning and look at the demand from the Revenue. There are often ways round such problems. George and I will walk your acres tomorrow after church and bring our own expert in antiquities to advise on books and things. He's writing up the history of this place and is down at the mill this morning looking around. Knows what he's about and no mistake.

'Can't thank you enough and it's Cissie to me friends. No more of this Lady Cecelia business, just because me pa was an Earl.'

★ ★ ★

With Lady Cecelia gone, Luke heaved a sigh of relief. Perhaps now he'd enjoy a little peace and could follow his own interests but on entering the kitchen in search of coffee he found Mrs Cherry and her husband clucking and tutting over Joseph who, shirtless, was having large and rapidly purpling bruises anointed with witch hazel and zinc.

'Hello. What's this then? Luke enquired.

'Horse bites, Guv,' George replied. 'That savage her ladyship rides.'

'Good grief. It did that to you? Needs to be muzzled I reckon. Anything broken? Need the doctor?'

'No bones or anything like that,' Mrs Cherry said, 'but just look at these marks. A good job Joseph had a thick coat on.'

'Indeed yes. Why did it go for you like that?'

'Stallion, Guv. Never bin gelded. Bit like a bull in some ways. Temper can be off. Could've got a whiff of the ponies or something.'

'I see. Glad I don't ride the thing. You'd best take it easy for bit. Go and have a drink,' and Luke slipped a half crown into Joseph's free hand, guessing he'd not mind time away to call on his young lady of the moment, whoever she might be.

★ ★ ★

Monday saw Luke back at Gresham House as usual with things to think about and Lady Cecelia's finances to discuss with Walter and Digger who, even at that moment was on his way upstairs.

'So 'ow's things down on the farm?' he enquired, with his ever cheeky grin.

'Oh, still sorting out the plans. I've learned that Hill Farm is part of the estate but the farmer's died. Widow wants to move out. Sheep, mainly. It could fit in.'

'You didn't know it was yours, then? Nice present. Much land with it?'

'No idea. George is off to have a look round so I'll know at the end of the week. Hope it doesn't need a lot spending on it or I'll be running short.'

'Use the Trust Fund. Ready and waitin' ain't it?'

'Thought about it. Tempting but not sure I should. Mind you, Lady Cecelia needs a bit of help at the moment, so it'll come in handy for that.'

'And what's 'er ladyship been up to, might one ask?'

'Nothing dramatic. Just no idea of handling the readies. Completely foxed over taxes. Facing foreclosure and that sort of thing. Paying through the nose for a mortgage she doesn't need and sitting on a pile of valuable books her brother bought. Old Bentinck-Searle went into a swoon when he had a look. Rare first editions. Originals of stuff Shakespeare wrote and Caxton printed. That sort of thing. All belongs in a museum or university he reckons. Couldn't haul him away from the place but he'll get it all suitably placed for the old girl.'

'And that'll sort 'er problems out?'

'With a bit to spare. The Trust can take over the mortgage short term as soon as Walter can get it organised and she can settle down in peace with that brute she rides. Do you know, it bit Joseph something rotten when he stabled it. Teeth marks all over him.'

'Sounds more like a dog ter me. Reckon if it bit 'er she'd bite it back,' and Digger dissolved into chuckles at the thought, spilling his coffee as he did so.'

'She might at that. Charlie mentioned the lad I sent along I suppose?'

'Yes. What do want done with 'im?'

'Oh just a bit of gentle help to get settled and make a fresh start. That sort of thing. He's the one got mixed up with that funny business when what's his name, you know, young Remnold topped himself at the Hall. Village wouldn't let it lie so he needs a change of air. No one's to know, mind.'

'Course not, Guv. Now, you sitting comfy like? Got news fer you. Beth reckons I shouldn't keep it ter meself so 'ere goes. Like you, I were dead curious to know why a certain party sent a ring back so I got the lads to look fer answers. Not going ter get mad are you?'

'Go on. I guessed you might do something.'

'Well, I got an address from the school and 'ad someone look around. Artist, as it 'appens. Landscapes and such like. Went ter try his 'and at those round a certain village in Norfolk. Had a drink or two with the locals and learned the story.'

'Which is?'

'Grace took 'er family ter stay with 'er brother who's a vicar but she died soon after she got there. She's in the churchyard.'

'Good Lord.' Luke was genuinely shaken. 'What happened?'

'Not sure about that. A sudden illness was all we could get.'

'So her family is with her brother. At the vicarage?'

'S'right. All there at church Sunday mornings. Oldest one's got work with a thatcher. Doesn't look too 'appy about it which ain't surprising. Other two go ter the village school and don't ask. The little so and so's as lovely as ever. Probably end up in a fen with a brick round 'is neck.'

Luke sat quietly, digesting this news, then, 'What's the name of the village?'

'Deepingham. About twenty miles from Norwich.'

Luke again sat quietly, deep in thought.

'Great Eastern, Guv. Liverpool Street. Platform 8.'

'Mm? What's that?'

'Guv, I know exactly what you're going ter do. You'll not rest 'till you've seen fer yerself and done what you thinks best.'

'I'm as predictable as that?'

'All the way and yer dead right. Beff an' me both thinks so and yer gets off at a place called Newton Flotman. You don't 'ave ter go right into Norwich and the station fly'll take yer to Deepingham. Just over two hours or so an' the pub's clean an' comfy. The ales good too, I'm told.'

'I shall probably need a drop of that before I'm finished. Train times?'

'Just say the word an' one o' the lads'll get yer ticket.'

★ ★ ★

The Reverend William Markham was a tall, spare man of early middle age with a careworn look about him. He

- 334 -

answered the door to Luke in waistcoat and shirtsleeves and looked surprised, as if expecting a different visitor.

'Reverend Markham? I'm Luke Gregory. You will have heard of me?'

'Oh, er, yes. Come in. A surprise, yes, a surprise,' and he led the way to his study, settling himself behind his desk leaving Luke to take the hard chair facing it. For a few moments they looked at each other, both wondering how best to start a difficult conversation. The vicar suddenly said. 'Grace passed away.'

'Yes. That's why I've called. May I ask how this came about?'

'Illness. Long standing. Grace had but a short while to live and felt it best to end any arrangement. She felt it would have been unfair to continue.'

'It would have made no difference at all.'

'Grace said you would say that.'

Luke nodded his understanding and felt, at that moment, very humble.

'And her family? I believe you now care for them?'

'I am her only relative so they are my responsibility. How did you learn of this address?'

'I knew that Paul was no longer at school.'

'And they divulged this information? Disgraceful. Quite disgraceful. They had no business doing so.'

'I am a governor of that school, Mr Markham apart from which I made enquiries. I had to learn the reason.'

'I see. Your visit is unexpected. Sudden. A surprise.'

'It was remiss of me to not write in the first instance for which I apologise. To present myself at your door in such a fashion was ill-considered but I thank you for your time,' and Luke stood up, ready to take his leave. This conversation was not what he'd anticipated and he began to regret making the journey.

'You would not wish to see the children?'

'You are their guardian, Mr Markham and I have no idea if they'd wish to see me.'

'Paul and Louise have spoken warmly of you.'

'But not Julian. No, that young man took an instant dislike to me for whatever reason.'

'There does not have to be a reason. How would you have coped with him?'

'I would have placed him in a suitable boarding school, possibly a naval one. He created such discord that he was no longer welcome in my house.'

'I shall administer a sound thrashing if I am able, the next time he insults my wife.'

'I should let someone else do what needs to be done and spare yourself the upset. There are schools aplenty that will have an answer to him.'

'Such a course is beyond my means. Boarding school fees are out of the question. This is not a wealthy benefice.'

'I would count it a privilege to fulfil my responsibility to Grace's family as I would have done had she not passed away. Would Paul, for instance, care to return to school?'

'Probably but I cannot allow you to take on such a commitment.' A pause then, 'Out of the question. I cannot allow it.'

'In that case, Mr Markham, I must wish you good day,' and Luke walked from the room leaving the Reverend Markham sitting behind his desk.

He would not, after all, stay overnight but would seek as early a return to London as the Great Eastern Railway Company could offer. He'd done all that he could or should. He could do no more. He knew the reason why, the event belonged to the past but he did wonder at his meeting with the Reverend Markham.

Barely polite. Certainly not friendly. No reason why he should be but not so much as a formal handshake and come to think of it, he'd kept his hands out of sight under the desk. Odd. He'd made a generous offer and had expected it to be accepted. Gratefully? Perhaps. Might have hurt the man's pride. Was he becoming smug and patronising? Self-satisfied? Could be. The very things he loathed in others. Perhaps he shouldn't have made this visit and just let life take its course. After all, Grace had made a decision and here he was poking his nose in.

Ah, but the ale was good, so was the rabbit pie and the landlord in his gig would have him at the station in time for the three twenty-five train to London. Time for another pot but as he looked up to catch the landlord's eye he noticed someone standing just inside the door.

'Ah, Paul', and he stood up with hand outstretched in greeting.

Paul walked uncertainly towards him. 'Uncle William will not approve of me coming here but I had to make sure it was you, Guv. I thought I saw you earlier,' he tailed off.

'Well, there's no sin and wickedness here and I can recommend the rabbit pie. Have you time to join me?'

'Well yes, Guv. I only help in the mornings. At the moment, that is.'

'Well sit yourself down,' and to the landlord, all eyes and ears at the arrival of this unexpected customer, 'A refill please and rabbit pie here.'

'You've lost weight, young man. Working too hard? Look, I really am most sorry about your mother. I've only just heard why she decided to end our relationship and that's why I called upon your uncle.'

Paul just nodded but set to enthusiastically when his meal was placed before him. 'They don't want us here. My uncle and aunt, that is. I heard them talking about us.'

'They do have their own family to consider and Julian can be difficult.'

'I know. He hates it here and he hates them as well.'

'He wasn't too fond of me.'

'I know. I don't know why.'

'Look, I'll be frank with you. I don't have long as I've a train to catch but I've offered your uncle any assistance he cares to accept. You must understand that he is your guardian and I have no right to interfere. I doubt he approved of me but I can't help that. If there's anyway in which I can assist then I'm happy to do so and you know where to find me. I must go now but slip this in your pocket. You may find it useful,' and Luke passed over a couple of half sovereigns as he stood up and prepared to join the landlord in his gig.

'Thanks ever so much, Guv. Do you think I should tell Uncle William I've seen you?'

'Your decision, Paul. You know how the land lies but news travels. Better he hears it from you than some busybody. Good luck, old chap,' and he again shook hands with him.

★ ★ ★

It was a relief to get back to Gresham House and soak in the bath. Travel always left him feeling uncomfortable, probably because the carriages were so grimed with soot.

He'd done what he should, he tried to convince himself but could he have done more? If so, what? He'd had no idea how things would turn out. Hadn't expected to meet Paul like that. Certainly wasn't looking too happy but that was understandable. No, what it was, he decided, he'd found Uncle William irritating. Quite odd in fact but then, many God botherers were. A lot of them didn't believe one half of what they preached and a good few more certainly didn't practice it. Forget it now, Gregory. Enjoy your dinner, read the newspapers and turn in when you feel like it. Tomorrow's another day and you've work to do.

★ ★ ★

Ah hah. Steam traction engines. The brochure's lay on the table awaiting his attention. Don't know about such things but always ready to learn. Fowlers, eh? Business-like machinery by the looks of 'em. Now what did he want one to do? Work a threshing machine and pull timber from the wood. Power a saw bench, pull out tree roots, work a chaff cutter and similar machines and then hire it out to others. Yes, it could earn its keep but he'd send someone off to the factory to learn about them before buying one but which would best suit?

There were Burrels, Marshals, Avelings, Wallis and Steevens as well as Fowlers. Best to ask around then see. Same with threshing machines or thrashers as some called them. He'd heard of Ransomes and Cases but who'd supply the best? More interesting enquiries to make. This farm business really could be something once he'd got it going.

Then there was the mill. Doctor Bentinck-Searle had again enthused over what he'd found. Definitely mediaeval in origin and probably earlier but it had been rebuilt at some time. In a poor state but restorable; he was positive of that. It had two undershot wheels, a stone-lined race to channel the flow of water and sluice gates to control the flow.

The machinery was all there; just needed setting up after a period of neglect. Iron cogs mainly but apple wood in places. No problem to replace those but what would he use the place for? Mill their own flour? Possibly. There might be a market in London for that, same as for vegetables and milk. There were possibilities without a doubt. He'd have a word with Pearson first and sound him out with the dairy side of things and take it from there.

★ ★ ★

A visit to the wharf with Digger showed all to be going smoothly. The flow of trade and demand for their lighterage services was steady, their staff reliable and content. Just as it ought to be, Luke thought, considering the way the enterprise had evolved. There'd been difficulties over the years with untrustworthy employees and enough villainy one way and another to test a man's patience but they'd worked through the bad patches and now all appeared to be satisfactory.

'You going ter tell me 'ow you got on yesterday or do I 'ave to ask?' Digger enquired.

'Oh, yes. Well I'm back in one piece but I'm not sure I shouldn't have stayed away. Wasn't exactly welcomed by the reverend sir. Civil enough I suppose. Didn't really know what to expect. Offered help but he wasn't enthusiastic. End of story, I reckon.'

'See the nippers, did yer?'

'Met Paul by chance. Told him I'd help if I could but his uncle is his guardian and I had no right to interfere.'

'Not so good then.'

'The way of the world. Life's a funny old business. No telling what's round the corner. Best laid plans of mice and men and all that. Know anything about traction engines? I'm planning on getting one.'

'You really going ter get one? I don't know what you'll come up with next but what yer going ter do with it?'

'Come on up and I'll show you. I'm going to drag the estate into the modern world. I'm going to improve productivity and efficiency. I'm going to experiment and try different crops and new ideas and gear everything to the London market. It's all there waiting to happen.

'Yeah, but aren't you sticking yer neck out a bit? I mean, you ain't a farmer are yer.'

'My dear doubting Thomas. I'm taking professional advice from the Royal Agricultural College at Cirencester no less. Their learned experts are guiding me through the whole process of modernisation from crop rotation to the most suitable breeds of stock and what to feed things on for best results. Before long you'll be enjoying Gregory's prime sausages, produced from happy piglets roaming free in pastures green and muddy.'

'Get on, Guv, you're a regular card and no mistake,' Digger said, laughing.

★ ★ ★

They were on the point of heading down to the kitchen for lunch when Walter knocked at the door and entered. 'Sorry to intrude Guv but I have a visitor downstairs who would very much like to meet with you.'

'Oh? And who might that be?'

'Mrs Markham, Guv. Wife of the Reverend Markham.'

'Good grief. What does she want?'

'Well, Guv, it's about your visit there, to the vicarage. Mrs Markham is most anxious to accept the offer you made to her husband. She has explained that he is in a most uncertain state of health and has difficulty in er, shall we say, functioning satisfactorily in conversation? I have assured her that your offer of assistance stands but she feels that she must speak with you personally.'

'Oh, my glory,' Luke said, looking at Digger. 'Well, better show her up then.'

Mrs Markham was a stout, rather fussy sort of person who dropped a quite unnecessary curtsey to Luke before being hastily shown to a seat in the visitor's armchair by the fireplace. Digger perched on a chair by the table and Walter started to withdraw, having made the introductions.

'No, please stay, Walter. We shall need your advice I know.'

'Mr Gregory, it was so good of you to visit and I must apologise for my husband's lack of hospitality but I am afraid he does suffer a problem with his health that affects his concentration. You see, he was formerly a missionary in Africa and contracted an illness that has left him impaired and with poor Grace passing away so suddenly it has left us in great difficulty.'

'Mrs Markham, there's absolutely no cause for apology whatsoever and I can well appreciate so sudden an increase in your family to be burdensome. As I explained to your husband, I would consider it a privilege to take responsibility for Grace's family, just as I would have done had our plans come to fruition.'

'Oh Mr Gregory it is so kind of you, it really is.'

'Not at all. Now I take it that Jean-Paul would wish to return to school? He would? Then he may do so without delay. Somewhere for Julian, I think is urgent. My experience of him was not a happy one.'

'Oh he is such a dreadful child. So rude and troublesome.'

'Indeed he is. Walter, would you find a suitable placement for him, please? Holidays with you, Digger?'

'You're joking, Guv.'

'Of course. We'll think of holidays later. And Louise?'

'Oh, I'm sure we can cope with Louise. She is very quiet and amenable.'

'Very well. Mr Brierly will attend to school fees and associated expenditure and will write to you directly when somewhere has been found for Julian. If there is anything else we can help you with please do not hesitate to contact Mr Brierly and we shall do our utmost to be of assistance,' and Luke went through the motions of half rising from his seat to signify the meeting was over, convention requiring that Mrs Markham make the first move.

★ ★ ★

Luke was soon to realise there would be resistance to change when he and William arrived at the Manor that next Friday afternoon. 'Fair bit of muttering about new fangled ideas,' George reported. 'Some as reckon you're no farmer and you'll be putting men out o' work.'

'Stupid bunch of thick-headed clodhoppers,' Luke muttered as he tackled a scone. 'There'll certainly be a few looking for other work if they don't do it my way. What's the state of the game up at Hill Farm?'

'Old man Daly's caretaking the flock but he's well past his best. Crippled with rheumatism so I take him up in the trap but he knows his sheep. Reckons all the pasture up there is sheep sick. Been over-worked, like most of the land round here. Doesn't think much of the flock either. Reckons Brownlow was known for keeping everyone else's scrag ends.'

'Not too good, then. There's thirty head at Higher Farm too. They any better?'

'A bit but not much. Mainly crossbreeds and a few blackfaces that could be anything.'

'I'm told I should go for Oxford Down ewes with a Dorset Down ram.'

'Daly reckons pure bred Suffolks would be right. Good wool and a decent carcass. Keep the Jacobs will you?'

'Yes. They're a bit different and not a bad commercial breed.'

'Daly said much the same. Seems like you're on the same tack there, Guv,' George said with a laugh. 'Reckons they're the only flock for miles around.'

'I'm getting something right then so let's give thought to clearing out the old stock and resting the grazing. Mutton boiled and baked for a bit, eh?'

★ ★ ★

'What's this, then Ticker? Been scrapping? Must have been some do.'

'It's me feyther, Guv. 'E's come back. Knocked our mother about too, and Robbie and Alf. I could kill the bastard. We were doin' all right 'till 'e turned up.'

'Can't have this. Won't have it. Where is he now?'

'In the Lamb. Been there all day. Drinking mother's money.'

'I see. Where is your mother?'

'Home, Guv. Sent me up to see yer soon as you got 'ome.'

'I'll come straight down. You go on in William. I'll be back directly.'

Life could be rough and tough, Luke well knew. Disagreements were commonly settled with a fist fight and a man could hit his wife more or less with impunity and on occasion it could be the other way round, but serious injury seldom resulted. He was shaken though when he saw the state of Mrs Donkin. With both eyes closed and purpling and her mouth split and bleeding she resembled a prize fighter in the losing corner.

'Good God!' he exclaimed. 'Has the doctor been? No? Fetch him, Robbie. Run,' and to Ticker. 'This has to be settled,' and he scribbled three words and the warehouse address on a page from his pocket book. 'Post Office, telegram. Round the back if they're closed. They'll deliver up to seven o'clock. Here, this'll cover the extra,' and he handed Ticker a crown piece.

'You want him out of the way, permanently?' to Mrs Donkin. 'Don't try to speak. Just nod or shake your head.' Mrs Donkin nodded. 'Australia far enough?' Mrs Donkin nodded again. 'Right. I've sent for the heavies. They'll be here on the last train. Ah, the doctor.'

'Good Lord, Mrs Donkin. I've heard what happened but this takes some believing,' and he carefully set about applying his medical skills.

'Robbie, everyone up to the house. Mrs Cherry'll fix you something to eat. Say I'll be up directly.'

'Ah, Ticker. Sent is it?'

'Yes Guv. He wasn't very pleased.'

'He never is. When the doctor's finished with your mother I want him to check you over.'

'Oh, I'm alright, Guv.'

'We'll see. Now, what's the verdict, Doctor?'

'Severe contusions as you can see but no bones broken. The swelling will have to subside before I can be sure of no long term effects but complete rest is required for at least three days. Cold compresses, of course. Mrs Donkin, let me help you upstairs. I'll leave instructions for your daughter.'

'When they come back Ticker, I want Robbie and Alfie to keep watch near the Lamb and if your father heads up this way they are to fetch me straight away. He's not to be allowed in. Then come up yourself for a meal. Alright?'

'Yes, Guv but what if 'e comes back later? When the Lamb closes.'

'The big lads'll be here by then and he'll be on the first train out in the morning, bound for Australia. Your mother thinks he should emigrate and leave the family in peace.'

And that is precisely what happened. Two large gentlemen in bowler hats, who might well have been mistaken for officers of the detective department, awaited a drunk name of Donkin, restrained same, locked him securely in an outhouse for the night and escorted him on the early train from Chidlingbrook to, within a week, the steerage deck of an emigrant ship bound for Sidney in Australia and was never heard of again.

★ ★ ★

'So how are things up at the Hall?' Luke asked Amos Burlington when he called to report. He'd been watching William riding in the field below with Ticker and his brothers. With the ponies not getting enough exercise, the weekends were spent riding them round the fields with everyone joining in under Joseph's watchful eye.

'Oh, not so bad, sir. Had to chase one or two for not pulling their weight.'

'Every crew has its slackers. Mrs Burlington alright?'

'That she is, sir. First born in the spring. April to May Doctor Fairleigh reckons. Over the moon she is.'

'Glad to hear it. You've gathered a few changes are in the offing. I'd like the Hall lands developed for vegetables on a commercial basis for the London market. A field of cabbages, another of cauliflowers and so on. Cut and pack on site then run sheep over the stumps before ploughing. Tom Pearson's going to run the dairying side of things so your cows'll probably go down to him.'

'You mean work on just one side o' things?'

'That's the idea. Hay carted down to him as needed and his yard sweepings removed to the fields. There'll be a new milking parlour and no more dung heaps round the place. It's clean, modern dairying I'm after. Milk maids in white smocks. Cows brushed down before milking and teats washed every time.'

'I get the idea. So no more corn up the Hall then?'

'In and out, yes. Ring the changes on the arable land. Use it to best purpose. With Meredith retiring I thought to base the horses there; mainly grazing and hay but nothing settled yet. It's best practice and better yields we need so wages can be improved. Got to earn it before we can pay it out. Father's short of help with you away is he not? Reckon he could use men from Higher? Save laying 'em off? I'll see to wages but how about a couple of days in London, to pick up ideas round the markets and see what's selling? Asparagus is in demand I know but there may be other things worth trying.'

That's settled then, Luke thought. Let that enterprising young man put his mind to it and watch for results. Encourage him and give him scope to develop ideas. He'd also see how flexible the work force would be, with a couple moving to Lee Farm when needed, and he turned his attention back to the ponies in the field below.

★ ★ ★

Not for long though for his next visitor was Doctor Fairleigh who clearly had business in mind as he stepped down from his gig and announced there were one or two problems over which he needed guidance, a neat enough way of sharing responsibility, Luke thought.

'There's sickness in the village that's avoidable. The Proberts are all laid up with severe vomiting and diarrhoea and I'm pretty sure it's from their water supply. I think their privy drains into their well, especially after rain and there are quite a few families drawing water from the river by the bridge and they have sickness on and off all the time.'

'Sounds like London a year or so back.'

'That's just it. I've followed the river upstream and apart from cattle pollution there are several properties in Chiddington draining directly into it.'

'Same with the mill. Doctor Bentinck-Searle tells me there's a two seater privy that empties straight into the river, to the benefit of Chidingfold downstream. Been the same for years I suppose. So what's the answer?'

'Well, Guv I was rather hoping you might have thoughts on the subject. Seems like the Rivers Pollution Act and the Public Health Acts are not acted upon, if you'll pardon the pun. Eighteen seventy-five and six respectively. No sewage to drain into any stream and a wholesome water supply for all.'

'And that's for me to sort out? Didn't know the village plumbing was my concern.'

'It's really the Sanitary Board's responsibility but the landowners have influence there so nothing's been done. I'm told Sir Brandon opposed any changes hereabouts.'

'He would. Not a pleasant type. Think I should have the wells filled in? Can't drink the stuff then, can they? They empty their cess pits onto the gardens so no point offering a honey cart for moving the soil. Tell you what. If they pay rent to me I'll get their wells emptied and cleaned and the sanitary people can pay for it.'

'That'll be a start, Guv but what about the river?'

'Not a lot I can do about that if the problem's upstream. Sanitary people again, I should think. Don't even know who owns what at Chiddington. Could find out, I suppose. Probably Lord Berrimond. Look, I'll get a surveyor to visit. You can tell him what's needed and we'll see what he comes up with. That satisfy you?'

★ ★ ★

No more visitors please, Luke said to himself as the doctor left. All they ever seem to bring are problems that have nothing to do with me. If these clodhoppers dig their cess pits uphill of their drinking water they damn well deserve to be ill. Don't the silly buggers know anything? He'd keep out of the way for a while and go for a good long walk after lunch and weigh up the possibilities of running pigs in the woodland. Pigs with long snouts for rooting around could do well there, he'd been told. Good, lean pork and bacon would find a ready market in fashionable London so let the locals enjoy their fat bacon if that's what they liked. He'd have his lean.

He'd have to give thought to Fred's worries, though as he hadn't heard from his father for nearly three months now. He knew they exchanged letters regularly every month so what was the problem, he wondered? He'd enquire at the warehouse as consignments from India arrived regularly enough. Cotton, some excellent silks last month and loads of hand made jewellery but three months was a long time.

★ ★ ★

Good surveyors tend to be thorough and George Ridgeway was as thorough as any. He'd scrutinised the village in detail, visited every occupied dwelling, pig sty and stable and duly noted water supplies and soil disposal arrangements. His verdict was that nothing had changed in a thousand years and improvements were needed to comply with the law.

'You'll send a report to the sanitary people will you? With your recommendations and let me have a copy.'

'I certainly will, Mr Gregory but I shall have to treat the river as a separate entity. A different body involved there, you understand.'

Examining the river however was not to be a straightforward process. The surveyor returned to the Manor in a distinctly dishevelled condition, limping and with clothing torn.

'Good Lord, Mr Ridgeway. What have you been up to? Come along in. You look in need of a restorative,' and Luke ushered him into the study and offered a choice of whisky or brandy. Ridgeway, it seemed had walked the length of the river as far as the railway terminus at Chiddington, making notes as he went but, once past there was accosted by Lord Berrimond's bailiff who'd abused him verbally for trespassing on private property and as he turned to walk away, had set his dogs on him. He'd been bitten twice on the right thigh and once on the left calf, and as Luke could see, his trousers and jacket were torn.

'I'll send for the doctor. Please come up stairs to the guest room. This is absolutely outrageous and something will have to be done about it,' which, in Luke's terminology, boded ill for those responsible. If Berrimond wanted trouble he could have it so he'd see that Ridgeway took a civil action for damages and get the constable to look into a matter of assault and injury to the person.'

A smile spread across John Fairleigh's face as he nodded his approval. 'I've met the bailiff in question. Barely civil when I was poking about the river but he gave me to understand his lordship would tolerate no intrusions from outsiders. I didn't mention this earlier but words are one thing, injuries another.'

★ ★ ★

In due course, Jabez Coultran, bailiff to Lord Berimond appeared before magistrates at Guildford and was fined ten pounds or thirty days imprisonment for causing his dogs to attack the surveyor retained by the Chidlingbrook Vestry.

It appeared that neither his lordship nor his bailiff were popular figures and there was much satisfaction when it was also learned that the surveyor had accepted an out of court settlement of two hundred pounds in respect of injuries to his person and apparel. There were, however, dark mutterings amongst the local gentry concerning one Luke Gregory, who was clearly intent upon upsetting the established order of things and something, they all agreed, would have to be done.

★ ★ ★

'Ah, there you are,' Lady Cecelia boomed as she caught sight of Luke. 'Got something to tell you. Best you should know. Hunt meeting. Big wigs of the district, you know. Got it in for you. Berimond's still ragin'. Wants to get back. Dirty tricks afoot. That sort o' thing.'

'And what have I done to rouse his lordship's ire?'

'Knows you were behind that business. Fellah being bit. Knows the Parish Vestry's come to life again. Complaints about the river. All that stuff. Quite right too. Time someone stirred things up. Had it their own way too long.'

'Ah. Well, yes. All sorts going in the river and causing illness. Against the law now so we're looking at drains and water supplies. Clean water for every cottage and waste taken well away from the village. No more cess pits draining into wells and causing sickness.'

'Got it all planned out if I know you.'

'Well, our surveyor has. His pipes and things need to cross Berimond's land. He's objecting and the sanitary people are reluctant to offend by insisting. Can't see why. They've got the law behind 'em.'

'You'll have an answer. Stake me life on it. Going to the hunt ball? Three weeks time. Event of the year you know.'

Mixing with the local hunting set was not something Luke had anticipated doing but, with both Lucy and Annabelle fast growing up he realised they needed to socialise. This would be their first venture into local society and they were wildly excited at the prospect. It could be an enjoyable outing, Luke decided for he did like to dance and he might even find a partner or two who'd welcome his attention. With Lady Cecelia in close attendance there should be few problems with the hot blooded local youth. Yes. He would, he decided, look forward to the occasion and if Digger and Beth did decide to join him, that would add to the pleasure.

★ ★ ★

Brightly lit by gas the ballroom was already filling up, the orchestra was putting the final touches to their tuning and cheerful groups stood about happily anticipating the opening dance. Luke was immediately aware of the interest shown as he and Lady Cecelia escorted the girls through the wide open doorway of the Assembly Rooms.

Older people commented together on their arrival, some acknowledging Lady Cecelia, whilst smartly dressed young men began manoeuvring with the intention of securing the girls as partners. In no time at all, both had well filled cards and looking around with an experienced eye, Luke realised they were two of the most attractive young ladies present. As a matter of courtesy, he partnered Lady Cecelia in the first waltz and was surprised at how light on her feet she was, despite her bulk.

'Nothing more than a waltz mind. I'm past the high steppin' stuff. Run out of puff, you know. Not so young as I was but Gad, Squire Gregory, you dance well.'

'Well thank you, Your Ladyship', and they both laughed at their jocular formality.

'That's me lot. I'll sit the rest out,' she declared as Luke escorted her to a seat. 'Get the gossip, you know. Plenty to be had. Keep me eye on the gels too. Those young fellahs are round 'em like flies at a jam pot.'

'I'll offer some competition before long. I've booked a polka or two. Show 'em how it's done.'

'I'll be watching so tallyho!'

★ ★ ★

It could and should have been a most enjoyable evening but, as supper was announced and the dancers moved towards the heavily laden tables, certain people made a point of standing where Luke could easily hear their disparaging and insulting comments passed for his benefit.

'Some guttersnipe from the London sewers, I've heard tell,' and Lady Cecelia stiffened.

Luke caught her eye and shook his head. He'd not be provoked by morons the worse for drink. Those involved though couldn't leave well alone and he was deliberately nudged, causing him to spill his drink. He turned to look at the one responsible, a man in his thirties who turned his back and remarked loudly to another that 'the place was being cluttered by riff raff. No business here. Can do without the type.'

'Brought some damn fine fillies with him. Wouldn't mind seeing what they could do over the jumps, what?'

Luke looked straight at the speaker, aware that he referred to Lucy and Annabelle.

'Know you, do I?' the man demanded, emboldened by drink and his companion's support and approval.

Luke continued to stare at the man aware that this would be seen as challenging. He would either look away and ignore him or seek to face him down. He chose the latter course.

'Who the deuce d'you think you're staring at?'

'Clearly not a gentleman.'

'Now look here, damn your insolence. Know who I am, do you?'

'I know you're a cad, sir,'

'I say, I'll have satisfaction for that.'

'You shall indeed. Name your second.'

There was a sudden hush and Luke realised that the altercation had attracted attention. He also realised that he was extremely angry at the insults directed at him but more so at the lewd comment towards the girls.

'Good Lord,' someone spluttered. 'They're going to duel. Damn me but I thought that went out years ago.'

'Can't do that. Against the law, isn't it?'

'Matter of honour, you know,' someone offered mischievously. 'Insults offered. Have to be settled.'

Luke turned away and saw that Lady Cecelia was on the point of exploding with laughter.' Gad, Luke Gregory, you're a one. A pleasure to know you. Never a dull moment. Serious are you? Duel and all that?'

'Most certainly. Insult and a challenge offered. Have to respond.'

'Now look here. There's no need to take things seriously. Social occasion, you know. No offence intended; things said in jest, what?'

The speaker was one of the group who'd guffawed at the challenger's comments and was now trying to play down the affair, but Luke was not to be deterred.

'If you sir, are that blackguard's second you may call upon mine and I shall expect a prompt settlement of arrangements.'

The man's eyes opened wide and he gurgled something incomprehensible and returned to his companions, grouped silently now around the challenger.

'Know who it is, I suppose?'

'Berimond?'

'The Honourable Gerald. Eldest son. Can't second you meself. Not allowed. Anything I can do? To help, I mean.'

'Best stand clear of this but you might put it about that I'm a crack shot with a pistol. Might cause him discomfort.'

They had scarcely turned their attention to their plates when they were again approached, this time by the Hunt Master who spoke bluntly to Luke. 'I think you should leave. Caused enough upset. Out of place. Bad form, challenging people.'

'I am the one challenged. I'm not the instigator of unpleasantness.'

'That's right, John. Berrimond insulted Squire Gregory here and then demanded satisfaction. Heard it meself. No choice but to accept.'

★ ★ ★

'Are you really going to fight a duel, Guv?' The girls were agog with excitement, wondering what was involved. 'But why are you going to fight?'

'Fellow made insulting remarks about you. Can't be allowed to get away with that or every popinjay in the district will consider you of no account and both of you are gentleman's daughters.'

'But Guv, won't you get hurt? I mean, what will you fight with?'

'Oh, feather dusters or turnip tops. Your Uncle Digger will arrange something suitable.'

Digger, though, was distinctly perturbed at the prospect. 'Aw, come on, Guv. Do you 'av ter do it? I mean, is 'e worth it and you're not as young as yer used ter be.'

'Don't write me off too soon, young man. I'm choosing cutlasses for the occasion. Had cutlass drill every week since I went to sea and I'll wager he's handled nothing heavier than a foil. Different business altogether and I have to make a showing. I've two young beauties on me hands and the local hot bloods have to know to mind their Ps and Qs.'

So, the meeting was arranged for the following morning, at seven o'clock in the field closest to the boundary with the Berimond estate. Doctor Fairleigh had agreed to attend but insisted on remaining out of view and uninvolved, unless his services were required. Lady Cecelia though, was no where near as discreet. 'Wouldn't miss it for the world. Nothing like it as long as I can remember.'

The Honourable Gerald, when he arrived, looked quite jaunty and sought to stare Luke down. As with many of his social class, he had a reasonable ability at fencing and had been reassured by the choice of weapons. Pistols would have been distinctly dangerous but now he felt he could teach that jumped up Gregory fellow a thing or two and had rejected the suggestion of allowing the law to intervene and prevent proceedings.

With their regulation naval cutlass in hand, the principals faced each other awaiting the signal to commence battle. Berimond had made a few flourishes with his blade and now took up a traditional fencing stance. Luke, set faced stood erect, left hand on hip, his blade held in a high guard pointing directly towards the ground. The handkerchief fluttered and Berimond immediately attacked with a lunge towards Luke's midriff.

It was exactly what he'd anticipated and he deflected the oncoming blade to one side, stamped forward and smashed the hilt and guard of his weapon into his opponent's face. End of contest as Berimond, his nose broken and minus his front teeth, collapsed bloodily on the turf. Luke turned away, took his jacket from Digger and walked off towards where George awaited him in the road with the pony and trap.

'You 'ad it all worked out, didn't yer Guv,' Digger commented.

'Of course. Home George. I'm ready for my breakfast.'

'I think Her Ladyship'll be joining us,' Digger said. 'I can see 'er 'orse back there.'

And Lady Cecelia did join them a short while later, beaming her delight at the outcome. 'Couldn't have done better meself,' she chuckled. 'Took him down a peg or two and not before time. Not well liked, that family, you know. Thought he'd fillet you at first, waving his blade about like that.'

'A brutal weapon, the cutlass, Cissie. Not built for fancy stuff. A line of good men can clear a deck with 'em. Thrust, stamp, slash. Very effective.'

'Still don't know why yer 'ad to do it,' Digger said

'Honour, sir. We squires have to act the part. No, it's not that at all. The Berimonds are a difficult lot. Lost the contest over our surveyor so were planning personal difficulties for my good self. Thought to push me about so had to learn the error of their ways.'

★ ★ ★

The Honourable Gerald, on behalf of his father, Lord Berimond, offered every possible hindrance to the Vestry's efforts to improve sanitation in the valley. An excellent source of fresh water was available from a spring by the Chidington station, which could have been piped alongside the railway track. Similarly with a sewer pipe that could carry effluent and so prevent it entering the river, but he would have none of it.

Ah now, the railway. He'd have a word with the railway company, of which he was still a substantial shareholder, and put to them a cost saving proposition. If Chidlingbrook were to be the terminus instead of Chidington, the company would save the expense of running a regular service to a little used station. Lord Berimond had, many years ago, insisted on the provision of the line for his personal convenience, that he knew. If he leased to the company, at a peppercorn rent, sufficient ground for an additional siding and turntable and leased from the company the track between Chidlingbrook and Chidington, the Vestry would be free to carry out its plans.

★ ★ ★

William Hurle was seriously ill. Lockjaw, it was rumoured and a bad case at that. 'Seems like he stuck himself with a dung fork while muck-spreading', George reported. 'Didn't take more'n passing notice at the time but a week later he were laid up real bad.'

'Where was this, then?'

'Up the Home Farm, at the Hall. They were doing one of the little plots ready for seed trials.'

'That's bad. Really bad. Let me know how he fares.'

But by the end of the following week, William Hurle was dead.

★ ★ ★

'As I see it, the Vestry meeting should be open to all ratepayers in the parish who'd be free to raise any matter for discussion but we'd need an agenda before-hand. Have to be business-like or we'll spend all night going in circles.'

Luke was in forthright mood. The first formal meeting had been hit and miss in his opinion and he was keen to see things more organised. He had insisted the Rector take the chair with himself and Doctor Fairleigh supporting. Pike the schoolmaster and Police Constable Hutton would add weight to proceedings for the future but they'd have to appoint a parish clerk as that role had been vacant for years.

He looked at his visitors for approval, saw that he had it and topped up their glasses.

'I still think you should take the chair,' the Rector said.

'Restarting the Vestry was your idea so you take the chair for your pains,' Luke replied with one of his rare smiles. 'And what's more I think you should become magistrate. I've twice now refused the Lord Lieutenant. Not to my taste at all, sitting in judgement.'

'Oh no, thank you very much. That would sit ill with my parochial duties but a doctor could surely find such a position congenial.'

'And I must decline that honour. As you know, at some point I shall move on. Probably seek to specialise in some field or other. Now if you want a really able candidate, why not Pike? There's rather more to our schoolmaster than at first meets the eye. Did you know he served in Africa? Youngest sergeant on Lord Chelmsford's staff at one time. Had charge of the baggage train or something. Served his time then took up teaching.'

'I had no idea,' Luke said, 'but I had wondered how he came to settle at a village school. Mm. Aloysius Pike JP. Has a ring to it. Yes. Why not? Good idea. I'll put his name forward,' which made all three smile and not just from enjoyment of the whisky.

★ ★ ★

'John, I'm so sorry about your father. It was quite a shock to hear of his passing. Anything I can do? To be of help, I mean.'

'Well, sir, mother doesn't know about the field. I mean she doesn't know what she should do with it.'

'Brothers not interested in working it?'

'No sir. Ronnie's going for a soldier and Jim says as he wouldn't know where to start and I know he wants to be considered for the traction engine,' and John coloured up, a bit embarrassed. 'After Rector gave it out in church, I mean.'

'Then he should come and talk to me about it and I'll have a word with your mother about the land. So Ronald's joining the army. Bit of a change there, I think.'

'He's fed up with just farm work. He wants to do something a bit exciting but father wouldn't let 'im. Now father's gone 'e's says he's off.'

'Understandable. Mother happy about it?'

'Yes, sir. Says as we can all have a bit more of a life now he's gone. He treated her hard, if truth be told. Heavy on us all, at that,' with a tilt of his head and a defiant glint in his eye.

'I see. Well, if I can be of help, just let me know and I've heard good reports of you at school so keep it up. Who knows where that can lead?'

★ ★ ★

'I have a letter that you might care to see,' Walter greeted Luke. 'Sad news, I'm afraid. The Reverend Markham has passed away and Mrs Markham is required to vacate the vicarage. It would appear that her next place of residence will be barely large enough for her own family and she would be happy to be relieved of further responsibility for her late sister in law's family.'

'Understandable, I suppose. Paul should be involved, I think. Telegram to the school. First available train here to resolve family matters and then I should be obliged if you would accompany him to the Markham household and finalise any obligation I might have towards the family. I'll leave it in your hands entirely, in every respect and no, I'm not about to enquire how his brother has settled. He can be mastheaded or keel hauled daily as far as I'm concerned.

★ ★ ★

Chapter 13

'There we are then gentlemen. We have progress.' Luke was addressing the assembled Vestry meeting in preparation for which, he'd been busy behind the scenes on what he called the 'spade work,' and was now outlining the immediate future to the principal members of the community.

'The railway terminus will soon be here in Chidlingbrook with whatever amenities the company chooses to install. I've taken a lease on the line to Chidington to enable the installation of water and sewage services alongside the track bed and I propose that Mr Ridgeway here be authorised to commence work on that as soon as possible.'

'Yes, but who's going to pay for all this, that's what I want to know.'

'Harrington, is it not?' Luke enquired, looking at the red-faced farmer sitting at the end of the table. 'The Sanitary Board has taken a loan to pay for necessary works.'

'Yes, but what's this about no more trains to Chiddington?'

'Oh, trains may still use the line, by prior arrangement with the station master.'

'But what about my milk churns?'

'Horse and cart to the station here?'

'This is monstrous. We'll see what His Lordship has to say about this,' and the irate farmer scrambled noisily to his feet and stamped out of the room.'

There was silence for a while, apart from scraping feet and a few muffled coughs then Luke again proposed an early start to necessary pipe laying.

★ ★ ★

'Er, Guv. Can I have a word?' George was clearly uncomfortable and had waited until Luke was alone outside in the yard. 'Er, it's like this,' he continued hesitantly. 'Young Lizzie's got 'erself in trouble. Beginning to show, like.'

'Oh? And who was her partner? Or isn't she saying?'

'That's just it, Guv. She is saying. Reckons it were Mr Wales as stayed 'ere.'

'What?' Luke was completely taken aback. 'Good God. You sure? I mean, is she sure? Knows what she's saying, does she?'

'Well, Guv, the missus got the whole story from 'er and Gertrude backs it up. You know, they share a room together. Seems like she visited late on. Said as 'ow she were invited, like. In a proper state she is. Scared stiff an all that.'

'As if I haven't got enough to think about. Well, these things do happen. I'll arrange something on Monday. No need for upset. Pass the word will you?'

'Righto, Guv. Will do,' and each, catching the other's eye, half grinned, as men of the world will, who understand how things are.

Luke though, was not well pleased. Was really annoyed, in fact. 'Why couldn't the fat freak control himself?' he demanded of Digger. 'A guest in my house and in my bed too and with one of Thomas's girls at that. All right, she's at fault but he should damn well know better.'

'Yes, too right,' Digger agreed diplomatically, 'but what you going ter do, that's the question.'

'Oh, I'll not cause a stir but I want him to know. Lizzie'll move to the Lodge House. There'll be no questions asked there but I expect him to make provision for the child. I'll leave you to arrange that. Damn feller. Worse than a barnyard cockerel.'

★ ★ ★

One week later and Walter was tapping on the sitting room door. Luke, occupied with the day's newspapers was still in his slippers, a half empty coffee cup by his chair.

'Sorry to intrude, Guv but Sir Reginald Fortescue is downstairs and wonders if he might have a word. Very apologetic at not making an appointment but says it is a most urgent matter.

'Oh? Do we know him?'

'Not that I'm aware of, and he declined to state the nature of his business beyond it being of a confidential nature.'

'Armed and dangerous do you think?'

'I would not have thought so,' Walter replied, smiling.

'Well best show him up then. Oh, wait 'till I tidy these things away and grab a jacket. He'll have to put up with my slippers.'

Sir Reginald was not an old man but he wore the slightly careworn and greyish appearance of advanced years and heavy responsibility. 'It is most kind of you to receive me at such short notice, Mr Gregory but I have the most urgent instruction to meet with you.'

'And what might be the nature of this instruction?' Luke enquired, cautiously.

'It is to do with an er, indiscretion on the part of one in whose household I hold a position.'

'Which tells me nothing, Sir Reginald. For which newspaper do you write?'

Sir Reginald's jaw dropped in utter surprise. Had Luke assaulted him with a wet haddock he could not have been more taken aback.

'I, I do assure you, Mr Gregory I have no connection whatever with any journal. None whatsoever.'

'I am aware you see, that sensation seekers will stoop to any subterfuge in search of scandal and as you have yet to state by whom you are employed and precisely your purpose in calling I feel unable to be of assistance.'

There was an awkward silence broken by the sound of footsteps on the stair and Digger appeared in the doorway.

'Hello Reggie. Hot foot from the office? Let me guess why.'

'Oh, Mr O'Dowd, I am relieved to see you. I'm afraid Mr Gregory is suspicious of my presence and believes me to be a newspaper reporter.'

'Oh, Reggie's alright, Guv. Works for 'is nibs. Gets the awkward jobs to sort out. That sort of thing. Coffee's on its way.'

'Ah. Right. Have to be careful. So, you'll be interested in arrangements for the future. Firstly, we keep the matter private. Those who know are either totally trustworthy or will be persuaded to maintain their silence. The lady's interests will be suitably looked after of course and I and one other will stand as God parents and will register the birth appropriately. Should the child be a boy then a reasonable education will be arranged and possibly, long term, a career in one of the colonies might suit. A sheep farmer in Australia, perhaps? If a girl then again, adequate provision will be arranged.'

'Mr Gregory, I can see that you have given the matter considerable thought for which I am truly relieved. Might I enquire the person's name?'

'The young lady's name is Elisabeth Farrell and is originally from Ireland. She was placed in my care by Thomas Barnardo to whom I have guaranteed employment and support until the age of twenty-one years unless suitably married prior to that. You will appreciate that should the matter become public there would be a most damaging outcry from both charitable and Irish interests, which is why I felt it advisable to bring this to his Highness's notice.'

'Oh indeed, yes indeed. I do see the wisdom of your action and I know that his Highness will be most appreciative.'

'Naturally I shall look for his Highness's support in these arrangements.'

'But of course, Mr Gregory. You may rest assured upon that.'

'And perhaps I might look for assistance on one or two other minor issues?'

'You have but to name them, Mr Gregory.'

★ ★ ★

Things were beginning to move, with Luke's plans well under way. The railway company had lost no time in curtailing uneconomic services to Chiddington and were well advanced with their depot work at Chidlingbrook and

Luke had his converted carriage on a small siding for use as the Farm Company office.

Tom Jackson the blacksmith's son and Jim Hurle were away at the Wallis and Steevens factory at Basingstoke learning about the traction engine Luke had decided to buy and much of the poorer livestock had been sent to market.

There had been the inevitable rumblings and grumblings. No one, it seemed liked the idea of change so Luke realised he'd have to call a meeting of all those who worked on the various farms and seek to explain his plans. He would have much preferred someone else to do this but in absence of an estate bailiff, he'd have to face the workforce directly.

Apart from those occasions when he was persuaded to attend church, Luke never came face to face with the village population as a body. Avoided doing so, in fact. He'd never again set foot in the Lamb Inn and now he must face them all and he wasn't looking forward to it. Slow to forgive? Slower still to forget? Probably, but that was his nature, he told himself.

* * *

'The Head wants the Upper School to propose someone suitable to present the prizes on Speech Day. We're all supposed to submit a name when we return and whoever is selected will issue the invitation on behalf of the school but I haven't a clue who to suggest.'

'How about Mrs Donkin?'

'Oh Guv, get on,' Richard exclaimed, laughing. 'No, seriously, I just don't know of anyone who would be acceptable.'

'HRH?'

'I couldn't ask him, could I?'

'I think he might be delighted to accept.'

'You really mean that, Guv?'

'Yes. If the Head is happy about it, let me know and I'll send you a draft invitation to copy.'

★ ★ ★

The meeting was set for seven o'clock in the evening in the schoolroom and Luke was dreading the occasion. He should, properly, have done something about it at Michaelmas when Meredith finished. Now it was the New Year, it was bitterly cold with snow on the way and he'd just have to get on with it.

'Oh my Lord,' he muttered to himself as he saw that just about the entire village had crammed itself into the main schoolroom. Perched on desks, filling every space, they hadn't even left room for him to walk to the front of the gathering in order to address them.

The room went silent as he stood in the doorway looking in. 'Well, let me through, then,' and a passageway was created as people squashed their neighbours even more tightly together. There were faces he didn't recognise, or did he? 'This is not a public meeting. It's for those who work on Chidlingbrook farms. You, Coultran, are not welcome and have no place here so leave and take your people with you.'

With red, glowering face, Jabez Coultran, bailiff to Lord Berrimond, elbowed his way towards the door, followed by half a dozen of his estate workers and encouraged by hostile comments from those around. Luke faced the meeting, satisfied he'd made a good start, but my, the stink. Did they never wash or was it the muck that clung to their clothes?

'From Lady Day the farms you work on will all be run by the Chidlingbrook Farm Company as one big farm to make the best use of the land. There's little money in farming at the present time and I don't have to tell you wages are low and hours are long. I'm not a farmer but I am a man of business and farming's a business like any other. So, the company plans to run all dairying at Church Farm, vegetables on the Hall grounds and horses at Lee or Higher for example. If you're a stockman you'll be looking to Tom Pearson for a place and if market gardening suits you then Amos Burlington is your man.

Some are saying I'll put men out of work. They're wrong. Firstly, employment will be with the company, not me personally and no man will be refused if he's prepared to work anywhere, at any task. That way costs can be cut. There's good Canadian bread wheat at half the cost of growing it here so there's no point wasting land on it but asparagus, or sparrow grass as I've heard it called, will fetch a good price on the London market. Just a different crop, that's all.

On the question of wages the company is being advised by Arch, the union man. You'll all have heard of Joseph Arch I'm sure and he has sensible ideas as to how things might be improved, with a regular wage all year round and no casuals brought in to undercut the regular workforce, but understand this. Wages are paid out of profits so the company will expect a fair day's work for a fair wage. Now, does anyone want to ask questions so far?'

There was a long pause with much scraping of feet and clearing of throats as everyone waited for someone to make the first move and the first questioner was one of the women present.

'Will there be work for us women, sir, if you don't mind me asking?'

'Yes. There'll be a new and bigger dairy so there'll be milking jobs and a lot more vegetable and poultry work, much of it part time, which might suit those with families to think of and women are better at some tasks than men so yes, there'll be work for you.'

'And what'll you be payin' the women?'

It wasn't so much a question as a muttered comment from within the crowd, but Luke saw it as a challenge. He'd meet it head on.

'That was a deep voice for a woman. So who wants to know what they'll be paid? Come on now, don't hide behind your mates,' which approach quickly identified the mutterer who was named and pushed towards the front. 'So, Thomas Leckington. You think you might earn more if you wear a skirt and bonnet.'

There was a roar of laughter at this and the discomforted man looked down at his boots. 'Company policy will be to pay for the work done and the responsibility taken. If a woman can pluck and draw six chickens quicker than a man why should she be paid less? Now, there'll a ploughing match in March, open to all. The rules'll be given out next week and the judges'll come from miles away so it'll be fair. The company'll be running pigs in the woods and there'll be no objection to anyone from the village walking there but no gypsies. They're not welcome and neither are gin traps. They're nasty, cruel and barbaric. Same with badger baiting. A cruel and cowardly game so lets have an end to it.'

★ ★ ★

'Ah, Mr Tate. I can guess why you've called. Come in, come in,' and Luke ushered Farmer Henry Tate into the study. 'Where do you fit in with the new scheme of things? I thought so. What did you think of the meeting last night?'

'Well, sir, it's caused a stir that's for certain and sending Coultran about his business went down a treat. Thing is though I'm not sure where it all leaves me.'

'Understandable. Yours is the last tenanted farm on the estate and that's how it stays if it's what you want but I can offer you the sheep side of things with the company, if you prefer. You'd finish your tenancy and run whatever sheep the estate will carry with a salary and a share of the profits. No more quarter days, rentals or tithes. The land here could be far more productive and the right men can make it so. What do you know of Chidlingbrook history?'

'Well sir, very little really. I know the family's worked Downs for many years but that's about all 'cept Hill Farm used to be with Downs 'till it was separated. 'T'was a shepherd's cottage one time.'

'I see. Well, I've had a historian looking round the parish and he's found some interesting things. This place was some sort of religious building that was closed during Henry VIII's time and it was bought by a wool merchant in Guildford called Hezekiah Tate. Could be an ancestor of yours and it's possible he turned all the land round about into one big sheep walk because that was where the money was. Wool and mutton. There's still plenty of good sheep country here and arable sown for winter feed is part of the plan. You'd have whatever help you needed at busy times, like lambing and shearing and breeds of stock would be up to you, just so long as I can keep my Jacobs.'

That made Henry Tate smile. He'd listened with interest to what Luke had said and was considering the possible advantages of joining the company over continuing the constant struggle to make ends meet on his own.

'I don't expect a decision now. You must think about it and perhaps offer a plan of what might work best. Hill would come back to Downs as a matter of course and you're free to look round any of the farms to weigh things up. It might be an idea to consider a permanent sheep wash and lambing sheds. It's all up for discussion. It's ideas I'm looking for based on quality and best practice.'

Not a lot to be done at the moment with twelve inches of snow on the ground and a fair amount of drifting. 'Ah, Joseph. Ride up to Higher Farm and have a look round, would you? I want to be sure the animals are cared for. If you think the horses would be better off here or at Lee move them around. The bullocks should be all right if they've sufficient to eat. Ticker and his brothers can give you a hand. Let me know when you get back.'

With no one actually in charge at Higher, Luke was uncertain just how responsible the staff there would be, unsupervised. One man had already been reprimanded for smoking in the hay barn and human nature would never change. But who to put in charge of arable, that was the question. He needed an older, experienced man for the position, but who?

★ ★ ★

'This is monstrous. Totally monstrous!' The lady uttering this condemnation towards Luke was fairly quivering with indignation. 'I am unaccustomed to being so inconvenienced and I understand you to be wholly responsible for this sorry state of affairs.'

'I beg your pardon, madam,' Luke replied, politely raising his hat, 'but were you addressing me?'

'Madam? Madam? How dare you? Do you not know to whom you speak?'

'We haven't been introduced, so no, I have no idea,' though the coat of arms on the door of the carriage in which she had arrived, escorted by liveried footmen, indicated only one possible personage.

'I am the Baroness Berrimond and never since my forebears came over with the Conqueror has my family been so put about.'

'And I am Luke Gregory whose forebears came with the Romans many years before William's hooligans brought destruction to a peaceful country. Should we not board the train? It appears ready to leave.'

Luke was hard put not to chortle out loud at the look of baffled fury on Her Ladyship's face as she entered her compartment. Well done, Dr Searle, for that small history lesson. An interesting man was Dr Searle, as he was content to be called. He was currently examining Church Farm from roof to foundations, now that Pearson had moved into his cottage. He was also supervising the restoration of the tithe barn and going into raptures over what he viewed as most important discoveries.

'Well, good luck, sir,' Luke thought. 'Just don't be too extravagant in your enthusiasm.'

★ ★ ★

'The doctor's in the study, Guv,' George informed Luke as he was about to take his place for breakfast.

'Bit early for a social call,' and Luke made for the study.

'Mr Gregory, I apologise for this early call but I felt I should acquaint you with Lady Cecelia's mishap. I've been at Burberry Court since late last night and I'm afraid she is in quite a bad way. Her horse returned to its stable alone and she was found lying unconscious in the snow.'

'Oh dear oh dear. Bad is it? Bones broken or anything?'

'I'm afraid so. Arm, leg and a large contusion on her head. She is such a large lady that the task of getting her home and into the warmth was far from easy and she doesn't have many staff to help.'

'So how have you left things?'

'Well, sir I have set the bones and she is on a couch downstairs but properly she should be in bed.'

'I see. I'll go over with a few strong men and see what we can do. She'll need a nurse, will she not? Will you arrange that? From an agency? Accounts or whatever to me and now come and have some breakfast or it'll all go cold and Mrs Cherry will be telling me off.'

★ ★ ★

'Joseph. What are your plans for the future? You'll not want to stay in the yard here forever. Have you given thought to anything else?'

'Well, Guv, funny you should ask that. I'm well enough settled I know. Enjoy working 'ere and all that but I, well, I 'ad wondered if there might be something else. Round 'ere, mind. I'd not want to move away.'

'We're on the same tack then because I wouldn't want to lose you but I want someone to look to the horses. All the horses. Breeding, buying, selling and readying them for farm work. Would you care to take this on? Unless you'd prefer pigs and poultry? No, I can see you wouldn't. So what do you think?'

'Well, Guv, yes, I'd like that very much but I don't 'ave that much experience really. Only what I've got to know round 'ere, sort 'o thing.'

'Which is a start. You read a lot and you've got it up here,' and Luke tapped himself on the side of the head. 'If you looked around other stables, attended horse fairs and the like, asking and listening, you'd learn all you needed to know. I'd thought to use Lee for this but Higher is vacant and would suit just as well. Anyway, give it some thought and let me know.'

★ ★ ★

'Rector's 'ere, Guv.'

'No peace for the wicked, George. Show him in.'

'And what problems bringeth the church this merry morn, might one ask?'

'Many and varied if you have time to listen.'

'I'm listening.'

'Firstly, the church bells. Work progresses well I'm delighted to report. Secondly I regret that your meeting has given rise to much consternation. Oh, I've had the fullest of reports on proceedings and it seems you have introduced a new catch phrase. How does it go, now? 'Leave and take your people with you.' It is being used on every possible occasion and is the cause of much merriment especially amongst the younger people but also, I'm afraid there is much opposition to your proposals, so much so that some intend leaving your employ. They fear that new ways will bring ruin to them all and they prefer to seek employment with traditional farmers.'

'I'd heard something of this. They must do what they feel to be in their best interests.'

'Will this not cause you problems?'

'Enough will sign on to keep the ship sailing. For them the company'll offer better pay and renovated cottages, the doctor when needed, wages paid if they're sick and pensions when they retire, same as my staff on the river but first I want their agreement. I want them working with the company not for it. By the way, your bodger's commenced his trade. He's taking over the mill once renovations are complete. Going to grind our corn, do some coppicing and make charcoal for us, so no opposition there.'

'Oh, that is splendid news. I really am delighted to hear it. This all sounds so promising but did you know there have been two deaths from the cold? Both widows on their own with no family to help them. There is such a need for outside relief but that is refused. It is the workhouse or nothing and many prefer to die rather than enter the house.'

'The church could change that if it chose, could it not?'

'Mr Gregory, you hit hard. Very hard indeed but I hope you will forgive my uneasiness at your decision to ban all gypsies from the estate. They are, after all, God's creatures.'

'I'll take your word for that but they're thieves and rogues to a man. It's their culture. They live by their wits with loyalty to their tribe and no one else. It's well known if something isn't nailed down or closely watched it'll vanish when they're about so we're better off without 'em.'

★ ★ ★

'Letter for you, Guv. Delivered by 'and and 'ad ter be signed for,' Sammy informed him as he stepped through the doorway of Gresham House. 'Mr Brierly sent word as 'e's unwell terday and so 'as Mr Digger.'

Must be the weather, Luke decided, hung up his coat and took his letter up to the sitting room, comfortable with its blazing coal fire. So who sends letters by hand, he wondered and slit the envelope. 'Good grief', he exclaimed. A solicitor acting for the late Bishop Augustus Quinney wrote to inform Luke Gregory Esquire that said Bishop Quinney had named him as beneficiary in his will, and so on and so forth and would he be so kind as to call to attend to formalities, and so on and so forth.

Why, Luke wondered, and not for the first time, did legal people use fifty words where one would do and why on earth should Quinney name him in his will? Would have thought he'd leave it to the dog's home rather than himself. He'd made use of him, certainly but he hadn't exactly endeared himself to the fellow. Odd. Very Odd.

★ ★ ★

'Mr Pike. You look despondent. What ails?'

'Well, sir, several things, actually. You know that I wish to marry but I'm told I may not do so and remain in my present position and quite frankly, I don't wish to move.'

'I would've thought a married schoolmaster to be highly desirable. I encourage that at the prep school. What reason is given?'

'I am told the position is for a single person only.'

'Ridiculous. It's a Board School now, is it not? Rector's a Board member. I'll have a word. See what I can do. Salary needs looking at too, I would have thought. Sixty a year? Not enough to marry on. Need eighty at least. Next problem?'

'I need more help than I have, especially with the younger ones.'

'One teaching assistant have you not? You need more space and a full time teacher at the very least. There's a need to stir someone up a little. Leave it with me. Anything else?'

'I'm having trouble with the older ones over attendance. They're for ever saying they're needed on the farms, to help out, but I'm not sure this is correct.'

'It shouldn't be the case. I've made my thoughts on the matter clear enough. I'd be interested to learn the details. There's week-end and evening work if they want it and if we do away with the school pence there'll be no excuses left. There's something else?'

'Well, yes sir. It's always difficult to maintain interest. I'm wondering what I might offer to encourage more attention to schoolwork.'

'Thought of sending a group to the market in Guildford? Get them to make notes and write it up afterwards? Prices of stock, corn, breeds, that sort of thing. Find out how auctions work? Train there and back? Amos Burlington would lead a group satisfactorily. Think it over and we'll set a date. What about Wednesday next. How would that suit?'

'My goodness sir, that would suit splendidly and it would certainly add interest.'

'Another idea. I'll send down a load of fruit. Oranges, dates and the like. Bananas too now they're becoming available. You run lessons on them then take a group to see where it's all unloaded. Leave Friday afternoon, stay overnight and return Saturday. Bit more interest and tell your older ones if they wish to work with the company when they leave school they must apply in writing stating what work they want and what they can do. Time to be moving on from knuckling forelocks for a pittance and hoping for employment.'

For Pike the school master was a different man from when he'd first arrived at Chidlingbrook. Gone were the assertive eccentricities that had so encouraged ridicule and in their place was a thoughtful, settled and caring teacher, respected if not actually liked.

In his thirties now he'd decided to settle in the village seeking, he had realised, a quieter and more fulfilling life than soldiering had offered. He'd witnessed the carnage of the Zulu war in South Africa and now openly questioned the morality of colonial policy.

'I'm not unpatriotic, Mr Gregory but on the one hand we say 'Thou shalt not kill and on the other, we slaughter all who stand in our way,' a theme that struck a chord with Luke who, in consequence, was happy to offer whatever support he could.

★ ★ ★

In one of his contemplative moods, Luke sat comfortably on his settle, watching the ever-changing flames of the log fire, just allowing random thoughts to drift as they would. He could hear the girls giggling together in the kitchen where they were making toffee. Louise was settling in well enough, he thought. She'd been an unhappy little thing when Paul had brought her from their aunt's house in Norfolk. 'Depressed', was the doctor's opinion. If toffee making was the answer they could make as much as they wished.

James had moved on and was spending most of the week in school now as a boarder. 'Getting stronger by the day,' and his mother's visit had helped enormously. All the way from India to see him after his bout of diphtheria. He suspected the Rector had corresponded with her and exaggerated his involvement. Still, a pleasant lady.

More than could be said for Adrian's step father. They'd met at the Hall on Adrian's last speech day before he moved on to Bramsden. Mrs Townley had appeared pleasant enough but was clearly terrified of her husband, a tall, thin disapproving man who'd spoken of putting his stepson to work of some sort.

'There is little to be gained from furthering his education. Nothing but a hooligan at the best of times.'

'I'm surprised to hear this,' Luke had replied. We have seen no behaviour of that nature and he conducted himself impeccably when dining with the Prince of Wales.' That shook the fellow and Luke again chuckled to himself at reaction to this name dropping.

'You, you mean that he has dined with the Prince of Wales?'

'Oh yes. His Royal Highness visits from time to time and Adrian has joined us on occasion. His Royal Highness thinks him a splendid fellow. They have a mutual interest in horses, you know and Adrian is quite knowledgeable on the subject.'

That was it, Luke recalled. Lay it on. Not too much, of course. Just enough to suggest that such contacts were of no great moment to them. There'd been no further talk of 'putting the boy to work' and he had actually shaken Adrian by the hand on leaving. Now he was firmly settled at Bramsden and had taken to rugby football like a duck to water.

The Rector had been right when he'd said some of the older men would decline his new contracts on Lady Day and now there were long faces as they did the same work for their old wage whilst others enjoyed the new wages he'd agreed with Arch, the union man and he allowed himself a smile at the expressions on the faces of those who'd called at his railway carriage office that morning.

Basic weekly pay for a general farm worker, twelve shillings and sixpence, ploughman, stockman and carter eighteen shillings a week. Skilled hedger, seventeen shillings, and so on. Dairy maids, one and nine pence for two milkings a day and fresh milk and butter. He might be out of pocket this first year but then, maybe not. He had a definite advantage financially without a doubt with very little land tax, thanks to those Redemption Certificates.

He could just about cope with the local rates at a shilling and three pence in the pound and the way Ben was using his accountancy skills, income tax wouldn't be much of a problem, and he smiled comfortably to himself. After all, if you didn't look after yourself no one else would.

His investment was showing promise as already the new, red topped milk churns were finding favour, with their contents guaranteed clean, fresh and offered on a sale or return basis. Not being left with unsold milk was a definite attraction and any that did come back went straight to the pigs, to their advantage.

Not a speck of muck to be seen anywhere. All sweepings carted away and slurry pumped from the pit into containers by the yardman and tipped on the fields. A good start and changing over to Red Polls with heifers to bring on, long term contracts to supply would be feasible. Arthur, your days are numbered.

A few more long faces when Harrington's head ploughman had taken first prize at the ploughing match. Chiddington had been cock-a-hoop at their man's success. No bad thing. It'd wake a few up. All fair and square with judges from the Agricultural College. A decent plough pulled by a pair of clean-legged Suffolk Punches. The judges were impressed.

Have to get that butcher organised, though. His place is a disgrace to civilisation. A new building needed, further out from the village. Proper slaughter facilities. Steam cleaned like the dairy and boxes of lamb chops wrapped in white paper for the top end of the market. If he won't do it my way he can go.

★ ★ ★

'Invited to visit at Eton. Boat day or something. Fourth of June. One's people expected to attend you know. Nicholas asked me. Not up to it. Go would you? Hold your own; no problem.'

'Eton, eh? Well of course, Cissie. Happy to do so if Nicholas approves.'

'He will. Sure of that. Not ready to travel yet. Still aches and pains. Knew it'd come to this some day. Horse all right?'

'He's fine now his leg is healed and he's in demand at stud. We've had enquiries from Hunts as far away as the Midlands. Belvoir and the Quorn amongst others. All looking for fresh blood for their stables. You'll make your fortune!'

'All due to you. Can't thank you enough. Expect you've heard about Berrimond? Fell asleep at his club in St James and didn't wake up again.'

'I suppose the Honourable Gerald'll succeed to the title. Might help him grow up a bit.'

'Doubt it. Doubt it. Never been much good, that family.'

Something was certainly lacking in these interbred aristocrats, Luke thought to himself. Like half the village population. For hundreds of years they'd married round about for as far as a man could walk on a Sunday, with everyone related to his neighbour. No wonder some were on the slow side.

★ ★ ★

After a trying week in London, Luke was relieved to be back at the Manor for Digger was unwell and he'd had to see to much of what he was normally responsible for. Beth, he knew, was becoming increasingly concerned over his health. 'It's one thing after another and he just will not take things easy when he should,' she confided to Luke.

'You'll have to be firm with him. He must remember that bout of cholera left its mark. Just tell me when he's off colour and I'll take care of things down the wharf.' A bit of a nuisance, that but by and large most of their enterprises ticked along comfortably enough but only, perhaps, because they were closely supervised by one or other of them.

Now it was George wanting a quiet word when he had a minute, which meant something had cropped up here. 'Had a visitor the other night Guv, after dark. Stephens, who won the ploughing match. You know, works for Harrington. Asked if there's any chance of employment with you but he's scared stiff Coultran'll find out he called round. Reckons as he'd lose his place, cottage an all. Seems he's a very angry man as well. Said as Coultran took most of his prize money. Two guineas for the horses, another for the plough and one for himself for letting him take part.

'I thought it was Harrington's tackle he was using.'

'It was but Harrington's afeared of Coultran and his lordship. Seems he's not a well man. Reckons as Harrington'll quit before long.'

'Sounds a bit odd to me. D'you reckon Harrington sent him? Can't think what for. Best we stand clear but say we'll bear him in mind if he comes back.'

'He said his lordship's up in arms as well over the rates of pay here. Raging about farm servants on forty a year and more and paid every week come rain or shine. Said as 'e's planning to make trouble over it with other employers who'll be after your blood for discontenting the men. Reckons as you'll have a hard time of it afore long.'

And Luke didn't have long to wait for the court summons awaited him when he arrived home after another busy week in London. With Digger still unwell, he found himself fully occupied, not with major events but with a host of issues requiring decisions or advice. Should he delegate more responsibilities, he wondered? Difficult and with their varied interests, not altogether advisable. The personal touch had always been their winning card. He'd make the effort to keep on top of things himself but maybe, just maybe, he'd make a surprise visit home mid week.

Would have to now. The summons required his attendance at Guildford Magistrate's Court to answer an allegation that he, as owner of a heavy locomotive had used, or caused to be used, said locomotive upon the highway without warning banner or attendant walking twenty yards ahead of said locomotive, contrary to the Locomotive Act of 1865.

'Er, young Jackson has to appear as well, Guv,' George told him. 'A bit worried 'e is, too.'

'Someone's doing a bit of needling and I can guess who. Nothing for Jackson to worry about. He just has to get himself there on time, clean and tidy, then we'll see what's what.'

★ ★ ★

'Ah, doctor. You've beaten the Rector to it this morning. He's usually first at the door with matters to resolve. So, what's on your list?'

'Well, sir, it's partly about the Rector I've called. You see, he's unwell and I cannot for the life of me find a cause. All the symptoms point to poisoning but I cannot see how that maybe. Also, there are other, similar cases throughout the village that became apparent at more or less the same time.'

'And you think that I may be of help?'

'Well, sir, I can think of no one to whom I may speak without causing alarm. It can no longer be due to polluted water so it must be something else that has been consumed by those laid low. The one thing all have eaten is bread from the bakery. I've spoken with Bartlett but he was unhelpful and took offence at my enquiries.'

'I see. So what would you like me to do?'

'Support me in obtaining samples of his flour and other ingredients and ascertaining from where he obtained them.'

'Have we a legal right, I wonder? If there's nothing wrong with what he uses he might demand redress. Better to be sure of our ground first, don't you think?'

'I am sure. I've done a basic analysis of the bread and I'm certain it contains chalk for a start.'

'Really? You're certain? Mm. Were I a magistrate I could issue a warrant, of course but I respect your judgement so we must pay friend Bartlett a visit. Tell me, though. How will you test whatever we remove from the bakery?'

'There is an authorised analyst in Guildford now. He also attends at the laboratories at Barts. so his findings will be reliable.'

'Very well. Give me a minute to find collar and tie and we'll get under way.'

★ ★ ★

The village bakery was something of a hand to mouth affair offering a few loaves daily baked in an ancient oven in the back room of a cottage. Bartlett, who termed himself a baker, also kept pigs and chickens, the evidence for which lay upon the unswept floor. Shades of the Manor kitchen, Luke thought, as he looked at the dirty table and unwashed utensils.

Mrs Bartlett, tight-lipped and disapproving, sent for her husband who was cleaning out the henhouse. In due course he appeared, looking wary and defensive.

'Ah, Bartlett. There is illness in the village and we wish to be sure that your bread is not the cause so the doctor would appreciate samples of your ingredients for analysis.'

'There's nothing wrong wi' my bread. Never 'ad complaints from no one,' he said indignantly.

'I didn't say there was anything wrong with your bread but there is a need to be sure that whoever supplied your flour didn't sell you poor quality that might cause illness. It's in your interests to co-operate. If all is well here then we must enquire elsewhere until the cause of the illness is found.'

'You've no right accusing folk of usin' bad mixin's. You're no magistrate and you don't own this 'ere property so you've no right ter be 'ere at all.'

'No one's accused you of anything. Public Health Regulations allow anyone suspecting food to be unsafe may obtain samples for analysis. I know there's chalk in your bread so it's possible your flour is suspect. I can send for the constable and make this a police matter if you wish. Your decision.'

'T'aint right comin' 'ere causin' trouble fer 'onest workin' folk. Jus' cus you 'ave money,' he whined.

'Just show us your flour sacks, Bartlett. If there's nothing wrong there's nothing to fear. What else do you use, now? Salt, sugar, yeast, water. I want to see it all. Right, doctor. Take your samples. What's in this box here?'

'It's fer the rats. Arsenic.'

'Next to the salt and sugar? On the same shelf and not labelled? I hope you've not put that in your dough instead of salt or you'll be in deep water.'

★ ★ ★

Accompanied by Walter Brierly, Luke duly attended the magistrate's court sitting at the Guildhall and together with Thomas James Jackson, a Locomotive Engineer residing at The Forge, Chidlingbrook in the County of Surrey, entered a plea of 'Not Guilty' to the charge of using a locomotive upon the highway other than in accordance with the statutory provisions governing the usage of such mechanically propelled vehicles and so on and so forth. Long winded, pompous, formal, legalistic claptrap, Luke thought. Just what sort of mind puts such rubbish together? Ah, so Police Constable Hutton had observed their road mending activities, with stones picked from the fields being rolled into the potholes with a large roller towed by said steam propelled locomotive.

His evidence was supported by another witness. 'Call Jabez Coultran.' So, there it was. Lord Berrimond was behind this petty business. Walter took each witness through his evidence again, establishing exactly the stretch of roadway to which they referred then addressed the magistrates.

'Your Worships, this allegation is made quite erroneously, the information having been laid by a hostile and malicious party. The roadway described in evidence is not a highway within the meaning of the act but is a privately owned byway belonging to the defendant, Mr Gregory, who had engaged his employees upon the task of repairing and macadamising the surface of the roadway under the direction of his surveyor. No offence has therefore been committed and I ask that Your Worships dismiss the charge levelled at my clients.'

★ ★ ★

'This will be the best place, you say? Right, follow Mr Ridgeway's instructions and see how much you can shift in a day.'

Dry summers were a problem. Cool they might be but without adequate rainfall, the level of the river was often low and last year several wells had dried up, and then, of course, there was rain at harvest time just when you didn't need it. The obvious answer then, was to store water when it was plentiful against the dry times and Ridgeway the surveyor had proposed a reservoir on the hillside that could be filled from the river by means of a hydraulic ram.

Logical, Luke thought and it would partly fill from winter rains running off the higher ground behind. Full of ideas, our Mr Ridgeway, Luke mused as he watched the turf being stripped away by the working party detailed for the project. Ah, the beauty of a flexible work force that could be put to whatever task was most pressing! Next project would be a borehole with the prospect of tapping into underground supplies.

★ ★ ★

'So, what's the verdict?' Luke enquired of Doctor Fairleigh.

'Arsenic, but only in the bread. I had a telegram to this effect as I had stressed the urgency of the situation. It would appear that someone's been taking from the wrong box as you suggested and used rat poison instead of salt.'

'So, what's to be done? No one's died, have they?'

'No, there was just enough to cause illness in those sensitive to it and all are recovering. The trouble is, the news has leaked out and there's trouble brewing for Bartlett.'

'I thought telegrams to be confidential.'

'They should be. I can only think the post office has been careless.'

'Thank goodness I'm not a magistrate or I'd be up to the elbows in sorting it out. I think we'd do well to stand clear and let things settle.'

'I'm afraid I cannot. I'm duty bound to inform the authorities.'

'I see. Yes, I suppose you're right. Tell the constable will you and let him do the dirty work? I've no idea about such matters myself.'

★ ★ ★

Digger was still unwell. This was worrying, Luke decided, for not only did he miss his partner's cheerful presence but his side of the business would suffer from his absence and keeping an eye on everything himself was becoming tedious, yet he couldn't bring himself to delegate more to others, no matter how able they might be. So, if he couldn't delegate he'd just have to get on with it.

'Came in a box of that there joolry, Guv. Bangles, beads and the like. 'Ad your name on it so thought it best to bring it on up.'

It was a small, varnished wooden box with the lid firmly screwed down and with his name neatly printed on a waxed paper label. 'I wonder what?' Luke muttered to himself. He'd need a screw driver before he could explore the mystery of its contents so pushed it to one side and turned his attention to the letters that also awaited his attention and his first one caused a raised eyebrow for Paul could possibly be heir to a property in France, one that had been in his father's family for generations.

The world was full of surprises but why, he wondered had he not mentioned it before, whilst he was at the Manor? It appeared that his mother had written him a last letter before she died but his uncle had kept it from him. Strange man that but it had been amongst items he'd collected on his last visit to the vicarage with Walter, to tidy things up and of course, rescue his sister from her unhappy position there. Much on his mind, he supposed.

Anyway, as far as his mother was aware, his father's older brother had died, of wounds from the war with Prussia, she believed, so that Paul was now the eldest male in line of succession to the family estate, though French law might be different in such matters. In short, what should he do? Luke knew exactly what he would do and passed the letter to Walter for his opinion and also to see if they possessed a screwdriver. No. No screwdriver of any size. No tools at all, come to that so Sammy was despatched to buy one and returned an hour later with one of the required size.

Now, Luke thought to himself, let's have a look in this box and hope there'll be no unpleasant surprises of an oriental nature; shrunken heads or the like. The wood was hard. Teak, Luke thought and the lid must have been fastened by a gorilla but, by leaning his full weight upon the screws he managed to loosen them, and sat back for a breather after the struggle. What, now, was inside? Raw cotton for a start, packed firmly around some hard object, then, 'Good God,' he exclaimed as he held up the biggest ruby he had ever seen.

He'd heard of one the size of a pigeon's egg but this one must be half again as big and cut with many facets that caught the light from any angle. What else was in this box of surprises he wondered and pulled out the rest of the cotton packing to reveal two more rubies, smaller than the first but cut in identical fashion.

What on earth is this all about, he wondered. No note or letter. Nothing. From India with a consignment of bangles and beads, which could only mean Fred's father, who hadn't written to his son for an unusually long time. Letters could get lost, of course but this was all very odd and for once, Luke was completely at a loss.

★ ★ ★

'Ah, Rector. Up and about again. Glad to see you recovered.'

'That's kind of you to say so. I was most surprised to learn the nature of my illness. I had hardly expected to be poisoned and I understand others suffered the same misfortune.'

'They did indeed and no wonder but we have an able practitioner in Doctor John. There should be no recurrence now the bakery's closed. Bartlett is to appear at the Sessions charged with using adulterated ingredients. There was both lime and alum in his flour would you believe and when word got out, Hutton had to take him into protective custody. The village was really up in arms over it.'

'Lime I know but what is alum?'

'Something used to whiten flour and made from human urine would you believe?'

'Good Lord. That really is dreadful but what, I wonder are we to do now for not many folk bake bread.'

'No problem. Bread is to be sent daily from Guildford and Hopkins' wife will sell it from the station waiting room. What do you think to that?'

'I think it's a splendid idea. Indeed I do.'

'We'll have a bakery again but properly set up and moreover, clean. Bartlett's was anything but. We also need, I think, a shop selling everything and anything but who to run it?'

The Rector laughed. 'You'll have us all organised I can see but yes, a general store would indeed be most welcome.

'Building team's about set up now for repairs round about. Law says I'm responsible for decent housing so they'll work through all the estate cottages and get them ship shape with iron cooking ranges for those that want them so tell me what I've missed.'

'Alms houses and a hospital, perhaps? No. I jest but I really am delighted that you have found work for some of the older men.'

'Ah, yes. Light work. Repairs and painting. The company tackle will be kept in sound condition at all times. No rusty, ungreased axles and the carts will be painted green with red wheels. All ship shape and Bristol fashion

★ ★ ★

Chapter 14

'Sir! Mr Pike said to ask you to come quick. There's
trouble. They're smashing up Bartlett's and they're going to
burn it down and she's inside!'

'What? Who is? Good Lord! Richard, Peter! There's a
row down the village. They need a hand. Joseph? You'll join
us? Good man. Get down there quick as you can. No time to
harness up. I'll follow.'

As soon as Luke reached the road he could see the glow
of a fire on the far side of the village and he made his best
speed towards it, quickly aware that at fifty years old he was
not in great condition for running. Puffing hard he arrived at
the edge of a crowd of onlookers in front of what had been
Bartlett's Bakery. By the light of the fire, he could see that
the windows of the cottage and the front door were smashed
whilst several youths cavorted around the burning
outbuildings in pursuit of pigs from the sty whilst others,
one of whom appeared to be wearing a policeman's helmet,
chased around after birds from the hen house.

'They're drunk, Guv,' Joseph reported. 'Drunk as tinkers
at a fair.'

'I see. Where's the constable? Have a look for him, will you? And the schoolmaster. Ah, Pike. What's all this about?'

'As far as I can tell sir, some of the wilder ones decided to drive the Bartletts out of the village, on account of that bread business only there's just Mrs Bartlett and her family here, as you know.'

'So where's the constable? I thought he was keeping an eye on things.'

'He's inside, sir. Guarding the family. He did his best by all accounts but he couldn't do much on his own especially when they set fire to the sheds.'

'Well this has gone far enough. We need to round up those fellers before they do any more damage,' and to the bystanders, 'Who'll give a hand to stop this? Come on, before someone gets hurt,' and Luke moved towards those nearest the fire.

At first, no one moved then someone called out, 'Come on lads. Give Squire an 'and,' and there was a general move by the men present to follow Luke.

'Round 'em up. All of 'em and let's see who they are.'

There was a bit of scuffling as the drunken revellers were manhandled into a group, a couple of lanterns held high shone on their faces and names were called out along with exclamations of surprise and condemnation.

'Good God. Archie Burlington,' Luke exclaimed in surprise as he recognised the young man sporting the policeman's helmet. He knew Amos's younger brother to be on the wild side; harum scarum he'd been called and his father would be horrified at this episode.

Three of the group were from the village, the others coming from the nearby hamlets and judging by their bottles of gin they had well and truly indulged. But what to do next? Thank goodness he wasn't a magistrate or he'd be arranging custody for all concerned but everyone seemed to be looking to him for a lead.

'Where's PC Hutton?' he asked, as much to give himself time to think as from interest.

'He were 'urt,' someone said.

'Got 'arf a brick on 'is 'ead,' someone else added. 'Doctor's with 'un inside.'

'Ah, Rector. A bad business and I'm wondering what's to be done. Look, you all know these fellers,' he said, speaking to those around. 'The constable knows 'em too and there'll be warrants out on Monday. Riot, arson, damage to property, injuring a police officer. They could get twenty years for this.'

'If they joined the army smartish they'd be out of the way. Could be safe in uniform. A few years in India would be better than rotting in jail.'

They all looked at Pike the schoolmaster, who appeared to be gazing up at the stars. There was silence at first then muttered comments as the idea was considered, discussed and, welcomed. After all, the miscreants were kin and related to village families. Blood was thicker than water, was it not? What they'd done was wrong but twenty years in stew? That didn't bear thinking of.

'Mr Pike, you're a hero,' Luke said. 'Leave it in your capable hands? Good man. You know where to stay in London and I'll send down the necessary. Now look, all of you. Things need tidying up and quickly. Jim Palmer here, is he? Repairs first thing Monday if not sooner. Live stock needs tending and play the game there. This has shamed the village so get things put right. A word with you, Rector?'

Alone with the Rector, Luke put things plainly to him. 'The law'll come down heavily once it gets started. Injuries to policemen always affects courts. Could you, I wonder, talk to Mrs Bartlett and see what she considers best from her point of view? I doubt she'll want to stay round here after this upset but I don't want to be openly involved in any arrangement that might be helpful, if you see what I mean and I don't want to know too much, especially where Hutton's concerned. I just hope he's not badly hurt.'

'I think I understand. Yes. We may achieve a better outcome between ourselves. A bad business though. I shall have something to say from the pulpit tomorrow. I'm sure this could have been avoided if others had been more responsible.'

Very likely, Luke thought but enough of this village nonsense. He'd stay clear and spend the week in London. Plenty to do there and with luck Digger might put in an appearance.

And Digger did, but there was no bounding up the stairs now and though he looked distinctly peaky he was determined to start work again, which suited Luke well enough.

'Beth thinks we should move to the country,' he confided. 'Bit worried about the young 'uns with all this sickness about.'

'Nothing to stop you. If that's the answer you must do it. Start handing over some of your side of things. You'll know who can best take it on and there's a nice, quiet little place I know of called Chidlingbrook. Might be worth having a scout round there. Organise the farm office, maybe?'

'Come on, Guv. You know I'm no good at clerking but Beth wouldn't mind a move there.'

★ ★ ★

'He were right, Guv. Harrington is quitting. His lordship's put the farm up for sale and another the other side of the park. Heard tell it's to do with paying duties after old lord died. Succession duty or such like.'

'So Harrington could be holding a clearance sale, unless it's sold as it stands. Wouldn't mind that plough team of his if he does sell. They were lovely animals and I know next to nothing of such things.'

George grinned. 'I reckon you knows more'n you let on, Guv but that's as nice a team as you'll find anywhere. Matched and balanced just right for the land hereabouts. I'll say that for Harrington. Knew 'is animals well enough and kept 'em well, which is more'n you could say of some.'

Luke left it at that but, as always, his mind was racing, seeing an opportunity and debating the possibilities. Did he want more land and could he afford to buy more? He'd invested most of his capital in what he already had and you could go too big and over reach yourself and end up in shoal waters. It was tempting though. The land adjoined part of Lee Farm but that was next to Berrimond's estate and there was no telling what mischief might result if he bought it. Best to stand clear and play safe but he'd still give it some thought.

★ ★ ★

'Not the blasted Rector again,' Luke muttered to himself. 'What's he want this time as if I can't guess. Money. Well I haven't got any. Spent up so he's wasting his time.'

'Ah, Rector. Good morning to you,' he greeted his visitor diplomatically.

Returning the greeting but reading between the lines, the Reverend Greenway settled himself in the offered chair and wondered how best to open the conversation. Straight to the point he decided.

'As you know, Lord Berrimond is selling some of his land and Harrington has decided to retire. There is concern round about and, frankly, the hope is that you will purchase some, if not all of the land and continue to offer employment.'

'I'm fully committed already.'

'I was fearful of that. You know that Coultran has been dismissed? It appears he has been defrauding the estate for years. Harrington finally found the courage to inform upon him to his lordship who, I understand is somewhat embarrassed financially.'

'That's another reason for keeping clear. Troubled waters there.'

'Oh, without a doubt. You will probably be aware that the family circumstances are far from happy?'

'I know little of the family and have no wish to learn more. I've been well berated by Lady Berrimond. Hoity toity old dame. Claims her forebears arrived with William of Normandy, as if that were a recommendation.'

'Ah yes. The dowager Lady Elisabeth. Rather conscious of her social position. No, it was Lady Penelope whom I had in mind, the new Lady Berrimond.'

'Such people create their own troubles so must learn to live with 'em.'

'Indeed yes but permit me, I beg you, to explain. The Berrimonds have a son of some eight years of age. His father, Lord Berrimond is not well disposed towards him as he appears insufficiently robust to ride to hounds, amongst other requirements. He is determined to send him to boarding school to make a man of him. His mother, Lady Penelope, is protective but has little choice in the matter. One possibility would be for the boy to attend the school at the Hall but knowing of the er, feeling between yourself and her family, her Ladyship is fearful of your refusal to allow this.'

'Her fears are groundless. Admissions are the headmaster's responsibility and I wouldn't dream of interfering. Judging me by their own standards I think. Now, Mr Joseph Arch has accepted an invitation to open the new chapel. May I take it that you'll join with us on that happy occasion?'

★ ★ ★

Now just how much could he lay his hands on and how much would Harrington's fetch at auction? He could use the trust fund and call it an investment and there was that eleven thousand or so the Bishop had left him. Nowhere near enough even with a discounted sale. He could borrow against those rubies. They must be worth a bit. He could call in a few loans, sell his shares, mortgage the Manor. No, that wouldn't do. Scraping the barrel and for what? Land he didn't need. Another farm for which he had no use. Forget it Gregory. Don't get greedy and over do things. Enough to cope with as it is. Be sensible. Half your time spent in the City with your warehouses and a partner in poor health. No, it's time to shorten sail else you'll never make old bones and dammit, he was over fifty so he'd talk things over with Digger and Beth and take stock.

There we have it, then. I'm trying to sail two courses at the same time. You need to take things easy and Beth wants country living. You know the village. Enough going on there to keep you both busy. Good prep school for the nippers. Choice of houses to settle in. All we have to do is sell or lease out the wharfing side of things and the other bits and pieces. Straight forward I should think.'

'You make it all sound so simple,' Beth said.

'It is, if you don't go into the realms of what if and maybe. If we're in agreement just make your decision and act on it. There's even a good farm on the market, Harrington's, if you want to be independent.'

There was a long pause then Beth said, quietly. 'That's the problem, Guv. We're near skint. Got the house and that's about it.'

At first, Luke didn't think he'd heard correctly but one look at Digger, seeming even smaller than usual as he huddled in his chair, said it all. 'Care to tell me about it?' he finally managed to ask.

'Lost it, Guv,' Digger almost whispered, his humiliation plain to see. 'Got caught with the 'orses. Should've known better. In too deep. I know what you're thinking.'

'I'm thinking anyone can get carried away. Just pulled back myself from making one deal too many. Look, me old mate. We're still partners. We've got businesses running. You've a house, clothes on your back, food on the table and the best wife anyone could ask for. Could be worse, couldn't it?'

'Oh, Guv,' and Beth began to sob.

'None of that, now. Tales of woe yes, but weeping and wailing definitely not.'

'Just can't 'elp it, Guv. Thought it were all roses in the garden,' as she dabbed her eyes.

'And still is. Now, we settle up the businesses here and you move to Chidlingbrook. More than enough to occupy us there and you sir, need to get your strength back. If you've had this on your mind it's no wonder you've been ill. Come on now. Let's get on with it.'

★ ★ ★

'Ah, Amos. Harrington's clearance sale in three weeks. Care to attend and do a little bidding for me? Prefer to keep clear myself but I'd like that plough team. You know the one. Plough, horses and the ploughman too if he's interested.'

'Course I will, sir. Happy to do so.'

'If there's anything else of interest, at the right price mind, I'll leave you decide. There's viewing anytime I understand so I'll leave it with you and banker's drafts the day before.'

'I'll get father along too, sir. He's a keen eye for most things. Er, I know there's some first rate beef cattle. You want me to look 'em over?'

'Anything that's of use to us and if Harrington wants private arrangements I'll leave it with you.'

Clearly, with one thing and another this was going to be a busy time and Luke was wondering if he'd over committed himself. He had to show his face at Eton then oversee his nib's visit to Bramsden for the speech day and prize-giving. The head had almost swooned when that was arranged, Richard had reported. There was still no word of Fred's father, which was a worry, yet cotton and other items were still arriving at the warehouse. Most odd and his enquiries at the Colonial Office had offered nothing. Should Fred go off looking for his father? He'd know his way around, he supposed. He'd think it over.

Then there was Paul and his possible inheritance in France. He'd have to go with him to see what that was about. Closer to home at least but he wanted to be back in time for the harvest and see how his new ideas worked out. Not a good time to go charging off to foreign parts and here was the blasted Rector again to bother him with church bells and burial plots, or whatever. It was nothing so mundane though, and Luke was intrigued by what he heard.

'I just thought if you were aware of the situation it might be possible to well, oh, I don't know. Perhaps I'm wrong to call but I know so little of commerce and next to nothing of farming matters.'

So His Lordship couldn't sell his farms as both were mortgaged by his late father and the quarterly rentals served only to cover the interest payments. With Harrington selling up there'd be no rent and whoever held the mortgages was unwilling to foreclose as a sale wouldn't cover what was owed. Also, the farm workers would be without employment.

A familiar story, Luke thought but not his concern. Could he though, turn it to his benefit? Not easily, yet he'd gained from other men's follies before. The Manor here, for instance. Perhaps he'd make enquiries. No harm in that.

Meanwhile there was muttering over 'this 'ere new fangled cuttin' o' grass early stead 'o leavin' it fer 'ay', with which to contend but then there would always be muttering over new ideas and Luke was trying out the clamping of fresh cut grass to let it ferment for winter cattle feed. 'Pack it down tight', he'd instructed the bemused and doubting mowing team, 'so no air can get in'. Black molasses mixed in as well in one clamp, cut out of the solid chalk and sheeted down with tarpaulins weighted with timber and stones. If the animals liked it the milk yield could be maintained through the bad weather. If not, it would be hay, turnips and oats. These things had to be tried, never mind the mutterings.

'Ah, Dessy. Come on in and give me your news,' and Luke turned his thoughts from feeding cattle during the winter to what his chief spy had to tell him.'

'It's like this, Guv. The feller holding the mortgages on the farms is bankrupt. Cleaned out. Land speculator from Essex named Taylor. Bought too much thinking he could sell it on for building then found he couldn't. Borrowed a fair old bit, Ben says. Creditors queuing up by the mile. A couple of banks but mostly private investors hoping for a quick profit.'

'Some burned fingers, eh? Interesting. You've done well. Mr Brierly in the picture?'

'He is that, Guv. Been checking out land prices too, look you. Just in case, see', and Luke nodded his appreciation of the thoroughness of the enquiries, quietly amused by the Welsh lilt that Dessy had never lost despite living in London for years. Quite a team there. Ben, Dessy and Walter Brierly. If there was information needed, they'd ferret it out and, what was more, evaluate it before passing it on. Dependable, that was it. Thoroughly dependable.

★ ★ ★

'Ah, Amos. Had a good look round? What do you reckon then?'

'Well, sir, first of all, Harrington's had another turn. With his heart, that is. Word is, the strain of selling up is getting to him.'

'A trying time I should imagine. Going ahead with the auction, is he?'

'So far as I know but he wouldn't mind an offer for the lot and save the costs and everyone trampling all over. Never did like folks round his place. Don't suppose you know about him, do you sir?'

'Not a thing apart from he's said to be a good farmer.'

'Oh, he's that all right but hard on his men. We never had dealings with him as father reckons he's not respectable. We're chapel, you see and well, Harrington's got a bit of a name round about.'

'Go on,' Luke prompted though he wondered what all this was leading up to.

'He's got an idiot son in the asylum. Blamed his wife for that and treated her right badly then lay with every maid he could get hold of. There's any number of Harrington bastards in the valley and they're all wanting a share of the farm now he's selling up.'

'His past catching up with him, eh? So how does that affect things?'

'Well, sir. Father reckons you should be in the picture if there's any buying and selling. In case someone claims what they say wasn't his to sell, if you see what I mean?'

'Ah. Yes. I'm with you. Well thank you for that. So, what sort of offer is he looking for?'

'We never got round to a price. He dickered a fair bit over all sorts. I reckon he's wanting as much as someone'll give.'

'Understandable. Now, this is between the two of us. I've taken a five year lease on the farm from the Bankruptcy Court. There's all sorts of legal shenanigans going on but that's not my concern. How would you feel about taking it on? Separate from the company but with no rent or tithes and the same benefits as you have now. I'd like to see what can be done compared with the estate. You'd employ who you wanted of course, at whatever rate you set.'

'You mean as manager, sir?'

'No. As farmer. Take over from Harrington as if you'd bought the place and run it as you see fit but keep tight records of everything. As I say, I want to make a comparison.'

'Well sir, what can I say but yes. I'd like that, I truly would,' then, pausing 'but what about the vegetables? What I'm doing now?'

'I have someone in mind for that side of things. Mrs Foster. Capable woman. I think she'll cope admirably.' Which move set the tongues wagging when it became known.

'There's some as say they'll not work under her, Guv,' George told him. 'They'ver never heard the likes of it, having a woman in charge.'

'They can always seek work at Harrington's and when Amos moves out Digger and Beth'll be on hand if she needs support.'

A slow smile spread over George's face. 'I reckon you've got 'em weighed up, Guv.'

'Well, there's one or two not pulling their weight up there. They spend more time leaning on their hoes than plying 'em but I'll not let 'em hold back others who want to earn a bonus. First sign of trouble and they can sling their hook.'

★ ★ ★

'Er, Guv. Have a word, can I?' Dessy was hovering in the doorway of the sitting room, respectful and deferential as ever.

'Come on in. What's on your mind?'

'There's someone been asking questions about you. Making enquiries, see. Been going on for a while now. We thought it might be the Dicks but it's an enquiry agency. Been watching this place, the wharf and all stops on the main line seems like. Checked up on share dealings, customs and excise, who you know, where you go. The lot.'

'So who's the interested party?'

'That we don't know yet, Guv. Being very careful they are, see but we reckons they want to get something on you, to give you trouble.'

'So if they had something they'd show their hand? Blackmail? Always possible, I suppose. Revenge? Possible again but for what? Any ideas?'

'We could dangle a juicy worm for the fish to bite at? Ben says there are several possibilities.'

'What would I have done in the old days now; invite the enquirer in for a chat, perhaps? A frightened man will sing or take a better offer. I'll leave it in your capable hands and many thanks. I'll look forward to the outcome.'

★ ★ ★

The grain dryer now. Would it work when needed, Luke wondered? Several ideas had been proposed but he'd opted for the simplest and cheapest design. This was unexplored technology that might or might not work. The Romans had them, he was told. Something after the pattern of their under floor heating, with the grain constantly raked and moved to get the surplus moisture off. Trial and error, he supposed. Anything was better than losing a harvest through wet weather but what was going on outside?

'Guv, the lads've moved that gang of gypsies on like you wanted. Picked up a couple of gin traps and any number of snares while they was at it.'

'Good. Well done. We're better off without 'em. Thieving rogues. Nothing safe when they're around.'

'They left something behind, though. It's a bear.'

'A bear?'

'Straight up, Guv. Brown one. Half dead it is. In a bad way.'

'What've you done with it?'

'It's in the yard outside. The lads reckoned you'd want to see it so they got it in the float and brought it up here.'

'This I have to see,' then, 'It is in a bad way. Old too, by the looks of it. Ugh, just look at that,' as he saw the oozing infection on its nose and jaw where a metal control ring showed through the swelling. 'Bloody people with their dancing bears. Never did hold with that. Cruel in my book. One of you find the doctor will you? Give him something new to practice on and call in at the forge for someone to cut that ring off. Right, bed it down in the cart shed and we'll see if we can do something for it,' and Luke started back inside, still muttering about distasteful gypsy ways then turned back. 'Who's going to look after it?'

'I will,' both Robbie and Alf Donkin answered together and grinned at each other then set about the task of seeing to the bear's needs. They bathed its nose, fed it porridge sweetened with honey, brushed its shabby coat and several days later reported to Luke. 'Reckon it'll make it, Guv. Skinny, though. 'Arf starved it is but it's moving about now. Osses don't like it, mind.'

'Well, if it's in the land of the living you'll have to decide what to do with it. The doctor says they eat most things, just like pigs so you'd best set up a sty for it. Oh, and is it church or chapel? Should liven things up on a Sunday either way,' and he allowed himself one of his rare chuckles.

★ ★ ★

The seasons were moving on and most of the early hay was safely in. A question of dodging the showers and turning it constantly, one field at a time and all hands on deck as needed, milkmaids included. He'd make this business work whatever the weather and now he'd got that Eton visit out of the way he could give thought to Bramsden and his nibs.

'Ahoy, there!' Lady Cecelia, trying a nautical greeting broke in on his thoughts. 'Thought I'd ask how it went. Downright grateful to you for going. Aches and pains one thing. Figure of fun without a doubt. Would have embarrassed the boy.'

'Oh, come on Cissie you're doing yourself down. No need for it. You're straight and honest and no one could ask more than that.'

'Know what I'm saying. Heard enough over the years. Any way, tell me about it.'

'Oh, an interesting outing. Everyone dressed up to the nines and strutting about on their dignity. Definitely a social occasion. Lords, Dukes and Honourables all over the place. Some reasonable jollifications on the water. Nicholas is a wet bob. That's their term for the boating fraternity who were all intent on getting wet one way or another. Everyone is a bob of some sort, it seems. Dry bobs play cricket and slack bobs do very little. Anyway, it turned out well for me personally. Met up with someone who's been avoiding me. I hold his note, you see and now he's come into his inheritance he's well able to redeem it. Bad form to let things slide so.'

'Indeed, indeed. No gentleman should avoid his responsibilities. Glad you stand to benefit. Damn glad.'

★ ★ ★

'Come on, Guv. Give us something ter do. I can't just stand around admiring the view.'

'Do what you've always done, Digger me old mate. Be my eyes and ears. Get to know everyone. See who's doing what. They're not all happy with the changes I've made.'

'I getcha, Guv. Get mud on me boots.'

'As much as you like. George'll show you around. Pony and trap everywhere mind and take your time. Don't go overdoing things.'

'So who's not happy, then?'

'Some are set in their ways. I don't think they want better conditions. They'd rather work long hours for a lord than earn more with me but I'll not put up with their nonsense. I've invested everything I have in this and its got to pay its way.'

'So what's the form with Harrington's?'

'Ah, interesting, that one. I couldn't afford to buy it so I'm leasing it, on favourable terms, I might add and Amos is going to run it as if it's his own. Ben has an interest, working it in with some of his client's investments. He's a sharp one. Best day's work when he signed on.'

'It'd take a good 'un ter catch him out,' Digger muttered. 'Pity I didn't listen to 'im meself.'

'Forget that. Water under the bridge but it's got the Rector off my back. Moaning on about men without employment with Harrington finishing and all that but you know my thoughts on everyone doing a day's work. Got the girls learning clerking skills now. Sent for one of those new fangled writing machines. Type writers I believe they're called. I want 'em to learn to keep business records and such. You never know when they'll find it useful.'

★ ★ ★

And so to France. Not a journey he wanted to make but Paul's need to meet with his relations was important but had he left everything in order during his absence? He'd tried to consider every eventuality, everything that might need his attention. Ugh, but he'd lost his sea legs he thought as he clutched at the rail of the cross channel packet, pitching and bucking in the choppy conditions. Hadn't been to sea for years and hadn't missed it either. Eight hours from London to Paris, they'd said. They couldn't arrive at Boulogne soon enough, never mind Paris.

Fred would have to wait for his return before he gave further thought to his problem. Digger and Beth were on hand and Richard and Peter were back from school. George was there so what was he worrying about? Learn to delegate, you half-baked muffin and hang on to your hat or you'll lose that as well as your lunch!

He'd never landed in France during his travels and Paul had never visited despite his fluency in the language so it would be a new experience for both but just how the visit would turn out he couldn't imagine. They'd not be made welcome judging by the tone of the letter Paul had received from someone who was possibly an aunt. There was no invitation to stay so they'd have to hope for the best and hope too that this really was the train for Paris. It was but it was no cleaner or more comfortable than the one from London and he looked morosely through the grimy window at the countryside and decided he'd never travel for pleasure. With luck, they'd arrive at Orleans by early evening and he began to look forward to a relaxing hot bath, a decent meal and a comfortable bed.

'Non, monsieur.' The hotel could not offer a hot bath but a jug of hot water might be brought from the kitchen. The food was reasonable but his bed creaked and the mattress was lumpy and Luke spent a restless night, longing for the comfort of a shipboard hammock.

'Getting soft, Gregory', he told himself. Accustomed to easy living and a flush lavatory, not the horrors of a malodorous hole in the floor of a privy in the rear yard. Mediaeval, but he managed to exchange a wry grin with Paul as they wandered around the town having decided the afternoon to be the best time to venture out to the Chateau Grivelle near the village of Sandillon. At least the coffee wasn't bad, he decided, as they sat outside a cafe, comparing the dress and mannerisms of those nearby with those at home. Thank goodness Paul spoke the lingo. He'd be all at sea on his own.

'Now, let's go over things again. Your father was born at the chateau and was the younger of two sons. His older brother was a soldier and died in the war with Prussia. He was unmarried and had no children so possibly you're the eldest male descendant of the family but inheritance laws here are a bit different, except for taxes, of course. Nothing new in that but there's no telling what we're about to discover so best we make the first visit short and formal.'

★ ★ ★

First impressions were of a run down property that might once have been prosperous. Tall, rusty iron gates in a dilapidated stone wall at the end of a short gravel driveway, the building of a modest size of honey coloured limestone but nothing like the extravagant chateaux of illustrations in books.

An elderly woman wearing a black dress and large white apron opened the door before they could reach the bell pull and wordlessly beckoned them to follow her across a tiled hallway and into a large drawing room. Opposite the door sat another elderly woman in a high backed wooden chair flanked by two more women, both standing and all dressed completely in black. They stared disapprovingly at Luke and Paul but offered no greeting.

'Who are you and what do you want?' the seated woman suddenly demanded in rapid French.

Paul, somewhat taken aback, introduced himself and explained that he had hoped to meet members of his family.

'Who is this person?' the woman demanded, indicating Luke with a contemptuous wave of her hand and Paul named Luke as his guardian.

'A bas les anglais,' with another dismissive and contemptuous gesture.

'No need to translate that,' Luke said. 'I gather we're not welcome.'

Paul though was clearly nettled by their reception and began to enquire the reason for the obvious hostility, though Luke had no idea what was actually said.

'You might do better if I withdrew,' he suggested, 'but first I want you to translate exactly what I have to say. Tell the lady in the chair that I think her the rudest, most unpleasant old woman I've ever met and I wish her good day. Go on. Just as I said it.'

Looking a little worried, Paul did as instructed. There was a sharp intake of breath from one of the black-clad trio. Three pairs of hostile eyes focussed on Luke who gave a half bow, turned and walked from the room. He'd barely reached the door when there was a cackle of laughter and a voice calling out and Paul, catching up with him by the open front door, explained that he was asked to return.

'No thank you. Not today or any other. I shall walk around a little. The air is sweeter out here. Best of luck.'

My, but it was hot outside and dry. What wouldn't he give for a dip in cool water. Cool water? Ah, but there was a river nearby. The Loire, Paul had told him. Couldn't be worse than the Thames, surely and he started to walk in that direction across meadows where a few cows grazed round about. Bushes by the water's edge. No one around that he could see and he peeled off and slid into the water. Ah, bliss. Sheer bliss. Didn't taste too bad either, as he ducked his head under. No salt anyway and he swam a few strokes into deeper water where there was a bit of a current but felt cooler.

He lay back and must have drifted further than he realised for when he looked up he was well away from where he'd left his clothes. Clothes? What was that old woman carrying? His clothes and he struck out for the bank with all his energy, scrambled out of the water and shouted 'Oi! Come back!'

Nothing for it but to go in pursuit and the old woman was nearly a hundred yards away and making steady progress. Hell, he thought. Here he was, a middle-aged man without a stitch on chasing over a field after some old peasant woman who'd nicked his togs. After what seemed an eternity he managed to catch up with her and made a grab for his clothes but she wouldn't let go. A larger size Mrs Donkin he thought. Good job she was wearing those wooden clog things or he'd still be chasing after her but the more he pulled at his belongings the tighter she held on to them and then started a high pitched squealing of protest. God dammit! What did he have to do? Thump her? Not the thing but he couldn't go on struggling there with the old witch, not in his exposed state.

Things came to a head quite suddenly as a big man in a blue smock came lumbering up just as Luke's shirt tore as he pulled at it. The old woman went over backwards, legs in the air, Luke staggered and was knocked flying by the big man who followed up with a kick aimed at his head. Never in a month of Sundays had he thought to find himself in such a ludicrous position, stark naked and with an assailant intent upon trampling him into the ground with his wooden footwear.

Rolling desperately away from attack he found himself alongside the prostrate possessor of his clothes, screeching blue murder still, or so it seemed. He was no where near as nimble as he used to be but he managed to get into a crouch as the next kick was aimed at him and then it was bar room rules and the big man stopped in his tracks with eyes and mouth wide open in pained surprise.

Slowly he doubled up, clutching his offended regions and Luke, on his feet now brought his knee up sharply into his opponent's face. The man fell over on top of the woman who, still screeching, flailed at him with her arms and Luke grabbed his clothes, picked up his boots from where they'd fallen and staggered away to get dressed.

Why, he wondered, as he made his way back towards the chateau, was life so full of unpleasant surprises? Who would've thought that a quiet, cooling swim would lead to such a fracas? You offer a helping hand and end up with a torn shirt, sharp thistles where you didn't want them and bruises you could have done without. Maybe he'd see the funny side later, but not just yet. Paul was waiting for him by the chateau gate and saw by his dishevelled appearance that he hadn't enjoyed a peaceful stroll in the sun.

'I'll tell you later but I've had a most trying experience. Are you ready to leave? Finished your business?'

'Well, Guv, actually it all turned out very well but yes, of course if you wish to go I'll get my hat and say good by.'

'That cafe in the village up the road, the one we passed earlier with tables outside. We'll settle there and you can tell me your news.'

'Yes, Guv but what happened to you? You've got blood on the side of your face.'

'I have? Oh. Not surprised. Went for a swim and some old biddy ran off with my clothes. Had to chase after her. Not a stitch on. Wouldn't hand 'em over either then some great oaf came along and set about me.'

'Yes, but how did you get away, I mean?' and Paul's face betrayed his thoughts as he pictured the scene.'

'Oh, well may you laugh, young man. I reckon if it'd been someone else I'd find it amusing. Ridiculous even. Couldn't make it up.'

Paul, openly laughing now, persisted. 'But how did you get your clothes back, with the man going for you?'

'Oh, managed to down him long enough to grab 'em. He landed on top of the old duck who let go of 'em. No beauty, that one. Long black stockings but no drawers. I've seen lovelier rear ends in pig sties.'

Paul was almost helpless with laughter now and Luke, despite beginning to stiffen up was forced to chuckle along with him as they approached the cafe and settled at a table shaded by a tall tree.

'Order something filling, will you? I'm peckish and beer for me. I could sink a barrel.'

★ ★ ★

That they were objects of curiosity was soon obvious. Few strangers passed that way and English-speaking visitors were an undoubted novelty but after his second glass of beer Luke felt ready enough to exchange nods with others who began to settle at nearby tables. Perhaps this was the local watering hour, he mused as soup, bread and sausage was placed before him. Mm. Plenty of garlic there. That'd keep the flies off. 'So, young Paul, tell me all about the chateau.'

'Well, Guv' Paul began then 'Look out!' he shouted urgently, as a large man in a blue smock rushed at them brandishing a thick cudgel and clearly intent upon beating Luke to a pulp.

Even middle-aged men can move smartly when sudden danger threatens and Luke ducked beneath the descending cudgel, which surely would have brained him had it landed. Ye Gods, he thought, it's him again, his earlier opponent. Having missed the first time, the man raised his cudgel for another try, which was a mistake for Luke was too close to him and his knee came up sharply. For the second time that day the big man doubled up, his eyes bulging in agony.

'A knife. Get me a knife,' Luke called out to Paul who passed on the request to those nearby, all standing now, well away from the action.

A knife was handed to him and as his opponent started to straighten up, Luke hoisted his smock and cut his braces and the broad leather belt that kept his trousers in place. There was silence then a babble of excited voices and Luke, replacing his fallen chair, felt a great weariness sweep over him.

'Get me another beer, would you? And something a bit stronger.' He really was too old for this sort of thing. Far too old and he hardly noticed his late opponent hobbling away, one hand clutching his nether regions, the other holding up his trousers.

'Cognac, monsieur. Complements de la maison.'

'You all right, Guv?' a worried Paul enquired, nearly as shaken as Luke himself.

'I'll live but who was that maniac?' and Paul began to speak with those around.

'He's known as Big Louis Guv, and everyone's scared stiff of him. This is the first time anyone's got the better of him and they think that cutting his braces was magnificent.'

'Well, 'tis a known fact a feller can neither fight nor run if he's holding up his britches.'

★ ★ ★

They were back at their hotel before Paul felt able to speak of his visit to Chateau Grivelle. The elderly woman in the chair was indeed his paternal grandmother and her lack of hospitality was due to an intense loathing of foreigners. During the war of 1870, Orleans was occupied by the Prussians, some of whom had behaved very badly and had nearly wrecked the chateau.

Her husband and her eldest son, that's my grandfather and my uncle, my father's brother, were killed in the fighting and my grandmother was very angry that my father had stayed in England instead of returning to France to fight. She was even more angry when my father married mama who was English so she refused to have anything to do with us. My grandmother says now she is too old to carry on a feud and must forgive and forget so I am welcome in her house. She wishes to proclaim me as the new Seigneur de Grivelle, whatever that means. A bit like lord of the manor, I think but there are many problems to be overcome.'

'And what are they?'

'There is no money. The estate has not been worked since the war ended. Whatever money my grandfather had is held in a bank by law. My grandmother can have only what the estate produces during her lifetime, which is very little. There are taxes to be paid and she believes the government offered compensation for damage to property by the Prussians but no one will tell her about it as she is a woman. There is a lawyer here in Orleans who knows of everything but he is unhelpful. A twisting villain is how grandmamma describes him.'

'I see. So there's skulduggery afoot. I should imagine your appearance on the scene'll cause a flutter. I think this is something we should pass to Mr Brierly. He'll find a way to clarify things, from a legal standpoint, you understand. Now I shall get myself to bed. I'm sure I'll sleep tonight despite the lumpy mattress.

However, at four in the morning, Luke was racing down to the privy, hoping he'd get there in time. Something he'd eaten? River water? Whatever the cause he was feeling unwell. By nine o'clock, when he hadn't left his room, a bright and cheerful Paul knocked on his door to enquire if all was well.

'The answer is no, I am quite unwell. I've spent too much time in that damned privy to be well so I'll stay where I am for a while. The sooner I'm home the better so it's the overnight train to Boulogne for me. You'll be off to see your grandmother I expect. Don't be too late back and get someone to sponge my suit off, will you? It's in a poor state.'

Luke hadn't felt so ill for a long time and had few memories of their return journey but by Felixstowe, Paul had also begun to wilt and by London they were a most unhappy pair who hauled themselves into a cab and sought sanctuary at Gresham House. 'Something they'd eaten', was the doctor's opinion, prescribed foul tasting medicine and ordered complete rest and a miserable diet for a week and so ended Luke's first and only visit to France.

★ ★ ★

Paul though, was full of enthusiasm over his visit, had written down all he'd learned of his family connections and was now preparing to visit his brother at the naval school he attended at Portsmouth. Walter Brierly had dutifully visited there regularly and had tentatively hinted at a wish on Julian's part for a better relationship but Luke wasn't interested. That young man had caused so much upset to so many members of his household that he couldn't accept the inevitable opposition to even a short visit to the Manor. There was William to consider as well as Rory, Lizzie and James never mind Adrian who still visited whenever he could escape from home, a much more accepting home now that a measure of respectability had been established in his stepfather's eyes.

HRH doing penance at the Bramsden College Speech Day had been bemused by Luke's thanks, unaware that certain people had been specifically lined up to be presented. The look on Major Townley's face when his stepson had made the well rehearsed introduction had been impossible to describe and Luke still enjoyed a private chuckle over it.

'My dear Gregory, you are the one deserving my thanks. I felt utterly ashamed of my misconduct on that occasion and I am so grateful for your understanding.'

'These things do happen, sir and no great harm has been done.'

★ ★ ★

Walter Brierly's eldest son Edward, reading law at Cambridge and intending to follow his father's profession, had seized upon Paul's need for advice on French law with a view to adopting this as his thesis subject, much to Luke's relief.

He personally wished for no involvement whatsoever in the legal affairs of the Chateau Grivelle and would prefer to forget about the place. A different story with Fred, though. With still no word from his father, and with no information from the Foreign Office, Fred was a despondent and unhappy young man.

'Right, young Fred. This has gone on long enough. You'd better book yourself a passage to Bombay and see what you can discover yourself. Your mother's side of the family might shed light on things but be careful. Be aware of the risks and there's something you can do for me whilst you're out there. Cargoes continue to arrive at the warehouse as if your father had despatched them but there's never been any explanation, which remains a mystery to be solved. Whatever course of action you decide upon is fine with me but be sure to keep in touch.'

★ ★ ★

Digger, he found, had taken on the task of organising activities for those boys who remained at the school during the holidays. Parents abroad was the usual reason and who better as an entertainer of small boys than Digger? He was beginning to regain his cheerful, light-hearted approach to life now he and Beth were safely settled in the Home Farmhouse at the Hall and wished they'd made the move earlier.

There were five at the moment, including James, who would shortly be moving to Bramsden, plus William, Rory, Lizzie and little Chloe, who had arrived rather later and 'quite unexpectedly', Beth had claimed, with a twinkle in her eye. 'Woke up one morning and there she was, all pink and smiley'.

Before long there were rumours of wild goings on in the woods with grubby urchins cooking things over fires, swinging from trees and camping out with the minimum of adult interference.

'Good for 'em,' Lady Cecelia boomed. 'Join 'em meself if I was younger. Not allowed in my day. All sitting around being ladylike. Not a happy time. Take me word for it.'

★ ★ ★

Financing all his activities and outgoings was beginning to exercise Luke's mind more than usual at this time. He'd committed himself heavily and had less in the bank than he found comfortable. True, there was a steady flow of income from his various investments and enterprises but it would be at least two years before the estate produced a worthwhile return.

Ben Driscol though, was reassuring. 'You don't need to worry, Guv. You're doing all right. The Revenue'll hold off for as long as need be and the Church Commissioners are happy with our arrangement. All you have to do is keep things ticking along steadily, but you'll have to watch your back. It's Berrimond after your blood. We have an understanding with those making enquiries. All very civilised, of course. Seems you've upset the man and he hopes to even the score.'

'Ah, well yes. We're not exactly on speaking terms. Any idea what he has in mind? Best not to be caught on a lee shore with that sort.'

'Nothing we know of but we could set him up, if you like. Feed him something interesting to act upon then pounce. It's been done before but you'd probably ruin him.'

'Prefer to avoid that if I can. Rather the feller left me in peace.'

★ ★ ★

'Bit of needling going on, Guv.' George reported. 'Between Master Nicholas and Richard. Something about Eton being superior to Bramsden. Getting a bit heated at times, I reckon. Won't leave off. Fur'll fly presently if it doesn't stop.'

'Bad as that, eh? He's welcome to come over and join in but he has to mind his manners. I'll keep a weather eye on it and have a word.'

Not an easy situation Luke mused. No family, a tidy little estate in trust but no real say in affairs. About ready to leave school, not sure what he wants to do when he does leave. Army, perhaps or university, or just play the gentleman of leisure but he could do without him causing upset here. He'd ask Walter to advise.

As so often happens though, things came to a head shortly after. Nicholas had stayed the night and at the breakfast table made some pointless and unnecessary remark clearly aimed at irritating Richard, who tensed and glowered at his plate but said nothing. Luke seized his opportunity. 'I've heard it said,' to no one in particular 'it's what you do with your education rather than where you receive it.'

There was little further conversation but within the hour, Nicholas had packed his bag, saddled his horse and ridden off without so much as a word to anyone. Odd, Luke thought but not his problem. He'd mention it to Lady Cecelia when they next met.

★ ★ ★

'Rain on the way', he was told and the oats were ready for harvesting.

'In that case let's get 'em in. Make a start in the morning first thing. Thresh and bag in the field then spread 'em on the granary floors to dry off properly. I know it's not been done before but we'll give it a try and once we start we'll not stop 'till the last bag's under cover.'

'You mean work after dark, sir?'

'I mean just that. The electric affair that runs off the traction engine'll give light enough. All hands on deck; horses to work in relays. Plenty of time to rest when it rains, eh?'

So, working in shifts, nearly forty acres of prime oats were harvested and stored under cover before the rain arrived. Four hours on and four off for man and horse with the traction engine and thresher going full tilt. A constant procession of bag-filled carts heading for the different buildings designated as granaries, tea, bread, cheese and lemonade within easy reach and, to everyone's surprise, a carnival atmosphere. Somehow, working non-stop through the night had caught the imagination and there was a collective determination to get the job done, to beat the weather and 'show 'em what Chidlingbrook folk can do.'

'Quite remarkable,' the Rector observed. 'I really am amazed. Is there nothing I might do to assist?'

'Best to stand clear like me,' Luke replied. 'This is their trade. They know what they're about and we'd only be in the way.'

'But it's all so organised.'

'Indeed. Each man to his task with another covering. No more than half an hour on the thresher at a time. Dangerous things machines. Don't want accidents through carelessness so there's no alcohol allowed. Drink all they like afterwards.'

'Are you allowing gleaning?'

'If they're smart about it. There's a catch crop of something or other to be sown straight after, for late grazing.'

The barley crop had earlier been harvested in more leisurely fashion during a welcome dry spell and was already spoken for by a Guildford brewery. Now it was the turn of the potatoes and again, it was all hands on deck to lift and store the crop before the weather made life difficult and by the end of November, Luke was reasonably satisfied with the company's first season, the earlier grumbles at new fangled ideas subsiding with the increased wages offered.

The grazing was much improved by reseeding and fertilising and the nucleus of the chosen livestock breeds were all in place ready to increase their numbers in the spring but as always, Luke and Digger took a close interest in every aspect of the company's activities, as much to learn as to supervise.

That had been the winning formula on the river and they'd follow the same pattern on the estate. There'd been resistance by some to having a woman in charge of the market garden side of things but Mrs Foster was a big woman with a forceful personality who was determined to prove her worth and make a success of her department.

The Rector had enquired as to his thoughts on a harvest supper or celebration of some sort but Luke had no interest in any such tradition that might or might not have been customary round about. 'You organise whatever you wish, Rector but leave me out of it. I'm running a business and treating people fair and square but I'm not hob nobbing with 'em. I know full well how the land lies so we'll leave it at that.'

★ ★ ★

Chapter 15

December already? Good Lord! Where had the year gone? Christmas would be upon them before they knew it and the weather was already much colder. Frosts, fog and rain. No weather to be outside but there was still work to be done. Sprouts, cabbage, carrots and parsnips to be readied for market. Hay to be carted, muck to be spread, cows to be milked and tended and hedges to be laid.

It was never ending but it was becoming more tightly organised and the whole enterprise promised to be productive and profitable, never mind tales of doom and gloom round about. There was resentment from neighbouring farmers and landowners over the higher wages the company paid. Jealousy too, over the mechanisation and investment already showing results but this was nothing new to Luke. It'd been the same on the river when he and Digger started out and tried new ways of working. Invest in the right tools, meet your customer's needs and treat your workforce fairly and you had a good chance of success but watch your back, for no one else would.

Knowing it was Lord Berrimond actively seeking ways to injure him made Luke more wary and ready to respond to any provocation that might arise. There was an attempt at creating a boundary dispute on the far side of the wood, and an allegation of sheep stealing made but Walter Brierly had dealt firmly with both counts. To clarify matters, Luke had the whole of the estate surveyed and a detailed plan produced so was pleasantly surprised to learn that the complaining neighbour had, in fact, encroached on nearly an acre of grazing belonging to the estate and had been obliged to make restitution.

To help guard against such mischief, Luke organised mounted patrols to check on all the boundaries and comb the wooded areas for trespassers, a task gleefully undertaken by Richard, Peter and the Donkin boys that gave exercise for the ponies and something useful to do over the Christmas and New Year holiday.

The company had given a bonus of a week's pay to every employee, not that it could really be afforded but there was no doubting the popularity of the idea, according to reports. No harm in pleasing folks, Luke mused as he sat by the fire and gazed at the bell hanging close by.

That had been his Christmas present from Digger and Beth and a more pleasant surprise he could never have received. They'd watched him closely as he opened the box and stood holding it in amazement. The ship's bell from the Dorien Bee, the first ship on which he'd sailed as galley boy all those years ago and to think it had been his task to polish it. There was the lettering. Dorien Bee.1836. The year he was born.

'The old girl was broken up at Blackwall a while back. Thought you might like a keepsake,' Digger had said, almost shyly.

★ ★ ★

Funny thing, fate, Luke mused when he heard that Berrimond was no more. 'Came off his horse,' Lady Cecelia told him. 'Broke his neck. Two of 'em gone in no time at all.' A relief in a way. Should put a stop to unpleasantness from that direction but just what was young Richard going to do with himself? None too academic. Not interested in university and no real ideas of his own. His friend Robert would follow in his father's footsteps and join the Indian Army. Understandable, that, but Richard wasn't sure of such a move so he'd have to accept whatever was thrown at him.

He could start by moving into the warehouse and learning the wharfing business from the bottom up. That should concentrate his mind, Luke thought and nodded his approval at the idea. Then there was young John who was academic and hoped to become a teacher and was being encouraged by the Grammar School to work for a Cambridge scholarship, never mind a teacher training college. A University Degree for a farm labourer's son, now. That would be an achievement but he'd need help.

★ ★ ★

Now George was ill and seriously so. Hemiplegia, the doctor said, which meant paralysed down one side. Something called a stroke. Wasn't that what Brandon Remnold had suffered? But he was known for hard living and a nasty temper whilst George Cherry was as equable a fellow as one could hope to find anywhere and was certainly not known for harmful habits.

There was just no telling. One day a man could be hale and hearty, the next he could be down and out. If it wasn't illness it could be an accident. A horse might bolt, a train might derail, you could be struck by lightning. Oh, come on Gregory! You must be getting old, thinking like this. Get off your tail end and do something useful, like drawing up an agenda for the manager's meeting he'd called.

He wanted those organising the various sections to meet and discuss progress. He wanted ideas from them to improve efficiency. He wanted co-operation between them all to make everything run smoothly. Was hay getting down to the dairy on time? Were there enough hands available for lifting a crop when it was ready? Were there horses, ploughs and carts available when needed? Who would look to the pigs in the wood? Tamworths he had in mind. Long snouts for rooting around but inclined to be frisky. Closest domestic breed to wild boar he was told.

They'd have lunch beforehand or would it be better after business matters were cleared? No, luncheon first. Put everyone at ease. Ale and cider on hand. Problem. Mrs Foster would be the only woman present. Might feel uncomfortable. Unused to this sort of thing. Ah. Beth and Digger. The girls too. They could join in then withdraw when work started. No. What was he thinking of? Secretarial skills. They'd record the meeting. Good practice and get 'em involved. Family business. That was it. Keep things light and easy. Not too formal.

★ ★ ★

Luke was sitting in the orangery when Lady Cecelia arrived. He liked it out there with the scent of the orange blossom and the warm, airy spaciousness. His bit of personal luxury no matter what the weather was like outside.

'Ah, Cissie. Come in, come in. Nothing like a hot house when it's chilly outside.'

'Glad to, glad to. Like this. Wouldn't mind one meself. Brought you a problem. Know you'll help if you can. Know you'll be straight if you can't.'

'Sounds ominous. Drop of the usual?'

'Had a visitor. Lady Penelope. You know. Berrimond. Nice gell. Nice gell. Badly used by that fellah. Don't feel so bad not being wed. Better off without fellahs like that. Don't mind me telling you this, do you?'

'Not at all.'

'Two of 'em gone. Finances in a mess. Estate badly managed. Creditors pressing. Doesn't know where to begin. Like me. Never had to, you know, deal with money. Told her how you got me ship shape. Wondered if you'd, well, give the gell a hand,' and Lady Cecelia flopped back in her chair having outlined the problem in her staccato fashion, then examined her glass closely. 'Know your thoughts on 'em. Not her fault. Not her fault.'

'What do you wish me to do?'

'Talk to her, would you? Without the dowager? You know, Lady Elisabeth. Difficult, that one. No help at all. Be all manner of well, hell to pay if she got to hear.'

'I can well imagine. We met briefly once and it wasn't friendly. Probably best if I stand clear and get Walter Brierly to call. He'd ask all the right questions so if you'd let me know where and when? Better still, why not call on him? Go up to London. Stay at the house for as long as need be. All the right advice to hand there and no interference from the dragon. How does that sound?'

With Lady Cecelia gone to organise her side of things, Luke sat musing on this latest event, his book neglected. Finances in a mess. Well, he'd gathered that but desperate enough to seek his help? What, he wondered might the possibilities be? He'd no money to spare; wouldn't have for a couple of years at least but there must be some sort of opportunity here.

He'd send Walter a note. Give him an idea of what his visitors required. Urgent though and confidential. Better send someone with it but who? The boys were back at school, Richard down the wharf. Ah, the girls. Why not? They could be relied upon. Just time for the afternoon train if they moved themselves. Telegram for the cab to meet them at Waterloo.

Right, that should work out, but what, now, to do about poor old George? Mrs Cherry was in a state and the doctor couldn't reassure her about his recovery. How would it be if they moved back into the house and he engaged an attendant to see to George's needs? Lifting and washing and so on? That might be a practical arrangement. Only right to do all he could for him. Done a good job here at the Manor. Didn't care to see him like this. Unable to speak or move. A bad business indeed.

It's a less than perfect world he mused and here was Robbie Donkin wanting a word. 'So it didn't wake up and the rats have had a go at it. Well it was an old thing after all. You did your best for it but get it buried quick as you can and well away from here.'

That was the bear gone, then. It'd provided a bit of fun during its short time with them. Had amused the village children no end playing around in the river. Been a devil with the bee hives though but Mrs Donkin had its measure and one screech from her would send it scuttling. Oh well. It'd added a bit of interest. Now what about a few ostriches around the place?

But here was the doctor with, Good Lord, a black man carrying a large valise. 'Come in, come in,' Luke invited trying to conceal his surprise. You didn't see many black faces round here so what was this all about?

'Mr Gregory, may I present Mr Dennin who comes highly recommended by the agency in the care of the incapacitated?'

'Ah, come to look after George? Good, good. Start straight away? Excellent, excellent,' but why was he looking at him like that and why was the doctor smiling?'

'You don't remember me, sir?'

'Er, we've met before? At sea or the warehouse maybe?' Luke was struggling with his memory trying hard to place the man. Big, broad of shoulder, finely boned features and a deep bass voice. No, he couldn't place him he decided.

'You remember a house with bars at the window and a big fat man?'

'Good God!' Luke exclaimed. 'You mean you're,' and he tailed off in utter surprise, his mind going back to one night years before when he and his strong arm men had raided the fat man's fortress, the Lodge House, the 'house of ill repute', as the Chinese mandarin had aptly termed it.

'Thaddeus Percival and the Lodge House. Good Lord. So you're Tommy? What a small world it is,' and he held out his hand in happy recognition.

'Look, drop your bag and come and have a seat. This is just incredible. Tell me, how come you to be with the agency? What, it must be, well, how long I shudder to think. Last I heard you'd gone to sea.'

'That's right, Guv. After I left the Doctor's I signed on as a galley boy, just like you. On a steamer though. Went on to be a steward and sick berth attendant. Suitable work for a nigger, that, mopping up after other folks but I didn't mind. Found it interesting and stayed ashore. Ended up with the agency. Heard your name mentioned and here I am.'

'Well it's not me who needs the helping hand as Doctor Fairleigh will have told you but poor old George is laid up pretty bad. If you can do something for him I'd appreciate it and it'd be a big help to Mrs Cherry. Come on and I'll introduce you.'

★ ★ ★

The girls were back, flushed with the success of their visit to London. They were surprised to say the least when they met Tommy but quickly relaxed and accepted him as part of their busy lives. Clerical duties in the company office now occupied some of their time and on Friday they were to pay out the wages. The routine was for someone to call at the bank in Guildford, collect the wages bag and return to the railway carriage office, closely escorted by a couple of strong young men from one of the farms, with intense competition for this privileged role as a welcome break from normal routines.

Delegation was the secret, Luke kept telling himself and an ability to turn your hand to anything but he was often hard put to follow his own advice, though he'd insisted from the start that the girls learn to cook and take their turn with the laundry for there was no telling when they might find such skills useful.

He'd maintained their social position though by use of the prefix 'Miss' before their name so it was Miss Lucy and Miss Annabelle to the village. Likewise it was Master Richard and Master Peter to those outside the family but everyone, in his opinion, was better for being busy, including himself, intent as he was on keeping his eye on every aspect of the enterprise and this still included the wharf. True, the Downing brothers had taken over the lighterage side of things but no one had acquired the knack of encouraging profitable cargoes into their warehouses.

The Parsons clan kept immaculate records of everything but lacked the confidence and ability to bargain and trade the varied items they had always carried so there was nothing for it but to make regular appearances as the resulting income was very much needed. He'd taken on a lot and a steady cash flow without the need for borrowing was essential.

He'd hoped that Richard would find this scene interesting but the grim surroundings and rough nature of the wharfing trade were clearly not to his taste. Still, he was making an effort and a few evening visits to the card rooms in search of profitable notes offered distraction. All of which left Digger, and to some extent, Beth, to keep an eye on the estate, a reversal of roles, but George was sorely missed. Surprising how you came to rely on one person, Luke mused but Tommy had assured him that George's condition wasn't hopeless.

'If the man wants to get better, he will, I knows that. Not the first one I've met like him. Sure thing, I'll keep him clean and tidy, no problem but he has to exercise and fight. I'm hard on him, I knows that but I'll have him back on his kitchen stool if he'll work at it.'

★ ★ ★

Ah, here it was. Walter's report and assessment of Lady Penelope Berrimond's visit. Not a rosy picture. Why were these titled folks such hopeless housekeepers? Why did they squander their resources in such a fashion? They'd never had to work for it, that's why, he decided.

Virtually bankrupt. Value of the estate probably less than creditor demands. So who were the creditors? Ah. Her Majesty's Revenue after succession duties or whatever. The Church Commissioners after their tithes, Poor Law Rates unpaid, Club fees, Hunt fees, tradesmen's outstanding accounts. Good Lord! £327 – 10s – 6d owing to a tailor in Saville Row. Ye Gods! Time these people came down to earth, no doubt about that.

A footnote. The Lady Elizabeth was violently opposed to the making of any changes whatsoever to her accustomed mode of life. Refused absolutely to recognise the dire financial position, and so on. Just about fits the old biddy he'd encountered at the station. She'd probably be a match for Paul's French grandmother.

Recommendations. Ah. If persuaded to involve at any level, proceed with extreme caution. Well, that was sensible enough but what could he offer? Liabilities aplenty. Resources minimal. If declared bankrupt and the place were sold, creditors would still be out of pocket so what on earth was to be gained by any involvement?

Luke's scheming nature began to work overtime. Here he was with his own potentially profitable estate with farming and land usage at the core. He'd avoided borrowing to fund it all but had a lease on one farm. The Berrimond estate was two thousand acres or more producing what, exactly? A deer park for show. Hunters for chasing foxes and four farms. Now, what if that estate were to be run, like his, as a company? What if creditors could be persuaded to wait whilst solvency was restored over, say five or even ten years?

If he took ten per cent of the gross as his fee for organising it all? There were possibilities but he'd avoid personal financial risk so what, he wondered could Ben come up with? And Ben, as ever had ideas to offer.

'Put it this way, Guv. As you know, I specialise in enquiries of a confidential nature and there are many financial irregularities to be found. I'm discreet over my findings but I'm never party to misdeeds and my investments are in honest enterprises, just as you taught me. Farming, for instance but never racehorses. I'm interested in estate management and could probably lose both revenue and church demands, which would put things on a more reasonable footing.'

'Are you serious? Wouldn't that be risky? I mean, for you, personally?'

'No, Guv. I have only to whisper in receptive ears. An entry in a ledger, a receipt on official paper and all is painlessly accomplished. It's how things work actually, though all is outwardly upstanding and respectable. You'd never believe the ways of those in high places. It all starts at the top and works down to the lowly clerk with his ledger, for gentlemen never discuss money. They merely oblige one another. Nothing more but Freemasonry helps, which is why I joined.'

'Well, what can I say? Without those millstones round its neck that estate could prosper but I must know that you're not putting yourself at risk. I must have your assurance on that. I've no love for the revenue or the church but you in the dock, well that doesn't bear thinking of.'

'Guv, you have my word on it. No pigeons'll come home to roost on me. The risk, if any, will be elsewhere.'

★ ★ ★

'Lady Penelope. I'm delighted to make your acquaintance.' They were meeting at the Manor, Luke, Digger and Lady Cecelia as the Dowager Lady Elisabeth was on the war path, bitterly opposed to any change and unable to comprehend the parlous state of the family finances.

'The appraisal of the estate leaves few options,' Luke commenced when all were seated. 'Bankruptcy and surrendering the estate to creditors is clearly the least palatable one and something to be avoided. There is a possibility that by making the estate pay its way, creditors may be persuaded to accept deferred payment for a stated period.'

'There is hope then?' Lady Penelope asked.

'It would mean making changes and I understand the Lady Elisabeth would oppose these.'

'I have my son and daughter to think of, Mr Gregory. It is their future that concerns me and as my late husband held both title and estate I believe I have the right to overrule whatever objections might arise.'

Luke nodded his understanding. 'You are correctly advised. Your son, the present Lord Berrimond, is nine years of age. If the target date for solvency were to be fixed at his twenty-first birthday, or earlier if possible, that would guarantee his education and your continued occupancy of The Towers.'

'You think this to be possible?' There was hope in her Ladyship's voice now.

Again, Luke nodded. Yes, it is possible. Eleven or twelve years of hard work, full utilisation of the land and an end to all extravagance could make it achievable.'

'There is nothing I will not do to enable this. It is far more than I expected to hear. What would you have me do?'

'There are two possibilities I'd suggest to you. Firstly, turn the estate into a farming company along the lines I'm following myself. That would mean the deer in the park being replaced by cattle, sheep or horses; whatever stock that will create income, both to impress your creditors and to maintain your family. The second aspect is the house. I believe The Towers has potential in its own right but I have yet to give further thought to the possibilities.

There was a pause as Lady Penelope grappled with the implications of Luke's suggestions but there was to be no further peaceful discussion as the sound of horses hooves and metal wheels on the gravel outside distracted them. Moments later came a vigorous clanging of the doorbell and Digger got up to peer through the window to see the nature of this disturbance.

'Er, Guv. It's Her Ladyship's carriage and the footmen look set to knock the door in.'

Lady Penelope went pale, Lady Cecelia bridled protectively and Luke stood up. 'I'll see to this. Just sit tight, all of you,' and he deliberately left the study door open so that all might hear what passed.'

'Where is she? I demand to know. I will not tolerate her scheming. Let me pass. Stand aside this instant. Forbes,' to the bell-ringing footman, 'remove this person and allow me entry.'

One look at Luke's expression was sufficient to deter the man and an unmistakeable inclination of the head made him step back from the doorway. 'You forget yourself, madam.'

'Madam? I am the Lady Elisabeth Berrimond.'

'Then stop behaving like a fishwife and I'll accord you your title.'

The Lady Elisabeth appeared to swell with fury but finding that she couldn't stare Luke down controlled herself with some difficulty.

'If you wish to speak with me Lady Elisabeth then you are welcome to enter.'

'I seek my daughter in law, the Lady Penelope, whom I believe to be making quite improper arrangements regarding my affairs. My affairs, sir and I will not tolerate it.'

'I beg to disagree, my Lady. The Lady Penelope has a clear understanding of the state of your family finances and seeks to remedy matters. I have been asked to assist and have offered my services. Will you not take a seat?'

'I demand to see my late son's wife. Immediately.'

'You do not make demands in this house. Either you conduct yourself in a civilised fashion or you will leave. Now hear what I have to say. At this moment in time the Berrimond estate is bankrupt. Your creditors are pressing and a High Court Order awaits the transfer of all assets of whatever nature, and that includes your carriage and even the rings on your fingers.

If the court order is served and you have no friends to take you in then you may find yourself in the workhouse with your status less than that of one of my dairymaids. The Lady Penelope is doing her utmost to protect both you and your grandchildren from such indignity yet you obstruct and decry her at every turn.'

'I do not believe one word of what you say.'

'That is your privilege but when was your staff last paid? Your bankers called upon you last week did they not? At the behest of the High Court, I might add. Your affairs are no longer as private as they once were simply because you are no longer solvent. Now Look. Please do take a seat. I can well understand how perplexing this is to you but be assured, there are those prepared to help if you will allow.'

As Luke had hoped, the bubble of anger and outrage was deflating and the Dowager Lady Elisabeth suddenly looked old, tired and defeated.

'But how has this come about?'

'Both your late husband and son were extravagant and maintained lifestyles beyond the estate's ability to support them. Farming is difficult at this time with incomes reduced. Your bailiff was dishonest. Taxes and tithes are always with us and nothing was put aside with which to meet them. Your late husband had mortgaged Harrington's Farm and one other and had probably disposed of other assets. Eventually all these outgoings had to be accounted for.'

There was a long silence then and Luke found himself actually feeling sorry for the lady.

'What then must I do?' It was no more than a subdued whisper.

'May I suggest that you make your peace with Lady Penelope? I know she would welcome this. You might then work together to improve matters and above all, maintain your social standing and dignity.' That, Luke hoped was the right tack to take. Emphasise social position, the one thing that really mattered to such folk.

'Very well.'

'I will call Lady Penelope.'

★ ★ ★

'I know what you're going to say, young Richard. Warehousing and wharfing are not to your taste. Right?'

'Well, yes, Guv. To be honest I find it all a bit depressing. Interesting, though,' Richard added hastily. 'It's just, well, I can't see myself settling down to that sort of life.'

'Understandable but I know you've learned from the experience. Seen how managers manage and teams work together without some beak in a gown waving a stick, eh? Different world altogether.'

Richard nodded a trifle gloomily. 'I almost wish I'd done the same as Robert and gone into the army but I'm not sure that would have been a good idea.'

'Plenty of time to make decisions. The trouble with schools is they cut you off from real life and you have to start learning how the world works once you leave. Now, thought about estate management? Outside in the open air most of the time keeping an eye on things? Directing, encouraging, making decisions? Hard work being a good bailiff, mind. Not for the idle or dishonest.'

'You mean here? Looking after all this?'

'Possibly. Now, let's be frank with each other. Had things been different you might well have travelled or spent a year or two in the army or gone to university then waited around to inherit the place, a bit like Berrimond. Well, you have to earn your living, same as Peter and the girls. William too, in case you thought he might be having the lot. Same for Fred and Paul. I'll help, of course but you could make a good life for yourself minding other people's land and farms. Might even aim to look after one of HRH's estates? You'd have to learn the trade, mind, with the agricultural college, to look at new ideas. Very much a changing world and it's no good battling with stick in the muds if you don't know what you're talking about'

'Well yes, Guv. Do you think I could try that?'

'Certainly and I could use a bit of help whilst George is laid up. The first thing I'd suggest is to work alongside Amos Burlington. He's a bright fellow who's known farming from his earliest days but he has an open mind. You could learn a lot from him and he'll need a fair bit of help with the plans I have in mind.'

And now to Digger. 'Feel up to having a cosy chat with Lady Penelope? This is what I have in mind for The Towers. Offer it as a country retreat for the up and coming social climber. Not quite an hotel but somewhere to relax, keep a horse, chase foxes, play the country gent and be entertained by her ladyship, for which they will pay handsomely. Shooting parties too. Discretion, naturally. All by word of mouth but not the same as the Lodge House. Mustn't lower the tone. What do you think? Feel like taking it on and helping her work it up? You have the contacts and his nibs might even wander round. No? Asking too much there perhaps, but you see the possibilities?'

'Guv, where do you get these ideas from? I think it's a corker. Ye hip! Get Beth to join in?'

'By all means. Could be an enjoyable enterprise.'

★ ★ ★

'Rector, this is not a subject with which I have much sympathy. I believe I fully discharge whatever obligations I might have by supporting him where he is. I found him to be the most distasteful and unpleasant boy I have ever met and that view was shared by every member of this household.'

'I see. Yes, I see. I had of course heard a little of the distress the young man occasioned. There are few close

- 438 -

secrets in so small a community as you well know, but the letter I received from the chaplain of the naval school was most pressing and I assured him that I would use my utmost endeavours to er, seek a more forgiving attitude?'

'Forgiving? I can forgive but I'll not forget in a hurry.'

'He was but eleven or so years of age at the time. Not an age of great maturity and he very much regrets the unpleasantness he displayed. You see, he was deeply affected by the loss of his father and just could not accept another in his place.'

'I've never been overbearing as a guardian. Quite the opposite, I would have thought,' Luke responded huffily.

'Indeed yes. Oh, if only he had been able to see that. Unfortunately he felt at the time that his mother was being disloyal and he readily admits that he did his utmost to prevent your union.'

'Well, he didn't manage it and he'd still have been placed where he is had the wedding taken place. I was determined not to allow his disruption to mar our relationship.'

'Is time not a healer?'

'Look, Rector. No matter what my feelings are, I have to bear in mind those of others. There would be precious little enthusiasm for renewed contact, of that I am sure.'

'Would it be possible, no, may I beg you, to enquire of the others of your household to at least consider, oh how may I put it other than forgiveness? Mr Brierly, your solicitor, pointed out to him that you had no legal responsibility for him or for his brother and sister and that his continued expressions of hatred towards you were quite unwarranted. Given the chance of a career at sea instead of the workhouse when his uncle died, surprised him profoundly. It was something he had never even considered.'

Luke was silent for a while, then, 'What's behind this, Rector? You're not usually so pressing.'

'Mr Gregory, I had not intended to mention this but I feel now that I must. The young man in question attempted to kill himself, hence the contact from the chaplain. Apparently he was so unhappy at his situation that he decided to end his life. He is currently confined to the sick berth under close supervision and it is felt that only one thing will prevent a further attempt. Forgiveness and acceptance.'

'I see. Well, you took your time coming to the point,' Luke said, gruffly. 'Leave it with me.' As if I haven't enough to think of, he brooded, once the Rector had gone. Damnation but surely it wasn't his fault this had come about? How could it be? Told me to my face he hated me. Hated being with his uncle's family. Probably hates being where he is. Better than the workhouse though and that's where he could've ended up, together with his brother and sister. Where anyone could end up if there was no one else, he supposed. Even William.

Good God! If he'd said he didn't want to know, his own son would have ended up in St Olaf's. That place of stinking drains where the Warner family found themselves. He'd have to do something but what? Visiting folks who'd tried to top themselves wasn't his cup of tea no matter who they might be. He just wouldn't have the right approach. Wouldn't know where to start. Ah! Digger and Beth. He'd persuade them to do something; visit or whatever. That's it, he decided. Delegate. The art of good management. Pass the rotten jobs to someone else. Whatever they thought should be done would be fine by him.

★ ★ ★

A busy but useful week at the wharf. Two cargoes of rice, another of dried fruit and one of spices, all on top of cotton, jute, coffee and hides. Spring was in the air and trade was picking up. A pleasant evening at the Lodge House, purely to see how things were, of course and Luke had a spring in his step as he left the carriage at Chidlingbrook station. Lambs, piglets and foals had been arriving when he'd left and he looked forward to hearing all the news.

'Ah, Digger. Not train spotting surely, or are you greeting me with good news or bad?'

'Well, Guv, depends 'ow you look at it. You did say ter do as we saw fit.'

'Go on. Ruin my weekend.'

'Well, we brought 'im back with us.'

'What, here?'

'Yes. Now before you blows yer top, we decided it was fer the best. It's not permanent and I reckon you'll 'ave a surprise. I never thought I'd feel sorry fer that young 'eathen but he's just not the same feller. E's just a frightened little scrap. No steam in 'im at all. Talk about 'ave a few rough edges knocked off 'im. E's dead smart in 'is uniform but 'e's so thin 'e could 'ide behind a broom 'andle. Doctor's given 'im the once over. Said 'e's underweight an' overwrought, whatever that means but you can see 'e's not well so we got 'im sick leave and Mrs Cherry's doing what she does best.'

'So what's the state of the tide? With the others. William and the girls.'

'No problem. No fuss at all. Just said 'Hello' and carried on with what they were doing. Beth settled 'im in and 'e's scarce moved from the kitchen since. Funny thing, though. He an' Tommy took to one another straight off. Talking ships an' barnacles an' such like. Oh, and another surprise for you,' Digger's diction improving as his confidence grew, 'George is back on his stool two hours a day. I reckon Tommy's working miracles, I really do.'

'Well that I am glad to hear, really glad but what course do I set now? Plain sail or storm canvas?'

'Calm weather, Guv. He knows what train you'll be on and he'll be waiting for you top of the drive to make 'is peace. Just him. No one else. Boots shined up special like. Been told what to say an' how to say it an' I've got a tanner on it with Tommy as to what you'll do an' say.'

'I'm that much of a dead cert am I?'

'All the way, Guv. Me tanner's safe.'

'You don't leave me much choice. Coming up are you?'

'We'll be up later. We're booked in for dinner. Seven courses Mrs Cherry's promised.'

Well, honestly, Luke thought to himself. Feelings of trepidation at walking up his own drive, to his own house. This, he hadn't reckoned on but the course had been plotted and he'd just have to steer it and hope the compass was true. And there, just at the top, as he rounded the bend was a slim figure in cadet uniform of dark blue jacket and trousers and short-peaked cap. If he had been apprehensive then the figure in front of him, saluting now, most clearly was and he raised his hat in formal acknowledgement.

'So, young Julian. You've returned to the fold. Good to see you again,' and he held out his hand in greeting.

'I, I want to say, sir, how sorry I am for everything I did. I really regret it, sir, I really do.'

'That's alright. We all make mistakes. Made plenty myself. Water under the bridge. Start again, shall we? Come on. Let's see what Mrs Cherry's got for us,' and with his arm round Julian's shoulders they walked up to the kitchen door.

★ ★ ★

There was talk already of the Queen's Golden Jubilee celebrations and there was nearly a year before that royal knees up. It was a load of old nonsense in Luke's opinion. A sheer waste of public money that would be better spent on improved housing and wages for the very half-wits who'd be in the front row waving flags and drinking themselves silly, in celebration of what? Fifty years of doing nothing useful but interfering in matters beyond her comprehension.

The Irish question could have been settled had she not refused to tolerate any form of self government. Refused even to believe there were prostitutes, pimps and homosexuals, she was so out of touch with her adoring subjects and hadn't the least idea of the living conditions many endured, surrounded as she was by snivelling sycophants intent on maintaining their undeserved privileges. Ugh! Here was ample reason to dodge taxes at every opportunity!

His heretical thoughts on the subject at least served to while away the tedium of the journey to Waterloo at the start of another busy week. All appeared to be running smoothly around the estate now Digger was making his presence felt. He was a dab hand at cheerfully chivvying those who might have applied themselves more diligently for where Luke would have growled, Digger's wit and good humour achieved the same, if not better, results. He had Lady Penelope eating out of his hand and even the Dowager Dragon was beginning to respond to the plans for opening up the family seat for a useful purpose. But where was the cab? Was Joe unwell? Or the horse? Most unusual not to be met and he muttered in annoyance as he climbed into a cab from the rank.

'Dead in 'is bed, Guv. 'E were found this morning,' he was informed when he arrived at Gresham House. Well there was a fine start to the week. Poor old Joe. Another casualty of the war in the Crimea, where he'd left most of one leg. What with George laid up and Joe gone he was losing his best men. Funeral arrangements to be made, for

Friday. Yes, of course he'd attend and he'd let Digger know. He'd been a good, steady member of the team who neither smoked nor drank and treated his horses like family. There were few like him. He'd be missed.

So who to run the cab? Did they really need one now? They did. Whilst they still worked the wharf their own cab was a must for there was never one to be found round there when needed. Now, people to see. Cargoes to discuss. The stock exchange to visit. It really was time those South African mining shares showed a return and there was that continual unpleasant mood of discontent on the river. Their employees were treated well enough, with their regular work and decent pay, but the casual system in the big docks was increasingly resented. It'll blow one of these days, he reckoned so what, if anything, should he do to protect their interests?

Digger's strong arm boys were still with them under the direction now of Euan Mackenzie, a large and forbidding Scotsman. They would protect his staff and look after the warehouses should trouble erupt but better by far to head things off and let disturbance pass by. He'd keep his ear to the ground.

★ ★ ★

Digger was with him on Thursday in good time for the funeral next day.' All quiet at home?'

'All quiet, Guv. Beth's in charge and the Lord help anyone who steps out o' line.'

Luke nodded. 'Shame about Joe but we need to keep the cab going, for a while at least. Any ideas who might step in?'

'Oh, Billy. Billy Hocken. You remember One Eyed Titch?'

'He still around?'

'Never moved out. Still dosses with the 'osses. You couldn't get 'im in a proper bed for love nor money. Hay sack fer a pillow an' a pile o' straw on top. Hoss blanket now and then if it's really cold. Set 'im on, shall I?'

'Please do. Didn't care to fix anything up 'till Joe'd gone and I haven't needed a cab. I've been busy up here.'

★ ★ ★

'Well, Tommy, you can tell him there's to be a Board of Enquiry into the mistreatment of junior cadets. HRH wants to know about it so it's all being taken seriously.'

'Digger said you'd be stirring things up with a very big spoon.'

'Did he now. It's clear Julian was persecuted. Mr Brierly has seen the records and they don't make comfortable reading so changes will most definitely be made and he should stand a better chance when he returns but that'll not be until he's fully fit.'

'He doesn't want to go back, Guv. Reckons it'll be just the same.'

'Well it won't be. There'll be no more nailing his boots to the deck or cutting one leg of his trousers short to make him late for divisions and most definitely no more nonsense round the heads. That really did raise a few eyebrows I can tell you but I think he should arrange to visit Paul at school and also polish up his French if he hopes to visit his grandmother. She has a poor opinion of English speakers and her disapproval could take the varnish off the furniture.'

★ ★ ★

May Day celebrations? He knew the Rector was keen to revive the old customs of the area but why could he not just organise whatever took his fancy and leave him out of it? He didn't mind if folks took a day off to wave bunches of flowers at each other just so long as the routine milking and feeding was carried out and the whole village could drink itself silly and sing and dance all day and night as far as he was concerned.

He had more pressing matters in mind with HRH wanting to send a couple of his nags down to be mollycoddled and they'd need protection. Fred had written to say his father had died and an uncle on his mother's side had taken over as agent in his place, which explained the continuing flow of merchandise, but not the rubies.

Odd, that. The trouble was, the uncle was hostile to Fred becoming involved in the business. What did the guv advise? Then there was Lady Elisabeth being difficult, Nicholas Hurlingham had got some young lady in trouble and Lady Cecelia was wondering what she should do about it. Problems, problems.

Simplify it, Gregory. Simplify it. Digger and Beth to dance round the maypole and distribute sixpenny pieces to the schoolchildren, a round the clock patrol of the horse pastures and stables for which his nibs would get the bill. Fred to report to the local constabulary and inform Uncle Singh that he had not been appointed as agent, should open all accounts and records for inspection, or else, when Fred would take his father's place if he so wished.

Lady Elisabeth would move into a Dower House on the estate whether she liked it or not and Master Nicholas would get his superior backside into the army pdq until he reached his majority and would be responsible for his own follies. There, that was it. All neat and tidy.

★ ★ ★

It was a warm, sunny day at the Manor and by way of distraction Luke was gently scraping away at weeds poking up in the gravel at the front. Not his job, of course, but fiddling around at such tasks helped him relax. The sound of a horse on the drive interrupted his thoughts and he leaned on his hoe as a smartly dressed man on a very shiny horse cantered towards him.

'You. Fellow. Take my horse,' the smartly dressed one ordered as he dismounted. 'Well, come along. Jump to it!'

'Where shall I take it?' Luke asked, innocently, half amused at the man's arrogant manner. He was, after all in his shirt sleeves and wearing one of his ancient deck caps so probably looked like the hired help.

'Damn your insolence! Here. Hold it,' and as Luke sauntered over to take the horse's bridle, 'I shall speak to your employer,' then turned and tugged vigorously on the bell pull by the front door. This could be amusing, Luke thought and wondered who might be around to open the door. Ah, Tommy.

'I wish to speak with Squire Gregory,' and Luke put his finger to his lips and pulled a face at Tommy.

'Certainly, suh. May I take your card, suh?' Tommy responded, playing the well trained negro serving man.

'Card? I have no card with me.'

'Ah, suh. Master will not see you without a card, suh.'

'Damnation. Inform the squire that Major Sir Jocelyn Gortbury, equerry to his Royal Highness the Prince of Wales wishes to speak with him.'

'My regrets, suh, but master never sees equerries without a card, suh.'

'God dammit, man!' The visitor's voice rose and he appeared to swell with fury. 'Are you an imbecile? I am equerry to His Royal Highness. Now inform the squire immediately. This instant.'

'My regrets, suh but no highnesses or equerries without a card, suh. I must wish you good day, suh,' and Tommy closed the door, leaving the visitor gazing at the ancient oak panels in sheer disbelief before turning to seize hold of his horse's bridle.

'Give me a leg up,' he ordered.

'Not without a card, sir,' Luke replied and stepped back hurriedly as the man lashed out at him with his riding crop. This was getting beyond a joke, he thought and prepared to defend himself but the horse was now occupying his rider's attention. A spirited animal, it was unsettled by the raised voice and the blow aimed at Luke and began to dance around as the man attempted to get his foot in the stirrup. The more he cursed and snarled at his mount, the more it danced and circled with ears laid back. Finally losing his temper completely, the smartly dressed equerry struck the horse a resounding thwack with his crop. It reared up, knocking him over and took off down the driveway, tail up and stirrups flying, leaving his rider sitting open mouthed on the gravels.

'The price of bad manners,' Luke quietly observed.

'What? What's that you say?'

'Best look for your horse else you'll have a long walk.'

Without a word the man got to his feet, picked up his hat and with a look fit to scorch the grass set off down the drive after his horse. Mm, Luke thought to himself. If that jackanapes was an equerry then his nibs might well be visiting nearby. Plenty of titles and estates within a brisk horse ride, he supposed. So what could old Tum Tum be after? More horses for safe-keeping? He'd learn soon enough.

★ ★ ★

For once, Luke had promised to attend morning service at the church. Not his favourite pastime, though he enjoyed a good sing if the hymns were lively and the organist did them justice. Now, with the ritual over he, as required, led his household in the exodus from the ancient building, keenly anticipating his lunch and a tankard or two of their latest cider.

Just through the lych gate he caught sight of a carriage nearby with a pair of grey horses held by a liveried groom. Not one he recognised but unusual and he was continuing on his way when who should approach him but the smartly dressed rider of the previous day.

Coming face to face, the man's jaw dropped in utter surprise as he recognised Luke, who looked enquiringly at him. Was he, he wondered, about to be challenged to riding crops at dawn or something more lethal?

'Er, er, excuse me sir,' he finally managed to say 'but His Royal Highness wonders if you might spare him a few moments of your time,' and Luke realised then who it was in the carriage.

'But of course,' and turning to his party, 'nip on and tell Mrs Cherry visitors for luncheon,' and added 'All hands on deck.'

'Ah, Gregory. Good day to you. Hope you don't mind my appearing like this but I need to talk with you. Need your thoughts on a delicate matter and I can think of no one more qualified to assist.'

'Happy to help, sir. At any time. You'll join us for luncheon, will you not? The usual gathering; Digger, Beth and family, so we shall be well entertained.'

'O'Dowd, and Mrs O'Dowd. Most happy to see you again. Missed around Town you know. Place is far too quiet without you. You know Gortbury, do you not?' indicating his equerry, who appeared to have shrunk in stature.

'Yes. Sir Jocelyn and I are acquainted.' Luke replied, straight faced. No point in embarrassing the fellow further. 'Digger, Beth, Sir Jocelyn Gortbury, Equerry to His Royal

Highness. Now, let's make sail and head for home. I'm starving and I'm sure you must be too.'

Luncheon was the main meal of the day at the Manor on a Sunday, which allowed Mrs Cherry to attend her chapel meetings and Luke's injunction of 'all hands on deck' saw arrangements for unexpected visitors well in hand as he led the way inside. Richard directed coachman and groom to the stables, where Alfie Donkin awaited them to assist with unharnessing and to show them into the back room for their meal. Tommy, in clean shirt and spotless white apron stood ready to carve. Lucy, Annabelle and Louise were putting the finishing touches to extra places at the table whilst Julian carried up wine, ale and cider from the cellar. An organised and well run ship's company, Luke decided, approvingly.

'May I present Julian Eugene, sir? You will, perhaps, recall a board of enquiry?'

'Ah, so you are the young man behind the Portsmouth business,' and he shook hands with a trembling Julian. 'A bad business and one that will be put right, you may rest assured. Ah, thank you,' as Luke handed round chilled sherry.

After lunch Luke and the prince strolled around outside where they could talk undisturbed.

'Tell me, did you know my father?'

'No sir. I never met him.'

'But you acted for him on occasion? In regard to myself?'

'Yes,' Luke replied, wondering what this was all about.

'A certain young lady persuaded to try her luck on the New York stage? Care to tell me why? I'm curious, that's all. Came across records due to be destroyed. Had the opportunity to peruse some of them. Learned a few answers to puzzling questions.'

Luke thought fast. He well remembered that business Magistrate Morden had set him on. 'The lady in question enjoyed a number of admirers, one of whom was believed to have an infectious disease. You were at risk of contracting something unpleasant.'

'So the danger was quietly removed and a safer facility provided.'

'Exactly, sir. We all have our needs.'

'You know, Gregory, you are a remarkable man. You are incredibly helpful, totally trustworthy and understanding yet you never seek to take advantage. I appreciate that. I really do. On top of which you show real initiative and all flavoured with the most devilish sense of humour. Now, my present problem. My eldest is quickly earning for himself a troubling reputation. I am the last person to look askance at a young man's amorous activities but there is a dividing line over what society might look away from and what would be condemned outright.'

'So you need to know what the young man is about, with whom he associates and should the need arise, offer assistance?'

'Gregory, you have read my mind.'

'I'll set the wheels in motion but how am I to report to you? There must be nothing in writing and with Digger mostly here a link is missing.'

'Ah, yes. Of course. You have a suggestion?'

'Below stairs at Clarence House?

'Capital and much appreciated. I will ensure that you are not turned away! Now, have I time to visit my yearlings? I'm staying over at Burkwood. You know, Elsingham. It is his carriage I have commandeered. Expected back for dinner, of course.'

'You know, Guv, I really would like to try my hand in the army. For a while, at least.'

'You could do worse See a bit of the world and you're used to being organised boarding school wise. Straight lines and routine, that sort of thing. Avoid the Guards or cavalry, though. Very expensive.'

'Do you think I'd get a commission?'

'I don't see why not. You've a reasonable education. You ride to hounds and on a good day you'd pass as a gentleman.'

'Oh Guv, get on.'

'Make your number with the Rifle Volunteers or Militia or whatever they call themselves these days. The Surreys have a depot somewhere or other I believe. I've seen uniforms in Guildford often enough. Bound to find someone to tell you what's what.'

★ ★ ★

George had gone, the telegram told him when it arrived at Gresham House. 'Died in his sleep', despite Tommy's best efforts. So, two old soldiers of the Crimea were no more. Two veterans of the charge against the guns. Joe and George. Both badly wounded by the same canon ball. Both survivors of the Scutari hospital shambles and both left to fend for themselves by an ungrateful nation and Luke shook his head sorrowfully. Not altogether unexpected but it would leave something missing from the Manor.

★ ★ ★

Chapter 16

'You have nothing whatever to worry about, Mrs Hurle. Your lad's got the ability and the company'll see him through. You don't have to find a penny piece and it's not charity. Whoever told you that is just out to cause you upset. He really impressed in the interview and scholarships to Cambridge have to be earned. You know, his work on country dialects interested them no end; the way folks speak in different places and the different things they say. No, you give him your blessing and let him do what he's best suited to. Choice is the thing. Square pegs in square holes. T'would be a happier world if all could follow their own course so you look out for something smart to wear when he graduates.'

★ ★ ★

'Before you start on me Rector, I've spoken with Mrs Hurle and John's all set to go up to Cambridge. The company'll see him right for expenses so his mother has nothing to worry about.'

'You know, Mr Gregory you really are the most remarkable man.'

'I keep hearing that. I merely wish to see things happen as they should. Too many barriers to progress. Don't hold with 'em.'

'You are certainly demolishing some of those. You know, Mrs Hurle might easily have found herself in the workhouse when she lost her husband. It would have been a real struggle for her family to keep things going and John would never have been able to even think of university.'

'Her man died in my employ. It's only right she be helped.'

'But a pension of five shillings a week is most generous. I just wish others shared your view. Er, I expect you have heard about the mishap in the wood?'

'No. What mishap?'

'With your pigs, the brown ones you have running free.'

'Oh? The Tamworths? What about them?'

'Well, it appears that some children from near Chidingford tried to catch one of the piglets and the mother attacked them. Then the boar joined in and there are some quite serious injuries as a result. Badly bitten arms and legs. That sort of thing.'

'I should imagine an angry porker to be a handful. They'll perhaps keep away in future.'

'The new constable, Harker I believe, is intent upon reporting them for attempted theft.'

'I suppose that's his job. Ah. My piglet. That means a complaint and a court appearance? No thanks. He's sure they were trying to nick it? Not just playing around? I'd've thought a few piggy bites would be ample deterrent.'

'It isn't quite as simple as that, I'm afraid. The family concerned, whose offspring were injured, are local outcasts. They live, or exist, in a makeshift camp by a track in the woods. Askett by name. Mad Jack, with a brood of nine children and presumably a wife somewhere but kept out of sight. They are just within the parish boundary so I am bound to show an interest but quite what I should do I am unsure.'

'And you want me to suggest something? You can tell 'em to leave my Tam'orths alone. I've high hopes of them. Lovely lean tender pork; full of flavour.'

'Er, yes but when the doctor called to offer his services he was refused entry and was roundly abused although he could hear a good deal of weeping from inside. You see, the postman reported all this. He's a sober enough soul who considered the injuries he saw to be quite severe.'

'If the man refuses medical assistance that's surely his business?'

'But these are children and he is at best an unstable character.'

'So isn't that a matter for the Board of Guardians? Or a magistrate or someone?'

'If such injuries are not treated promptly they could result in serious illness. Death even and by the time any public body becomes involved it may be too late.'

'So what you're saying is that I should do something about it?'

'You can be very persuasive Mr Gregory when the need arises.'

'Damnation, sir. They trouble my animals, get themselves bitten and I'm expected to do battle with some lunatic? Just what is the world coming to?' Luke found himself decidedly exasperated. He was quite busy enough without involving in matters outside of the estate. Damn these do gooding God botherers expecting folks to get mixed up in other people's follies. Why couldn't he do something about it for heaven's sake?

'Well whose land is he on, anyway?'

'Yours, Mr Gregory. As I said, they are just within the parish boundary.'

There was nothing for it then but to get this business settled as quickly as possible and with the doctor and Rector discretely out of sight, Luke approached a makeshift windowless cabin cum brushwood lean-to tucked out of sight on a woodland pathway. A sacking and tarpaulin affair appeared to be the entrance and he called out to make contact with whoever might be inside.

'Get you gone. I want no dealings with you,' a voice replied.

'Well I want dealings with you. You're on my land and you've been after my pigs so get yourself out here and explain yourself.'

The voice rose an octave and repeated the instruction to 'get you gone' with a number of embellishments and Luke's sorely strained patience snapped. Just what was he doing here bandying words with some idiot lurking in this shanty?

'Jack Askett. Get your arse out here now or I'll kick your blasted hovel down about your ears. Now, sir. This minute. Do you hear me?'

Silence, then the sacking at the front moved a little and a face peered out. 'What you want?'

'You! Out here. Now!'

The face withdrew behind the sacking, which moved a little more and a scarecrow figure of a man appeared. Luke had seen human wrecks in his time but few could compare with the skinny, ragged, barefoot creature that now stood before him, head turned sideways, peering at him from under an unkempt shock of hair.

'And about time. Now. Your children disturbed my pigs and were injured. The doctor is going to examine them and treat their injuries, so bring 'em out here.'

'You can't order me. You're no magistrate.'

'You know that, then. Well, you'll also know that a magistrate is constrained by his position but I'm not so do exactly what I tell you or my men'll burn this heap of rubbish you live in and you'll find yourself in the county asylum before the day's out. You're a disgrace, Askett, living like this. Why don't you find work and live decently?'

'They're all agin me. All of 'em.'

'Well I'm not but I'm against the way you're carrying on so get your family out so's the doctor can see 'em.'

If Askett was truly unhinged he had wit enough to realise that Luke was not to be trifled with and reluctantly and sullenly he turned towards his hovel, muttered something incoherent and a gaggle of skinny smaller scarecrows shuffled into view, some limping and all looking fearful and apprehensive. Luke waved and the doctor appeared, leading his pony and trap and Luke spoke again to Askett as Doctor Fairleigh set to work.

'I can find you work if you want it. There's no reason why you can't have a regular wage and somewhere to live. Food on the table. Boots on your feet. Decent living. Come to the office in the morning. You know, the railway carriage in the station yard and we'll set you on. Folks'll give you a chance if you'll let 'em,' and ignoring the Rector, Luke walked away towards where his own pony and trap waited, not a little shocked at the unhappy state of the doctor's patients but he'd done his bit and more. Now it was up to others to sort things out.

'You've really hit it off with Lady Penelope, I hear. A little bird tells me the project is taking shape quite nicely.'

'Well, yes Guv. We get on alright and Beth's giving 'er lessons in the practicals. Yer know, these toffs 'aven't a clue about running a house. Any house. Couldn't darn a sock or boil a kettle to save 'er life,' and Digger shook his head in mock disbelief. 'Mind you, Tommy's making 'imself useful. Plays the part like a good 'un. Adds a touch of class to the household 'er ladyship reckons.'

'I'm glad he's settling in. Got right upset at losing George like that. Thought he'd failed and let us down. Rubbish of course. He couldn't have worked harder. Now, how's the estate side of things? Everyone doing as they're told, are they?'

'Reckon so, Guv. Amos has 'em toeing the line an' no mistake.

'Good. Well I'm away on the afternoon train. Keep 'em hard at it and don't let the Rector get you do-gooding. Offered that crack pot fellow work and he upsticks and disappears. Still, he's off our patch and good riddance. Complete waste of time the whole business.'

Not though, that by the river, with all the usual cargoes arriving at the wharf. A note from Fred to say that yes, he would very much like to take his father's place as agent, that he had the measure of his uncle and was sending samples of different items for Luke's appraisal and was playing cricket with the local club. Good. An energetic and enterprising approach should be helpful.

A contract to supply leather to a boot company in Northampton. Nothing like Texas longhorn hides for soles apparently. Flour contracts to two biscuit manufactories, enquiries for whale oil and tallow when they became available. Tea, coffee, rubber, cotton; all moving through the wharf. Mining shares now. Plenty of activity in South Africa. He hadn't done badly there.

Rumblings of discontent round about, though. All to do with low wages and poverty in general. Nothing new there. Loads of unskilled folks chasing work and employers paying as little as possible. Been like that in the docks as long as he could remember. Ben was on about it the other day. Knows folks around the docks and in the match factory apparently but that'd be government business, not his. Now, time to visit the stock market and pick up the latest news.

★ ★ ★

'Papa, do you think I could do the same as you?'

'Doing what?'

'Well, being in charge and going into town and running businesses.'

'Billy Boy, there's nothing I'd like better than for you to take over from me but it's hard work, I'll warn you of that.'

'I know. Richard said. He didn't like the warehouses at all.'

'It's not to everyone's taste but trading is a good way of making a living. I enjoy it well enough. Lots of interest. Always something new round the corner but you've got to keep your wits about you. Know when there's an opportunity and when to leave things alone.'

'Is that why Uncle Digger had problems?'

Luke paused in their strolling. 'Someone been talking? Wouldn't be Rory would it? If it is, you tell master Rory if I hear one word of family business spoken I'll be down on 'im like a ton o' bricks. Your Uncle Digger was very ill and someone took advantage of him. Cheated him and I'll be settling that score by and by. Without him I'd never've got started. We've been close partners ever since I left the sea and we'll be partners to the end. He's good at the things I'm not good at and that's how we've prospered. That and straight dealing.'

Luke was frowning now and William was uncomfortably aware that he'd stepped on uncertain ground. Like most others he was wary of his father's displeasure and sought to avoid it at all costs. No great problem there for Luke was easy going enough, 'provided folks steered a straight course', as he was wont to say.

'Any way,' his frown fading as quickly as it had appeared, 'come along with me whenever you feel like it and have a closer look at what it's all about but if you're starting at Bramsden in the autumn I fear you'll have a very busy life.'

'You didn't go to school, Papa but you're still in charge.'

'True, but it would've helped if I had. I learned the hard way and made mistakes. Anyway, it's a fast changing world. A rough-cut sailor would have difficulty starting in business today but an educated gentleman is halfway there. You've met the next king have you not? What common sailor would manage that, eh?'

★ ★ ★

'Ladies and gentlemen. You must have the confidence to make your own decisions.' Luke had called a meeting of the estate managers to say firstly how well things were shaping up but also to encourage a more adventurous spirit that would try out new ideas without fear of dismissal. They had the skills and expertise and he wanted to see them fully applied. If Ryland sheep might suit in the scheme of things, try them. If new fertilisers would improve yields, set up a trial and compare results.

'Now, we've this jubilee business to reckon with', he continued, 'and the company'll help make it all go with a swing so I want you to take a lead in organising things. There'll be sports, competitions, fireworks and an evening entertainment. Dancing, of course and an ox roast so give the Rector a hand to set things up will you?'

Following which meeting Luke set out on one of his tours of inspection, always alone and on foot. He liked to just quietly appear, not he told himself to catch people out but to get a flavour of what was going on and Mrs Foster had asked him to call in at the cabbage patch, as it was light-heartedly termed, at the former Hall Home Farm for all the ground there was now given over to market gardening and the return from sales of vegetables at the London markets was promising indeed.

'I'd like you to see this, sir if you'd step this way,' and she led Luke over to an area of ground fenced off with hurdles. 'We've made a start on a herb patch with just about all sorts coming on. Things to cook with and others to cure ailments, like. Elsie's in charge of it,' and she indicated a girl of fifteen or so who was hoeing between rows of drab looking plants and now approached, dropping the regulation curtsey to the squire.

'I see. So tell me about it,' Luke invited.

'Well, sir, 'tis all things what folks use an' mos'ly 'as in their gardens like, but we reckons as folks in cities would want 'em too. Lunnon and the like,' and she tailed off, not knowing how Luke would view the idea.

'Like this one, sir. Lavender,' and Mrs Foster offered a leaf and flower. 'It's the scent folks likes.'

'Ah, yes. We have that round the house,' as he took a sniff. 'Of course. It all goes with market gardening,' as it dawned on Luke what they were offering.

'An we thought, sir,' Mrs Foster continued, encouraged by Luke's approval, 'to dry and package things up during the winter. With labels on to say what was in and what it could be used for. Elsie's gran knows all about it and she's teaching Elsie.'

'Well I'm blessed,' Luke said. 'Packets of different herbs for sale. Yes indeed. Labels. Coloured labels. Yes indeed,' as he thought ahead to the marketing of a new product. 'What a splendid idea, Mrs Foster. I knew you were the right one to run the show. No man would've thought of this,' and Mrs Foster swelled quite literally with pleasure at the compliment.

'Now Elsie, if your gran knows all about herbs do you reckon she'd write everything down about them? In a book?'

'She don't write, sir.'

'But you do. If you wrote it down for her we'd have something for the labels and a new book on herbs might well be printed for sale. 'Grandmother's book of herbs.' How does that sound? Office'll give you a notebook or whatever you need. Gran on the books, is she? Should be if it's her knowledge we're using.'

'Well if you say so, sir,' Mrs Foster said, approvingly.

'Right. Good. Well done. You're on the right lines. Good day to you both.'

★ ★ ★

Yes, that was it, he mused as he walked away, well pleased with what he'd seen. Give 'em a free hand and a good dose of encouragement backed up with a decent wage and they wouldn't go far wrong. Horses now, up at Higher Farm and young Joseph talking of getting married. Good for him. He had an excellent team of horse handlers to support him and what, between them, they didn't know about nags wasn't worth mentioning.

With the deer gone from the Berrimond park, mares and foals of all shapes and sizes now roamed free. The nursery,

Joseph called it with working horses based mainly at Higher but stabled round about, according to the work in hand and there was a fair bit of land being worked now when you came to think about it, either part of the estate or associated with it.

Then there was the school. Settled nicely now and feeding on regularly to Bramsden. Offering a caring program for pupils with families abroad was meeting a real need and enquires for placements were regularly received. Did no harm to name Lady Penelope and Lady Cecelia on the governing body either. Titles meant a lot to many, no doubt about that.

Time was it to appoint a bailiff, to oversee the whole lot and give him more free time? No. Better by far for he and Digger to do their own supervising as they had at the wharf and maintain the personal touch. Bailiffs were for the idle rich and Richard hadn't the grasp of it at all so he couldn't use him but he'd have to settle to some gainful activity before long. No room for a gentleman of leisure in his household.

★ ★ ★

'Ah, Cissie! Just been doing the rounds. Join me in a snifter? I'm ready for one. Covered a mile or two today. Good for the figure, I'm told, walking. You're looking serious. Something amiss?'

'Hope not but I have me worries,' Lady Cecelia replied as she settled her ample proportions into one of the study chairs and accepted the malt whisky Luke handed her.' It's young Nicholas. Going off the rails. Tried to talk to 'im but told me I'm old fashioned. Told me to my face, the impudent young puppy.'

'I see. Hasn't been round here for a while. Bit of friction with Richard. Walter did tell me he's seeking an increase in his allowance. Not sown more wild oats has he?'

'Not heard of any. Once is enough. Racing around with fellers from school. More money than sense, some of 'em. Upset him, but feel a bit responsible, y'know.'

'And how did you manage that?'

'Didn't want to know so I registered the child in his name. He's a Hurlingham now. Baptised as well. I'm the Godmother. Family honour. Said the gel was only a milkmaid so it didn't matter. Think it does, meself.'

Luke chuckled his appreciation. 'Cissie, I like that. I really do but there's nothing you can do but hope for the best. If he's turned wilful and won't listen he has to learn the hard way. Walter's tried to point him towards university if he doesn't want the army but he can only have the income his estate can produce. What he does when he's of age is another matter.'

★ ★ ★

'How time flies,' Luke commented to Digger and Beth. 'November already. Be Christmas before we know it and a new planting season.'

'Listen to the farmer will you?' Digger quipped. All sheep pens an' muddy boots 'e is.'

'That'll cost you a comic turn at the concert. It's to be all home grown talent I'm told. Cracked voiced old men singing country songs and the misses whoever reciting their own poetry. You'll have to liven things up a bit or I'll be called away on urgent business.'

'You will attend, Squire Gregory or you'll be seen as insulting Her Majesty,' Beth said with mock severity, wagging her finger at him, 'and you're expected to offer more than a big top for the occasion so start practicing your singing and no saucy sea shanties either.'

'They'll be more than saucy if you call me squire. Makes me sound like one of those numbskulls with a couple of fields and a worn out nag for chasing foxes.'

'Committee's got all sorts planned,' Digger said. 'Ox roast, fireworks, sports for the youngsters, competitions, dancing, singing, swings, roundabouts and that sort o' thing.'

'School's putting on a play,' Beth added. 'A jolly time'll be had by all or me name's not Beth O'Dowd. Rain or shine it'll all go with a swing. Just like a shindig down the wharf.'

'And all because the old girl's sat on the throne for fifty years,' Luke groaned. 'Still, there are worse excuses for a knees up. Tug o' war across the river? Chidlingbrook against the rest?'

'Now yer talking, Guv. Hadn't thought o' that one,' Digger enthused. 'Good fer a laugh any time, that.'

'Women to take on the men?'

'Oh come on, Guv. That wouldn't be fair,' Beth remonstrated.

'No? Even with a small pony or two hooked on? The fellers'd never live it down.'

'Oh Guv. You're a demon,' and Beth doubled up with laughter at the thought.

★ ★ ★

'Cissie, you look upset. Come in and share your troubles.'

'Shows, does it? Never been so cross in me life. Insolent young puppy. Told me to mind me own business, stop interfering in his affairs and keep me distance. That sort o' thing.'

'Master Nicholas, I presume? I see. So what's he been up to lately?'

'Signing notes against his property. Gambling debts. Drinking too much. Keeping bad company. Tried to talk to him. Sent me about me business would you believe.'

'I see. Indeed I do. No wonder you're vexed. Getting well out of hand. Well, his notes are worthless whilst he's under age but if he's taken money they're still debts that'll have to be met. Right. As his legal guardians, Walter will write requiring that he meet with us and explain himself and we'll suspend his allowance to ensure he attends. We shall have to remind him of the terms of the Chancery ruling and if there's any nonsense we'll return the question to the court. How's that sound?'

'Splendid. Splendid. Knew you'd have the answer. Needs a curb to his bit before he comes a cropper.'

★ ★ ★

Ah, the Rector. Now what can he want, I wonder? Not more bells for his tower, I hope. Quite enough noise from those he already has. 'I can read your mind, good sir,' Luke greeted him jovially. 'You hope for a line of chorus girls to entertain us on the big day.'

'No, nothing like that. The Bishop would surely frown upon the thought. No, my problem is of a more basic nature. You will recall the incident of the pigs in the wood, I'm sure. Well, a certain young man in the Rectory grounds this morning tells me he has run as his father is "fetched" and he wants no more of him. He recalled that you offered his father employment and in short, wondered if you might offer him work of some sort but he is too apprehensive to make an approach. He fears he will be chased away, as that has been his previous experience round about.

'I see. So where is this willing worker?'

'He awaits me on the road, quite certain you will refuse him. You see, he is as ragged as ever, barefoot and unwashed. Famished too.'

'I've met a few like it over the years. Should never be, not in this day and age. Perhaps Mrs Donkin'll help. Good hearted soul and room to spare. We'll have a word. Get her to tidy him up and rig him out for starters. That suit do you think?'

★ ★ ★

The hay was mostly in, the weather settled and warm after late snow and a cold spring and but a week to go before the Golden Jubilee celebrations. With the actual date falling midweek, Luke named the following Saturday for the big event to allow Sunday free for settling the inevitable hangovers. Hancock the butcher would have charge of the ox roast, the marquee was in the siding awaiting volunteers to haul it away and erect it, the cricket field behind the school would be the centre of events with the pitches boarded over to protect them and give a firm surface for dancing.

The evening concert, now. The Rector would be master of ceremonies, the local talent had all been organised, their efforts to be supplemented by a couple of invited performers and with Roddy as guest pianist. For his part, Luke insisted on keeping well clear of all such matters, firm in his stance of having neither time, talent nor interest in such frivolity. Quite sufficient, in his opinion, that he, or rather the company, was paying for all the nonsense.

Behind the scenes though, and under strict security, he was organising a suitable contribution to appear on the program as a ballet performance and a visit from a distinguished operatic singer all the way from Italy. Humour, clowning and slapstick were his guiding thoughts with memories of shipboard entertainments from his youth and music hall turns providing inspiration. The tug o' war was the one event hugely anticipated as the initial event was to be between Chidlingbrook and their old rivals Chidington from up the valley but with the winners facing a one pull challenge from the women.

To this end Mrs Foster had been openly practicing with her heftiest market gardeners to the astonishment and disbelief of the men of the valley who just could not accept that a 'bunch o' haybags' could provide any possible opposition. The thought of all the gells ending up in the river though gave rise to much rough humour.

'Queen's in charge o' the country so we'll show 'em 'oos's in charge round 'ere', was the challenge,' and 'they'll find out 'oo wears the britches come Sat'day,' was the response.

★ ★ ★

And to the City once more and Luke reluctantly took his seat in the eight twenty train. Like it or not he had to ensure all was in order at wharf and office before the jollifications began. There'd be precious little work done over the next few days with plenty of irresponsible behaviour round about but this journey was becoming irksome to him now, with the estate and its activities preferable to the grimy drabness of the wharf . He was relieved then to finally arrive at Gresham House and make his way upstairs to his sitting room to where his post awaited him.

'Nothing from India,' he muttered to himself and hoped all was well. Had been so far. Perhaps he worried too much. Now what was this? South Africa? He had a few shares in gold there. Mm. He liked gold. Safe currency. Oh?

'Dear Sir, Word has reached me that you are a gentleman both trustworthy and enterprising. I seek at this time the assistance of one familiar with the trading rooms of London and with reliable business contacts who might care to act on my behalf in all respects. Sincerely, De Beers.'

Luke's mind began to churn. De Beers? Mining. Gold and diamonds. Was this an attempt to sell him worthless shares or implicate him in some shady enterprise? Plenty of villains about. He was familiar with stock market shares and knew the risks and he glanced at his waste paper basket for this was no time to take chances. Then, on the other hand, one never knew and he who ignored a beckoning opportunity might well regret it.

The address. Johannesburg. Need to make enquiries at first hand. But how? Ah. Send someone reliable. Who, now? Richard. That's who. Give him something to do. Get him there before any reply to this letter could arrive. Take the writer by surprise. If it wasn't genuine the cost of the journey would be well spent so, on his return to the Manor, 'Richard. Visit South Africa for me will you?'

Richard gulped. 'South Africa, Guv?'

'Yes. I want you to call on someone and ascertain their requirements. This letter arrived for me yesterday. It might be connected with fraudulent activity or it might offer an interesting business opportunity,' and he went on to explain about the mining activity in the area he'd visit; mainly gold and diamonds, that De Beers was a company heavily involved and it was possible Rhodes might be the author of the letter.

'I know little of him beyond reports in the press but if it is he and he desires private representation in this country I might be interested, provided it's legal. This is in the strictest confidence between us. Your passage is booked on the mail ship from Southampton the day after tomorrow. You'll be travelling second class and you must avoid attracting attention from anyone. Having made your enquiries I wish you to return promptly and advise me. Travel light. Avoid whisky and wild women and not a word to anyone.'

★ ★ ★

Luke lay in bed reflecting on the events of the big day which, by and large, had passed off well enough. A few things unforeseen. Young Saunders knuckling a rival over some girl or other. A child nipped by a dog and a tent collapsing when a guy rope parted, or was it cut? He didn't care. He was just glad it was all over.

A procession to the sports field with the school children waving flags. A tedious speech or two and the singing of the national anthem. He'd forgotten how many verses there were. Races, competitions and prizes handed out by Lady Penelope, representing the highest level of society round about. Dancing. Ah, yes. Bridie, the minx. Mrs Bridie Roberts now she'd married the Rector's gardener handyman. Showing off her dancing skills and calling out 'Come on, Guv. Show 'em how 'tis done,' so, joined by Digger, Beth and Lizzie he'd found himself jigging away Irish style accompanied by an accordion and a couple of fiddles.

That had made folks gape but not as much as the tug of war and it was the Chidlingbrook team who ended up in the river, to their extreme chagrin. It had then been up to the women to regain the honours and regain them they did with Lady Cecelia calling the moves and Luke chuckled to himself once more.

His scheming had worked perfectly. A pulley wheel fixed in the ground concealed by a table, the garden ponies behind the marquee and a patent hitch to the end of the tugging rope. A group of women added further concealment with their voluminous skirts and the astonished Chiddington team found themselves dragged through the river to roars of merriment. With all attention on the men floundering in the water the hitch was cast off, the ponies whisked away out of sight behind the school and few were the wiser. Doubtless the truth would leak out but the joke was there to be enjoyed, for a while at least.

And then the concert. Half past six in the packed marquee, the audience replete with roast beef , the Rector as master of ceremonies and Roddy seated at the school piano, well briefed for the occasion. Another rendering of the national anthem, patriotic poems, recitals and singing by the talented and not so gifted, a patriotic play by the prep school and another by the village school and then a little humour.

For weeks, Digger had secretly rehearsed a chorus line in the privacy of the prep school. Not a music hall line of young ladies but one of muscular farm workers, bribed with a guinea apiece, wearing hob nailed boots, ballet tutus and long lacy drawers and flowing wigs. To give them their due they performed perfectly, not a step or move out of place and the audience was completely convulsed with laughter. Nothing had prepared them for such a departure from the formality of the proceedings until then and they loved it with encores demanded.

Little Maisy Cooper had followed, wearing an enormous satin bow in her hair to sing a popular ditty but instead of her piping voice it was Tommy's deep bass behind the scenes, all beautifully mimed and utterly ridiculous. Then it had been the guest singer's turn. It could all have gone horribly wrong but with Digger and Beth organising things the enormously fat, top hatted opera singer, Signor Mucho Pomposo, had appeared on stage to politely hushed anticipation.

The aria had begun safely enough but then strange things happened with lady's stockinged legs appearing from behind the side curtains to mild amusement then painted flowers popping up from beneath the stage behind the singer. More amusement and subdued laughter as the puzzled singer glanced sideways to find the cause of the merriment but saw nothing, as legs and flowers had disappeared. A cardboard dog moved across the stage behind him pausing only to lift his leg before disappearing at the far side. This time howls of laughter as the singer made play of shaking a dampened trouser leg whilst continuing to warble without interruption.

Whatever next? A bird with gently flapping wings had appeared directly above the singer's head and deposited the inevitable message onto his shiny top hat. The audience was convulsed with merriment at this slapstick performance with the singer missing not a note until the appearance behind him of Jack, the stud donkey who, with his muzzle removed, let out an enormous braying eeaw, eeaw of protest.

The timing was perfect and the fat singer made an exaggeratedly dramatic departure and scuttled off to a nearby tent. A short while later a soberly dressed and dignified lord of the manor joined the Rector in thanking all those who had performed and announced that the beacon fire would be lit as soon as it was properly dark and advised that spectators should keep a safe distance from the fireworks display.

★ ★ ★

A couple of months is a long time to wait for news, though Richard had scribbled a short note to say he'd arrived in one piece at a place called Kimberly, the end of the railway line. Most of the corn harvest was in with just the last of the oats soaked by a sudden thunderstorm. Welcome enough, he supposed after a dry summer, with the river running low but rain now might save the root crops after all.

No matter how the religious prayed in church and chapel, life depended on sun and rain at the right time, which made farming on its own a precarious business, so interests unaffected by the weather were a real boon and Luke was depending on the wharf to maintain his cash flow. Any other safe and reliable source of income would be most welcome and he waited impatiently for Richard's return from South Africa and then, there he was, dishevelled from his travels but smiling widely. Mm. Looking older and more confident? Could be. Now let's hear what he had to tell him.

'Well, Guv. Had a bit of luck actually. It was Mr Rhodes just as you thought and he was in his office in Kimberly, not at Jo'burg as they call it. Bodyguard wouldn't let me in at the front so I went round the back and surprised him at his desk. Had a bit of explaining to do but he said he was impressed. Took me straight off to a diamond mine; quite a small one but busy enough. Asked me all about you. What you did exactly. Who you knew. Who you associated with, whether you were religious. Did you vote Liberal or Tory and even what you thought about home rule for Ireland.

Wanted to know about me, of course. I told him everything, as you said to and he kept nodding. I think he knew already. Then he said that any commodity had a higher value if it was in short supply. Too many diamonds on the market and prices dropped. He wished to maintain prices so it would be helpful to have a trading arrangement for the finest gemstones, separate from the local open market. He thought you would be the right man to undertake this for him. Nothing in writing but he assured me it was perfectly legal. The diamonds would be his property that you would place to best advantage in London or elsewhere as you saw fit. As a gesture of earnest he sent this,' and Richard rummaged down the front of his trousers and produced a small wash-leather bag containing six reasonable sized uncut diamonds.

Luke's mind raced as he considered the possibilities and looked for problems. 'So who else knows of this?'

'Just the three of us, Guv. No one else. If you are agreeable I would be the intermediary. Collect the stones. Return with the proceeds or credit his London account. Private and confidential arrangement. Actually, I got on rather well with Mr Rhodes.'

'Did you now. You've done well. Very well indeed. Better than I'd hoped. So what's the next step?'

'Well, Guv, Mr Rhodes invited me to join him as an assistant.'

'He did? You must have made an impression but the decision will be entirely your own. If a career in mining interests you then by all means go ahead. You could do very well for yourself.'

'Mr Rhodes said I would need to learn Dutch. Proper Dutch, he said not the kitchen sort spoken in the Transvaal and I'd also have to master the local lingo, you know, what the blacks speak.'

'You've got some work ahead of you then. How would it be if you took these diamonds to London for an opinion, started language lessons then went across to Amsterdam to make your number there. I can provide you with introductions to get you started.'

'Guv, that's a lekker idea.'

'Lekker, eh? Sounds as though you've already started.'

★ ★ ★

The news came as a complete shock. Lady Cecelia had passed away. Heart failure, he was informed, whilst climbing the stairs. Had fallen backwards. Nothing whatever to be done for her. Mrs Trumpton, her housekeeper heard the fall and sent for help.

'Poor old Cissie,' Luke mused. He'd been fond of the old girl. Quite a character in her way. He'd miss her and she couldn't have been that old though she did carry a lot of weight. Make's you wonder how long you've got yourself. Well yes, of course he'd make the arrangements if there was no one else. Young Nicholas Hurlingham should see to it all really. Next of kin after all but goodness knows where he's to be found at the moment. Better talk to Walter. Legal opinions and all that.

The family vault appeared to be at Wisley Priory, the family seat going way back to the year dot so there must be other relatives surely, even distant ones but there'd been neither enquiries nor offers of assistance from anyone and Nicholas hadn't replied to Walter's telegram, so it was down to muggins again. The least he could do for a friend, he supposed. Decent send off naturally, but funerals were not his cup of tea. Never had been. Too much top show with everyone copying the nonsense of Prince Albert's end all those years ago. Anyway, the undertakers had it all in hand but he'd get Digger and Beth to go with him and he'd assured Mrs Trumpton, she was welcome to join them.

Seemed she'd served the Burberry-Harcourt family for years and had known the Lady Cecelia quite well before she went to India. Family retainer, Luke mused. Must be getting on herself. Let's hope she's been provided for. Too many loyal servants ended up in the workhouse thanks to uncaring employers.

★ ★ ★

'How's it working out Mrs Donkin? I've seen him helping you around the place.'

'Well, sir, 'tis a surprise 'e's settled so well but 'e's better now doctor's cured 'im. Got a flat worm out of 'im nigh on a yard long. Mind you, I can't get 'im in a proper bed. Sleeps on the floor wi just a coupla blankets but 'e's no bother at all. Sez 'e 'opes for a proper job but 'e's that shy 'e's afeared to mix in wi a crowd 'cus they allus tease 'im like. On account of 'ow 'e lived, before, like and 'is name.'

'What, Askett?'

'No sir, 'is first name. Abednego.'

'Oh. So how old is he?'

'Born in seventy-six 'e thinks which'd make 'im bout fourteen, fifteen or so. Never bin to school but 'e can tell all the psalms off be 'eart.'

'What, all of 'em?'

'Every one of 'em. We've tried 'im but 'e's never bin in a church nor chapel even.'

Luke shook his head wonderingly. You learn something new every day, he thought but an idea was forming in his mind. 'Reckon he could take on the pigs in the wood? Feed 'em, tend 'em. Set up proper winter shelters so they don't go wandering off? He could keep a weather eye open for strangers lurking about whilst he's at it. Have a word. See what he thinks.'

★ ★ ★

'Yes Walter. I have time to attend to a little formal business, as you put it. What momentous dramas await my attention?'

'Lady Cecelia's will, Mr Gregory.'

'I assume she made one?'

'Oh, yes indeed and I am executor and you are the beneficiary.'

'What? Are you sure? Well you must be or you wouldn't be telling me this but I don't understand.'

'Well, Lady Cecelia made a new will following that unhappy meeting we had with Nicholas Hurlingham. Her feelings were that he was unready to accept further responsibilities and wishes you to make suitable arrangements, dependent upon his future conduct.'

'I see. Hold things in trust until he settles down or comes to his senses? Understandable I suppose. Heard he's signed more notes to cover his gaming debts, silly young fool. He'll have nothing left the way he's carrying on.'

'I fear that may well be the case. The moment he comes of age his creditors will seek settlement but he appears unable to understand or accept this. He would heed neither Lady Cecelia's pleas nor my own counsel and became quite agitated on occasion.'

'I'd better see about buying up those notes but it's something I could do without. Very well, I'll speak with the staff and leave things as they are at Burberry Court. Time will likely offer a solution.'

★ ★ ★

'Good Lord. Look at this, Digger,' and Luke held out a letter he'd just received.

'Blimey, Guv. Not mincing 'is words is 'e?'

'I've been called rude names before but wicked, greedy, dishonest, scheming, rotten to the core, thief, typical villainous tradesman, never a gentleman, scoundrel? Cheating him out of his inheritance? Criminally influencing his late relative to leave what is rightfully his to your disgusting self?'

'Drunk d'yer reckon? Look how it's written. Starts off straight then goes bigger an' bigger an' slopes down. Must've bin pissed as a newt unless 'e's off 'is chump.'

Luke shook his head in wonder. 'And this was the schoolboy worried about Uncle Godfrey selling the family silver. Makes you wonder why we bothered to help but how does someone change so completely and in so short a time?'

'Beats me, Guv. You've always done the right thing by 'im. Done more'n others would an' this is the thanks you get. Chuck it in the fire, will you?'

'No, I'll pass it to Walter. This is personal so it's formal legal contact from now on. Quite old enough to know what he's about so I'll have no further dealings with him.'

It'd been a busy year Luke mused as he locked up the company office and set off for the Manor in the evening gloom. November was seldom a bright and cheerful month, with winter just around the corner, but he was pleasantly reassured by the way things were turning out.

He'd been going through the books for most of the afternoon, looking for areas of success and those that might be improved upon, largely with the Christmas bonus in mind.

An extra week's pay all round was well enough but would it be possible to improve upon that or would it be better to increase wages by sixpence or a shilling a week?

Preoccupied by this and with his coat collar turned up he was only vaguely aware of someone close by and started to turn to see who it might be when the first blow from a cudgel hit him on the shoulder, making him stagger.

Almost immediately he was struck another blow on the head and he collapsed unconscious in the road. His assailants, two heavily built men, began then to systematically beat him with their cudgels, adding brutal kicks and even stamping on him for good measure, before calmly walking away towards the station.

★ ★ ★

Eubelus Williams was now the village doctor in place of John Fairweather who had returned to London to further his medical training. Doc Williams, as he became known, was a small, wiry Welshman, quick of movement and searching and thorough in his diagnoses. Sponsored in his medical training at Barts by the churches and chapels of his home area he had taken the position as locum practitioner for a year to gain experience in a rural setting.

'Practice upon the English', was how he'd put it but with such obvious good humour that it hadn't in the least offended anyone and with his attentive bedside manner had even served to gain him quick acceptance. Called to attend Luke, when someone eventually stumbled across him, he organised a party to carry him home on a gate and spent most of the night assessing the damage and wondering how best to treat the many severe injuries, nothing of which Luke knew as he was out cold and would remain so for several days. Only later would he learn that the village was in turmoil over the attack whilst the police arrived in numbers and questioned all and sundry.

Tommy moved back in as nursing attendant, firmly declaring 'this is my business'. Digger called his team of specialists, vowing vengeance on whoever was responsible and Doc Williams sent for Professor Lambourne to check his work and to advise, whilst Luke lay comatose, splinted and bandaged from head to foot.

It was soon established that the attackers were not local men as both were seen to leave on the next train, cool as you please. Described as big, heavy men with London accents, one of whom spoke with an unusually high pitched voice, the essential lead that set Digger's team on their trail. Familiar with the strong arm men of the various factions around the river areas, their attention settled on a particular suspect and his companion.

One Ball Hannigan and Darrel O'Shea were enforcers used by bookies, loan sharks and those needing a certain kind of protection. They were of Irish stock from the Seven Dials, had a reputation for brutality and were known to work for the mob across the river from their warehouses and with whom they had a mutual agreement.

Was that agreement now at an end, Digger wondered? Were they planning a take-over of the South side? Their side? Did that mean war between them? He'd have to find out and fast, which was how the guv would play it. First make sure of the facts but be ready for action. Carry the stone for as long as need be but be ready to throw it, hard. He'd make enquiries and prepare for the worst.

★ ★ ★

Dimly, Luke heard muffled voices and the sound of groaning that seemed to float around as he slowly regained consciousness, then a voice told him to 'Stay still, Guv. You've bin knocked about bad.'

Gradually he realised that he had indeed been well knocked about, that he couldn't move his arms or legs, couldn't see clearly or speak and had the most disgusting taste in his mouth. Tommy, that's who it was close by. What was he doing here? Couldn't ask him. Couldn't speak. Was he dreaming? No. Too much pain. Pain everywhere and it was his groans he could hear. Then it was Tommy speaking again.

'Bout time you come back, Guv. Had us worried. Now get this straight. You can't move. You've got broken bones everywhere. Your jaw's busted in two places so you're all tied up 'till it's mended. It's everything through this 'ere tube for a while. You ready to swallow?'

And Luke was. He had a raging thirst, felt ghastly but knew Tommy was good at tending the sick even if he was firm as a jailer and for a man of Luke Gregory's active nature he was as confined as if he was in a straight jacket. Digger and Beth were his first visitors the next day and Luke wasn't sure he appreciated Digger's humour at that moment.

'Cor, Guv, yer looks like one o' them Egyptian mummy things with all yer bandages.'

'Give over, Diggs,' his wife admonished. 'It's bad enough without you poking fun.'

'Sorry, Guv but we're well on with catching up with them as did it to yer and mark my words, there'll be a reckoning an' no mistake. The whole village is cheering fer you. Didn't know yer were so well thought of but everything's running like clockwork. Not a thing out o' place, neither 'ere nor down the wharf so just you get better quick. Oh, an' 'is nibs's interests are up ter date. All organised and confidential so over to you, Tommy. 'E's all yours.'

★ ★ ★

Christmas came and went and followed its usual form with the tree up and every member of the household present and though he was in no fit state to join in the festivities, Luke felt quite overwhelmed by the expressions of sympathy showered upon him. Genuine too; not just superficial tokens offered as a formality, which was a puzzle to him for he'd never have claimed to be particularly popular with anyone. Far too direct and uncompromising for that, he would have thought.

Still, Tommy was allowing him to be carried downstairs more now and had hinted that in a week or so these wretched bandages might be removed. The sheer discomfort of his whiskers growing unshaved beneath them was something he wouldn't wish on anyone.

★ ★ ★

Digger, making one of his now frequent visits to the wharf, had finally decided to approach the North bank organisation, had written a suitably diplomatic note outlining events and naming the perpetrators and, in effect enquiring 'what about it?'

The response was immediate, denying any involvement whatsoever and stating categorically that the South side was free to take any course deemed appropriate, with their blessing. Clearly, the precautions taken by the team had been noted and pondered with some unease for strife between the two sides was in no one's interests. So, if this wasn't a mob job, for whom were Hannigan and O'Shea working? Only one way to find out and those two worthies duly disappeared from their usual haunts for a quiet and very private chat.

Naturally, Digger left such business to those best qualified but was totally taken aback when given the results of the questioning. Yes, they'd done it. Some toff had paid them twenty thick 'uns apiece to knobble the geezer. They'd been recommended by a bookie who was owed money by the gent. And the name of this gent?

'By all the saints. The guv'll never believe it. We can't tell 'im 'till 'e's well, if then. I can't get over it. He gave 'em twenty sovs each? You fellers sure of this? And the bookie confirmed it? Hell's bells. The rotten son of a whore.'

★ ★ ★

At last. The great day had arrived and the room was filled with Doc Williams' chatter as he laid out the tools of his trade, the tools that would slice through bandages and splint bindings and start to liberate Luke from his confinement. But it was only a start for he'd never felt so weak in his life. His voice was a croak, he could barely open his mouth and those damn bedsores seemed to be worse, now he could move a bit more and yes, he had to agree, when given a mirror, his face would never be the same again, so he'd keep his beard to hide the damage.

Someone though, was going to pay for all this misery but who? He'd made enemies over the years but he hadn't upset anyone recently, surely? Not enough to earn such treatment as this. Yes, he'd dealt out the heavy stuff when driven to it but nothing lately and Digger thought it wasn't local business. Anyway, Berrimond was gone. Sir Jocelyn? A possibility. He'd been humiliated enough, he supposed. Fenians? They'd bear a grudge for ever and a day. Not

O'Halloran. He'd gone down with that Yankee ship; same with Jonas Davey so who then? Local gentry and farmers. That could be it. He'd upset 'em all by raising the wages and no man went home now with less than fifteen shillings.

Then there was Lady Elisabeth. Ye Gods! The Dowager Lady Elisabeth! She loathed both sight and sound of him but would she go this far to settle the score? She was an unpleasant old dame and never missed a chance to disparage him. 'Ordered around by some common tradesperson would you believe? Whatever is the world come to? Outrageous!' But if she was behind it what on earth could he do about it?

★ ★ ★

'Well sir, 'tis like this 'ere.' Mrs Donkin was clearly struggling. 'I bin awaiting 'till you wus better like an' Mrs Cherry said t'would be alright now if you don't mind me speaking, like.'

'Of course not, Mrs Donkin. What's on your mind?' Luke, moving about carefully on crutches now, was seated in his favourite spot before the fire, well padded with cushions. He was very stiff, had lost a great deal of weight, was not yet allowed outside but was taking an increasing interest in what was going on.

'T'is about my boys, sir. They's growin' fast now and my two oldest 'ave both got young ladies but yer see, sir, if they should think o' getting wed like, things could be ockared fer 'em 'cus me an' Donkin wus never wed as yer know an' none o' mine 'as bin baptised nor nuffin' an' gals from decent families won't fancy goin' wi' someone like that. Folks still says as we ain't respectable an' that but I goes to chapel meetin's regular wi' Mrs Cherry an' she said as you might 'ave an idea or two on it an' that,' and Mrs Donkin, unusually flushed from delivering this difficult speech, looked hopefully at Luke.

'I can see your problem and it's all about appearances. You know, how the world sees you. Doesn't matter much whether you're good or bad just so long as you look right. Well, we'll make a start by getting you married off. Don't look so worried. Donkin'll do as he's father of your family. It only takes an entry in a parish record to put things right but you have to get your story straight and stick to it. Do you reckon your lads would put up with being baptised at their age? Not round here, mind. Somewhere quiet and miles away. All nice and private. Easy enough to arrange with a friendly preacher. Be all above board so then they can choose church or chapel or whatever. How does that sound?'

'Oh sir, I don't know 'ow ter thank yer, deed I don't,' and the tough, hardened little woman started to weep. As if on cue the redoubtable Mrs Cherry appeared and Luke thankfully sank back on his cushions as the ladies retired to the kitchen. He had plenty of time to think, stuck inside as he was and the thought of making Mrs Donkin respectable in the eyes of the world tickled his sense of humour. He'd get Digger to set it all up, work out dates of birth and such formalities and from now on it would be the respectable widow Donkin of Chidlingbrook. Thinking of Digger, it was high time his partner told him all he knew and stopped palming him off with excuses of 'still working on it, Guv'.

★ ★ ★

'You sure yer ready for the gory details? You're in fer a surprise I can tell yer.'

'Well get on with it then. Who knocked me about, that's what I want to know.'

'Hannigan and O'Shea from the other side.'

Luke considered this information but Digger cut in on his thoughts. 'I know what yer thinking but it was a one off job an' nothing ter do with the firm. Swore blind it was none o' their doing an' they don't want a war.'

'So who put 'em up to it?'

'You ain't going ter believe this, Guv but it was Nicholas Hurlingham.'

Luke just stared at his partner in sheer disbelief.

'We had a little chat with One Ball an' 'is mate. They were recommended by Smerdon the bookie as top rate knobblers an' Hurlingham paid 'em twenty sovs each fer the job. Friend Smerdon was happy ter sing and named Hurlingham then pointed 'im out to us when we took 'im up St James. Owes 'im a fair old dollop too and 'e was blaming you fer not allowing 'im to settle with Smerdon. They were just supposed to rough you up so you'd increase his allowance, but those two don't know when ter stop.'

'This'll take some getting over,' Luke eventually said. 'I'd no idea he'd go this far. You spoken to him about it?'

'No Guv. So far as I know 'e's none the wiser we're on to 'im but 'e's gone right off the rails an' no mistake. Dismissed his bailiff fer no good reason. Threatened Walter over 'is allowance too and spends most of 'is time round the card rooms with 'is cronies.'

'Police know anything?'

'No, Guv. We've kept it to ourselves.

'Keep it that way, will you and I'll give it some thought. So how long 'till he's of age? Can't be far off now.'

'Best part of a year. Then 'e'll have ter face the music, the number of notes 'e's signed. Ben's got some of 'em but there's bound to be more. Just about signed away the whole bleedin' show I reckon.'

'What happened to his bailiff?'

'Thought you might ask. He's up at The Towers giving Amos a bit o' help. Came ter see me when 'e were turned out. In 'is sixties now and bin there fer years with never a word against 'im. Too old ter try fer another position at his age.'

Luke nodded his understanding, then, 'I have it. Several fellers took the shilling to dodge the law not long back. Master Nicholas can do the same. A few years in the ranks'll make or break him and I'm sure Aunt Cecelia would approve.'

'In the ranks, Guv? Ee, a gentleman ranker! Cor, Beth'll fall about laughing. Just the ticket. So who's goin' ter tell 'im?'

'The Rector? He's preached forgiveness at me and turning the other cheek. No, perhaps not. Dessy or one of his mates can tell Master Hurlingham he has two days to enlist otherwise the law'll have him. Warrant out for his arrest. Thirty years hard for attempted murder if he stays around and he's dead meat if I so much as see him. Gather up his notes and we'll run his place in with the others and if I'm still around when he gets his discharge I'll see how good a mood I'm in. That suit you Cissie?' and Luke looked up at the ceiling. 'Ah, and what of Hannigan and his mate?'

'Left the country, Guv,' and it was Digger's turn to look up at the ceiling.

★ ★ ★

Chapter 17

A fine spring day and Luke was glad to be alive as he leaned on his stick looking out over the valley, accompanied by the ever attentive Tommy. He was lucky to be this well and was grateful for the care he'd received. It'd been a close call and he realised just how vulnerable he was and how much he had to do before he ended up wherever folks like him ended up.

William's future needed to be secured as did all of those for whom he had responsibility. The girls had a following of admirers, at least Lucy and Annabelle had and Louise had found favour with her grandmother in France who declared that she looked just like her when she was a girl.

Richard seemed happy enough assisting Cecil Rhodes, up and coming now in South Africa and Peter was just longing for the day he could leave school and try his hand at farming. No problem there, Luke thought. Julian? A career at sea if he applied himself. Paul? Hoping to take on the family estate and restore the chateau. A lifetime's hard work there for certain. So what should he now do to ensure all plans came to fruition and above all to ensure security for everyone in an uncertain world?

Gold. That was it. Accumulate gold for that gave security. But wasn't that what he'd always done? Of course it was. He must have had a bang on the head to be wondering about it. He'd just carry on the same and trade and scheme and play the markets as before for land was fine if it yielded a profit but it was gold he liked and understood. It held its value and you could turn it into anything you wanted.

But was it safe in the bank? Any bank? There'd been failures and panics enough. Should he withdraw what gold he had and keep it himself, in the cellar? He'd lose interest but the coin would be safe. That's it. He'd be his own banker. Now, was Rhodes into gold or was it just diamonds? Richard would tell him.

'You all right, Guv?' Tommy enquired, hearing Luke mumbling away to himself. It would take a while before he got over that beating. Best get him inside again.

★ ★ ★

Now Digger was unwell and here he was still hobbling around and nowhere near his old self. The thought of travelling up to London appalled him but he needed to know how things were or he'd fret himself into a fever worrying and wondering. Who to send? Who knew their way around the wharf? Who could talk to Ben and Walter and the Parsons on equal terms? Beth. That's who. She was sharp and they'd all show her respect. My word, they would!

That was it. He'd run things from here. Send others to gather the news he wanted. Even get one of those new fangled telephone things and speak direct to Walter or Ben or whoever. Plenty in the newspapers about them. NTC they called themselves. National Telephone Company. Cost about twenty pounds a year. Take off the cost of train journeys and he might even save a shilling or two.

Acting on the idea he had all the main books and ledgers moved up from the office in the siding to the study. That would be the hub of the wheel from now on and folks would report to him there. He'd keep his finger on the pulse without rushing about the countryside. He'd know how many ewes had lambed, how many potatoes were planted and what price milk was fetching and he'd pass over the trade with India to William and get him started in business.

Straight forward enough. Fred would send goods to the warehouse, deduct his commission and Bill would sell them on and take his cut. Not too demanding. Plenty of staff to do the fetching and carrying whilst he was at school.

Feeling pleased with his planning, Luke settled on one of the rustic seats at the front of the house facing over the valley. Might as well enjoy the sun, he thought as he reached for his coffee cup, the latest copy of the Times on his lap. And to think that he'd come close to never enjoying any of this again, but he'd have to get some stronger reading spectacles or he'd give himself another of those damned headaches.

Movement caught his eye. Now who was this walking up the driveway? Good Lord. A black woman and two black children. What on earth? Hesitantly and apprehensively the trio approached the house and cautiously moved towards him.

'My pardon, sir,' the woman said. 'I look for Tommy Denin. I is told he here.'

'Well yes,' Luke replied, getting to his feet. 'Tommy's here. And you are?'

'I's Francesca. I's his woman.'

'Oh, I see. Well, have a seat and I'll go and find him,' and picking up his stick he limped into the house to find an agitated Tommy, who'd seen his visitors from the billiard room window. 'Surprise, surprise, Mister Denin,' and Luke offered one of his rare chuckles.

'No, go out the front door you goose and take your guests round to the back room. If I'm not mistaken they're in need of more than coffee and biscuits.'

With the morning post in his hand, Luke retired to the study but it wasn't long before Tommy appeared in the doorway looking less than his usual confident self.

'Have a seat,' Luke invited, 'and I do not want to know of your private affairs. None of my business so no explanations but may I hazard a guess?' and Tommy nodded. 'You were at sea, as I was. You had regular ports of call and you had friends ashore?' and Tommy nodded again, his eyes fixed on Luke's face. 'Difficult business, seafaring. Not easy to keep contact but I can see the likeness. Handsome family and come to join you. I'm glad for you so what arrangements have you in mind?'

'Guv, I er, just didn't know how you'd see it. Should a said somin afore but didn't know if she'd come. Sent the passage money close on a year since.'

'So what plans have you?'

'Well Guv. Find work and somewheres to live for starters.'

'Plenty of work round here of one sort or another but no rush. Use the guest house while you sort yourselves out.'

'What, the house out back?'

'No one in it. Won't hurt to be lived in.'

'Thanks Guv. I'm real grateful to you.'

'Tommy, after what you've done for me it's the least I can do. Off you go and settle in.'

★ ★ ★

'Mrs Cherry. You have something on your mind unless I'm mistaken.'

'Well, Guv. Oh I don't know how best to put this but I don't like all these black people in my kitchen. Don't seem clean, some'ow. Oh I know as how Tommy looked after George so well but, well he was only one and now there's these others.'

'Ah. See what you mean. Well Tommy's taking his family up to The Towers any time now. His wife's a lady's maid and his daughter's a seamstress so they're going to help Lady Penelope. His lad wants the stables and horses and Tommy's going back again as footman.'

'Oh, my Lord. What have I been saying?' Mrs Cherry was clutching at her throat in horror. 'His wife! I didn't know they was married. I didn't know such folks did that. I thought, oh I feel terrible. I didn't know. Really I didn't.'

'Well they're civilised enough and I've known Tommy since he was down here and they're part white. Mulattos from the Caribbean, not cannibals cooking missionaries in pots. Mrs Denin was a lady's maid in a big plantation house. She speaks French and Spanish and a bit of Italian too. She's known a different way of life of course but it's the same for folks the world over. Think of Fred in India. He's half English half Indian and you liked him well enough.'

'Oh Guv, I feel so ashamed, I really do. I don't know what came over me thinking like that.'

'You're not the first, Mrs C and you won't be the last so not to worry over it. We don't see many black folks round here so we don't know much about 'em and you can't believe all you read in the newspapers.'

★ ★ ★

'What's the score now then?' Luke asked, when his visitors had settled themselves in the study ready for a business discussion.

'We have an inventory and very approximate valuation of the Hurlingham estate as it stands at present,' Walter replied, holding a sheaf of papers. 'There are two farms of around a hundred or so acres that provide rental together with one at the main house, which is really more of a large farm house than a mansion. There are several cottages nearby, one of which is occupied by the bailiff who looks to the home farm.

Value on the open market at present? Perhaps fifteen to twenty thousand but that could be improved upon I'm sure. Funds in trust are eight hundred and seventy pounds from which the school fees were formerly met and from which Master Hurlingham's allowance is made over to him. Then there is the income from the coal mining interest in Wales, which appears to be rather variable.

Ben has so far acquired signed notes for nearly four thousand pounds but believes there to be others. Of course, our responsibilities as trustees end in less than a year's time but the odd thing is he hasn't collected his allowance for nearly three months. As you know, I required his signature for whatever he received following his unpleasantness but it is quite unlike him not to call promptly.'

'Most odd,' Luke agreed. 'No news of him round about, is there, Digger?'

'Not a thing, Guv.'

'I fear we shall have to inform the police that he is missing if he fails to appear shortly,' Walter continued. 'As trustees and in effect, guardians we do still have a responsibility.'

'I could get someone to ask around the clubs and card rooms,' Digger offered.

'Yes, that would be helpful. We must be seen to do everything possible to ensure his welfare, before the police become involved.'

'Indeed yes,' Luke agreed once more. 'I'll ask someone to enquire of his bailiff but it's possible he's staying with friends. I believe he knew several landed people from his school days.'

★ ★ ★

A letter from a Bernard Hastings of Stroudly Manor near Godalming enquiring if he might call upon Luke Gregory Esquire as his eldest son, also named Bernard, would appreciate permission to call upon Miss Annabelle Gregory.

Oh ho, Luke thought. Romance in the air and formalities entered upon. He'd have to explain to the man that Annabelle wasn't his daughter and neither was she a wealthy heiress, in case the eldest son had ideas of coming into a fortune through marriage. That, of course, would be Annabelle's own decision but he'd protect her as far as possible from an unhappy union and the first move, even before speaking with her or replying to the letter, would be to get Dessy to make his usual exhaustive enquiries about the family.

Be doing the same for Richard or Peter before long. All growing up fast but Lucy appeared more interested in the business side of things than fluttering her eyelashes at eligible bachelors, sensible girl that she was.

Of more immediate importance though was the prospect of another very dry summer like last year. Winters were cold enough and spring late coming so they'd have to plan carefully and watch their water usage. Sheep wouldn't mind, though. They liked it dry and the returns from the enlarged flock were promising. Be interesting to hear what new ideas Peter would pick up at the agricultural college. A two-year course he was committed to, which should keep him out of mischief and then perhaps he could begin to take on some of the responsibilities of the estate.

★ ★ ★

So, 'Squire Gregory', for so he was known, whether he liked it or not, ruled his little empire carefully and cautiously from the safety of the Manor, sought to maintain a contented work force and to integrate all and sundry into satisfying niches from where they could give of their best. Annabelle, completely smitten by the dashing young Bertram Hastings was married and living over at Godalming, or more properly near Farleigh Green at one of the farms the Hastings family owned.

They were substantial landowners in the area, members of the traditional squirearchy who rode to hounds and followed the traditional customs of the countryside so were by no means disappointed in Annabelle, who was well and truly countrified and could turn her hand to most things, even those not normally required of a gentleman's wife. Eyebrows were raised though, at her preference for not riding side saddle. 'Hardly the thing, you know. Most unladylike.' But then, eyebrows were raised at young women in general who rode bicycles or smoked cheroots or even, horror of horrors, aspired to a university education or sought the vote.

Perhaps Luke's contempt for social pretension was responsible and had rubbed off on his household but all this had been brought to the attention of the prospective groom who hadn't thrown up his hands in horror but had welcomed 'a little fresh air from the stuffy conventions of the old days', which appeared to Luke to be a promising start.

The wedding had been the social occasion of the year in the village but Luke had struggled to play the attentive host to the groom's side of the family, some of whom were of a distinctly sniffy disposition, affecting airs and graces on very meagre grounds.

★ ★ ★

A surprise visit from Dessy Williams in early July had him concentrating hard.

'It's like this, Guv. As you know we've been keeping a close watch on a certain person and he's been going to some funny places. There's one I knows of where the queens go and meet up with, well customers. You know, like a bawdy house only it's all fellers, look you.'

'You mean a male brothel?'

'Yes, Guv. They pays to go in and then pays for a partner for as long as they like.'

'Go on. He been there, has he?'

'Yes, Guv. There's some real toffs there too sometimes. Lords and Honourables and such only I've got word the law is asking questions. I wouldn't want to be there if they visit, if you see what I mean.'

'I do indeed. You're quite sure of this?'

'Yes, Guv. I've been in there and seen some of it and I knows a couple of 'em. They works for the Post Office. They reckons it's easy money. You don't think I'm mixed up in it do you, Guv?'

'No, Dessy I don't and I'm grateful to you for telling me this but you must be careful. There's two years with hard labour for anyone caught at it so best keep clear. Why not make a visit home? Well away from here. Out of the area. I'll come back with you on the next train and report to his nibs but there'll be a bonus in this for you.'

★ ★ ★

'Gregory! I'm delighted to see you recovered. I was really shocked to hear of your misfortune, you know. Really shocked. Are the police any further on with their inquiries?

'Not that I'm aware of, sir. There really was so little for them to work on. Two unidentified strangers in the dark,' and Luke shrugged philosophically. 'I have serious news to relate I'm afraid and would suggest that a certain young man be confined somewhere safe for a while at least. As you know his inclinations are socially questionable and I understand the police are shortly to visit a house of ill repute. A male brothel, in fact. It would be disastrous were he present at the time.'

'Good Lord, Gregory. Are you certain of this? You must be, you must be. Disastrous is putting it mildly. It could threaten the monarchy's very existence. The scandal would be unimaginable,' and the Prince of Wales put his hand to his head in horror and despair.

'Tell me. What would you do in my position? You have such a fertile mind in such situations.'

'Arrange for something to be added to his food. A severe stomach upset would see him confined to bed and would leave him weak and listless for a while. Once he is recovered bring forward, if possible, his visit abroad and have him in the clear for when the storm breaks.'

'Gregory, you really are a marvel. You should be in government and solve a few of our national problems.'

'One other thing, sir. A member of your staff is likely to be named and possibly one or two other prominent figures.'

'I just cannot tell you how indebted I am to you for your assistance. The nation too. I would dearly like to offer you an honour but I know well your thoughts upon the subject.'

'I appreciate the thought, sir but I'm content as I am.'

★ ★ ★

Serious unrest was at last brewing in the docks with energetic agitators urging manual workers to action over their low wages and poverty for if the match girls and gas workers could achieve improved pay and conditions why not the dock workers? Six pence an hour and eight pence for overtime were rates proposed but unsympathetic employers were resisting the very idea of change, though Luke couldn't see why they were being so stubborn for the labourers had a genuine enough grievance.

Should a strike be called though, all work on the river would cease so it would be as well to clear as much stock from the warehouses as possible for no insurance would cover damage from riot should things get out of hand. He was though, prepared to offer his support to help bring an end to any dispute and would seek to speak with someone from the other side, one of the organisers if possible.

'Ah, Mr Tillett. Thank you for calling. I'm happy to offer support over better pay and conditions in the docks, provided your means are within the law. My staff enjoy reasonable terms so I'm looking to stand clear of whatever action you decide upon but I can offer you the proceeds of any trading I undertake, for the benefit of families affected.'

Accustomed to hostility from just about every waterside employer, Ben Tillett considered Luke's words suspiciously. None of the riverside bosses could be trusted in his opinion. They were greedy, grasping and uncaring, interested only in profit and to hell with the welfare of the working man. No. There must be a united front right from the start, whatever the cost.

'Not interested. Trying to buy your way out is typical of your class and we won't stand for it. You and your kind have gone too far and we're going to put an end to your exploiting of honest men. A good day to you,' and Tillett climbed back into the boat that had brought him over.

'So there we are,' Luke said to John Parsons and William. 'A fair offer of financial help and it's been rejected. You'll see it's made known, will you Mr Parsons?'

'Yes, of course, Mr Gregory. I think he was most ill advised. I understand there to be no funds available to support any refusal to work and I think that his remarks to you were quite uncalled for. You are well known for your fairness to your employees.'

'A blinkered man. Six pence an hour is his target and nothing else matters to him. It's a worthy enough aim but he needs to consider the broader picture.'

'What will they do, Pa?' William asked, his curiosity greater than his understanding.

'They'll probably stop work at some point but so will their wages. There'll be no money for food and their families'll go hungry. Anyway, if a strike is called we'll close the warehouses and moor up the lighters and barges 'til things are settled. Normal wages for our people of course but they must be available to safeguard our property. In other words, we'll ride out the storm but I'll speak with Lafone at Butlers and see what his thoughts are. Who knows, with luck it'll all be quickly settled and may not even come to a strike at all.'

Luke's optimism though was ill placed as he soon found. 'There we are then, young William. The strike has started and no ships are being unloaded in the docks. It's a labourer's dispute but they want everyone on the river to join in. We can go along with that provided it's peaceful and not too long. We've the Surrey Commercial on this side but everyone else is in wharfing and lightering, which is a bit different. Mind you, a lot of the barge men are badly done by and may look for better terms as well.'

'But ours are all right, aren't they? I mean, they're well paid.'

'We've always tried to be fair. I reckon the dock owners need to take that on board.'

'Yes, but what if the Indian ship comes in and Mr Abu arrives with fruit? It'll all go bad, won't it?'

'I've a few ideas in mind and so has Mr Lafone but we must get ourselves home and see the harvest in.'

★ ★ ★

A telegram from John Parsons set Luke thinking. One of their regular ships was moored in the river with the captain anxious to unload, as were many others, all waiting for the strike to end. Nearly three weeks now and apart from meetings, parades and attempts at mediation, there was no end in sight.

'Right, Bill, I'm off to stir things up. Coming?'

'You bet, Pa. What are you going to do?'

'Unload a ship. Get things moving by example. Ask someone to get your Uncle Digger here, would you? I'll let him know what I'm doing.'

Digger though, was far from happy about Luke's intentions. 'You're sticking yer neck out, Guv and yer not really fit yet, are yer. Why not leave things settle down on their own? You'll never learn, will yer?' Probably he never would learn but his scheming nature saw an opportunity and he'd grasp it, come hell or high water.

'Right, Mr Parsons, off and buy the cargo for me will you? Everything she has on board and we'll unload over the side. No tugs, just lighters. If she still has steam up get her as close as possible but not alongside any wharf. I'm off for a word with Lafone.'

It was risky for there was no telling how other watermen would react but all this time with no pay and very little in the way of relief may have altered men's thinking. He'd soon find out as he and William joined the crew of one of the lighters. The ship's crew would help unload and booms and cradles were already swayed out with sacks of maize and millet, which would go into their number two warehouse. William, perched in the forepeak of the steamer, had the task of keeping watch for any hostile approach on the water, for news of their activities would quickly be known.

Henry Lafone, General Manager of Butler's Wharf shared similar feelings with Luke over working conditions on the river and had early accepted the basic demands of the dock workers for six pence an hour and, despite widespread derision, was actually paying over three hundred of his striking workforce a shilling a day hardship money as a gesture of support. Never, it was claimed, had any employer ever paid the very people who were striking against him. The man must be mad but Henry Lafone just nodded and ensured that the loading doors of the wharf were open.

★ ★ ★

'There's three boats coming, Pa. Full of men,' William called down to Luke where he stood in a lighter rapidly filling up with rubber. The moment of truth, Luke thought. 'No rough stuff,' he advised his helpers.' Self defence only.'

Tillett was in the leading boat, megaphone in hand. 'You're breaking the strike', he called out. 'You're letting your workmates down. You're a bunch of scabs and blacklegs and should be ashamed of yourselves.'

'Clear off, Tillett. This is a private party. There's no one here working for slave wages and never have done.'

'Oh, it's you,' as he recognised Luke. 'I might 'ave known. Just like I said. Typical, but there'll be a price to pay, you mark my words.'

'If you're threatening me you're wasting your breath. I own this cargo and these lighters and I'm doing nothing unlawful. I offered you support at the outset but you turned me down. All you're interested in is making a name for yourself. We've agreed the tanner an hour over here but that's not good enough for you is it? The longer you keep men out of work the bigger your name'll be so hop off and leave us in peace.'

The delegation departed in sullen silence but that was not the end of the matter as later that day another man called at the home warehouse seeking a word with Luke. Almost like the old days he thought as he perched on the edge of a table with a mug of tea, tired and grubby but satisfied with the day's work, whilst William watched John Parsons complete his bookwork and the regular staff sat around enjoying their evening meal.

The visitor was a tough looking man with a heavy moustache, not particularly big but with an air of assurance about him as he enquired, politely enough, if he might enter and speak with the manager. Luke nodded his agreement to John Parsons who enquired how he might be of service.

'I see you're engaged in unloading a ship,' the man said. 'I thought everyone had agreed to support the worker's dispute with the dock employers.'

'We do support it,' Luke said, taking over from his manager. 'and you are?'

'Tom Mann. I'm on the strike committee and organising the South bank.'

'Luke Gregory,' Luke said, standing up and offering his hand. 'I've heard of you. Cup of tea? Your dispute is with the dock employers not us wharfingers. We've agreed your terms in full as you know from talking with Henry Lafone.'

Tom Mann nodded. 'True enough but we've the dock owners to convince.'

'We're helping by example. If they see us unloading in the stream no ship owner will want to enter the docks and if you look around you'll see quite a few wharves busy enough. This is the third week of your strike and you haven't made a deal of progress though I wish you well with it.'

'Do you mind telling me the owner of the ship you're working on?'

'Sampsons, but I own the cargo. It's one of my regulars and I own the lighters we're using and these gentlemen here are all full time members of my staff. Not a casual amongst them and that's how it's been for the past twenty-nine years. Ask around if you wish.'

'You don't have casual labourers here?'

'No. I retain a dozen or so preferred men at Butler's for when something big comes to us and they've no other work. Shilling a day, same as Lafone's paying his men. Not a lot but there's a limit and full rate when they're working, of course. One more thing, we work an eight hour day here. No slave labour, like I told the other feller, Tillett.'

'You didn't get on with our Ben, then.'

'I did not. Uppity feller. Offered my support before the strike was even called but he turned me down; didn't want to know. That right, Mr Parsons?'

'It most certainly is, Mr Gregory and he was extremely uncivil about it. Refused a regular cash payment to help feed the families and accused Mr Gregory of trying to buy his way out of supporting the dispute.'

'I reckon you'd best put your efforts into the Commercial down the road. They're receptive from what I've heard. Get them to agree your terms and it'll help force the other's hands.'

★ ★ ★

That did the trick and from then on Butler's and any number of other wharves on the South side started work again but honouring their lightermen's eight hour day. The strike proper though, rumbled on for another two weeks before the dock companies reluctantly conceded improved conditions for their work force.

From Luke's point of view it had been a worthwhile settlement as, by purchasing the ship's cargo at a time of shortage and high demand he'd made a welcome profit, far in excess of any from merely unloading and storing. That, he told William, was the art of successful trading. Look for an opportunity, weigh up the odds and put it to the test but always leave the back door open in case you have it wrong.

'But what if things had become unpleasant, Pa?'

'We'd have stopped unloading but then the world would've seen that people were being threatened and they'd have lost public sympathy. We helped shorten the strike by showing the dock companies they were on a losing wicket. There's more than one way of winning a battle and Tom Mann had the wit to see it. I just hope things'll settle down now. I'd much prefer to play the farmer and leave the river to others. Time we went home.'

★ ★ ★

'I reckons yer back to yer old self,' Digger said, when they next met. 'Didn't think yer'd manage it, not after that business. William told Rory all the gory details, facing 'em down an' that. Got to hand it to yer, Guv. You're a winner an' no mistake.'

'Couldn't let things slide. We could be ruined by that. Got Henry to do the formal stuff. You know, meetings with committees and so on. Happy with that once he knew he wasn't on his own. Good man, Henry. Straight and fair.'

'Rory reckons he missed all the fun.'

'He didn't miss a lot but I reckon Bill learned more in a couple of weeks than a whole term at school. Seems wharfing's caught his fancy. Be glad to pass it over in due course.'

'Rory's wondering if there's anywhere he might fit in. You know, in the whole set up.' Digger was digging for naturally he had his own son's interests to think of and Beth would be nudging her easy-going husband to broach the subject.

'Now let me see,' Luke replied, with a twinkle in his eye. 'A chip off the old block if I'm not mistaken. Work alongside Bill as we've always done but I reckon we need a contracting agency. Ben thinks we've a war or two ahead of us before long so there'll be government contracts out for everything an army needs and the right man with a contact or two could do well. We've one already to supply leather for boots to that factory in Northampton and they have a contract with the army so, if father were to start building on that, son could join him and learn the business.'

'Guv, where do you get these ideas from?' Digger's eyes were wide open in astonishment. 'It's my nasty, scheming mind and a love of gold. I had a good look round this last couple of weeks, at the markets and auction houses and I reckon they're stuck in a rut. A farmer has six beef bullocks to sell to meet his rental or whatever. He gets them to market and he's at the mercy of the auctioneer and whoever's willing to give as little for them as possible. If you contract with the farmer to raise those six beef bullocks that you will buy from him at an agreed price you remove the auction cost and the uncertainty.

Do this on many small farms and you have enough beef bullocks to meet a government contract. Do the same with cavalry mounts, draught horses, hay and oats. An honest man with the right approach? Why not make a start with what we have on the estate?'

★ ★ ★

'Morning , Guv. So you're out and about again. Glad to see it too.'

'Ah, Richard. Yes, thank you. Yes, I'm getting about more now. Keeping busy. How're things with you? Thought you were going to sleep for a week.'

'I was tuckered out I must admit. All this travelling about you know but that's still the most comfortable bed I know. A real pleasure to come home to.'

'As it should be. So how's the ambitious Mr Rhodes these days? More about him in the press now. Not all complimentary either. Keeping clear of villainy are you?'

'So far, Guv but there's competition and some folks are just downright jealous of success. I'm actually employed by the British South Africa Company, now it's up and running.'

'So what's your position? What exactly do you do?'

'Frankly, Guv, a bit of everything. Mr Rhodes is in Cape Town much of the time so I carry messages to various people all over the territory on his behalf and then report back to him. He wishes me to learn as much of his operations as possible so I'm back now to visit banks and diamond brokers in the City as he believes personal contacts to be better than written notes that might go astray.'

'Interesting. I can understand his thinking.'

'He also wishes me to sound you out on something. As you know, diamonds are his main interest but he also now has gold claims and workings. Quite small in their way but he would like to bank in this country, confidentially if at all possible.'

'Smuggle it in, you mean?'

'I wouldn't put it quite like that Guv but if someone were to extend credit based upon the value of gold they were looking after, it would be appreciated.'

'You, young man are learning the devious arts of diplomats and politicians. Well, I'm no stranger to such ways

I suppose just so long as no one is injured. How then might this be arranged? Sacks of South African maize, millet or other produce delivered to a wharf in London? In the middle of certain marked sacks a bag of something else? Maize is a useful animal feed so I'd naturally inspect such an import to ensure its quality. Need I say more?'

'No, Guv. You make it sound so simple.'

'Such ploys are but I'd need prior notice to ensure careful unloading and storage.'

'One other thing, Guv. Mr Rhodes wishes me to introduce myself to Rothschilds the bankers and to be honest, I'm a bit out of my depth there. I wondered if you wouldn't mind coming with me. I have a letter of introduction but it's all to do with finance for some of his ventures.'

'No problem. Just say when.'

★ ★ ★

A hand delivered note from Ben warning him to remove any deposits he might have with Baring Brothers Bank as they were in trouble over failed loans and investments in Argentina that might lead to a panic, with a run on their reserves.

It was just such information that Luke valued so highly and he thought again how fortunate he was in having someone like Ben to keep him ahead of events. He had no actual account with Barings but he did hold Argentinean stock that might suffer from adverse publicity and he wrote a note to his broker to sell, for Ben's assistant to take back with him. If South American stock did fall he could always buy again at a lower price later on. It was all part of the game and he didn't care to make a loss.

★ ★ ★

La belle France was picking herself up still from her disastrous defeat by the Prussians and Paul was busy doing his bit with the family estate. What money had been held in the bank but denied his grandmother had at last been released but it was nowhere near sufficient to restore the property to its former state. What would the guv do in his shoes?

Simple. Get the land earning again. Forget work on the house unless the roof leaked. Live small and leave the rusty gate swing on its broken hinge. Get those grape vines sorted out and whatever else would grow there. Start making wine again. Buy in wine from small producers round about. Send him samples for appraisal. Aim to get it right and become a producer and supplier.

Hard work but there was a goal to aim for and no, he really wouldn't care to visit. Not until he had progress and results to show and he really had quite sufficient to occupy his mind here, with winter approaching. It was far too mild for November so it could well be a hard winter but then, he always planned for the worst. Shorten sail early just in case was ever the maxim at sea, with a valuable cargo in the hold.

Winters lately had certainly been sharp enough but careful planning had avoided disasters so he again ordered extra stocks of coal and coke, bought in more hay and animal feed and checked that the traction engine was in good shape ready for snow clearing when needed. Last February they'd cut through a deep drift blocking the railway line so trains could keep running and had kept the road open between the village and Chiddington up the valley. A useful tool that, without a doubt.

Those who muttered that 'squire were fussing like an old maid' quickly changed their tune when, almost over night, the temperature dropped to well below freezing and stayed that way day and night until nearly the end of January. It was down to minus seventeen at times and by the end of the month there was a further twelve inches of snow on top of the fall shortly before Christmas.

'Never known it this bad', was a frequent comment as men piled on extra clothing and blew on numbed fingers to warm them, for outside work had to continue and with the frost and snow there was no grazing for the animals, so feed had to be carried to them all. Water supply became a problem with everything frozen solid but the sheep were all down on the lower ground, the cattle under cover with only the beef bullocks roughing it behind hedges and hurdles against the penetrating North East wind. Just so long as they were well fed and watered they'd come to no harm he was assured.

The younger members of the community of course revelled in the icy conditions with slides and snow fights everywhere, even skating on the mill pond, whilst home-made toboggans added to the fun on the hillsides. There were mishaps of course with a couple of broken arms from falls and a cut leg from a hay knife whilst one unfortunate caught the end of his muffler in the cogs of the turnip cutter. Only quick thinking by his companions saved him from severe injury or worse. Then, as ever, spring arrived and the routines of ploughing and sowing and tending newborn stock occupied everyone's minds, the discomforts of winter forgotten.

★ ★ ★

Time to take stock, was it, for time just seemed to fly by, with season following season and here he was, sixty odd and slowing down. No getting away from that but he'd just about achieved the comfort and security he'd always craved; security in a hostile world. A fast changing world too, with all manner of new ideas to be considered but his planning and investment in the estate had paid off and his bank balance was comfortable once more.

He'd had to persuade, cajole and insist to achieve acceptance of change but, finally, the doubters had been won over. It was all so different from his earlier world by the River Thames where he could easily oversee his barges and warehouses. Here, it was all spread out with little in view, but Peter now did the running around, keeping things moving as he desired whilst Lucy had taken over the administration; thrived on it in fact and had everything at her fingertips.

She'd moved into the carriage office when he'd been laid up and now had charge of staffing, wages and liaising between the different sections and when 'Miss Lucy said', that was it and no one argued, though she was carefully polite and courteous towards everyone, no matter who. She was certainly no lady of leisure and in no particular hurry to marry it seemed, though she had friends and admirers enough. Perhaps she was deterred by Annabelle's unhappy marriage.

However that might be both she and Peter were prominent in village affairs and to his relief had organised every aspect of the diamond jubilee celebrations of ninety-seven. Peter also sat on the parish council that had replaced the Vestry whilst his sister organised the running of the Manor; routines, meals, staffing and even told him when to buy new underwear as Mrs Jeffrey reported 'his drawers not fit to be hung on the line.' No arguing there, not with both of them after him!

He was simply no longer so spry since his mishap and seldom left the Manor by choice though he kept a weather eye on everything under the guise of 'The Company', employer and arbiter of local affairs. A problem? A need? The Company would help. Never the squire. Always 'The Company.'

The village, now. A different place from when he first visited, for every cottage had its own water supply, wash house, iron cooking range and connection to the sewer, though that had led to complaints as ordure from family and pigsty had traditionally nurtured the vegetable plot. Some even had bathrooms but this was, for many a move too far. Dark mutterings claimed such were for women and infants only and sitting in a bath of water would weaken the back.

'Probably keep ducks in 'em if fitted', Digger reckoned but it proved the old adage that 'you may lead the horse to the trough but you can't make it drink,' or in this case, wash overmuch. However that might be, as the estate had prospered so had the work force, with regular wages of well over a pound a week or more for most and modest rentals too, provided decent standards were maintained.

No one now entered the workhouse because of old age or infirmity, with medical care and pensions for employees and their families; all part of the contract between them and the company, for the Quakers had set a fine example that Luke had quietly drawn upon, though he made no demands of religious observance upon anyone.

That, he left to the Rector and his curate, an earnest and energetic young man who sought to fill every pew in the church on Sundays and any other day too, if he could find an excuse. Luke though, remained aloof from regular attendance or close contact with the village and its affairs, though he promised to review his stance should he ever become gentry.

Richard, firmly established and prospering in South Africa, was warning of further trouble with the Boer population. Bound to be friction, Luke reckoned, with a pushy fellow like Rhodes. Still, Richard would stand clear of hostilities that might arise. No point in collecting a bullet from an argument not your own. Enough poor devils had paid the price from the follies of ambitious men. Thank goodness William was settling firmly into the wharfing side of things, an increasingly complex business these days but a damn sight safer than fighting with angry Dutchmen.

It was a pity Digger's health was now so poor. Whilst he did all he was able it was one thing after another, almost like continuous influenza and so depressing for Beth, with her worries over Rory who was turning out to be quite irresponsible. Likeable and popular maybe but not an asset to any part of the business. Too fond of carousing with his friends or anyone for whom he bought beer at the Inn. So what to do about it? He had a few ideas but it really wasn't his place to interfere.

With his secure and privileged upbringing he should be doing better whilst John Hurle, as a farm labourer's son, had achieved a first class university degree and was now teaching English and History at Bramsden College. That really was something to be proud of though many in the village couldn't bring themselves to acknowledge it, blinkered hobbledehoys that they were.

Beyond the village, Luke knew he was thoroughly loathed because his successful farming struck at the very roots of the land-owning fraternity, whose wealth and influence depended upon the subservience of the farm labourer. To actually encourage his workforce to join the union and support Joseph Arch was the gravest heresy and meetings were held by bailiffs and others to condemn him and seek ways of combating his damaging behaviour.

Accompanied by Peter and William he'd attended one of these meetings out of curiosity, or was it devilment? Standing quietly on the edge of the gathering he'd heard himself vilified in no uncertain terms and when a show of hands was called in support of legal action on the grounds of his inciting civil unrest, he'd readily raised his own hand in support, which attracted the attention of a hovering newspaper reporter, anxious for first hand testimony for his journal.

'Have you knowledge of this fellow, sir?' he was asked.

'Oh, most certainly.' Luke replied. 'Know him well. Thorough going mischief maker. Votes Liberal, you know. Full of Jack's as good as his master and such rot. Uneducated rascal. No background, no people. Not from the best of circles. Definitely not gentry.'

'Indeed not,' agreed the scribe, scribbling furiously in his notebook, delighted to have such comments to publish. 'And might I enquire your name, sir and where you reside?'

'Oh yes. Gregory. Chidlingbrook Manor.'

The reporter got as far as recording Chidlingbrook before it registered and he looked up, his mouth opening wide as he saw Peter and William both helpless with laughter and Luke politely raising his hat and bidding him 'good evening'.

★ ★ ★

Then out of the blue, or so it seemed, Lucy announced that she wished to marry one of the masters at the prep school and here he was thinking he knew all that was going on. The Manor had always been more or less open house to anyone brave enough to cross the threshold but of course he'd met Charles Marchant. Had interviewed him when he'd been appointed. Asked him often enough how things were at the school, hadn't he? Decent enough fellow, he supposed. Came from Dorchester if he remembered rightly, so where did they plan to live, he wondered? 'Railway carriage in the siding?' he teased Lucy. No, they could choose a site and he'd have a new house built. That would be his wedding present to them.

But what had become of Nicholas Hurlingham senior? He didn't care that much but his sleuths reported he'd enlisted in a cavalry regiment, wisely using his mother's maiden name but to placate Walter Brierly, ever the stickler for the legal niceties, Nicholas St.John Hurlingham had been duly reported missing to the local constabulary and his estate placed in chancery for the benefit of his son, also Nicholas St John Hurlingham, a scholar at the Chidlingbrook Preparatory School at The Hall.

His milkmaid mother, in service at the Towers, now a thriving and well patronised country club for the discerning, was learning from Lady Penelope, the necessary social skills that would benefit her son as he grew up. A reasonably tidy arrangement would you not agree, Lady Cecelia? Certainly it was one that caused Luke to chuckle from time to time but just what his cavalry trooper father would think, if and when he learned of it, he had no idea but neither did he care, for memories of that beating remained with him and his was not a forgiving nature.

★ ★ ★

A cold winter, a late spring and a dry, hot summer with less than the usual rainfall and the river was running low with some of the wells drying up but, thanks to that borehole, there was ample water for the village for Ridgeway the surveyor had again proved his worth.

With most crops safely in and the weather staying fine, it came as a shock to the country to learn that open warfare had started in South Africa with a Boer commando firing on British troops and bringing to an end the so called peace and plenty boasted by the government. Both William and Ben had earlier warned of the deteriorating situation and had secured worthwhile contracts for supplies to the army, as Rory and William had fallen out over their working arrangement.

Funny, Luke mused how the sons could so reflect their father's personalities. There was William actively seeking cargoes and contracts and applying himself from early morning to late at night, as he himself had done, whilst Rory maintained a cheerful light heartedness and avoided any serious responsibility. Inevitably there'd been words between them, especially when a cargo went to a rival wharf and Rory had walked off in a huff, to hang around the village, kicking his heels.

Then Beth had arrived in a flurry of skirts and worry to seek Luke's advice as Rory had decided to join the army and enjoy both freedom and adventure, making disparaging remarks over the tedium of the workaday world.

'Tell him not to be an ass,' Luke advised. 'Any fool can wear a uniform and get himself shot. The army's not fit for battle so Wolsely says. I read it in The Times. The Boers have better rifles and know the ground so tell him to go out there as a civilian and see what Richard can do for him. I'm sure he'll find something to suit.'

So the restless Rory was gone, along with a couple of the village lads who took the shilling, keen to be soldiers of the queen and teach those Boers a lesson, for patriotic fervour ran high. Jingoism was it called? Load of nonsense in Luke's opinion for he well remembered the horrors of the Crimea. Be better if those who called for conflict did the fighting but if they must have a war he'd help supply the troops and turn a profit for if he didn't, someone else would.

It wasn't long before Lord Wolsely's opinion was proved correct, with the Boer forces running rings around the lumbering British army and its unimaginative commanders. It was soon learned that Kimberly and Ladysmith were besieged, that transport links were tenuous and many more troops would be needed to replace casualties and contain their highly mobile opponents. All very embarrassing and the cause of much worldwide satisfaction as the Imperial British Lion had its tail well and truly tweaked, and largely with the aid of modern German and French weaponry, it was learned.

But what of Richard and Rory? Beth was in a real tiz through lack of news but then it was reported that Cecil Rhodes was in Kimberly seeking to safeguard his mining interests from the encircling Boers, which meant Richard was probably there with him. Ruinous battles marked the turn of the century with heavy loss of life as the army attempted to break the siege and then it was over, the Boers retreated and with the railway line to the Cape restored, letters could be sent out once more with here, a month later, one from Richard.

A light-hearted account of battle and derring do but of greater interest was an account of how one Rory O'Dowd had strolled into the besieged town having passed unhindered through the Boer positions. Told that Cecil Rhodes was there and with instructions to look for Richard he'd followed the railway line for a week towards the distant sound of artillery until challenged by a very surprised sentry. Talk about the luck of the Irish, Luke mused and sent for Beth to share the news.

★ ★ ★

So the queen had died and old Tum Tum would be king at last. Perhaps he'd lean on those military blockheads to end the fighting in South Africa. Be a damn good thing if he did and an even better thing if he got someone to sort out the army from top to bottom but here was Peter announcing an interest in a young lady and would the guv mind if he brought her to visit?

Apparently her family were frequent visitors at The Towers and Peter had met her near the stables during his rounds, had learned that she liked to ride but not to hounds, that her father was something in the city who'd taken to the country club idea with enthusiasm and that she was under pressure to marry one of his associates, whom she detested.

Natural enough at his age, he thought and wondered when William would get around to it so was happy to meet Miss Isabelle Baddersley one afternoon as her parents snoozed off the excesses of a heavy country club lunch. A pleasant, rather shy young lady he thought as, dutifully chaperoned by Tommy's wife as decorum decreed, she was introduced by an attentive Peter.

There was a rumpus though when the snoozing parents learned of their daughter's excursion, made without their express permission, and both guests and staff enjoyed the voices raised in discord, the upshot of which was an unannounced visit to the Manor next day by the displeased parents.

Peter got wind of it and confided in Luke, who prepared for whatever battle was forced upon him but the encounter turned out to be no contest for when the irritated father came face to face with Luke he displayed every sign of acute discomfort, went quite pale and gurgled something incomprehensible.

'Ah, Baddersley. You have something you wish to say to me? Perhaps we should talk in private. Come into the study.'

Whatever passed between them Luke didn't reveal but, once he'd seen his visitors on their way, he was chuckling as he clapped one very puzzled young man on the shoulder and informed him he was free to pay court to Miss Baddersley without parental opposition, if not quite with their blessing.

'Put it this way. Yes, I've met the man before but I've agreed to set my feelings aside for the time being, conditional upon his good behaviour, so off you go and saddle up but be sure to follow the rules. You know what I mean? Most important.'

★ ★ ★

'Guv, is there nothing we can do for Annabelle? She really is having a most dreadful time.' Lucy, with concern in voice and expression had cornered Luke in the hothouse where he was admiring an orchid just coming into bloom.

'Mm? 'Tis not reckoned proper to interfere between man and wife, you know. It can lead to problems. So what's the latest?'

'He's hit her. She still had a bruised face when we met. He's got another woman in the manor house and pushed Annabelle out to that farmhouse with the children without even a maid or a cook and he's sending Oliver to a school in Yorkshire and said there'll be no holiday visits home. He's doing everything he can to be unpleasant.'

Luke listened to this recital with growing concern. 'Not exaggerating is she? Can't be if she has bruises. If it's that bad she'd better come home. Can't have that sort of thing in the family. First though, send a telegram to Dessy. I want a full picture before I decide what's best to be done.'

With Lucy gone, Luke resumed his study of the orchid, with its subtle colouring and shape but with this new problem in mind. Ever since his father had died and he'd inherited the estate Bertram had begun to change, had taken to frequenting the London clubs and treating his wife with indifference.

What gets into these fellers, Luke pondered? Almost as if lack of the parental hand brings out the true character and this was the dashing young man who'd swept Annabelle off her feet not so very long ago. But dammit. She'd been his ward, which was the same as family and he'd have no one treating them in such fashion and she with three young children as well. No, something would have to be done and Dessy would paint an accurate picture to guide him.

And a very clear picture he did present for Bertram Hastings was sick man who'd been behaving irrationally for some little time. Increasingly violent and persistent headaches had troubled him for which he'd sought relief from the bottle until he finally collapsed and failed to regain consciousness. A tumour of the brain was the medical opinion and as he hadn't made a will there was immediate family squabbling over the estate, with all and sundry attempting to grab a share.

With Lucy to support her, Annabelle passed the problem to Walter's solicitor sons and Ben's accountancy company, all known to each other and in face of which, opportunist claimants were quickly sent packing. Handy to have such skilled resources available, Luke thought. Not only handy but downright comforting.

★ ★ ★

The Crimea all over again, Luke thought as news came of the death of one of the young men who had so rashly volunteered for service in South Africa, not from wounds received but from dysentery. The village went into mourning and began to realise that people died despite all the flag waving and cheering and for what? So the likes of Cecil Rhodes might increase his wealth? Best keep such thoughts to himself for they weren't shared by much of the country if The Times was to be believed. Still, Rory had found a niche with the British South Africa Police, which caused Digger some amusement for 'he'd never have thought his lad would make a Peeler.'

Then one of Ben's assistants arrived with unwelcome news. 'Not safe to send a telegram or letter, Guv but Mr Driscoll said to get all record books up to date as someone's put the finger on you over tax and such like. Said he'll come down soon as he can and put you in the picture properly.'

Such warnings were not to be taken lightly and Lucy spent the morning checking through her records and accounts when, at midday, three grim looking men accompanied by police constable Studley arrived at the carriage office.

'I have a Treasury Warrant empowering me to examine all records of transactions,' she was told by one man, who waved an official-looking document under her nose. 'You must stand aside whilst I conduct a search of these er, premises. Constable, kindly detain this person the while.'

Lucy though, being a fit young woman and no shrinking violet, ignored the constable and set off back to the Manor at her best speed to warn Luke, arriving well ahead of pursuing officialdom who came hurrying up demanding immediate entry 'in the name of the law'.

'What law?' Luke asked, 'and have a care,' as one man attempted to push past him.

'I have a warrant authorising me to search these premises and remove items of an incriminating nature and you, sir must stand aside and not impede my assistants in the execution of their duty.'

'Show me the warrant and no one enters until I'm satisfied of its legality, and if you attempt to push past me', to one of the men, a stocky, heavy featured individual, 'there'll be consequences, I do assure you. Now. Let me see it.'

A document adorned with a crest was thrust towards him and as Luke reached out to examine it he was barged aside and staggered backwards as the trio of intruders moved quickly into the study and began collecting up books and records and placing them in canvas bags whilst the constable stood in the doorway, incomprehension showing in his expression.

That squire should be pushed around in his own house by men who required his official support was beyond his understanding and he was still wondering what he should do when Lucy returned to the hall accompanied by Mrs Cherry with her kitchen helpers and the yardmen.

'What do you think you're about, Constable, allowing this? Who are those men and by whose authority are they here?'

'This is disgraceful,' Mrs Cherry added. 'Come and sit down here, Guv. Bessy saw what happened and just who do you think you are, coming in here and causing upset?' as the trio emerged from the study with their canvas bags.

'We are here on official business, madam and have a Treasury Warrant, so stand aside.'

Luke began to realise what was afoot. 'Who are you? You'll take nothing from here without the fullest explanation.'

'I represent the Board of Inland Revenue and am charged with the investigation of financial irregularities, fraudulent practice and evasion of taxes due to Her Majesty's Government.'

'And your name?'

'Montmorency. Algernon Montmorency, principle investigating officer.'

'Well, Mr Montmorency, I find your practice high handed and offensive. My tax affairs are in order and my records complete and I require an itemised receipt for every item you have so improperly collected. Lucy, would you please list every item in those bags? Take your time. I want nothing missed. Empty them out, would you,?' to the yardmen.

'I cannot delay,' the taxman protested. 'I intend leaving on the next train.'

Luke ignored him and noticed that several more of his staff had joined the gathering, enough now to restrain these unwelcome intruders, for already he was planning his moves. This was his patch and he'd been roughly used so there'd be a reckoning.

'The inventory will first be made but I may as well demonstrate a civilised approach to your visit and offer you refreshment meantime,' and he gave Mrs Cherry a wink and accompanied her into the kitchen.

With the books and files piled now on the big banqueting table, Lucy began a detailed list of everything seized, interrupting the task for a leisurely luncheon despite the impatience of the men from the treasury who frequently consulted their pocket watches then realised they were too late for the afternoon train they'd planned to take. The next one wouldn't leave until eight o'clock that evening but they were somewhat mollified by the delights the kitchen had to offer them.

Peter, horrified by what had taken place whilst he was out readily fell in with Luke's scheming, having difficulty in containing his mirth. That the unwelcome visitors had consumed sufficient openers to keep them busy for some time, including a dose of the stuff they used for worming the pigs, was well enough but now there was to be a landslip that would hold up the evening train half a mile along the track, one that couldn't be cleared until the morning.

With all doors closed against them the trio would have to make do with carriage accommodation over night, when all their canvas bags would mysteriously disappear, for word that the treasury men were here to reduce their wages ensured total hostility.

★ ★ ★

Ben, when he called to put Luke in the picture, showed real surprise at hearing of the visit by the treasury men. 'Good Lord. If they sent Moses and his gang, someone high up is after your blood.'

'Moses?'

'That's what he's called, behind his back of course. Don't know why but he works for the top table and it pays to be wary of him. Not a pleasant fellow. Inclined to be vindictive and what, may one enquire is so amusing?' as Peter was bubbling over with laughter.

'I believe he found the country air disagreeable,' Luke offered, straight faced. 'Can't think why. Oh, go on, tell the tale,' to Peter, which left Ben near helpless with laughter in his turn.

'Oh, my glory. It doesn't pay to upset you, Guv. Oh, that's priceless and you got all the books and things back as well and hold his receipts for them. Oh, wonderful. That really puts him in a corner and just as well. You see, I'm retained to investigate you and your financial affairs by a city lawyer acting for some unnamed party.

Nothing unusual in that but it could be the Board of Revenue. Then again it might not for I've got wind of gold shipments from South Africa that may have been used for credit against the supply of weaponry to the Boers.' That shook Luke and it must have shown for Ben cocked an enquiring eyebrow. 'Something in that is there? You'd best tell me of it.'

'Well, yes. An arrangement I have with Rhodes. He sends me the yellow stuff and I arrange credit for him but it certainly doesn't go to the Boers so how did you get wind of it? Richard knows of course and William but no one else. Not even Digger. Peter, you've heard nothing, understand?'

'This is the worrying bit. It came first from the warehouse direction then with a whisper from the Cape. Something about a substantial sum sent to France.'

Luke felt jolted again. Bill wouldn't let anything slip. Not his own son. 'Good God,' he suddenly said. 'Rory,' and Ben nodded. 'How could he?' Luke muttered. 'Falling out with William is one thing but this is quite another.'

'The beer goes in and the sense goes out,' Ben commented quietly. 'But about the money sent to France.'

'All above board. I lent Paul five thousand for his vineyard, nothing more. It shows as a transfer to his account with a bank in Orleans. Seems like most of his vines are diseased and have to be replaced with local types grafted onto American rootstock. Something to do with Philox something or other. All above my head to be honest but listen. No word of this to Digger and Beth. It'd shatter them. Your word on it?'

★ ★ ★

Chapter 18

Coronation year and his nibs was to be crowned at last. Taken his time about it but he'd kept his word and declined to take the throne until that wretched war was over and that was probably helped by Rhodes keeling over. Disapproved of both the man and the war, unofficially, of course, but was surprisingly popular as he showed a human side that went down well with everyone, for he'd speak as warmly with a labourer as with a duke, so full marks there. Probably be high jinks to celebrate the occasion but he'd stand clear and let others organise things.

'Ah, Beth, me dear. You're looking very solemn. Digger all right is he?'

'Yes, he's ticking along as usual. It's just that I've got something to tell you before you gets to hear it from someone else.'

'Sounds ominous. Go on.'

'It's about Neeson, up at the school, the feller who looks to the ponies and teaches riding.'

'What about him? Nothing bad I hope.'

'It's not his real name. It's Nicholas Hurlingham. I thought you'd best know straight away.'

The effect on Luke was much as Beth had expected. He sat bolt upright with what she always described as his 'dangerous look' on his face, one that usually preceded hostilities.

'Hurlingham, at the school, right under my nose? In the stables? Good God. Is he tired of living? How come we didn't recognise him?'

Beth shrugged. 'The beard, walks with a limp, working clothes. Keeps himself to himself. No reason to think he wasn't just some soldier invalided out and given work with horses.'

'Yes, but how did you find out?'

'This is where it gets interesting. Someone found a letter in the stable addressed to Nicholas Hurlingham Esq., thought it belonged to the boy and handed it in at the school. Of course, young Nicholas didn't have the first idea and the head asked the Rector if he could shed any light on it and he spoke to me and Digs. It's a letter from a lawyer acting for Cousin Hubert, who's claiming the family estate, as Nicholas junior is illegitimate and has no legal right. Oh, and the letter, was collected from the post office in Guildford, not delivered to the stable.'

'Yes, but how come Hurlingham's working there, at the school, of all places?'

'Ah, now promise not to explode? Hurlingham wrote to the Rector, from India. Told 'im what 'e'd done, how sorry he was about everything. Wanted to know about the girl he'd wronged and the child and all that. Got 'imself wounded and invalided out and the Rector put in a word for the stable job so's he could see his son. Seems he's met up with our Mary as well.'

'That damn, blasted God botherer! They just can't keep their bloody noses out, can they and all behind my back as well. I feel like pulling his damn bells out of the church tower and wrapping them round his blasted neck! Leaves me looking a prize fool, not knowing about it and damn it. I own the blasted school and that bloody man's working there, laughing at me from round the back end of a horse. Here, get me a whisky, will you?'

Luke was in a rare old lather but Beth, knowing he'd calm down as quickly as he'd worked himself up, poured him a decent measure of his favourite malt, and waited.

'So where do we go from here?'

'Well, first off, Guv he's not laughing at you 'cus we told 'im you knew about 'im being there all along, which stopped 'im doing a runner on account of that warrant fer his arrest. Didn't tell 'im, mind, there wasn't one and never 'ad been. He can go on thinking you're a nice, forgiving sort o' feller, even if you're not an' if you grinds yer teeth like that you'll have none left.'

Beth was, perhaps, the only person who could treat the 'old man' like this and get away with it. Sharp, astute and strong minded she enjoyed enormous respect for her good sense and practicality. 'So that's how it is, Guv. You can do nothing if it suits but if that there Cousin Hubert gets his way everything you've done so far'll be wasted. Young Nicholas'll have no inheritance an' his mother'll remain in service an who pays the school fees if there's no income from the estate?'

Luke, his thoughts racing, looked straight at Beth then nodded his acceptance of her reasoning, got to his feet and wandered around, glass in hand. 'So what do you reckon, Cissie?' he asked, quietly. 'Mm. Yes, but would that work? Well, if you say so that's how we'll play it.'

'You all right, Guv?' Beth asked, looking at him sideways.

'Perfectly. I was merely consulting with Lady Cecelia and her advice is that Hurlingham should marry Mary Ellis without delay, to legitimise his son, then reside at the family seat and live quietly and happily ever after.'

Beth just stared at Luke open mouthed. 'Here, I don't drink whisky but I reckon I needs a drop. You were talking to Lady Cecelia? Straight up?'

'You may think what you wish but you brought a problem, sought an answer and now have a wedding to arrange well away from here and funded from the Hurlingham account. Details to be passed to Walter and his sons, who will attend to all legal niceties now that Hurlingham has returned from service abroad. I personally am not involved and the groom should give me a wide berth. That I want clearly understood and the warrant will be withdrawn as the main suspects are deceased, so I wish you good day,' and Luke bowed in elaborate and comical fashion.

'Oh Guv, get on with you. But yes. Right. I'm on me way. Ta ra.'

★ ★ ★

So the Jacksons were taking an interest in these new-fangled, petrol-driven horseless carriage things. Well, Luke supposed, blacksmiths reckoned to turn their hands to most things made from metal but the thought of them becoming as popular as bicycles was surely a bit far fetched, though someone called Wright had actually got off the ground in one, in America of course, so there was no telling where all this inventing would lead. What with the electrical lighting and the telephone in the study and even messages being sent without any wires at all, it was clearly a changing world.

Probably all down to more education, with women trying for the professions and making a fuss over not having the vote. Plenty of huffing and puffing in The Times on that score. "They should know their place and stop seeking to change things" appeared to be the general view, but he knew women with a good deal more sense than many men so why not?

Perhaps if they had more of a say there wouldn't be so many wars, with everyone picking fights with their neighbour, like Russia and Japan, for the only yield would be a load of dead and wounded men, just like the South Africa business. At least, they could rely on King Bertie to keep the country clear of conflict and those Sinn Feiners in Ireland sounded more peaceable than the Fenians so perhaps a settlement was now possible.

★ ★ ★

'The Old Man about, is 'e?' Luke heard a voice enquire of Alfie Donkin who was busy grooming a pony in the yard. Luke, looking around the stable, admiring the swallow's flying skills as they swooped in and out to their nests, heard a muttered reply to the enquiry. Old man? What old man? Then it dawned on him. Old? Well he was getting on a bit, he supposed and he'd be seventy next year but was that what folks were calling him? Impertinent crew and walking out to the yard, glared at the young station porter and demanded 'Well?'

That young man, his uniform still shiny and new, had the grace to go bright red and stammered that a wagon load of fertiliser had just arrived and was in the siding ready for unloading. Luke just nodded, not deigning to reply and the subdued bearer of the message slunk away, well aware that such discourtesy could earn him instant dismissal from his employment, should a complaint be made.

Luke though, never too concerned about his status was far more interested in this new type of fertiliser than causing a fuss at the station. Made from dried fish, ground up bones and animal blood from the abattoirs it was claimed to boost crop yields even more than the guano they'd been using.

Expensive mind, but if it gave the results claimed and repaid its cost he'd be well pleased, for the reputation of their produce for top quality ensured a steady demand, with its equally steady yield of gold, and that was the true test.

A pity about Tom Barnardo though. Worked himself to death but what a difference he'd made. No, he wouldn't attend the funeral and Digger wasn't up to travelling. Seldom went out now; just a shadow of his former self but Joseph and Bridie would go. Would want to for both were his and they always spoke of him with fondness and gratitude.

Then it struck him and stopped him in his tracks. He was nearly seventy. People he'd known were passing on. How long did he have left? Who would inherit the estate when he was gone? He'd have to give serious thought to this. It wasn't just a case of leaving it all to William, for he had other responsibilities. He'd discuss it with Ben as soon as possible but now there was an election pending with talk of heavy going for wealthy landowners no matter who was elected.

So, who to support? Liberal or Tory? Not that he ever voted for he'd avoided inclusion on the register and had never appeared on any census return. Illegal? So what. He was his own man and would remain so. Same with religion. It was a free choice to attend church or chapel or none at all or vote for who he pleased or not bother. In neither case, to his mind, would it make a scrap of difference in this world or the next, a viewpoint that sometimes led to lively discussion, especially with Lucy, who of course couldn't vote.

'Best move to Finland then,' Luke had teased her only last week. 'Women have the vote there now, so I've read but you'll have to wait for Tum Tum to move on before you'll get it here. He's quite set against it. It'd take a San Francisco sized earthquake to change his mind.'

★ ★ ★

'Ah, Bill. Serious talk time. Let's walk shall we? No eavesdroppers then.'

William, on one of his increasingly rare visits to the Manor cautiously fell into step with his father, wondering what this was all about.

'Been redrafting my will and I want your thoughts before I sign and seal. Different world when your Uncle Digger and I made ours in case one of us went overboard. Bit more to it now with investments, the estate and the warehouse side of things. I could just leave the lot to you but there'd be ill feeling and that's to be avoided. Follow my drift?'

'I think so, Pa. You must do as you see fit.'

'Hoped you'd say that,' and Luke went on to describe how he'd like everything kept together as one company with a chairman, directors and managers, to avoid, where possible, the taxes imposed on wealthy individuals when they died.

'Two types of people in this world; those who create and earn and those who try to take it from 'em and the government's one of the second lot, especially if Gladstone gets his way and imposes death duties. Aimed at the idle rich but it'd catch us too and I want to see you and yours benefit, when you get around to it.'

There was a lengthy silence then between them, so lengthy in fact that Luke looked hard at his son wondering what he might have said to cause it.

'Pa, I've been meaning to tell you but well, I just wish I didn't have to but now I must. You see, I've got a son. He's only a few months old but I'm not married and I can't arrange anything. I've made a mess of things and I can't forgive myself for it and oh, I don't know.'

Luke had had a few surprises in his life but this one left him open mouthed and uncomprehending as he took it in and looked hard at William, gazing at the ground now, deflated by his admission.

'You mean I have a grandson? You rascal you. So tell me about him. Why the secrecy?'

'Well Pa, I, I just didn't know how you'd take it. I mean I'm so ashamed, I really am.'

'Why? Were not your intentions honourable? Marriage and all that?'

'Well, yes Pa but you see Elsie's not yet of age and her father's forbidden marriage but he's also thrown her out. Said she's a disgrace to the family name and he never wants to see her again'

'How very Christian. So where is she now?'

'Gresham. Look Pa, I really am sorry. I really am. I didn't intend anything like this, honest.'

'I'm sure you didn't so stop apologising and start organising. Tell me straight. Do you wish to marry Elsie and does Elsie wish to marry you?'

'Yes, Pa.'

'Then get off back and have the banns read somewhere and organise your wedding. Your Aunt Beth'll give you a hand with the arrangements and for heavens sake cheer up, man.'

'Pa, you mean you're not mad at me over this?'

'William Gregory, I've been disreputable all my life. I'm the last one to be making judgements and I do know how the world works. Mind you, I had hoped you'd be more conventional but clearly you're a chip off the old block so you'll do for me. Come on. Back to the house. Enough of this other business. It'll all keep.'

'Yes, Pa but what about Elsie's father? He'll kick up an almighty fuss.'

'Leave him to me. I want a legitimate grandson.'

★ ★ ★

Dugdale Evintrie fforbes-Manton, partner in a private bank catering to the needs of minor royalty and others of aristocratic descent, dwelt in an exclusive area near Hampstead Heath. He enjoyed a comfortable lifestyle with a staff of five in his many roomed house but was of a Calvinistic turn of mind, thinking and acting along straight and inflexible lines and recognising no deviation from his view of right or wrong. He was a pillar of the local community, sidesman at the parish church and a leading light in the anti drink interest.

This much Luke learned from Ben Driscoll, who knew the man professionally. He also learned that it was fforbes-Manton who'd introduced his daughter Elsie to William, who happened to be with Ben at some meeting or other and Ben had recognised that both were strongly attracted to each other. The attraction had blossomed, probably clandestinely, with the present unplanned result and the outraged father opposed the usual answer to such a situation as retribution for the wickedness tarnishing his family's good name.

Strong stuff, Luke mused as he set out to meet the ogre in his lair. He'd have a hard time of it and not much to bargain with but, as the Rector had once said, he could be very persuasive. He hoped so, as the cab dropped him by the imposing iron gates and he wasn't encouraged by the chilly reception when shown into the august presence, who declined to shake hands with him.

'What, sir, is the purpose of your visit here?'

'My son wishes to marry your daughter.' No point in beating about the bush, Luke decided. Straight to the point and be damned.

'Your son, sir, is a reprehensible scoundrel and blackguard who has brought dishonour upon this house'

'That, sir, is an unfortunate comment. Had my son sought to evade his responsibilities it might be so but he is registered as the father of the child and has offered marriage, which you choose to oppose. True, his actions were not what either of us would have wished but the situation is easily reconciled and the child is, after all, our grandson.'

'I sir, had looked for a better match for my daughter than with some riverside trader.'

Count ten, Gregory and resist the impulse to thump the fellow. 'International trading is but one of my interests sir, an occupation in which my son is involved at this present time.'

'That is of no interest to me whatsoever. He is clearly an irresponsible character with whom I shall entertain no contact. I see no purpose in continuing this meeting and I wish you good day, sir,' and jerking an embroidered bell-pull, a manservant opened the door ready to usher Luke from the house.

Very well, my friend, if that's how it's to be, Luke thought to himself as he walked back to the waiting cab, so be it. The gloves can come off.

Some two weeks later, on a Wednesday evening, Luke, accompanied by two large men in bowler hats entered a restaurant of a certain type on the edge of the Paddington area and looked around for someone he expected to see.

'Good evening Mr ffinch-Manton. Are we working late, this evening? Pray introduce me to your daughter. Oh, it's not your daughter. Of course not but you, young lady should not be consorting with respectable family men who hold

- 533 -

strong views on moral issues and surely that is not intoxicating liquor you are consuming? Upon my soul sir, you do surprise me. What would the vicar say? Or your lady wife? Or your professional colleagues? Perhaps a word together outside might be appropriate?'

★ ★ ★

'Mrs ffinch-Manton has visited her daughter? And it was a happy occasion?'

'Pa how did you manage it? I just can't get over it. Elsie said nothing would change her father's mind and she's really terrified of him. So's her mother for that matter.'

'Oh, every man's open to persuasion and with Dessy on his tail he didn't stand a chance. I'll tell you about it some time but a quiet wedding at which her father will be delighted to give his daughter away is to be arranged as soon as convenient and the fond parents are visiting at the Manor this next week-end, in your absence naturally. One step at a time. Now, where do you wish to live, when you're not at Gresham, I mean. Give it some thought will you?'

'You mean they're staying at the Manor?' William was incredulous.

'Yes, and I'm not looking forward to it. I dislike entertaining as you know but we have to be friendly with the other side, do we not? I shall put on a show for their benefit; carriage at the station, Lady Penelope to dine and all that so you, young man are to be thoroughly respectable from now on. Understand?'

The weekend turned out to be not as difficult as Luke had expected but the Friday evening to the Sunday was quite long enough he reckoned as he lay in bed going over it all again. He quite liked Mrs ffinch-Manton and had been careful not to embarrass her husband. He'd unashamedly boasted of the company's financial standing and connections, for the riverside trader jibe rankled deeply.

'You mean William is known to His Majesty?'

'Oh yes. As Prince of Wales His Majesty visited frequently. Has occupied the very chair in which you sit and we have care of some of his thoroughbreds, on the horse pastures across the valley.'

He really enjoyed that and rubbed things in when relating their trading interests by nonchalantly showing the three rubies in their padded box. That really had made their eyes pop and Luke knew he'd have no further difficulty with the wretched man especially when he'd grandly proclaimed the company to be its own bank, apart from some depositing and investing with a select few, of course.

Had he over done it? Not really he decided then realised he had, in fact, been elaborating on his future intentions regarding the company, his interests and his will. Yes, he was satisfied now that he'd hit upon the right balance, with safeguards, should anyone take to the bottle or otherwise go off their head and jeopardise the enterprise.

One company, based at the Manor with a board of directors. Peter to look to the farming side of things, Lucy the clerical and administrative work, Richard the South African side, with diamonds and gold interests, Paul on the continent with his vineyard and Fred in India whilst William would oversee the wharfing and warehousing, chair the enterprise and pull it all together.

Salaries, dividends and bonuses based on annual profits. It looked well enough on paper but would it work? It would if they all pulled together. Ah, Digger and Beth. Mustn't leave them out but he'd be cautious over Rory who showed all the tendencies of the waster and ne'er do well.

★ ★ ★

Dessy, sixty odd now and no longer so spry, had built up a team of smart young fellows who did the running around so would the guv mind if he retired home to Wales? Of course the guv wouldn't mind but hoped he'd keep in touch. After all, he reflected, they were all aging, all of the old team. John Parsons had finished work, Walter too, had stepped down and poor old Digger no longer took part in anything. Just hanging on, the doctor told him, in confidence, of course.

So there he went again, making himself miserable with doleful thoughts. Snap out of it Gregory! You've organised things. You're reasonably healthy so cheer up and let the younger ones get on with it. So what to do? He didn't wish to travel and no longer looked to the Lodge House for recreation. Lost his falorem, or was it dingdoram, according to that saucy song? No matter but he'd get out more. Around the estate. Up on the Downs and yes, dammit. He'd join a club. A gentleman's club. But which one? Spoilt for choice there but he enjoyed intelligent conversation, was liberal in thought so, The Liberal Club, if they'd have him or, better still, the Reform. Now who could he get to propose him?

Then Digger, his partner for so many years passed on. It came as no surprise, was almost a relief really, though he was greatly saddened by the news. Then came a real shock when Dessy Williams was pulled from the River Thames. Been in the water a week, Ben's letter told him, for he'd been called to identify the body and there was to be an inquest. So he'd not made it home to Wales after all.

Poor old Dessy. He'd been an invaluable helper over the years and had worked closely with Ben on all manner of confidential business. An absolutely natural ferret where information gathering was concerned but how and why had he ended up in the river? Not suicide, of that Luke was certain. He was well provided for a comfortable retirement, though he'd never married, but he'd moved in a twilight world and might well have made enemies. He'd very much like to know and if he learned anything he'd certainly even the score.

Then the king died suddenly and it really was the end of an era. Luke had often been critical of the man but had liked him nevertheless and they'd certainly made good use of each other over the years and no, he wouldn't join in any national mourning. Losses closer to home meant more to him and he grieved still for that irrepressibly cheerful little Irish mudlark who'd helped him get started in trade and who'd been such a loyal partner over the years.

★ ★ ★

It was though, turning out to be an eventful period, with all these new motor driven vehicles replacing horses and asteroids landing in Russia and new inventions making the news almost weekly but at last there was to be a national pension scheme for people over the age of seventy and about time too, but seventy? Many were past work well before that and not all reached sixty but it was a start, though nothing like the terms offered by the company.

What really concerned Luke though, from his reading of the newspapers, was the number of conflicts in the world that continually threatened trade. If it wasn't frontier fighting in Northwest India or the Americans in the Philippines or squabbles between the Balkan countries there was always unrest in Ireland with continual demands for home rule. Why oh why couldn't folks live in peace with one another?

Why, because Great Britain had new battleships did Germany have to build them as well? The French and Americans would follow suit and then some clown would want to try them out and see who had the better ones. Madness. Nothing but madness with everyone vying for supremacy and making treaties and agreements that would drag every man and his dog into confrontation, whether they wanted to involve or not.

Then, almost inevitably, the spark started the fire and folks were rushing about cock a hoop because there was a war, but one that'd be over by Christmas, once the Germans had been sent packing from Belgium and France, but it was an ill wind that blew no good and orders for any and every item the company could supply came piling in from government departments.

Conversely though, the casualties began to mount as the battlefield tactics of the past two hundred years were practiced in the face of modern weaponry with masses of men walking towards machine guns behind barbed wire under a deluge of high explosive shells.

Cannon-fodder. Nothing but cannon fodder as young men round about began to appear in uniform then disappear never to be seen again, except for those who were wounded and as the number of these increased so officialdom began to seek out suitable buildings to serve as hospitals and convalescent units, which was how the prep school at the Hall was transformed almost overnight from a seat of learning to one of suffering.

Nothing for it but to accept it, Luke decided but what to do with the pupils? Couldn't just send them home, with parents abroad, so the Manor became a temporary prep school, Beth moved in to help, medical staff moved into the farmhouse at the Hall and Luke found himself pressed into service as a temporary school master when two of the teachers departed for military service.

What a pickle he thought, but was happy enough with something useful to do until Bramsden could make provision for the prep school but his main concern was for those nearest to him who might have to join the slaughterhouse in France.

Peter, he felt sure would remain exempt, both by age and essential occupation, for food production was enormously important but William might be dragged into some branch of the service so how, Luke wondered might this be avoided. There were women going around offering white feathers to anyone not in uniform and the last thing Bill wanted was to be considered a coward shirking his duty but, as Luke well knew there was no glory to be had in the trenches.

Ah! Supplies. No army could exist without supplies and William was skilled at handling goods of all descriptions in any quantity needed. That was it. Into uniform my lad and help create an efficient supply service to those who needed it for there were tales of bungling and stupidity going the rounds with crates of cutlery taking priority over much needed shells and rifle ammunition. A word with Stafford at the ministry should take care of that.

Then problems arose closer to home when Mrs Cherry, retired now but still full of get up and go, organised a working party to offer assistance at the Hall, but was told 'this is a military establishment and we cannot have civilians interfering', on top of which, Mrs Hutton and her kitchen staff had been replaced by army cooks. To say that the ladies were indignant was putting it mildly and Luke was required to do something about it.

'Well, Mrs Cherry, we must conduct an inspection of this military establishment and we'll start quietly at the back door. No time like the present so ask Alfie to harness up, will you?' Beth joined them for the expedition and together they entered what had formerly been the servant's hall in its days of grace and were confronted by piles of soiled and stained clothing and bedding all of which, according to Beth, should have been in the laundry across the yard.

In the kitchen, three men in a mix of chef's clothing and uniform lounged about smoking whilst pans and kettles bubbled on the stove. All three stood upright and straight when they entered and sought to conceal their cigarettes as best they could.

'We're having a look round to see how things are,' Luke informed them. 'You are the cooks, I take it? Regular qualified cooks?'

'Well, sir, no sir, not zactly sir,' the oldest of the trio offered, playing for safety. 'We was sent 'ere as there was no one else, sir 'cus we was in the cook'ouse at the depot, sir.'

'I see. So who's in charge here? Who's the commanding officer.'

'Major Duffield-Cranton, sir. You'll find 'im in the office, sir. Can I show you the way, sir?'

'No need, thank you. We know our way around well enough,' and Luke led the way up the back stairs to the dormitories on the first floor, then recoiled at the smell. 'Good God,' he exclaimed and looked around in disgust. Extra beds had been placed in the first one, where eight boys had previously slept, so there was barely room to move between them and in or on each one was a bandaged man, some with limbs missing or with bloodstains showing on shirts or hospital-type gowns. Luke and his companions looked at the men who looked back silently, pain and suffering on every haggard face. Men? They were little more than boys, no age in 'em at all and all smashed up here and for what?

'My name's Gregory. This is Mrs Cherry and Mrs O'Dowd. We're looking round to see how things might be improved. Anyone care to offer suggestions?

Silence at first then an older man with one leg missing above the knee said 'The food, sir. It's wus'n in the trenches.' That started the torrent of complaint and the visitors heard of everything from continual pain and rough handling from ill trained orderlies to a lack of bed pans and washing facilities and a rigid military regime unsuited to their disabled state.

With assurances that he'd 'do something about it', Luke led his party back downstairs to what had formerly been the headmaster's study and without bothering to knock, went in, to find a smallish man in uniform seated at the desk shuffling a pile of paperwork.

'What is the meaning of this intrusion?' the uniformed one demanded, getting to his feet, his moustache bristling with indignation. 'How dare you, sir. You have no business upon these premises so leave directly.'

'Major Duffield-Cranton? In charge of this circus? I, sir, own these premises as you call them and it is my desk at which you sit. I made this building available for the care of wounded men and what I find is quite unsatisfactory.'

'What do you mean, sir? I am in charge of this military establishment and follow my orders most carefully using whatever resources are made available to me.'

'This was a well set up school with a competent staff accustomed to dealing with large numbers and you've seen fit to discard their services. Now the place is unclean, the food is disgusting, there are piles of unwashed bedding and a lack of personal attention to badly injured men who deserve better. Shades of Scutari, sir. Oh yes. I saw Scut. I helped carry wounded men from Balaclava to what passed as a hospital and I saw Miss Nightingale at work improving conditions and that is the need here. Who, now is your superior officer. To whom do you report?'

'That is no concern of yours, sir,' the uniformed one snapped, face pale with anger, moustache bristling even more as he vigorously rang a hand bell to summon an orderly who, appearing immediately, had probably had his ear to the door.

'Then I shall speak to the king and see what His Majesty has to say about this disgraceful state of affairs,' Luke snapped back. 'Good day to you. You will hear further I can assure you.'

That must have rattled the man for next morning a full colonel of the Army Medical Corps was ringing the doorbell of the Manor asking for Luke.

'Good Lord. Steven and in uniform. Come on through. Never mind these ruffians. We're a school now so it's coffee in the kitchen.'

They decided the orangery to be more suited to a discussion and Steven Lambourne related how he'd been dragged out of retirement to organise facilities for the thousands of men wounded in the fighting in Belgium and France, described the shortages of trained nurses, doctors and attendants, of ambulances, equipment and suitable facilities.

'In short, Guv, we just weren't ready for the scale of this business and the wallahs at the top seem to have no understanding and put every obstacle in the way so what you found yesterday is probably the tip of the iceberg. Poor old Duffield-Cranton is completely out of his depth. Hauled out of retirement to take charge of something he hasn't the least idea of, so what's to be done?'

'At the Hall? Simple. Put all the staff back in post, feed everyone from the farms and gardens, let the ladies in to clean, help nurse and attend to whatever needs doing and collect all the equipment needed. Bed pans top of the list. All volunteers welcome. Soon get it ship shape again.'

'Guv, you should be doing my job. You make it sound so simple but would you, er join me in a visit to the Hall? To set things up amicably? Leave Duffield-Cranton to keep the books and answer the phone but leave the care side to you and yours? With a few army bods of course, for lifting and turning. That sort of thing and you to keep an eye on it all for me?'

★ ★ ★

Well-directed enthusiasm can achieve a great deal in a very short space of time and so it was with Mrs Cherry's working party for just about every able-bodied woman in the village turned out to help transform the Hall, motivated by the thought that it could be one of theirs in need of a place there. No longer were there heaps of laundry in need of attention, meals improved over night and flowers were placed in every room.

'Like a bleedin' 'otel', one cheerful attendant told Luke. 'Can't go over there cus I got flat feet, see? Yer can't shoot fellers wiv flat feet so I 'as ter take me chances 'ere, like.'

It seemed to be going well Luke thought but kept as low a profile as he could, offering suggestions that ensured more room between beds, collected every wash stand, chamber pot and commode for miles around for use there, had a railway truck converted to handle stretchers between Guildford and Chidlingbrook and a baker's van adapted as an ambulance to work between the station and the Hall.

Those who were able and wished to attend church were taken there on Sunday and a similar routine established with the Lamb Inn as destination. 'Purely medicinal, you understand,' Luke assured the major, who was tea total and disapproving but they'd settled for a formal working relationship and avoided each whenever possible. Much that was needed though required signatures in triplicate and reminded Luke of the tedious army bureaucracy he'd encountered in the Crimea.

Thought back to when, as a sixteen year old apprentice he'd been sent ashore at Balaclava to find someone, anyone, prepared to take the cargo of ammunition the ship had carried from Woolwich but was not allowed to discharge because too few officials had signed too few bits of paper and in any case, the ship must wait its turn in the queue.

He chuckled again to himself at the outcome of his trek up to the tented lines of a Scots regiment whose fiery colonel had exploded with rage, for his men were down to three rounds each and the enemy but five miles away. A company of highlanders had marched back with him to the harbour and no one stood in the way as every last item was carried off to where it was needed. My, but that whisky had tasted just fine, he well remembered!

Then, with an empty hold, they'd carried sick and wounded men to Scutari, the crew adamant that of the two cargoes, the danger of explosives was preferable to carrying wounded men in a bare ship's hold, with sea sickness adding to the squalor of dysentery and festering wounds, yet here they were again with a house, if not a cargo, of sick and wounded men not yet properly provided for.

Get hold of yourself, Gregory! You know how to go about it. You need wheelchairs to move folks about. There are wheelchairs in a warehouse at Wandsworth that William knows of so move your old bones over there and get a dozen sent down to Chidlingbrook, with or without a company of highlanders.

★ ★ ★

But the problems encountered at the Hall were not the only ones presented by officialdom for Peter was in hot dispute with some upstart demanding that he sow all fields, including pasture, with wheat and nothing but wheat, despite being told that much of the ground was unsuited to the crop.

Another had appeared to commandeer their plough horses for the army but they'd got wind of that visit and had all but a few safely hidden in the woods for they had a strong suspicion that compensation for many of the items taken for the war effort was minimal yet the same resources were being sold on at inflated prices, giving certain people a tidy profit.

That was probably the case with those seeking to fell their trees under the pretext of supplying much needed timber for trench supports. The last thing needed, he learned, was beech timbering as it splintered dangerously when hit by bullets or explosives, being hard and brittle by nature. Plenty of soft wood in France, he learned. Forests of it and plenty of steel and concrete too, so the would-be timber exploiters were seen off in short order and the pigs left in peace among the trees.

But the war dragged on with casualties increasing to incredible levels as the same old tactics were followed battle after battle; utterly futile, utterly pointless and all Luke could do was offer help at the Hall with its maimed and suffering inhabitants. By now, they had achieved as high a standard of care as was possible but Luke was deeply concerned over provision for the injured when they moved on. To where? Home, wherever that might be? From where so many had cheerfully signed on to do their bit for king and country? What would the future hold for young men who could never earn a living by physical work? How would a family cope in a small, poverty-stricken cottage with someone needing constant attention? Was government considering such issues?

It was to help arouse greater official concern that he'd attended a meeting in London but had left feeling frustrated and angry at what he viewed as apathy by both politicians and officials who really would have preferred not to be told the uncomfortable facts. Oh, they'd listened to him politely enough but he could see from their wearied expressions what they thought of the old fogey prattling on. His hearing might not be as sharp as it once was but he'd heard disparaging comments along the lines of 'past it, got a bee in his bonnet, thinks we can wave a magic wand,' and so on.

What if he was over eighty. He cared deeply and to be belittled by young know it alls with their superior attitudes was galling to say the least. This would be the last time he'd make the journey, he decided. He hated travelling and being jostled by noisy crowds, hated strange beds and not having his own things around him and hated not to be taken seriously, so he was in a decidedly prickly mood when he came upon a scene that roused his ire even more.

'Again! Get your arm straight and stop that damned shaking.'

The sharp commands attracted his attention as he walked past the Burlington Arcade and he stopped to look, with increasing disgust, at the spectacle of a tall young subaltern in immaculate uniform and highly polished riding boots upbraiding a uniformed private, requiring him to salute him correctly.

To his jaundiced eye the situation was clear. Here was some beardless youth with the red tabs of the staff on his lapels throwing his weight about. There were many such types posing in uniform around the society venues, enjoying soft home postings because of family influence, safe from active service in Flanders.

Five young men from the village had already been killed and seven wounded never mind those listed as missing and here was some privileged upstart pitching into someone who'd already been in the thick of it and been injured to boot.

'What the devil do you think you're about, sir! Can you not see this man is under hospital care? Can you not see he has the shakes? Do you not know what causes it? Not been out there yourself that's quite plain. You should be downright ashamed of yourself. You're a disgrace, sir.'

'This man failed to salute.' The tall young subaltern drew himself up indignantly in face of this heated reprimand. 'Discipline must be maintained and civilians have no business interfering in military matters.'

'Damn your impertinence, sir and stand to attention when you address a senior officer. I am General Callerton-Walker, and were I twenty years younger I would not be skulking around Town in a staff appointment. I have just left Horseguards, advising on questions of morale and here you stand, the clearest example of what is so wrong with the conduct of this war. The king shall here of this, indeed he shall. His majesty will take a very dim view. Your name, sir?'

The tall young subaltern appeared to shrink. 'Trumpington-Caldwell, sir. I, I did not realise, sir. I do apologise, sir, most sincerely.'

'Rot, sir. You will go directly to your commanding officer and apply for an immediate posting to an active unit. Prove your worth to your country. Off you go,' and responding to an immaculate, parade ground salute from the discomfited subaltern, Luke dutifully raised his bowler hat then turned to the pale young man standing silently beside him.

'Come along, young man. We'll have lunch at my club. Happen to know there's chicken on the menu, courtesy of the Chidlingbrook Farming Company. Turner, isn't it? Thought I recognised you. Small world. So what was all that about, back there?'

'I didn't see 'im. Just didn't see 'im and he were on me. Made me keep saluting 'im. Said as I didn't do it proper, but me arm's still stiff. I were lookin' in a shop winder. Don't know what were there. All I could see were the trench side blowed away an' Tommy with 'is guts 'anging out an' screaming an' then it all went black.'

'That feller wouldn't know about that. He'll maybe get himself out there and learn something.'

They walked in silence for a while, not hurrying then, 'Was you really a general, sir?'

'Course not but he didn't know that. Wet behind the ears. Bark at 'em, drop names and they fold up.'

'And the king, sir?'

'I've met him but I can't abide the little shrimp. Should've been strangled at birth. Could've kept us out of this business if he had half the brains of a tuppenny rabbit. Not a patch on his father for all his faults. Anyway, here we are so make yourself at home. I'll sign you in.'

★ ★ ★

'Come on, lad, eat up. It must be better fare than you've had lately.'

'I'm not hungry, sir. I keep thinking about it all and going back. They said I'll be fit enough and I couldn't stand it', and Luke felt his arm grasped tightly in a shaking grip and looked into the wildly staring eyes of an almost hysterical young man.

'You're not well enough to go back. I can see that. Who said you have to return?'

'The medical officer said he can't have lightly wounded cluttering up 'is wards and I only got a few bits o' shell in me.'

'But you've got the shakes. I've seen a fair number up at the Hall with the same thing.'

''E said I'll get over it.'

'You probably will but not if you go back over there. Now cheer up,' as Harry Turner hid his face in his hands. 'We'll have a second opinion,' and Luke beckoned to a waiter to ask for pen and paper. Now, take this note to Colonel Fairleigh at the Herbert Hospital at Woolwich. Take a cab to London Bridge railway station and another at Woolwich if you wish. Here's your fare but be sure to hand this note to Colonel Fairleigh in person. Any problems, tell 'em you're ordered to report. Understand? This is the first step towards getting better. The colonel will do the rest. Off you go, now.

★ ★ ★

So, you are Private Harry Turner of the Surreys. The guv tells me you've been knocked about, been patched up and are to be sent back. Mm. No longer fit for active service. Got the shakes. I see. Well coming from him I'll accept that diagnosis. Now, let's have a look at you. Hold your hands out. Mm. Eyes. Follow my finger as I move it. Mm. You've had a whiff of gas too. Well, you young man are certainly not fit for Flanders Fields. Convalescence and light duties are my recommendation. Had any leave? No? So where is home?'

'Chidlingbrook, sir, near Guildford.'

'Well bless my soul. Chidlingbrook eh? Well, well. Tell me. Have you an Uncle John who nearly cut his leg off with a scythe? You have? Ah. I sewed him up after that mishap. I was village doctor, you know. A few years ago now. Fond memories of Chidlingbrook and a certain Squire Gregory. Could tell you a tale or two about him. Quite a character. Anyway, you go back to base and I'll set the wheels in motion. You can make yourself useful up at the Hall. Some really good work being done there, with chaps in a terrible state. Something you'll understand, I know. Good day to you.'

★ ★ ★

Eventually, like all bad dreams, it came to an end, a formal ending at a certain time on a certain day yet by all accounts both sides were shooting at each other right up to the final whistle. A game to some, it seemed, but not to others and injured men continued to move to and from the Hall. Luke, as weary of it as any, continued to offer whatever help he or the company could, and was taken up to the Hall daily but he had to admit that even getting in and out of the trap was becoming difficult. Stiffening up, was how he described it but, determined as ever, he continued to make the effort.

There seemed to be no rush to get the army back home in time for Christmas, a source of irritation to many but gradually, in the new year, in ones and twos the survivors of the conflict from round about began to return and seek employment. Peter, organising the estate, had the task of slotting them into suitable positions but it quickly became clear that several who'd previously worked for the company were quite badly affected by their experiences so had to be offered light work and varied hours. Time, it was thought, would be the healer but no one who was capable of doing anything would be refused.

Added to their problems though was the recurring threat of a new and more dangerous form of influenza that was spreading rapidly with apparently fit and healthy young adults most badly affected. Deaths were reported daily in the newspapers all over the world but their small village was not to escape for Bert Milton, having spent three years in the trenches without so much as a scratch, became ill and died a week later, followed by his married sister.

The lottery of life, Luke mused as he sat in his favourite place by the fire in the hall. Warm outside it might be but he was seldom warm enough now even in the orangery but old folks did tend to feel the cold and yes, he was getting old but he still had his interests, still read the Times right through and enjoyed the company of his grandson Josh. Nice name that, Joshua. Nearly ten now but just where did the time go? Be harvest time before he knew it.

More men around to see to it this year but there was talk of using things called tractors instead of horses for farm work. Didn't sound right to him. They had some of the best plough teams for miles around and the Suffolk Punch was well suited to their land and what was all this about setting the price of gold twice a day? Four pounds eighteen and nine pence an ounce was being quoted.

Odd. Very odd and would the prep school seek to return to the Hall now? He'd heard nothing but it was possible. Have to see about that. Have to get the cricket going again in the village and the football. Get things back to normal as quick as they could. Much to do. Much to do, and he dozed off by the fire.

End

By the same author

Wharfinger

With sail giving way to steam in the 1860s, Luke Gregory and his shipmate Jonas Davy plan to stay ashore and trade from a warehouse in Bermondsey. Davy runs out on Luke leaving him penniless but a chance encounter with a mudlark enables him to continue with his plans, aided by the small local Jewish community. Hungry for success and driven by a fear of the poverty and degradation he sees around him, Luke is prepared to  increase his wealth by any reasonably legal means, though on occasion he sails very close to the wind indeed. He faces conflict with business rivals, river pirates and Fenian activists and struggles to make sense of the bitter religious hostility round about. Twenty years of unremitting work sees him comfortably settled but still hungry for further wealth-making opportunities.